Obsessed

A Falcon Pointe Novel

Jennifer Harrison

Visit https://www.jenniferharrisonwrites.com

Cover Design: Hayling Bookstorm Ltd Services

Amazon: https://www.amazon.com/stores/Jennifer-Harrison/author/B0B9YP9743

Goodreads: https://www.goodreads.com/jenniferharrison
Instagram: https://www.instagram.com/jennifer.harrison.writes/

Facebook: https://www.facebook.com/jennifer.harrison.writes

TikTok: https://www.tiktok.com/@jennifer..harrison

Contents

Author's Note

Obsessed explores themes of love, loss, trauma, and survival. Some scenes may be difficult for certain readers.

This story includes depictions or discussions of:

- Emotional and psychological abuse

- Domestic violence

- Trauma related to intimate relationships

- Control and manipulation within marriage

- Grief and loss

- References to pregnancy and childbirth

- Mentions of substance use

While this is ultimately a story of resilience, healing, and love, reader discretion is advised. Please take care of yourself and read at your own pace.

Resources and support information are provided at the beginning of this book for those who may need them.

Resources & Support

If you or someone you know is struggling with issues related to the topics discussed in this book, there are resources available. Please don't hesitate to reach out for support.

National Domestic Violence Hotline

Call: 1-800-799-SAFE (1-800-799-7233)

Text: "START" to 88788

Website: https://www.thehotline.org

Substance Abuse and Mental Health Services Administration (SAMHSA)

National Helpline: 1-800-662-HELP (1-800-662-4357)

Website: https://www.samhsa.gov

Crisis Text Line

Text HOME to 741741 for free, 24/7 confidential support

Website: https://www.crisistextline.org

Soundtrack

Abby,

I don't know how to say this stuff out loud without sounding like an idiot, so I made you this. Every song is how I feel about you - some of them are fun, some of them are kinda heavy, but that's us, right? You're the best part of my days, and I don't ever want you to forget that.

Play track 1 when you need to smile. Play track 6 when you need me close. Play track 15 when you can't sleep.

This is me, trying to tell you that no matter what happens, it'll always be you.

-J

1. Love Like Woe - The Ready Set
2. Hey, Soul Sister - Train
3. I'm Yours - Jason Mraz
4. You Belong With Me - Taylor Swift
5. Everything Has Changed - Taylor Swift ft. Ed Sheeran
6. Chasing Cars - Snow Patrol

7. Need You Now - Lady A

8. Let Her Go - Passenger

9. Car Radio - Twenty One Pilots

10. Take Your Time - Sam Hunt

11. Mine Would Be You - Blake Shelton

12. Counting Stars - OneRepublic

13. I Don't Want This Night to End - Luke Bryan

14. Stay Stay Stay - Taylor Swift

15. Fix You - Coldplay

For anyone who had to learn the difference between love and survival.

Abby

I didn't have a choice when my parents dragged me away from the only
home I'd ever known, and forbade me from contacting the one person
who meant the world to me. I was forced to live a life I never wanted,
with a man I could never love.
Somehow, I learned to survive it...
Until Jackson Taylor finds me.
He's not the boy I remember. He's stronger, sharper, and asking questions I can't afford to answer. Being near him cracks open everything
I worked so hard to bury - especially the truth about why I left and
what I've been protecting all these years.
Because Wanting Jackson means risking everything.
And this time, losing him might cost more than my heart.

Jackson

She vanished, gone like a ghost in the night, and I never stopped
looking.

OBSESSED

Abby Park was my first love. The girl who owned my heart before life ripped everything else away.

Eleven years later, I've built a life I can manage, surrounded by people I care about, while never allowing myself to need anyone too much.

Until I finally track her down.

She's different. Guarded. Hiding something I can feel in my bones.

And the more I push, the clearer it becomes that Abby didn't leave me. She was taken.

I don't just want answers, I want her.

And I won't walk away again, not when the truth threatens to change everything I thought I lost forever.

Prologue

Jackson

11 Years Ago

I didn't think anything could be better than winning State. Football was everything, my love, my passion, my dream...

Turns out, I was wrong, because I just may have a new dream, and she was laying right next to me, her head on my chest, skin warm against mine. Abby's fingers traced lazy lines across my ribs like she was sketching something only she could see. The fan overhead clicked every time it spun, but it didn't matter; I felt like I was floating on cloud nine.

Her breath tickled my skin when she said, "I still can't believe we actually did that."

I laughed. "Pretty sure I believed it somewhere around the second time you said my name."

She smacked my stomach. "Jackson."

"What? I'm just saying... for a girl who used to scream if I touched her glue stick in kindergarten, you've come a long way."

"Ugh." But she smiled. That soft, sleepy kind of smile that made me want to memorize her face in every shade of light.

We'd been best friends since we were five. Knew everything about each other - favorite cereal, biggest fears, worst middle school haircut. I knew the mole behind her left knee. She knew how I cried when my dog died, even though I swore I didn't.

I thought it was the best day ever when I kissed her and she kissed me back. And now this. Now we were something else; something more.

"You're so full of yourself," she muttered, but her fingers didn't stop tracing.

I rolled toward her and tucked a strand of hair behind her ear. "Maybe. But you're glowing. I'm just observing the facts."

She didn't answer right away. Just looked at me like she was trying to memorize everything. I hoped she was. Because I sure as hell was doing the same.

After a moment, she asked, "You still planning to go to Georgia?"

"Yeah. If I don't blow it this season I've got a real shot."

She nodded, eyes dropping to the sheet between us. "My parents want me to stay close. Community college. Maybe nursing. They think I'm... easily distracted."

I reached for her hand. "They don't know you like I do."

"They'd flip out if they knew you were here." She smiled, but it didn't reach her eyes. "If they knew what we just did."

That landed in my chest like a brick.

I wanted to say it wasn't fair. That hiding what we had felt wrong. That I'd never done anything but love her; not in the loud, possessive way, but in the kind that watches and waits and memorizes every detail because it matters.

She matters.

But all I said was, "So let's keep it ours. Just for now."

She turned to look at me, something sharp and tender in her eyes. "What if it all falls apart?"

I brushed my thumb over her cheek. "Then we find a way back to each other."

God, I meant it. More than anything. She was the one thing that made me question leaving. The one person I'd give up everything for if she asked.

I kissed her then, slow and deep and certain.

And then the sirens screamed.

Sharp, shrill, and too damn close.

Abby bolted upright, grabbing the sheet. "Again?"

I was already on my feet, heart pounding. "Fuck, I thought it was over..."

She clutched my hand. "Jackson, wait. Stay with me..."

"Whitney," I said. "She wasn't home when I left. She told Mom she'd stay in, but I know she snuck out."

I pulled on my jeans, heart racing. "I have to find her."

Abby's eyes brimmed with fear. "Just... be careful. Please."

I leaned in and kissed her - fast and hard, everything I didn't have time to say packed into that one second.

"I'll be right back."

And then I ran.

Chapter 1

Jackson

Present

The sun wasn't even up yet, and I was already tired.

I killed the engine behind The Hideaway and just sat there, fingers clenched around the steering wheel like if I let go, something else might slip with it. The morning air pressed heavy on my chest, quiet, even for Falcon Pointe, where life moved slow and soft, like the whole town was still half-asleep.

I never came to work this early.

But I couldn't stay there.

Whitney was under my roof again. Broken, stubborn, and furious about it. I hadn't seen her in years, and the universe had decided the reunion should come with casts, bruises, and a hospital discharge I still couldn't shake from my head.

She'd fought me every mile back from Salt Lake, swearing she didn't need saving. Maybe she didn't. But there was no way in hell I was letting her crawl back to that scumbag boyfriend of hers. I'd given her my bed, shut my mouth, and pretended I knew how to handle any of it.

Turns out, I didn't.

So here I was, parked behind my bar, inventing reasons to go inside. Inventory. Vendor calls. Anything to avoid the past breathing in my house like it had every right to be there.

The Hideaway wasn't a dream. It was something solid I could hold onto when everything else fell apart.

My hands were still shaking. Not from the cold, it was the middle of August.

I leaned back and popped the glove box.

The old phone slid into my palm, cold and familiar. It was scratched, outdated, and stubborn as hell. I hadn't powered it on in months, but the cracked screen still flickered to life, dim and blue.

And there she was.

Abby.

Barefoot in the grass beside my truck, hair a mess from the wind. Her hands on her hips like she was daring me to say something stupid. I'd taken the picture when she wasn't looking. I never told her I kept it.

I unlocked the phone and scrolled to our last texts, the same way I always did, slow, and deliberate, like maybe they'd changed when I wasn't looking.

Me: God, I miss you. When can I see you?

I should've known something was wrong. The whole night had that gut-twist feeling, like waiting for a storm that never came.

Friday night lights and I was decked out in full pads. The weight of my helmet pressing down as I scanned the bleachers again and again.

Every time the crowd shifted. Every time the band paused. Every time we scored.

I kept looking for her.

By halftime, I couldn't take it anymore. I walked straight off the field and ran, my cleats slapping the pavement, lungs burning, her last text replaying in my head like maybe I'd misunderstood.

Her house was empty.

A FOR SALE sign leaned crooked in the yard, like someone had shoved it into the ground without caring how it looked. The curtains were gone. Her bedroom window, the one she used to sneak out of, was shut tight.

I knocked anyway.

Nothing.

I called her phone. It was disconnected.

No note. No warning. She was just... gone.

People talked about moving on like it was a choice. Like it was something you decided one morning and followed through on. But I still had the same old phone. The same cracked photo. The same damn playlist I'd made for her junior year playing on repeat every time I drove.

I hadn't moved on. I'd just stayed still while the world kept going.

I let my head fall back against the seat and shut my eyes. The old phone stayed warm in my hand, like maybe some part of her was still in there somewhere. Dark hair. Brown eyes. That smile she only ever gave me.

My real phone buzzed from the cup holder.

I opened my eyes.

Unknown Number.

My pulse kicked up. I stared at the screen for one second too long before answering.

"Yeah?"

A pause. Then, "Mr. Taylor?"

"Speaking."

"This is Carson Finch. You hired me a few months back to find Abby Park."

I sat up straighter. "I remember."

"I found her."

Chapter 2

Abby

The alarm went off at 5:15. I was up and out of bed before the second beep, same as every morning.

I moved like clockwork, making my side of the bed with quiet, practiced motions, careful not to wake my husband. I didn't even need to look at him to know he had one arm over the covers, his mouth slack.

I padded down the hall and opened Cole's door. The night light cast a dim glow on his face - the same strong nose, the same mouth - and my breath caught. I lingered a second longer than I meant to.

He stirred. "Mom?"

"I'm just checking on you. Go back to sleep."

"I'm ten," he mumbled, rolling over. "You don't have to check every morning."

I stepped into his room. "I'll always check," I said, and brushed his hair off his forehead.

He squinted up at me with those green eyes, and for a moment, everything felt lighter.

"I packed your lunch last night," I whispered. "Banana and PB&J, just the way you like it. Make sure you brush your teeth this time."

He smirked. "I always brush."

"Liar."

I kissed his forehead and stood to go, but his hand reached out, fingers curling around mine.

"You okay?"

I smiled because that was the answer he needed. "Always."

He didn't smile back right away. Just studied my face like he was filing something away for later.

Cole had always been like that. Quietly observant. Too aware of things a ten-year-old shouldn't notice.

I hated that I was the reason.

———

I dropped Cole at my parents' house just after six.

My mother barely looked up from her tablet. "He's wearing yesterday's shoes."

"He likes those ones."

She sniffed. "Your husband called. He wants gimbap for dinner."

Of course he did. He always called her instead of me.

"I'll make it after work."

She nodded, already back to her screen.

I waited until Cole was inside before pulling away.

They never said it out loud, but I knew they knew. You could see it in the way my mother watched him - measuring, comparing. In the way no one ever commented on the things that made him different.

It was the rule.

As long as he carried the last name Kim, nothing else mattered.

Cole didn't know. He'd never asked. And I'd never told him.

Some truths were dangerous just to think about.

As soon as I had him, my parents enrolled me in the nursing program at the community college. "It's practical," they said. "You'll always have a job."

They were right.

Oakridge Living Center made sense to me. Sheets, bedpans, pill schedules - expectations that didn't shift depending on who was watching. The residents didn't ask questions I couldn't answer. They didn't judge the polite voice I used too often or the bruises I covered.

They just needed care.

And I was good at that.

Mrs. Ortiz waved at me from her recliner when I arrived. "You're too pretty to be sad, sweetheart."

I smiled. "That line's getting old, Queenie."

She winked. "So are we."

Sometimes, I stayed late because here, someone noticed.

At home, everything had rules.

His rules.

Shoes lined up by the door. Dinner hot and ready by six. Voices low. Eyes down. Never contradict. Never draw attention. Be grateful.

I moved through the kitchen like a ghost - cleaning, plating, adjusting. The mistake he covered up by marrying, as he liked to remind me. "No one else would have taken you. You should be thankful."

My parents agreed. A man like him, they said, was stability.

Thankful.

Sung-ho acted like I owed him - for the roof, for the silence, for everything he'd decided to give us. Like he'd fixed a problem no one else would touch.

But Cole wasn't a mistake. He was my beginning.

Dinner passed in careful sounds. The soft clink of metal chopsticks. The muted television murmuring to no one. Cole sat straight-backed between us, eyes down, chewing slowly like he'd learned to.

I watched him more than I ate.

Sung-ho sat at the head of the table, immaculate and untouched by the tension filling the room. I'd made the gimbap just the way he wanted it - neat, precise, nothing out of place.

"Say thank you to your mother," he said without looking up.

"Thank you, Umma," Cole said immediately.

I nodded, forcing a smile. He was always careful. Always polite. But I saw the way his eyes flicked to Sung-ho every few seconds, like he was watching the sky for storms.

"How was school today?" I asked, needing to break the silence.

Then it happened - the innocence of a child, the kind of thing that wouldn't matter in another house.

"I threw the football over the fence today," Cole said. "It almost hit Mrs. Greene's cat."

I froze.

Sung-ho's chopsticks paused in midair.

"You were playing football?" His voice stayed calm. Too calm.

"Just a little," Cole said. "At recess. With some kids."

"You are not some animal on the street." Sung-ho's words were precise and sharp. "No son of mine runs wild like a delinquent."

Cole's shoulders stiffened. "Sorry."

I opened my mouth to defend him, but nothing came out.

Sung-ho stood, carried his bowl to the sink, and rinsed it in silence. Then he turned back to Cole.

"Finish your homework. No television."

He didn't wait for a response, just left the room, his footsteps disappearing down the hall. The bedroom door clicked shut behind him a moment later.

Cole stayed perfectly still.

"I'm sorry," he whispered.

My chair scraped as I pushed back. I knelt beside him and wrapped my arms around his small, tense body.

"No," I said quietly. "You didn't do anything wrong."

He didn't cry. He just leaned into me like he wanted to disappear. I held him like I was trying to keep us both from falling apart.

Later, after he was asleep, I sat on the edge of my bed and stared at my phone.

I didn't know what I was hoping for. Maybe a message from no one. Maybe proof I wasn't completely invisible.

I thought about green eyes and callused hands. About a boy who once told me I was the only thing that made sense to him.

For the first time in years, I let myself wish someone would come looking for me.

That night, Sung-ho hit me.

He waited until the house was quiet, until Cole was asleep and the walls had settled. One word, ungrateful, and then his hand. Open. Fast. Hard enough to snap my head to the side.

I cleaned the blood from my lip in the bathroom and didn't cry.

The next morning at work, Mrs. Ortiz frowned when I bent to change her blanket.

"What happened to your mouth, sweetheart?"

I told her I bit it in my sleep.

She didn't argue, but later I caught the nurse watching me when she thought I wasn't looking. Long enough to notice. Long enough to remember.

That afternoon, walking to my car, keys clenched tight between my fingers, the air felt different.

Like something had shifted without asking my permission.

Chapter 3

Jackson

I didn't realize I was holding my breath until Grady's motorcycle rumbled into the driveway.

Helmetless, reckless, and running - like always.

He was my best friend, my foster brother. One of the only people I cared more about than myself.

I sat motionless on the couch, gripping his helmet like it was the only thing tethering me to the ground.

Then the front door creaked open.

"Jackson?" Grady's voice was cautious, and raw.

I stood so fast I nearly dropped the damn thing. "Thank fucking God."

Before I could stop myself, I was hugging him - tight, and desperate, not giving a shit about whether it was awkward. He didn't fight it.

"I'm sorry," he said quietly.

"Are you okay?" My voice cracked as I pulled back and scanned his face. "You didn't answer your phone. I thought..."

"I just needed to think."

"Don't scare me like that, okay?" I looked away, trying to get a grip. "I..."

I stopped and shook my head, unable to finish the thought.

Grady narrowed his eyes. "I know you're not crying over me. What happened? Is Whitney...?"

"No," I said, and something in my chest cracked open. I smiled - wide, stupid, *boyish*. "She's fine. I found her."

His brow furrowed. "*Her*?"

"Abby," I said. "She's in Kansas. I have her number. Her address."

The words hung in the air like they were too fragile to land.

"Holy shit. That's... that's incredible. Have you spoken to her? Does she know you've been looking for her?"

I scratched the back of my neck nervously. "I want to go out there, see her in person."

"And you're sure it's her?"

I nodded, "Yeah. I got a picture." I pulled out my phone and un-locked it, showing him the picture the PI sent me. It was Abby, *my* Abby, and God was she beautiful.

"So what the hell are you still doing here?"

I collapsed onto the couch. "I can't. Not with Whitney here. The bar, everything..."

He sat on the coffee table, elbows on his knees. "You have to go. I can take care of the bar. And Whitney." He sighed, like he couldn't believe what he was offering. "I'll take care of your sister. You can trust me."

"I know I can trust you, it's just..." I looked at him, this man I trusted with my life, and still I was conflicted, stuck between doing what was right for my sister, and finally chasing my happily ever after. "She's still mad at me, Grady. She thinks I left her. That I didn't come for her. And now I'm just going to walk away again?"

"Does she know why you didn't?"

I shook my head. "Not yet." What I didn't say was I didn't know how to explain failing her twice.

"Then tell her. But don't let this stop you. You've been chasing Abby for how long?"

I scrubbed a hand over my face. "Eleven years."

"Talk to her," Grady said, his voice full of conviction. "Tell her the truth. Then go find your girl."

I didn't know which goodbye hurt more - the one I'd already said, or the one I hadn't.

I packed light. Just the essentials and the one photo I'd kept in my wallet for a decade. By dawn, I was already on the road.

By the second hour of flat landscape, my tires humming against the pavement, the excitement had burned off, leaving too much space for my thoughts to wander.

Whitney's face came back to me first, tight with hurt, like she'd already known how this would end.

I remembered the way her shoulders stiffened when I mentioned Grady. The way something closed off behind her eyes.

I flexed my hand around the steering wheel, my knuckles whitening.

I should have said more. Something better. Something that didn't sound like an excuse.

Instead, I'd hesitated.

And she'd turned away before I could convince myself I was doing the right thing.

I hated that the silence felt familiar.

Chapter 4

Abby

My parent's house always smelled like lemon polish and boiled eggs. Sharp, sterile, and heavy with expectation. I wrinkled my nose as we crossed over the threshold; somehow it seemed worse today.

"You're late," she said without inflection.

Cole slipped off his dress shoes without being told and crossed the living room to his usual spot, an old armchair in the corner near the dining room. He pulled a book from his backpack and folded himself into the cushions, legs tucked up, back straight. He didn't ask to sit at the table, and no one invited him.

That was the unspoken rule: children stayed quiet, especially ones who didn't belong.

I followed my mother into the dining room, greeted her with a soft, "Annyeonghaseyo, Eomma," and a slight bow. She gave the smallest nod in return and sat, tablet already in hand, the screen casting a blue glow over her face.

"Annyeonghaseyo, Appa," I added with a bow as I stepped past my father's chair.

He nodded without looking up, eyes still on his newspaper. His dismissal used to hurt. I was his princess once. But time is good at dulling things you can't afford to feel anymore.

"Your husband called," my mother said, scrolling across something more important than me or her grandson. "He said your galbijjim was dry yesterday. You really should pay closer attention."

I sat straight-backed at the dining room table, napkin folded neatly in my lap, fingers wrapped too tightly around a ceramic coffee cup I wasn't drinking from. "I'll do better."

"You know," she began, and I braced myself, "if you focused more on your duties at home, maybe your husband wouldn't get so... upset."

She didn't look at me when she said it. Just dabbed the corner of her mouth with her napkin and reached for another croissant. Her eyes never flicked to the thin line on my upper lip or the faint bruising blooming along my cheekbone.

That was the rule.

Across the room, Cole's fingers tightened around his book, knuckles white. He didn't look up.

"We're lucky Sung-ho is such a patient man," my mother continued. "You're not an easy woman, Ah-bi." She said it softly, but it hit like a slap.

I stared at my plate, forcing my jaw to stay loose, my shoulders still. I let her words slide over me like cold oil. She didn't want a response. She never did. All she wanted was a quiet daughter and a perfectly plated brunch.

"He's been working hard," she added. "You could do better."

"I'm doing my best," I said, quietly.

She clicked her tongue. "Your best is what got you into this mess in the first place."

The word *mess* hung in the air like a dirty secret. Cole turned a page in his book, too fast. I saw him flinch at the sound of her voice.

I forced a smile. "Thank you for the food."

My father nodded from behind his newspaper but didn't speak. The three of us ate in silence, the only sounds the scrape of silverware and the occasional soft cough from Cole's corner.

Afterward, I helped clear the dishes while my father scrolled through stock alerts and my mother pretended she couldn't see Cole sneaking bites of leftover fruit salad when he thought no one was watching.

"I'm going to take Ha-joon to the park for a bit," I said, hating the name they insisted on. The name that made him theirs.

"He needs more structure," she said without turning. "All that energy. You should enroll him in study classes. The Chen boys are already preparing for middle school exams."

"He's ten."

"All the more reason to start now."

I didn't answer. I gathered Cole's things, and we left without another word.

The moment we reached the open grass, Cole bolted. He tore off the starched button-down, revealing his favorite shirt underneath - Jackson's University of Georgia Football tee, one of the few things I managed to hold onto after everything happened. I gave it to him as a present for his last birthday, though I couldn't bring myself to tell him why it was special.

As much as I wanted to tell him the truth, the risk was too great. But small things, little secrets, were worth the joy I saw on his face.

Cole whooped as he circled around and tapped my arm. "Tag, you're it!" he shouted, already sprinting away.

I ran after him, feeling the oppressive weight of my parent's expectations float away with each step. We laughed with each near miss until he finally tackled me to the grass.

"Got ya!" He grinned, and I couldn't help but tickle his sides until he was wailing with laughter, tears streaming from his eyes.

"Come on, buddy," I grabbed his football, another secret of ours, and waved him away. "Go long!"

He shook his head as he ran, "You can't throw that far!"

"Watch me!" I laughed. He was right, I couldn't throw that far. But he could. The ball landed short, bouncing in the wrong direction, but that didn't stop him from snatching it up and throwing it back.

We threw the ball back and forth until my arms ached and my sides hurt from laughing.

It felt like breathing again.

For an hour, I wasn't Mrs. Kim or the obedient daughter. I was just Mom.

I checked the time - 5:02. *Shit*. We had to go. "Two more passes," I said, already pulling my hair into a bun. "Then we've got to hustle."

I couldn't help but watch the time as I wrangled him toward the car with my usual promise of snacks. We stopped by the corner store to grab some ice cream sandwiches, both of us windblown and grass stained.

The line was short, but every beep of the scanner echoed like a countdown. I'd have to cut the radish garnish if I wanted the stew done in time.

We got back to the car in record time. I had just closed my door when I saw him.

Tall. Broad shoulders. Worn baseball cap pulled low. Back turned. Something in me stopped.

I stared, my breath caught, heart suddenly racing without reason.

"Mom, what are you looking at?"

I turned to look at Cole in the back seat, carefully buttoning his shirt. When I glanced back out the window, he was gone.

I laughed at myself quietly and shook it off.

"Nothing, baby." I smiled, but something in my chest stayed tight. Like maybe it hadn't been nothing at all.

Chapter 5

Jackson

The town didn't look like much.

Flat stretches of road, a grain elevator in the distance, gas stations every few miles like mile markers for the bored and half-asleep. Stonehill, Kansas. It sounded quaint on paper, but so far it felt like concrete under boots. Quiet, gray, and waiting.

I'd been driving since dawn. My back ached, my right calf cramped from too much time on the gas pedal. I'd passed the town limit sign ten minutes ago, and hadn't seen a single soul who looked like her.

I slowed the truck and turned into a corner store parking lot, not for gas, just to breathe. My hands were shaking, and I didn't want to show up at her door looking like I'd come unhinged. Carson Finch said her last name was Kim now. I didn't know what that meant, but my first instinct was that she didn't want to be found.

Well too damn bad.

The inside of the store smelled like bleach and microwaved bur-ritos. I grabbed a Coke and some trail mix. The cashier rang me up without a word, eyes glued to a tiny TV mounted above the counter.

Outside, the late-summer sun was starting to dip, soft gold casting long shadows across the lot.

The Coke hissed as I twisted the cap. I leaned against the tailgate of my truck, bottle sweating in my hand. I should've been planning what I'd say when I saw her. *Hi, remember me? I was your best friend, the love of your life? The man you disappeared on eleven years ago?*

But I couldn't think. All I could see was her face, how it had looked when I left her bed that morning. How sure she'd been that I'd come back.

And how stupid I'd been to believe a tornado and tragedy could ever make her wait.

A soft, once-familiar laugh carried across the lot like wind, and my ears perked.

I turned, bottle halfway to my mouth, and froze.

There she was.

Windblown, feet bare in her usual plain white sneakers, hair pulled up in a messy bun, her shirt clinging to her side. Laughing at some-thing I couldn't hear. She opened the driver's door of a silver sedan and slid inside.

The breath left my lungs.

Abby.

I didn't move. Didn't speak. Just stood there like someone had kicked the ground out from under me.

And then reality hit me like a punch to the gut. I pulled my hat down low and climbed into my truck. I couldn't let her see me like this, not when she was so damn alive, and I... hell, I'd been a zombie for years.

I watched from the corner of my eye as the car pulled out, tires crunching over gravel, and she was gone.

But this time I knew how to find her.

The motel sat on the edge of town, wedged between a shuttered car wash and a bail bonds office. One of those one-story places with a flickering neon sign and a Coke machine out front that hadn't worked since the Broncos won the Superbowl.

But the room was clean. Mostly. The A/C kind of worked, and the water ran hot. That was all I needed.

The water was hot enough to sting. I stood there, hands braced against the tile, trying to clear my head, but all I could see was her.

Abby.

Not the girl in pigtails or the teenager who used to fall asleep in my truck. The woman I saw today. Windblown. Laughing. Shirt clinging to her side. Hips a little fuller. Her body softer in all the places I used to touch and dream about touching again.

I imagined her under my hands. Her mouth against my neck. Her legs wrapping around me like she used to when we were seventeen and stupid in love. Back before the world cracked open and swallowed everything whole.

My breath hitched. I closed my eyes and gave in, my hand fisting my cock. Fast. Desperate. Muscle memory and aching need. Her name caught in the back of my throat, but I didn't say it. I couldn't.

When it was over, I stayed there, chest heaving, forehead pressed to the tile, steam curling around me like smoke.

And then the shame set in.

Not because I wanted her. God, I'd always wanted her. But because it felt like I was still clinging to a ghost. A ghost who'd stopped waiting.

She didn't come to the game.

She didn't call. Didn't write. Didn't try.

I was the one who stayed behind. I was the one who kept the playlist, the picture, the same damn phone. I was the one who chased her through three counties like a lunatic with a dream he never outgrew.

And Abby? She'd laughed.

She'd laughed and climbed into her car like her life was just fine without me.

What if I'd made it all up?

What if it had meant more to me than it ever did to her? What if her silence was the answer and I just refused to accept it?

I shut the water off and stood there dripping, shivering despite the heat. Grief clawed up the back of my throat, as raw and fresh as the day she left.

I dried off without thinking. Just muscle and movement. The towel sat heavy around my waist as I dropped onto the edge of the bed, my head in my hands.

The room smelled like cheap soap and stale air. A window unit rattled in the corner, spitting out lukewarm air. Somewhere outside, a dog barked. A car passed.

I didn't move, I couldn't.

I felt hollowed out, like everything I'd been holding onto for the last eleven years had cracked in my chest and started leaking through the seams. The picture. The playlist. The promise I made when I left her bed that morning, barefoot, smiling and stupidly sure of forever.

Maybe I should've let her go a long time ago. Maybe I never really had her to begin with.

I rubbed a hand over my face and let my head fall back against the headboard. And just like that, I was five years old again. The memory snuck in without asking, like they always did. Soft and slow, wrapped in the scent of rice and garden dirt and that high, wild laugh I hadn't heard since we were kids.

Her house had smelled like rice and something sweet, like toasted sugar.

I'd worn a dinosaur T-shirt and scuffed sneakers. My hair was sticking up in the back. I stood in the doorway, while her mom watched me with suspicion.

Then she appeared. I didn't know it then. But that moment? That was the beginning of everything.

She was tiny, confident, and barefoot, with pigtails and a permanent scowl that made me think she hated everything. She walked right up to me, hands on her hips, and said, "You're late."

I blinked. "Sorry."

"Do you like bugs?"

I nodded too fast.

"Good. Let's go."

She grabbed my hand and dragged me to the backyard before I could say a word. We spent the whole afternoon digging in the garden, poking ants with sticks and naming every worm we found. She named hers after Disney princesses. I named mine after dinosaurs.

At one point, her mother called from the kitchen, "Ah-bi, come wash your hands!"

I looked at her. "Who's that?"

She rolled her eyes. "Me, dummy."

I tried to repeat it, but it came out slurred. "Abby?"

She laughed so hard she tipped over in the grass, and something in my chest cracked open for good.

"Say it again!" she squealed.

I did. Three more times. Just to make her laugh like that again.

After that, no one ever called her Ah-bi again. No one except her mom.

I blinked up at the ceiling of a motel in the middle of nowhere, heart suddenly pounding harder than it should.

Abby.

Not the girl in pigtails anymore. Not the one who stole my bug spray and my heart before I even knew what either of those things meant.

But she was still *her*.

Still the only thing I'd ever been sure of.

I sat up and reached for my phone. Opened the address the PI had given me. My thumb hovered over the map pin.

Tomorrow.

Tomorrow, I'd knock on her door.

And hope to God she didn't slam it in my face.

I didn't sleep much. The bed was lumpy, the pillow flat, and every time I closed my eyes, I saw her face.

By sunrise, I was in motion; I'd shaved, combed my hair, and changed shirts three times. None of it mattered. My palms still sweat like hell.

As I neared the address the PI gave me, a school bus passed going the opposite direction, yellow paint and red flashing lights in the morning sun. I slowed, heart already thudding like I'd run a mile. And then I saw her.

Abby.

She wore navy scrubs, a little faded at the seams, and the same plain white sneakers I remembered from yesterday. Her hair was pulled back in a low ponytail, a badge clipped to her front pocket, and a silver travel mug tucked in one hand. No makeup, no fanfare, just her. Not like she ever needed it.

My heart kicked hard in my chest.

She got into her silver sedan, the door groaning a little as it closed. I didn't move. Not until the engine started and she backed out, turning toward the main road like it was any other morning.

But it wasn't. Not for me.

I let her get a few car lengths ahead before I pulled out and followed, careful, slow, and quiet.

The Abby I knew drove something old and messy, music always blasting, sunflower decals peeling off the windows. She would've carried a bright purple mug covered in paint splatters and Sharpie doodles, not something sleek and silver that looked like it came with a 401k.

She used to talk about color like it was oxygen. Used to sketch constellations on her arms with ballpoint pens and swear she'd live in Paris one day, selling street art to tourists.

Now she wore navy scrubs and a name badge, just like her mom always wanted. She drove a quiet car with practical tires and no bumper stickers.

And me? I was still driving the same old truck, still wearing the same beat-up hat. Still listening to the same damn playlist from high school.

Still looking for her like some fool chasing a ghost, like I didn't know how to quit.

What the hell did that say about me?

I'd come all this way thinking I'd get my second chance, but maybe that wasn't who we were anymore. Maybe she wasn't the one who left everything behind.

Maybe I was.

Because somewhere between the girl I remembered and the woman I just saw was a chasm I wasn't sure I knew how to cross. And I couldn't stop wondering, what had happened to the girl who used to glow like firelight?

And what had she left behind to become this?

Chapter 6

Abby

My chest still felt tight from the night before, like whatever I'd seen at the corner store had followed me home.

The sliding doors whooshed open like they always did, cold air brushing my cheeks as I stepped inside the nursing facility. I was already tired. My back hurt, my shoulder throbbed from the way I'd slept, curled too tightly on the sofa under a throw blanket that didn't quite cover my feet.

We'd gotten home too late. I knew it the second I opened the door. There wasn't enough time to prepare the stew or even set the table. And worse, Sung-ho's shoes were already lined up by the door, silent and accusing.

He didn't yell.

He didn't need to.

His silence and cold eyes through dinner were enough. For once, Cole's silence wasn't just heartbreaking, it was essential. He cleared his plate when he was finished eating, grabbed his homework and disappeared into his bedroom.

Sung-ho glared at me and shook his head. "Sofa."

One word. That's all he needed to put me back in my place.

And now I was here. Badge clipped, scrubs straight, hair pulled back. Playing the part my mother had drilled into me. It didn't matter how I felt on the inside, what mattered is what people saw - and I made sure they saw perfection.

"Morning, Ah-bi," one of the aides called as I passed.

I nodded. "Morning."

My voice sounded normal. It always did. That was part of it - pretending everything was fine. Pretending *I* was fine.

I had gotten really good at pretending, but on the inside, I could feel myself dying a little more each day.

I went through the motions - grabbing charts, checking the white-board, the slow crawl of the routine settling into my bones like muscle memory.

Pain pills in 102. Help Mr. Henderson find his glasses again. Gently remind Mrs. Freedman not to call 911 just because her breakfast was late.

Oh yes, I could do this. I was really good at this.

I was halfway through sorting the morning meds when I felt it - this pressure in the air, like someone was watching me. I glanced up.

And froze.

Jackson.

He was standing just inside the front doors, looking lost, or maybe just stunned. His eyes locked on mine, and the breath punched from my lungs.

"What the..." I nearly dropped the chart.

For a split second, I thought my mind had finally snapped.

Without thinking, I strode across the floor, grabbed his arm, and dragged him into an empty patient room before anyone could see him.

The door clicked shut.

For a second, we just stared at each other.

"You shouldn't be here," I said. My voice shook, but my hands didn't. They were already on him, like they'd been waiting ten years for permission.

"I know," he said.

I swallowed. "I don't care."

My fingers curled into his shirt, then up into his hair, pulling him down to me like a breath I'd been holding for years. Our mouths crashed together, messy and hot, and I kissed him like I needed him to remember who I was - who we were.

I didn't care why he was here. Didn't care if I was dreaming.

All I knew was that he felt real and warm and *Jackson*, and for the first time in forever, I didn't feel invisible.

His hands gripped my waist, grounding me as my body pressed to his, all heat and memory. I made a soft sound - part ache, part hunger - and pulled him closer.

He was the only person who had ever made me feel like I was enough. And in that moment, I didn't want to think about consequences.

I just wanted to *feel*.

Wanted to remember what it was like to be wanted for who I was, not punished for falling short.

When his calloused fingers slid under my top, I didn't push him away. I leaned into it, like this would be the last time I got to be me, truly me.

Our clothes fell away in clumsy, desperate motions. My back hit the mattress, hands grasping, hips lifting, legs wrapping around him like they remembered the way. There were no words. Just gasps and heat and the quiet kind of ache that comes from losing something too young and never quite letting go.

He moved inside me like a promise I wasn't allowed to keep. And for a few breathless minutes, there was no time. No past. No present. Just this.

Jackson.

His name echoed in my head like a prayer.

We didn't speak as we came apart together. Didn't cry, though it felt like we could have.

And when it was over, when the silence started pressing in, I turned my face away and reached for my scrubs.

Jackson sat up slowly, running a hand through his damp hair. His voice was rough, like gravel. "Abby…"

I froze. No one had called me that in years.

He pulled his shirt on. "Can I take you out? Just dinner. We need to talk; I need to know what happened."

I squeezed my eyes shut. The shame hit fast, hot, and sharp. I shook my head. "No."

His brow creased. "Abby…"

"I can't," I said, voice barely above a whisper. I was already tugging on my pants, movements jerky, the rush of panic rising too fast. "We shouldn't have done this."

"But we did." His voice cracked. "You can't pretend this meant nothing."

"You don't get to decide what this meant," I said. "I already know."

I looked up at him then, and it almost broke me. The way he looked at me, like I still mattered. Like I wasn't the ghost I'd become.

But ghosts don't get second chances.

"You have to go," I said, reaching for my badge and clipping it back on with trembling fingers. "Please, Jackson. You can't be here."

He stared at me; lips parted like he wanted to argue. "At least tell me why."

"I need to get back to work." I started toward the door when his voice stopped me in my tracks.

"We didn't use a condom," he said quietly.

I swallowed. "I know."

The panic flared brighter now. My heartbeat tripped over itself. *What have I done?*

"I didn't mean..." His voice faltered, but I cut him off with a look.

"Jackson. You need to go."

The pain in his eyes nearly undid me. But he stood and walked to the door.

He hesitated with his hand on the handle. "Abby..."

"Don't," I whispered. "Please."

He left.

The click of the door shutting behind him sounded too final.

I stayed there for a long moment, breathing through the weight in my chest. Then I straightened my shirt and stepped out into the hall.

Mrs. Ortiz stood by the nurses' station, arms crossed. She didn't say anything right away. Just lifted one eyebrow and handed me a chocolate from her pocket.

"I'm not one to gossip," she said a note of humor in her voice, "but that was one fine specimen of a man. And correct me if I'm wrong, but he didn't look a thing like your husband."

I didn't answer, I couldn't, but the heat in my cheeks said enough.

I unwrapped the chocolate and popped it into my mouth.

It melted too fast. Like everything good in my life.

I turned to get back to work when her arm reached out and stopped me.

"I'd suggest fixing your hair, cariño," Mrs. Ortiz added gently, her tone softening. "Unless you want the whole floor whispering by lunch."

My hand shot up to the back of my head. God. My ponytail was a mess. Loose strands clung to my neck. I looked like I'd rolled out of a patient's bed.

Which, in a way, I had.

"I'm fine," I murmured.

Mrs. Ortiz didn't push, just gave me a look that said she knew better. "Suit yourself. But whatever that was... you might want to figure it out before it finds you again."

I nodded, throat tight. "Thanks."

By midmorning, I couldn't breathe. The air felt thick, the fluorescent lights like needles in my skull. I clocked out early, claiming a headache, and slipped out the back exit with shaking hands.

I didn't go home.

Instead, I drove to Cole's school and parked near the edge of the playground lot, far enough away to not be seen.

Outside, kids ran across the blacktop in bursts of laughter. I spotted him instantly, my son, all long limbs and wild energy, hair too much like his fathers for me to ever forget.

I pressed a hand to my chest, grounding myself.

I used to be like them once. Bright. Laughing. Full of big dreams and bigger feelings.

I gripped the steering wheel hard enough that my knuckles ached.

Seeing Jackson today had cracked something open I'd kept sealed for a decade. Being with him, touching him, had been like falling into the past, into a world where everything felt possible. But it wasn't real. Not anymore.

I had a husband.

I had a son.

And neither of them could ever know.

Cole glanced toward the street and spotted my car. His face lit up, bright as sunlight. He waved so big his whole body got into it, and I forced a smile, lifting my hand in return.

God, he deserved the truth.

But telling him would blow our lives apart.

So, I stayed in the car, letting the moment pass. Pretending I was just another mom waiting for the bell. Pretending my heart wasn't beating in two different worlds - half in the life I had, half in the life I'd been torn away from.

Chapter 7

Jackson

The air outside hit like a punch - hot, stale, and smelling faintly of asphalt and fryer grease from the diner down the block.

I stood there on the sidewalk, hands on my hips, staring at nothing. I should've walked away, gotten in my truck, kept driving until Kansas was in my rearview mirror.

Instead, all I could see was her.

Abby.

Her hands in my hair.

Her body against mine like we were seventeen again, stealing time before the world found us.

What the hell just happened?

One second, she was kissing me like she'd been starving for it, like she remembered every touch and wanted them all back. The next, she was shoving me toward the door, telling me we couldn't see each other again.

I'd been ready for anger. I'd been ready for tears.

But not... that.

She was hiding something. I could feel it in the way she wouldn't meet my eyes. The way her voice shook when she told me to go.

I shoved my hands in my pockets and started toward my truck, my jaw tight. Eleven years without a word, and now she was right in front of me, acting like I didn't deserve an explanation. Like what we shared didn't mean anything.

The drive back to the motel blurred. I barely remembered turning the key, barely remembered the miles of cracked pavement and stoplights between us. By the time I reached the room, my chest felt too tight to breathe.

I yanked my duffel bag from the corner and started throwing things in. Shirts, jeans, toothbrush. It didn't matter if they were folded. I just needed to move; needed to leave before the hole in my chest swallowed me whole.

But the farther I shoved, the heavier the bag felt, and the less sense it made. My hands slowed. The zipper stuck halfway. Finally, I sat down hard on the edge of the bed, elbows on my knees, head in my hands.

I could still feel her.

The press of her body against mine. The taste of her lips, her skin. The way her breath hitched right before she cried out my name like she did that day, back when we thought forever was guaranteed.

It had been like no time passed at all. And for a few minutes, I'd believed it.

My chest ached. My throat burned. I tipped my head back against the wall and let the memory roll through me like it always did when I thought about the beginning.

I was fifteen all over again, on the football field, running drills with the team. It was hot out - too hot, as early August always was. Sweat rolled down my forehead and as I swiped it away, I stole a peek at the bleachers, where I knew she would be.

Abby was always there. People joked that we were attached at the hip. Except she was a girl, and not at all into sports.

No. Abby was an artist.

She sat there, a bag of colored Sharpies beside her. She had one leg crossed over her in what most would consider an awkward position, hair falling over her face, her brows pinched in concentration as she drew on her once perfectly white sneakers.

Her mom was going to have a fit.

I picked up another ball from the pile beside me and launched it down the field, but instead of watching to see if it hit its mark, my eyes went straight back to her.

My heart stuttered when she bit her lip.

These feelings weren't new, not exactly. But when had Abby gone from being Abby, to being someone I thought about every night when I closed my eyes, and again the minute I woke up? When did she stop being just one of the guys, and become a girl?

I showered quickly after practice, and when I got out to my parent's car, she was already there, sitting on the hood, leaning back on her elbows, face to the sky.

One of the guys caught me staring and elbowed me in the ribs. "Later, Taylor," he chuckled, waggling his eyebrows at me, like he could read the thoughts that were forever running through my mind these days.

I rolled my eyes and shook my head. Abby wasn't like the other girls at school. She wasn't like other girls. She was special, and I couldn't fuck that up.

We didn't talk much as I drove back to her place. Her scent filled the car, and I had to roll down the windows just so I could think clearly.

I parked out front, but instead of saying goodbye, I asked her, "Wanna hang out?"

Her face lit up, and she punched my shoulder. "Last one to the treehouse is a rotten egg!"

She was out the door before I even had the chance to think. I chased her across the lawn, through the rusted gate that led to her back yard, only stopping when my hands brushed hers on the old rope ladder.

I followed her up, the boards creaking under our weight. I was honestly surprised it had lasted this long.

We crawled inside, backs against the far wall, legs stretched out in front of us. Dust and the faint smell of old cedar hung in the air. The carved initials of kids long gone scarred the walls, but it felt like ours. Our hideout, our place.

Abby tugged one foot into her lap, Sharpie still in hand, and started shading in the petal of a sunflower.

"What are you working on?" I asked, my voice rougher than I meant it to be.

She grinned and kicked her foot toward me. "Look."

Her sneakers, once blindingly white, were now a collage of color and memory. A football, lopsided but unmistakable. A sunflower, bold and bright. A Ferris wheel, tilted on the canvas like it was about to spin right off her toe.

"The carnival," I said, pointing. "That was the night you ate all the cotton candy and made yourself sick."

She laughed, brushing a strand of hair from her face. "Correction - you bought all the cotton candy. I just couldn't let it go to waste."

I leaned closer, tracing the drawings with my eyes, the scent of her shampoo wrapping around me. My shoulder brushed hers, just barely, and suddenly the space between us felt too small.

Something came over me. A rush. A pull I couldn't fight anymore.

Before I could think better of it, I turned my head and kissed her.

It was quick, and clumsy, more nerves than skill. But her lips were soft, and when she didn't pull away, the whole world tilted under me.

When I finally leaned back, my heart was hammering so hard I thought she could hear it.

She blinked at me, wide-eyed, and then a slow smile curved across her face.

"Finally," she whispered.

I swear I saw forever spread out right there in front of me that day, painted across the inside of that treehouse.

That was the day I knew. She was the one, and nothing that happened after, not the storm, not her disappearing, not the eleven years in between, had ever changed that.

The memory faded, and I was back in the motel room, the stale scent of cheap soap and old carpet closing in around me. My fists clenched against my knees, my packed bag waiting by the door.

I should leave. I should save myself the hurt, get back on the highway, and put Kansas in the rearview.

But I couldn't.

Because no matter how much time had passed, no matter how many walls she tried to put between us, I still felt it. The pull. The truth I'd known since we were kids sitting in that treehouse.

We were meant to be together. I knew it then. I knew it now.

Tomorrow, I'd try again.

Chapter 8

Abby

For the first time in what felt like years, I drove home with the window down and the music turned all the way up.

Agnus Dei by Samuel Barber filled the car, voices rising and falling breaking something open in my chest, a far cry from the sentimental Korean ballads my mother used to hum under her breath, or the polite classical pieces Sung-ho's parents piped through their house during family dinners.

This wasn't gentle, or careful.

It was overwhelming. And it made me feel alive.

Cole sat in the passenger seat, something I never let him do. His hair whipped wild in the wind, his face tilted toward the open sky, eyes bright as he soaked it all in, like he could feel the weight of it too.

"You should do that more often," he said, matter of fact.

"Do what?" I asked, glancing over.

"Smile." He leaned his head back against the seat. "It makes you look like... you."

My chest tightened. I reached over, brushed his hair from his fore-head, then fixed my eyes on the road before the ache behind my ribs could swallow me whole.

The song faded out, and before the next one could start, I reached forward and turned the volume down. By the time we turned onto our street, silence filled the car.

I rolled the window up, smoothed my hair in the rearview, and forced the grin from my face. The weight of the house at the end of the block was already pressing down on me.

Cole noticed. He always noticed. He straightened his shirt, smoothed his hair with both hands, and sat up straighter like he was preparing for inspection.

By the time I eased into the driveway, the fun was gone. The moment had vanished.

We were back in Sung-ho's world.

The house was quiet when we walked in, and relief swept through me like air after holding my breath for too long. His shoes weren't by the door. Not yet.

"You can watch some TV for a little while," I told Cole, softer than I meant. His eyes lit up, and he dropped his backpack by the couch before flipping on the TV. Football highlights flashed across the screen, the roar of a crowd filling the silence.

Cole leaned forward, elbows on his knees, eyes glued to the screen. When a quarterback threaded a pass between two defenders, he shot both fists in the air. "Yes! Did you see that, Mom?"

I smiled despite myself, drying my hands on a dish towel long enough to peek into the living room. "I saw."

He grabbed one of the throw pillows and mimed a pass, his face flushed with excitement, a grin wide enough to make him look years younger.

I pushed the worry down and moved to the kitchen. Dinner had to be perfect, especially after the past couple of nights. I tied my hair back, rolled up my sleeves, and started pulling out ingredients - rice, vegetables, and beef I'd stew just the way Sung-ho liked it.

The sound of the garage door rising sent a chill down my spine.

Cole reacted instantly, fumbling with the remote until the bright green of the field and the roar of the broadcaster vanished, replaced with the monotone voice of a nature documentary.

I wiped my hands on a towel and stepped into the hallway just as Sung-ho entered. His tie was still knotted perfectly, not a hair out of place.

"Welcome home," I said softly, leaning up to press a kiss to his cheek.

He stilled, eyes narrowing as they flicked over me like I'd committed a crime I hadn't even had time to think of yet.

Could he smell Jackson on me? Could he tell? God. I should've showered.

Why didn't I shower?

"Dinner's almost ready," I added quickly, forcing my voice steady, shoving those thoughts down in case he could hear them screaming in my head, and retreated to the kitchen.

The silence followed me, thick and heavy, until I could barely hear the simmering of the pot over the sound of my own heartbeat.

Cole kept his eyes glued to the screen, posture stiff, shoulders hunched like he could make himself smaller.

Dinner was perfect. Of course it was, it had to be. My knuckles ached from all the chopping and sweat still dampened the back of my neck. He ate without complaint. Cole stayed quiet. And I played my part.

My secret was safe - for now.

That night lying in bed beside him, I couldn't close my eyes. I listened as his breathing grew steady, then slipped into snores, but mine never evened out.

I told myself I wasn't thinking about him.

I was only lying to myself.

One moment I was staring at the ceiling, counting my breaths, and the next I was sixteen again, barefoot in the cool grass, the sky stretched wide and endless above us.

We'd snuck out past midnight, a blanket thrown over our shoulders, his hoodie hanging off me like it already belonged there. He kept pointing at the sky, naming constellations he didn't really know, making up stories when he got stuck.

"Ah-bi," he'd said, careful with the sound, like it mattered. "Did I say it right?"

I'd laughed and corrected him, and he'd grinned like he'd won something. Like learning to say my proper name was an achievement.

When the first streak of light cut across the sky, we both gasped. He grabbed my hand without thinking, fingers warm and sure, like there was nowhere else they belonged.

I remember thinking, stupidly, that moments like that didn't end.

I rolled onto my side and squeezed my eyes shut, forcing the image away.

That was the problem.

He wasn't just a man who'd shown up out of nowhere. He was my history. Muscle memory. A part of me that still reacted before my brain could catch up.

And history didn't care about rules or consequences. Or the life I'd so carefully built brick by brick just to survive.

Where was he now? Did he listen when I told him to go? Was he already on the highway, heading back to wherever he called home?

My stomach twisted. Why was he even here?

I pushed the rest away, the old dreams, the seasons that no longer belonged to us. Thinking about where he should've been only made it worse.

And then a colder thought slid in. What if he hadn't gone far at all?

I rolled to my back, stared at the ceiling, and prayed for sleep that wouldn't come.

After all these years and countless prayers that he would come save me, why now? Why when I'd finally managed to build a rhythm I could survive inside?

Morning came too early. My body felt heavy, but my mind wouldn't stop racing, even after the alarm blared. I slipped out of bed before Sung-ho stirred, moving through the kitchen on autopilot.

I boiled water for tea, the bitter smell filling the silence. My mother always said coffee was indulgent, lazy, too American... Tea was discipline. Respectable. Proper. I used to hate it, but over the years it became a small comfort - especially as I added a spoonful of honey and a sliver of fresh ginger. It was sweet and sharp. Comfort with an edge. And all mine.

Cole shuffled in, hair sticking up in every direction, still rubbing the sleep from his eyes. I slid a plate of toast across the table and kissed the top of his head. "Eat up, little man."

I finished packing his lunch while he got dressed and brushed his teeth.

"Bus'll be here any minute," I said, straightening his collar as he made a face, swallowing the last of his orange juice.

We walked outside together, the cool morning air brushing my face. I held on to the moment - him slinging his backpack over one shoulder, the way he waved as he climbed the steps of the yellow bus. He was still my baby boy, the only light in a house that had so little of it.

I stayed there until the bus disappeared around the corner. Only then did I let my shoulders drop.

I loved these mornings when I didn't have to drop him at my mother's house, when I could say goodbye and wish him a good day, the way I liked to - without my mother's watchful eye.

I climbed into my car and as I backed out of the driveway, I froze. "Shit," I muttered under my breath. Time was already limited on these mornings when I saw my son off, the last thing I needed was to forget something. I pulled back up into the driveway and hurried into the house.

I grabbed my travel mug full of tea. I could have left it, but one mistake, even something as simple as that, would have Sung-ho insisting I drop Cole at my mother's every morning. Let her see him off to school.

Let her fill his head with whatever nonsense she wanted.

Mug in hand, I slipped back out and locked the door behind me.

And that's when I saw him.

Jackson stood leaning against his truck on the opposite side of the street. His hat was pulled low, but I knew it was him. I would know him anywhere.

My stomach dropped, fear flooding my veins.

If Sung-ho saw him... God, no. I couldn't even think of that.

I glanced back at the house, then crossed the street in fast, clipped steps. "You can't be here," I hissed, my voice sharper than I intended. "You need to leave."

He didn't flinch. "I'm not leaving. Not without you."

The words hit harder than they should have. My breath caught, and for a second, I let myself believe him. Let myself imagine what it would feel like to grab Cole, run to Jackson, and never look back.

And God help me, I wanted it. I wanted him. The taste of his lips was still on mine, the echo of his touch still humming under my skin.

But that was the problem. It was a fantasy. A betrayal.

I shook my head, backing away. "I can't do this. I have to get to work."

"Abby..."

"Don't." My voice cracked. "Please."

The plea wasn't just for him. It was for me, too. If I let him keep talking, I might not be able to stop myself.

I turned, hurried to my car, and slipped inside with shaking hands.

As I pulled away, I saw him still standing there in my rearview mirror, unmoving.

Dear God, please don't let Sung-ho have seen him.

Chapter 9

Jackson

She told me to leave.

Begged me, really. Her voice cracked when she said it, like the words cost her something.

I stood there on the curb long after her car disappeared, hands in my pockets, her plea still echoing in my head.

I can't do this.

Bullshit.

I knew her. Even after all these years, I knew when she was lying, when something was wrong. And something was definitely wrong, least of all the perfectly landscaped, cookie-cutter neighborhood she lived in.

I pulled my hat off my head and ran my hands through my mess of hair. This wasn't the end of our story, not if I had anything to say about it.

I climbed into my truck and drove. Aimless at first, then toward a diner I'd passed on the edge of town. The kind of place that smelled like burnt coffee and bacon grease, where nobody asked questions if you sat too long and the booths were sticky no matter how often they wiped them down.

I slid into a corner seat and ordered eggs I didn't want and coffee I wouldn't drink, just to keep the waitress from circling back too often.

She lingered anyway. She couldn't have been more than a couple years older than me, her blonde hair teased too high, lipstick smudged at the corners. When she leaned across the table to set down my plate, her blouse dipped low enough to make the offer clear.

A month ago - hell, two weeks ago - I would've indulged. I would've let her distract me, let her pull me into the bathroom or out to her car, anything to forget for a little while.

But not now.

Now, I didn't even look twice. My eyes were already somewhere else.

I could picture Abby's morning as clear as if I'd been there. She'd be in that little house of hers. The kitchen would smell like coffee with way too much sugar, because she never did anything halfway. She'd have her music on, something upbeat, and she'd be dancing barefoot across the floor while she waited for the toaster to spit out her breakfast.

Pop-Tarts. She used to love those. Cherry or strawberry, never frosted, and slathered in butter. She believed the frosting ruined them.

And then she'd spend the morning painting, hair tied up messily, streaks of color across her wrists and jeans, the whole house turned into a studio. Tarps over the floors, canvases leaning against every wall, her laugh echoing through the space like it used to echo through my truck.

That's how I wanted to believe she lived. Free. Untethered. Exactly who she was always meant to be.

The PI had said her last name was Kim now, but I didn't want to believe it meant what it looked like.

No. She'd run, sure. Changed her name, obviously. But Abby married? With attachments?

I couldn't picture it. I wouldn't.

Not when every part of me needed to believe she was still the same girl I left in that bedroom, promising forever.

I pushed the eggs around my plate until the yolk ran cold, then tossed a few bills on the table and left.

By midmorning, I found myself parked just outside her work, in full view of the front doors. The Oakridge Living Center was a nursing home, brick and squat, with an awning that looked like it had been red twenty years ago.

If I hadn't seen her there just yesterday, hadn't been inside of her in one of those rooms less than twenty-four hours ago, I wouldn't believe it. What happened to the girl I used to know? The girl who had hopes and dreams the size of Texas...

I sat in my truck, playing our song on repeat - *Chasing Cars* by Snow Patrol. Over and over, until the words blurred into memory, pulling me back to junior year...

I adjusted my tie for the twentieth time that night as I stood outside her door, a hand-picked bouquet of flowers clutched in my sweaty hand. Her father opened the door, his disapproving stare like a slap in the face.

"Ah-bi, your date is here," he said, not taking his eyes off of me.

He never was my biggest fan, especially after he found out I kissed her. Thank God he couldn't read my mind, couldn't see all the other things I wanted to do to her.

Abby appeared at his side, and it was like all the air was sucked out of the room. She was breathtaking.

I handed her the flowers as I tried to form words. Finally I managed, "You look beautiful."

She smiled, a pink flush lighting up her cheeks. She passed the flowers to her mother who said she'd put them in water for her, and took my hand.

I helped her into my truck, and when I finally climbed in, it took me a couple of tries to get the key into the ignition.

"Everything okay?" she asked, a crease between her brows.

I shook my head and ran a hand through my hair. "Fuck, Abby. Have I told you lately how incredible you are? You take my breath away. How am I supposed to think, let alone drive, with you sitting there, looking like that?"

A sad smile flitted across her face as she smoothed her hands down her pink dress. "My mother said I looked cheap. My dress is too short, too low. Too everything..."

I reached over and tilted her chin up until her eyes met mine. "Don't listen to her. Don't you let her make you feel less than what you are. You're amazing. And that dress..." I grinned, leaning over and pressing a kiss to her soft lips. "That dress is stunning on you."

Homecoming was special this year for multiple reasons. Not only had our team won our football game, but for the first time, I had the most beautiful girl on my arm.

We danced until they announced Homecoming Royalty. They called my name, like they did every year, but I had zero interest. Not unless Abby was going to be up there with me, and we didn't have to stick around to know she wouldn't be. She wasn't one of the cheerleaders, the popular girls. She didn't have to be - she was perfect as is.

And she was mine.

Her hand fit perfectly in mine as we slipped out of the gym, her heels dangling from her fingers, my jacket draped over her shoulders. I drove us out to an old field, and we climbed into the bed of the truck and laid there for what felt like hours, staring at the stars and planning our future.

"I'm gonna play for the Broncos," I said, cocky as hell even though I knew I had absolutely zero control over what team I'd be drafted to, if I even got so lucky.

"I'll have my own display in the Denver Art Museum," she whispered, as though saying it too loud would be bad luck. But the light in her eyes said everything her voice didn't.

It had felt inevitable. Like destiny.

Now here we were, eleven years later, and destiny had lied.

The front door of the nursing home slid open. My head snapped up, still so perfectly in tune with her.

Abby stepped outside, a paper cup in her hand, her scrubs wrinkled from hours of work. She looked tired. Older. But she was still her, and I'd give anything if she were still mine.

I didn't give myself time to think. I turned the key, pulled forward, and eased up to the curb. The engine rumbled low as I rolled down the window.

Her eyes met mine.

"Get in," I said.

Her eyes widened, and she froze on the steps. The paper cup tilted in her hand, spilling a little over the side.

For a second, just a second, her face softened. Like she wanted to smile. Like she wanted to run straight into my arms and forget the whole world.

I watched as she changed in front of me as the fear crept in. Her gaze darted left, then right, scanning the street like she expected someone to step out of the shadows. Her knuckles whitened around the cup. She hugged it close to her chest like a shield.

I leaned closer to the open window, my voice softer now. "Please. Just a minute. Five minutes max, that's all I'm asking."

Her lips parted like she might say something, then pressed together again, pale with the force of it. She shook her head, small and tight.

I could see it, the war inside her. The woman she'd become, careful and guarded, at odds with the girl I remembered who used to climb into my truck without a second thought, laughing like we had forever.

For one long, breathless moment, I thought she'd do it. Thought she'd take that step and slide into the seat beside me like she belonged there.

But instead, she whispered something I couldn't catch, clutched her cup tighter, and turned away.

I gripped the steering wheel until my knuckles ached. I wasn't ready to give up. Not when she still looked at me like that.

Chapter 10

Abby

I couldn't breathe.

Jackson's voice rang in my ears, low and steady. *Get in.*

God, how I wanted to. For one wild second, I almost did - almost let myself believe I could climb into that truck and drive until the world fell away. Just me, him, and the road.

But the weight of everything he didn't know pressed down harder. Sung-ho. My parents. Cole. The careful, fragile life I'd built out of obedience and silence. One wrong step and it would all come crashing down, and I couldn't risk it, not when Cole's safety hung in the balance.

Sung-ho would never let him go. He would never let *us* go.

And Jackson wasn't just anyone. He was Jackson Taylor. Quarterback. A public figure and far too recognizable. If anyone saw us together - even here, in front of this small-town nursing home - it wouldn't just be Sung-ho I had to worry about. The whole world would know. And they would judge me, us, all of it.

And there was still that little nagging issue in the back of my mind - I was a *mom*. That wasn't going to change. And if, by some miracle, we did escape Sung-ho, and ran away with Jackson, I didn't even know who he was anymore.

So, I shook my head, fingers trembling around the paper cup. My lips moved, whispering words I wasn't even sure I meant. *I can't.*

I turned before I lost my nerve, heart hammering, pulse screaming with every step that carried me away from him. But before I could take even three steps, I heard the slam of a truck door.

"Abby." His voice was closer now. Too close.

I froze as his boots hit the pavement. A second later he was in front of me, blocking my path. My eyes trailed up his body; he was taller, broader, more solid than I remembered, despite being with him just yesterday.

My heart leapt into my throat at the same time his scent filled my nose.

"What are you doing?" I hissed, panic clawing at my ribs. "Are you insane? You can't be here!"

Couldn't he see what this looked like? The NFL golden boy standing on a sidewalk with me? Me, who wasn't even allowed to walk into my parents' house without shame clinging to my heels? If anyone snapped a picture... if Sung-ho saw... it would all be over.

"I'm not leaving." His voice was low, and fierce. His green eyes locked on mine like they could hold me in place. "Not without talking to you first."

"Jackson..."

"Two minutes," he cut in. "That's all I'm asking."

God help me, I couldn't breathe. My gaze darted around, terrified Sung-ho or one of the nurses would come around the corner and see him standing there, see me rooted to the spot, torn between obligation and safety, and a love that felt like home.

But was it? Could he possibly still love me the way I would forever love him?

"Fine," I snapped, even though nothing about me felt fine. I needed to know, but more than that, I needed to put him behind me for good. It was the only way. "Meet me around back in a couple of hours when I take my lunch break."

The fight went out of him just like that. His shoulders eased. His lips curved in the smallest smile.

I shoved past him before I could change my mind, back through the sliding doors and inside where the air conditioning hit my flushed face like judgment.

"You've got it bad…"

I stopped dead at the nurses' station. Mrs. Ortiz sat there with her crossword, eyebrows raised, eyes twinkling like she'd just solved a clue.

"What?" My voice squeaked out too high and too fast.

"You're glowing," she grinned, tapping her pen against the desk. "And don't even try to tell me it's that shitty coffee you've been drinking." Her eyes dropped down to the white cup I still held clenched in my hands. "I saw the way you lit up when Mr. Tall-Dark-and-Handsome walked in here yesterday." She nodded toward the doors, "And again today."

"What?" Heat rushed to my cheeks as I scrambled for something to say. "It's nothing," I lied, fumbling for the nearest chart.

"Mmhmm." She chuckled, settling back in her chair. "If that's nothing, I hope nothing walks in here for me, too."

I rolled my eyes, but I couldn't stop the tug in my chest. Couldn't stop the way my steps felt lighter, my pulse quicker every time I thought about him.

Jackson Taylor was dangerous. He always had been.

And not just dangerous to my marriage. He was a risk to my survival. To my son. To the life I'd learned to navigate. He was too big, too loud, and way too visible. A man who belonged to the public could never belong to me.

Yet, when my lunch break came, my feet carried me right out the back doors without a second thought or hesitation.

The lot was quiet, the sun beating down on the cracked pavement. His truck was there, idling in the shade. The driver's window rolled down, and there he was, waiting, just like he'd always waited for me.

My body moved before my brain could stop it. The door clicked shut behind me, sealing us off from the rest of the world, and for a fleeting heartbeat, I wasn't Ah-bi, Sung-ho's wife or my mother's disappointment.

I was Abby. Just Abby.

Suddenly I was surrounded by his warmth, his scent. My chest rose and fell too fast. His eyes found mine, steady and burning, and then I wasn't thinking anymore.

I leaned across the seat, grabbed his collar, and kissed him. It was reckless, stupid, dangerous, and God, it was mine.

His mouth was warm, familiar, and completely devastating. The taste of him hit me like lightning, and for one breathless heartbeat, I let myself drown in it.

Then reality slammed back in.

I tore my mouth from his and pressed a trembling hand to his chest, holding him back before he could pull me under his spell again. My pulse was a hammer in my ears, my breath ragged.

"Abby..." he started, reaching for me.

"No." I shook my head hard, fingers tightening against him like a barrier. "Don't."

His eyes searched mine, hurt flickering there, confusion and something deeper I couldn't name.

The taste of him still clung to my lips, and I hated myself for wanting more. Hated how alive I felt, because I knew it couldn't last.

I shoved him back with a trembling hand, my voice breaking before I could stop it. "What do you want from me?" The words cut sharper than I meant, brittle and desperate. Because if I gave in again, if I let him be the one thing I couldn't control, I wasn't sure I'd survive it.

I needed him gone. Out of my head and out of the hollow space in my chest where his name had lived for too long. Because if I didn't, he'd take everything with him when he left - including me.

Chapter 11

Jackson

"What do you want from me?"

Her words sliced through me, sharp enough to sting, sharp enough to leave a mark.

I could still taste her on my lips. Still feel the heat of her palm pressed to my chest, like she'd burned her shape into me before shoving me away.

What did I want from her?

Nothing and everything all at once.

I didn't want anything *from* her; I just wanted *her*.

I wanted her in my arms again, in my bed. I wanted her in Falcon Pointe, in my damn life the way she was supposed to be. I wanted the girl I kissed under the stars, the one who painted sunflowers on her sneakers and planned a future with me like it was a given.

"I want you," I said hoarsely, the words torn from somewhere deep and raw. "Just you, Abby. Come home with me. We can finally have what we always talked about…"

She shook her head so fast it stopped me cold.

"I can't," she whispered.

Her eyes darted to the building behind us, then back to me. Fear, sharp and real, flickered there. "I have a life here. My family…"

She didn't say who. She didn't have to.

My gut twisted as my gaze dropped to her hands. Bare. No ring. No jewelry at all.

"Abby…"

"I can't." Her voice broke this time. Before I could reach for her again, she pushed the door open and stepped out into the sunlight.

She stood on the cracked pavement, her shoulders squared even as her fingers twisted together. Then she looked at me, one last glance that felt like both a goodbye and a plea.

"Go home. Please. I can't see you again. I can't be seen with you again."

Then she walked away.

"Abby!" My voice rang out loud and desperate. "I'm not giving up on you. You hear me? I'm not done!"

But she didn't turn back.

She disappeared through those doors, leaving me alone with the echo of her name on my tongue.

Abby had never walked away from me before. She vanished, without a word, without a trace, but I'd never watched her choose to leave me standing there. I hadn't realized until now how much worse that could hurt. How final it would feel to see her feet carry her away like I was nothing.

I sat there for a long minute, parked in the shade. Pain bloomed in my chest and all I could do was hold on. I gripped the wheel so hard my knuckles ached, only letting go when the ache became tolerable. Then I let go and pressed my fingertips to my mouth, as if I could still hold on to the ghost of her lips.

For the first time in years, I felt hollow.

What the hell was she hiding from me?

I leaned back in the seat, the engine idling low, and shut my eyes. I could still hear her voice, cracked and breaking when she said she couldn't. Couldn't see me. Couldn't *be seen* with me.

Couldn't, not wouldn't.

That difference mattered.

My chest burned like I'd run a hundred yards flat out. Eleven years apart and she still kissed me like she meant it. Still looked at me like she remembered.

She could say no until her lips turned blue, but her actions told a different story.

After all this time, I still couldn't let go of the belief that what we had mattered, even if she couldn't feel it anymore.

I paced the motel room, back and forth until the worn carpet groaned under my boots. My stomach clenched with hunger, but I couldn't bring myself to leave, not when I knew exactly what would happen if I saw her again. I didn't trust myself to stay away.

And to make matters worse, Grady was still back home, waiting for confirmation that it was really her.

I stared up at the ceiling, at the water stains shaped like maps I couldn't read, willing the right words to come. Finally, I dropped onto the bed, thumb flying across the screen.

> **Me:** It's definitely her. She's exactly how I remember.

> **Me:** Except she doesn't want to talk to me.

> **Me:** I need more time.

> **Me:** You okay watching the bar for a little longer?

The reply came almost instantly, like he'd been waiting.

> **Grady:** Take your time, I've got it handled.

I let out a shaky breath and dropped the phone onto the nightstand. Then scrubbed my hands over my face until my skin stung.

I was so damn grateful for him, for the way he always had my back. I just prayed Whitney wasn't making things harder than they needed to be.

But Grady's words echoed anyway.

Take your time.

The only problem was, time was the one thing I didn't feel like I had.

I'd been chasing Abby for eleven years, and every time I thought I'd found her, she slipped through my fingers.

Once, back in college after my ACL blew and football was ripped out from under me, I spent weeks hunched over my laptop, searching like a man possessed. Football was gone. Abby was the only thing left that made sense.

Then I found it, a news article out of San Antonio, about an up-and-coming artist named A. Park.

My heart damn near stopped.

I skipped class, climbed in my truck, and drove twelve hours straight, convinced I'd finally found her.

But "A. Park" turned out to be Andrew Park. Some guy with paint on his jeans and a gallery full of people cheering him on.

Not Abby. Not even close.

My knee ached the entire drive back, stiff and swollen from surgery, the brace digging into my skin like punishment. It was the same knee that cost me football, the same knee that reminded me every damn day that dreams could vanish in a second.

That was the closest I'd come.

Until now.

And I couldn't shake the fear that if I blinked, if I let up even for a second, she'd vanish again.

My knee still throbbed, like it remembered the hours I'd spent behind the wheel chasing a name that wasn't hers. Maybe it always would. A reminder of everything I'd lost.

After she disappeared, I searched like a man who didn't know how to stop.

I called friends who didn't answer. Knocked on doors that stayed shut. I chased shadows across state lines, every Park in three counties blurring together until names stopped meaning anything at all.

Every trail went cold.

When I finally came back, something in me was different. Quieter. Sharper. I drank to forget, fought to feel something, went home with anyone who didn't ask questions.

But I never stopped looking.

Not after the way she'd looked at me that night when we were seventeen. Not after the promise I made when I left her bed and swore I'd be right back.

Back then it had just been football and a girl with paint-stained hands and a laugh that belonged to me.

Now it was more than that.

Now it was the one thing I couldn't let myself lose again.

I pressed the heel of my hand into my chest, right where it ached the most, and for the life of me I couldn't tell which hurt worse anymore - the knee that ended my future, or the girl who got away.

The thought of leaving her was too much to bear, something I didn't know how to survive.

Chapter 12

Abby

I wrapped up my day on autopilot, unable to get the look on Jackson's face as I walked away out of my head. He looked devastated, and it was no less than I felt. The drive home was a blur, and for the first time ever, I was thankful my mother picked Cole up from school on Wednesdays and took him to youth group at the church. It bought me time; time to breathe, time to smother my guilt in routine.

I tied my apron, rolled up my sleeves, and threw myself into cooking. I diced the vegetables precisely, stirred the broth, and wiped the counters twice over though they were already clean. If I could make dinner flawless, maybe it would erase the heat of Jackson's kiss still lingering on my lips, enough that Sung-ho wouldn't see it written across my face.

The garage door groaned open, and my whole body stiffened. Sung-ho stepped inside, his tie still knotted, his hair sharp as glass. He always looked the same - immaculate, deliberate, untouchable.

"Welcome home," I said softly, twisting my wedding band nervously around my finger. I took it off earlier today, afraid of what Jackson would think, and the guilt gnawed at me.

He came closer, close enough that I could smell his cologne, so much different from Jackson's. "How was your day?"

"Fine," I replied quickly. Too quickly.

He bent just enough to press a kiss to my cheek, and for one terrifying second he lingered, inhaling like he might catch some trace of the secret still burning on my skin. My pulse roared. But then he pulled back, his head cocking slightly, eyes narrowing like he was dissecting me under a lens. My stomach flipped.

He couldn't tell, could he?

Before he could ask anything else, the front door opened, and Cole's sneakers squeaked on the hardwood. My son slipped inside, backpack slung low, his shoulders already slumped. And trailing behind him was my mother.

"Ah-bi," she said with her usual clipped tone, "Ha-joon is behind on his Bible verses. The Chen boys recited three chapters tonight. Three. And he..." she shook her head, lips pursed and turned to my son. "You can't afford to fall behind. What will people think?"

Cole's eyes dropped to the floor. "Yes, Halmeoni," he murmured, voice small like he wanted to disappear.

I shot her a tight smile and took his backpack. "Thank you for bringing him," I said, though what I wanted was for her to leave.

She sniffed. "Maybe if you didn't spend so much time at that job..."

"I'll try harder," I forced through my teeth.

I bit the inside of my cheek hard enough to taste copper. That job was her idea. Her proof to the world that I was respectable, useful, that I could provide even if my husband didn't need me to. But secretly, I'd come to cherish the hours I was away from this house, away from her scrutiny, away from the sharp edges of Sung-ho's silence.

To her, Cole would always be a stain. To me, he was perfect.

Some days I'd give anything to grab him and run away. Just the two of us.

Sung-ho saw her out, their heads tipped together as they spoke in hushed whispers. I rolled my eyes at their turned backs and returned to the kitchen.

Dinner passed in brittle silence. The stew was perfect. Of course it was. Sung-ho ate without complaint, Cole sat quiet, barely picking at his food. And me? The weight of everything pressed down on me until I could hardly swallow.

Afterward, I placed a hand gently on Cole's shoulder. "Brush your teeth, then I'll meet you in your room for some reading, okay?"

He nodded, grateful for the reprieve, and scurried down the hall.

I started to follow but Sung-ho's voice stopped me. "You let him disrespect the Word."

My spine stiffened. "He's ten. He's trying."

"Trying is not enough." His words snapped like a whip.

"He's a good boy. He just..."

His hand clamped around my wrist, yanking me back. His grip was like iron, fingers digging into my skin until I winced.

"Do not walk away from me when I am speaking." His voice was quiet. Deadly.

Pain shot up my arm. "I'm sorry," I whispered, bowing my head.

Only when I submitted did he let go. I fled the kitchen, rubbing my wrist, heart pounding against my ribs. I knew better than to talk back or try to walk away from him. But for Cole, I'd risk myself every time. Because if anything happened to me... who knew what would happen to my incredible boy.

In Cole's room, the air felt lighter, safer, if that were possible. I pulled a worn Bible from his bookshelf, its slipcover fraying at the edges, and curled up beside him. His eyes lit up instantly as I opened it.

Inside was our little secret. This book wasn't scripture like the outside implied, but a book about America's greatest sport. The cover read *Football: Strategy, Legends, and Plays*, pages dog-eared from numerous late night reading sessions.

"You remembered," he whispered, something warm and surprised settling into his tired eyes.

"Of course I did," I whispered back. "Ready for the next chapter?"

He nodded eagerly, shifting closer so our shoulders touched. I angled the book so we could both see, and together we traced the glossy photo of a quarterback mid-throw.

"Look at that arm," Cole breathed. "Bet he could throw it all the way across the field."

I smiled. "I don't know... you've got a pretty good arm yourself."

His cheeks flushed, his grin widening. "Think I could play pro one day?"

I brushed his hair back, my heart aching with how badly I wanted to say yes without hesitation. "I think you can do anything you put your mind to. Just... maybe not where anyone can see yet, okay?"

He ducked his head but nodded. We turned another page, whispering about plays, about grit and heart, about how football was more than just a game. His laughter, quiet and stifled, still cracked me open.

This was who he was meant to be: light, hopeful, and unafraid.

I wanted to freeze the moment. To wrap us both in it and never let the outside world in.

When I finally closed the book, his lids were heavy, his body relaxed against me. "Mom?"

"Yeah?"

"Are you mad at me?"

"Why would I be mad at you?"

"Because of what grandma said. About the Bible verses. I promise I'll try harder."

I kissed his forehead, lingering for just a moment. "I could never be mad at you for something like that. Don't even worry about it, okay?"

"Okay."

"Goodnight, my sweet boy."

"Night, Mom," he murmured, already half-asleep.

I pulled the covers tight and turned off his lamp. But when the shadows closed in, so did the ache.

Because as much as I loved these moments, I couldn't ignore the truth. Cole deserved a father who cheered when he threw a ball.

Someone who showed up.

Someone who didn't make him flinch at raised voices or measure every word before he spoke.

I pressed my lips together, forcing the thought back down where it belonged.

That night as Sung-ho's steady breathing filled the room, the occasional snore rattling like chains, I lay awake, staring at the ceiling. I should have been relieved - dinner was flawless, and my secret was safe. But the silence was suffocating.

Because every time I closed my eyes, I didn't see my husband.

I saw Jackson.

The warmth of his mouth still clung to mine. The way his voice wrapped around my name. The fire he made me feel with just a look.

I turned onto my side, clutching my pillow like it could anchor me. God help me, I wanted him. Not Sung-ho, not this house, not this life.

Jackson.

And that was the most dangerous truth of all.

Chapter 13

Jackson

For three days, I didn't go near her.

Not up close, anyway.

I told myself I was giving her space.

There was a time I'd filled nights with anything that kept me from thinking too hard. Anything that didn't ask me to stay.

I didn't live like that anymore.

And the truth was, I couldn't stay away. Not when her voice still echoed in my head: *I can't see you again. I can't be seen with you again.*

So instead of chasing her like I wanted to, I parked across the street from Oakridge, far enough back that no one would notice. And every morning, I caught glimpses of her.

The way she pushed through the sliding doors with her badge clipped to her side pocket, her travel mug clutched like a lifeline. The way she stepped out back mid-morning, her shoulders sagging like she had to breathe before she could face the next round. The way she picked at a muffin, leaving half behind like it was too much.

Since I'd been here, she looked thinner. Not the kind of thin that came from diet or exercise, but the kind that whispered something was wrong. Yeah, Abby's body had changed since we were kids, softer in some places, stronger in others, but it wasn't her curves that worried me. It was the way she seemed smaller inside them, like the weight she carried was crushing her.

I hated it. Hated not knowing what was breaking her down.

Was it me?

Saturday came, and for the first time, I didn't see her go in. I sat there until nearly ten, watching the lot, until it finally clicked; it was her day off.

I drove back to the motel, the room stale and suffocating, and dialed Grady.

He answered on the second ring. "Jackson." Relief warmed his voice.

"Hey." I sat heavily on the edge of the bed, staring at the peeling wallpaper. "How's it going there?"

"It's good. Busy. Steven's been a huge help."

"Yeah, I'm not surprised. I've always liked him." I hesitated. Those words didn't feel like enough, but I refused to say more. "And Emily?"

Grady sighed. "Oh, you know..."

I didn't like the sound of that, but I let it go. His girlfriend, Emily, was poison. But he had to come to that conclusion himself.

Guilt gnawed at me as I shifted the subject. "How's Whitney?"

"I took her to the doc. Got her cast swapped for a walking boot."

"That's good, right?"

"She's happier," he said, and I could hear the smile in his voice.

"She still mad at me?"

He didn't answer right away. Then, gently, "Why don't you just tell her?"

"I can't." The words scraped out. "What if... what if things don't go the way I hope? I don't want her disappointed. I know how much she loved Abby, looked up to her, you know? If this falls apart..."

"Yeah. Yeah, I get it," he said. "Don't worry about Whitney. I've got her."

"I know you do. I appreciate you, man."

"Yeah, yeah." He cleared his throat. "So, how's it really going out there?"

"I don't know... I mean, I've seen her, held her, touched her. Fuck, man. I had *sex* with her. But something's wrong."

"What do you mean?"

I leaned forward, elbows on my knees. "First, she's hot, then she's cold. She says she can't see me again, then kisses me like no time has passed. Maybe I'm imagining things, making a mountain out of a molehill - or whatever that expression is."

"Well, it has been eleven years. Maybe she just needs more time?"

"Yeah, maybe." I stood and crossed the small room, picking up the remote for the TV I had yet to turn on. "Look, I should probably go. Thank you for looking after the bar, and my sister."

"Of course. Is there anything else I can do?"

I set the remote down and looked up at the water-stained ceiling. "Actually, yeah. Can you send me the latest sales reports? I might as well get some work done while I'm here."

Anything to keep me from climbing the walls.

After I hung up, I drifted into the bathroom and stared at my reflection in the cracked mirror. The man looking back at me was older, rougher, scarred. What did Abby see when she looked at me? Was I still the boy she loved, or just a ghost of what we were?

That day eleven years ago, I ran out of her house barefoot, my shoes clutched in one hand.

The sirens were already screaming. The wind hit first, hot and violent, like the world had decided to shove back. The sky had gone that sick green-black, the kind that makes your stomach drop because you know what's coming.

I told her I'd be right back.

But I never made it.

I didn't even get halfway down the block before the air knocked me flat, before everything I knew splintered apart. I ran toward home, toward Whitney, toward the noise and chaos, and by the time it was over, nothing was the same.

I lost her that night.

Not because I stopped loving her. Not because I chose wrong.

But because sometimes running isn't enough.

I pressed my fingertips to my mouth. I could still taste her. Still feel the heat of her palm against my chest.

I tried to tell myself I could walk away. That I should.

But every time I imagined leaving her there, watching her grow smaller under whatever weight she carried, something in me resisted. Not resolve. *Fear.*

I didn't know how to stop caring. I only knew that pretending I could, felt like a lie.

Tomorrow, I'd try again.

Because walking away from Abby wasn't an option I could live with.

Chapter 14

Abby

I don't know what I expected as I left for work the next day. Jackson was never one to give up, so when Thursday passed, and then Friday without even a glimpse of him, I began to wonder. *Did he really leave?*

It made sense. Not only did I tell him to go, but football season was starting soon. He wouldn't have time for me anymore.

And while he was giving me exactly what I asked for, it still hurt.

It didn't help that today was Saturday, a day I had always come to dread.

I knocked on Cole's door. "Hey, bud. You almost ready?" I pushed the door open just enough to peek in when I didn't get a response, then all the way when I saw my sweet boy, sitting with his shoulders slumped on the edge of his bed. "Cole?"

I stepped inside and closed his door. "Hey, why aren't you getting ready? Grandpa will be here any minute."

"Do I have to go?"

I sat beside him and nudged his shoulder. "I thought you liked Saturdays with your grandparents."

"I did, when we would go to the park, or the zoo. Now it's all about Korean school and the 'Chen boys'." He said that last part with air quotes.

"I know they've been strict with you lately, but that's because they only want the best for you."

"Did you have to go to Korean school?"

I shook my head. "No. There wasn't one where I grew up." What I didn't say was that them sending him to Korean school was their way of making sure he didn't end up like me - their failure of a daughter.

"You're lucky," he crossed his arms over his chest. "Why can't I be like the other kids, like my friends? They ride bikes, play sports, video games even!"

I wrapped an arm around him and pulled him into a sideways hug. "I know it's hard being different. I'll talk to them, okay?"

The doorbell rang and a pit formed in my stomach, not only for my son, but for what the rest of the day would bring. I kissed the top of Cole's head and stood up, grabbing his overnight bag. "How about we go to the park after I pick you up tomorrow?"

He jumped up with an unexpected burst of energy. "Can we?"

I nodded, forcing a smile. "Come on, let's not keep your grandparents waiting."

I walked him to the door, handed over his bag, and pressed one last kiss to his cheek before watching him climb into the back seat of my father's car. He gave me a half-hearted wave, and then they were gone.

The silence that followed was heavy. I shut the door and pressed my forehead against it, breathing in the quiet that wasn't peaceful at all. Without Cole, the house always felt colder, emptier, yet still suffocating, like Sung-ho's presence expanded to fill every corner.

I peeled myself away and went straight to work, my mother's voice echoing in my head, *A clean house is a happy house.*

Sung-ho spent Saturday afternoons golfing with colleagues, leaving me to my housework. I scrubbed the counters, vacuumed the rugs, dusted the mantle until it gleamed. Every motion was practiced and precise, meant to erase any trace of disorder, any hint that people actually lived here. When the house looked staged enough to pass a military inspection, I turned to myself.

I showered using the body wash and shampoo he bought me. I shaved every inch of my body then ran his preferred moisturizing lotion over my arms and legs. I straightened my hair, then went to the closet and pulled out the dress he liked - black with a collared neck, capped sleeves, and a belted waist, that hung just below my knees.

I applied my makeup the way he liked it - light but flawless, then finished the look by pulling my hair back into a tidy bun. Neat, but not severe.

I caught my reflection in the mirror as I fastened the necklace he'd given me for our last anniversary. The woman staring back was polished, composed, and untouchable.

A complete stranger.

But under the smooth fabric, my skin still hummed with the ghost of Jackson's touch, and no amount of powder or perfume could cover it.

The garage door rattled open, and I stiffened.

Sung-ho stepped inside a moment later, still in his golf polo and slacks. His hair was flattened from the cap he'd worn, faint lines pressed into his forehead where the sun had baked his skin all afternoon. He smelled faintly of grass, sweat, and cologne he'd no doubt splashed on without showering.

I smoothed my dress and checked the belt at my waist, wishing I could disappear into the world I visited in my dreams. Instead, I waited, like a good little wife.

His eyes flicked over me once. No compliment, no pause. Just his expectation that I be perfect. He slipped past me and reappeared a moment later in a crisp, white button down, still adjusting his tie. Suit jacket in hand, he gave the smallest nod toward the door. "Let's go, or we'll be late."

Late. I swallowed the bitter taste in my mouth. *He* hadn't even bothered to shower, but *I* was the one who would make us late.

His Mercedes purred in the driveway, sleek and dark, a car so polished it practically reflected the whole neighborhood. I slid into the passenger seat, its leather cool against my legs, and folded my hands neatly in my lap. My silver sedan, a sad comparison beside us, not even worthy enough to be parked in the garage.

Dinner was at the nicest restaurant in Stonehill. White tablecloths, glass chandeliers, waiters with stiff bowties. A place where every bite was supposed to taste like status.

Our conversation was clipped, as always.

"The meeting went well," Sung-ho said between bites of steak. "The merger will finalize soon."

I nodded. "That's good."

His eyes sharpened. "You should sit up straighter. People notice."

I adjusted, pressing my shoulders back, my stomach hollow.

Between sips of his wine, he continued, "Your mother tells me Ha-joon's not performing as well as he should be in Korean school. His pronunciation isn't crisp enough, and he's gotten lazy with his tones."

My jaw ached with the force it took to hold back my words. Cole was ten. He was trying. He was already carrying more weight than most adults I knew. But Sung-ho didn't want to hear that.

"He didn't finish his writing homework," he continued. "The Chen boys already know twice as many characters."

I swallowed hard. "He's trying…"

"Trying is not enough," Sung-ho snapped, his voice still low enough not to draw attention, but sharp as glass all the same. "Do you think Harvard will care that he *tried* when he cannot even master discipline? Do you think the elders at church will be impressed with excuses?"

I pressed my napkin tighter into my lap, fingers trembling under the table.

"And another thing," he went on, dabbing his mouth with his napkin like the words were casual. "She says Ha-joon was talking about football again. Do you encourage this?"

"No," I whispered quickly.

"You had better not." He set the napkin down beside his plate, eyes narrowing across the table. "I'll not have him wasting time on that… sport." His lip curled as though the word itself were dirty. "Football. Disgraceful…"

His eyes bored into me, unblinking. "Do you understand?"

I swallowed hard, forcing my shoulders not to flinch. "Yes.

He leaned back in his chair, satisfaction flickering across his face. Then he launched into another story about golf with his colleagues - how one had praised his swing, how another admired his watch. The world turned around him, and I revolved in silence.

When the bill came, he slipped his card inside the folder with a practiced flick. No tip, of course. Gratitude wasn't something Sung-ho believed in.

The drive home was quiet. He hummed along with the classical station, tapping two fingers against the wheel, while I stared out the window and wished I could see the stars. The glow of passing streetlamps slid across his face, unchanging, steady, while my chest tightened with every mile closer to the house.

When we pulled into the garage, he didn't wait for me to gather my things. He was already out of the car, jacket shrugged off, shoes placed neatly by the door the second we stepped inside. No pause, no conversation, not even the pretense of small talk about the evening. His hand found my elbow, guiding me down the hall with the same inevitability as every Saturday night.

There were no words. There was no tenderness. He led me to the bedroom like he always did, shutting the door as if that made us private. His fingers were perfunctory, tugging at the zipper of my dress with a sharpness that made me flinch, while I fumbled with the belt.

I forced my breathing to stay even, my smile to be small and demure, like this was what I wanted. Like this was who I was.

And as much as I hated it, it was. I was Mrs. Kim, and this was my duty.

His weight pressed down on me, his rhythm mechanical. There was no kiss, no gentleness. Just the sound of our bed creaking, his breath hot in my ear, the faint scent of stale cologne clinging to his shirt.

That's right - he didn't even take off his shirt.

Inside, I counted the seconds. One. Two. Three.

Outside, I arched my back, parted my lips, and made the quiet sounds I knew he expected. Not too much, never too loud. Just enough to keep him satisfied, to hide the truth that my mind was anywhere but here.

And in my head... it wasn't Sung-ho at all that was touching me, it was Jackson. The way he kissed me like I was something holy, how his hands trembled with restraint even when hunger tore through him. With him, I had always felt weightless. Here, I felt buried alive.

It didn't take long. It never did. He groaned, hips stilling, and I exhaled a breath I hadn't realized I'd been holding.

He rolled off me, already reaching for his phone on the nightstand, his attention gone the instant he was satisfied. "You've been tracking your cycle?"

"Yes," I whispered, staring at the ceiling.

"It's time." His thumb scrolled across the screen as if we were discussing dinner. "Keep your legs up."

My stomach lurched. Still, I shifted, propping my calves against the headboard. I did as I was told, keeping his seed in me long enough to satisfy him.

He looked over once, just long enough to confirm compliance, then turned back to his phone. "Good. Don't waste this chance. I want a son of my own."

The words gutted me. My chest caved as Cole's face flashed in my mind - his grin when we whispered about football plays, the light in his eyes when he believed in himself.

My son. My only reason.

I closed my eyes, legs trembling against the wall, and let the silence close in. But behind my eyelids, I saw green eyes, and heard a voice that had once promised forever.

Jackson.

And God help me, I wished it were him. The thought shamed me. But worse than that, it kept me alive.

Monday came too soon, the weekends never feeling quite long enough. Even still, work felt like the only place I could breathe, where the routine dulled the ache. But when I stepped out back for my mid-morning break, a mug of lukewarm coffee in hand, my breath caught.

Even from a distance, I could see the sunflower, bright, golden, and impossible to miss against the dull silver paint of my car. Its stem was tucked neatly beneath the wiper, the petals bent just slightly from the breeze.

I hurried across the lot to get a better look. That's when I saw it, a folded note tied to its stem.

I glanced around, pulse racing. The world looked ordinary; patients' families coming and going, aides on smoke breaks. But I felt exposed, like someone had stripped me bare in the middle of the day.

My fingers trembled as I pulled it free.

I pressed the flower to my chest and slid into the driver's seat, shutting the door before unfolding the note. His handwriting was the same - sharp, slanted, just messy enough that I could hear him rushing to get the words down before he lost his nerve.

    Abby,

      I know you asked me to stay away. I'm trying to respect that, even when it feels like I'm failing.

      I won't pretend I don't still care about you. I do. More than I know how to explain. But I hear you, and I don't want to cause you pain...

      If you ever decide you want to talk - really talk - I'll be here. And if you don't, I'll find a way to live with that too.

      I just needed you to know I didn't come back to

hurt you.

I'm at the motel off 6th for a few more days, room 117. If you ever want to reach me, you can call or text me at 970-555-0172.

Always,

-J

By the time I finished reading, my hands were shaking so badly I almost dropped the paper.

Room 117.

He was still here. Waiting for me.

A sob clawed at my throat, half desperate, half wild. God, I wanted to go. I wanted to see him, to feel him, to remember what it was like to be alive instead of just surviving.

But if Sung-ho ever found out... if my parents ever even suspected...

I crushed the note in my fist, tears burning the backs of my eyes. I couldn't breathe.

I wasn't Abby anymore. I was Ah-bi, the dutiful daughter. Mrs. Kim, the obedient wife. Mom, the quiet protector.

But staring at that flower, at the crumpled note from the only man who had ever seen me for me and loved me for it, I wondered, just for a second, if maybe I could still be Abby too.

Chapter 15

Jackson

I wore a path into the cheap motel carpet, back and forth between the bed and the door, the sunflower's absence from the dresser like a hollow ache in my chest.

Maybe my letter was too much, too bold. Maybe she'd found it and ripped it up, thrown it away. Maybe she hated me for pushing. I raked a hand through my hair, my shirt clinging damp to my back. I'd rather take her anger straight to the chest than her silence. I've lived the past eleven years in silence, and it was killing me.

The hours crawled by. Afternoon shadows stretched across the room like accusations, and I'd just convinced myself I'd made a monumental mistake when I heard a soft, almost hesitant knock, like it could've been my imagination.

But when I opened the door, there she was.

For a breath, we just stared at each other, the air between us charged and trembling. Then she moved, straight into me, her body colliding with mine like we were magnets finally closing the distance. My arms wrapped around her without thought, holding her so tight I was afraid I might never let go.

I pulled her inside, and kicked the door shut, but neither of us said a word. We didn't need to. Her lips found mine, and I tasted years of silence, years of what-ifs, years of prayers I thought had gone unanswered.

She was warm and trembling in my hands, and I couldn't stop touching her - her face, her hair, the curve of her back beneath my palms. I wanted to memorize her all over again, trace every line like I was afraid she'd slip away before morning.

When I laid her down on the bed, she looked up at me with those same wide, defiant eyes I'd fallen for when we were kids. But they were older now. Sadder. And still, I loved them all the same.

"Abby," I whispered, my voice rough, torn from someplace I hadn't touched in years.

Her fingers brushed my jaw, and her lips curved in the faintest, almost broken smile. "I missed you."

The words cracked me open.

I kissed her like I'd waited eleven years for it. Because I had. Slow, desperate, reverent. Every movement was careful, not because I didn't want her, but because I needed her to know - she wasn't just a body I was touching. She was the girl I had never stopped wanting.

Her breath hitched when I slipped my hand beneath her shirt, skimming the soft skin I used to dream about. She arched into me, pulling me closer, and I gave in, letting myself feel the way her body still fit against mine so perfect. Familiar enough to make me forget myself.

When I tugged her top upward, she raised her arms to let me pull it over her head. The sight of her stopped me cold.

She was the same Abby, and yet not. Fuller now. Softer. The years written into her body in ways that broke me. My eyes caught on the faint stretch marks feathering across her stomach, soft reminders that there was so much about her I didn't know anymore. My hand trembled as I traced them; I bent and brushed my lips over each one.

"I never should've left you that night when we were seventeen," I whispered against her skin. "I never stopped wanting you."

Her breath hitched, her fingers tangling in my hair like she didn't believe me but wanted to.

I pulled back just enough to strip my own shirt over my head. Her eyes widened, her hand lifting to splay over the tattoo inked across my heart - sunflowers in full bloom, their stems tangling around her name. I'd gotten it years ago, when I was young and angry and couldn't say her name out loud without breaking, but needed her close all the same.

Her fingers traced the petals, and I shuddered. She looked up at me, her lips parted, and I kissed her again, deeper this time, like her touch on that mark had struck a match inside my chest.

My hands slid to her waist, finding the soft bow of the drawstring on her scrubs. I took my time untying it, my fingers brushing her skin again and again, deliberate, and unhurried. She sucked in a breath, her hips shifting slightly, and I felt the tremor of it all the way through me.

I eased the fabric down her hips, then slower still, guiding it over her thighs, my knuckles grazing warm skin inch by inch. Goosebumps rose beneath my touch, her body responding before she said a word. I followed the path with my hands, with my mouth, kissing her stomach, her hips, until she was bare beneath me, breathless and waiting.

I knelt between her legs, my nose brushing the soft juncture of her thighs as I breathed her in. God, she smelled like memory and heat and something achingly familiar. Abby. Always Abby.

I pressed a kiss to her inner thigh. Then another. I lingered there, letting the anticipation stretch, my hands steady on her legs as her fingers tightened in my hair. Every instinct screamed to rush, to take, but this wasn't about that. This was about showing her I was here. That I wasn't going anywhere.

I slowly kissed my way higher, savoring every quiet sound she made, every shiver beneath my mouth. I wanted to learn her again, remind her of what it felt like to be touched like she mattered, like she was cherished.

Next time, I promised myself. Next time, I'd take her apart with nothing but patience and devotion. I'd worship her the way she deserved.

But not now. Not when my chest ached with the need to have her.

I eased back just long enough to shed my jeans and boxer briefs, slower this time, aware of her eyes on me, the quiet anticipation humming between us. When I came back to her, I didn't rush. I settled my weight carefully, like she was something fragile and infinitely precious, my forehead resting against hers as we both caught our breath.

"Look at me," I whispered. She did, those familiar eyes shining, vulnerable and brave all at once. "Are you sure?"

Her lips trembled as she nodded, her hands sliding up my arms, grounding me. "Yes."

I moved then, slowly, giving her time to feel every inch of me, to pull back if she needed to. Her breath hitched as I eased inside her, the warmth of her surrounding me so completely it stole the air from my lungs. I stilled there, holding myself steady, letting us both adjust, letting the moment settle.

"Jackson…" she breathed, my name like a prayer, and something in my chest cracked wide open.

I kissed her softly, deeply, like I had all the time in the world. When I began to move, it was unhurried, almost restrained, each motion measured and sure. I stayed close, my forehead pressed to hers, our breaths tangling as if we were relearning the rhythm of each other.

"You're it for me," I whispered, the words spilling out before I could stop them. "You're all I've ever wanted."

Her eyes fluttered shut, a tear slipping free, and she cupped my face like she needed the reassurance as much as I did. I kissed the salt from her cheek, then her mouth, her throat, the delicate hollow at her collarbone, every touch meant to remind her she was safe, cherished, and wanted.

Her legs wrapped around me slowly, drawing me closer, deeper, and I went with her willingly, losing myself in the way she fit against me like memory and truth all at once. This wasn't just sex, it was remembering, reconnecting, daring to believe that what we'd had was still here, still alive.

She whispered to me between breaths - missed you, love you, don't stop - and each word anchored itself somewhere deep inside my ribs. I brushed my thumb along her jaw, tracing down to her lips, watching her mouth part as I leaned into the sensation, just a little more, careful not to break the spell between us.

She gasped, her body arching beneath me, and the sight of her - open, trusting, undone - nearly unraveled me.

When it finally crested, it wasn't rushed. It was slow and overwhelming, like the release of something we'd both been holding for eleven years. She cried my name, and I followed her, burying my face against her neck as everything shattered and came back together all at once.

I held her through it, through the aftershocks, through the quiet that followed, like if I didn't, we might both slip away again.

For a long time, there was only the quiet.

Our breaths slowly found the same rhythm again, bodies still warm and slick with sweat, her heart thudding beneath my palm as fiercely as my own. I stayed exactly where I was, afraid that moving too soon might shatter whatever fragile peace we'd found.

Eventually, I shifted onto my side, careful not to break the contact between us, drawing her back against my chest. My arm wrapped around her waist instinctively, holding her there like she belonged. She settled easily, her cheek resting over the tattoo she'd touched earlier, her fingers tracing the ink in absent, thoughtful patterns, like she understood now what I'd never known how to say.

"I still love you," she whispered.

The words were so quiet I almost missed them, but they landed heavy, stealing the breath from my lungs. I stilled, my throat tightening around the ache they left behind.

"Then come with me," I murmured before I could stop myself. "We could still have the life we talked about." The words rushed out, hopeful and reckless, like I could will it all back into place just by saying them out loud.

Her body went tense in my arms, the warmth between us dimming, retreating. She shook her head, eyes squeezed shut, like she was bracing herself.

"It's not that simple," she said softly. "My life... it's complicated."

I eased back just enough to see her face, my hand still anchored at her waist, unwilling to let her go completely. "Complicated how?" I asked, gentle but desperate. "Abby, talk to me."

She lifted her hand and pressed it to my chest, right over my heart, like she was trying to quiet both of us at once. "Don't ask me," she whispered. "Please."

The plea in her voice gutted me. I wanted answers, needed them, but I couldn't bring myself to push her when she looked like that. So I nodded instead and kissed her hair, breathing her in, holding her close like she might vanish if I loosened my grip.

Time slipped by in fragile heartbeats. Then she stirred, carefully disentangling herself from me, reaching for her clothes. Her hands trembled as she dressed, movements quick and practiced, like she was already building up her walls again.

"I have to get back," she said quietly, still not meeting my eyes.

My chest tightened at the thought of her walking away, of this moment ending the same way everything else had. "Then see me after work," I said, the words tumbling out. "Please."

She paused, hesitation flickering across her face, then shook her head. "I can't." She leaned down, pressing one last, lingering kiss to my lips. "Will you still be here tomorrow?"

I nodded without hesitation. "I'm not going anywhere," I said. "Not without you."

Her smile was soft and sad all at once. "Then I'll see you tomorrow," she said. "Same time. Same place."

Before I could say anything else, she was gone, slipping out the door like a ghost, leaving the room impossibly quiet behind her.

I followed her only as far as the threshold, bare-chested, jeans half-buttoned, watching her walk away until she disappeared from view. The hollow in my chest deepened around a single word.

Complicated.

Whatever that meant, I was going to find out.

The next day, I was ready before noon.

The room smelled like cheap motel soap and nerves, the air conditioner rattling in the window like it knew how wound up I was. My palms were slick, my chest tight, every bit of me waiting.

When the knock came, I didn't hesitate.

She barely made it inside before she was in my arms, kissing me like yesterday had never really ended. I caught her, lifting her off the floor as the door shut behind us, her legs wrapping around my waist on instinct alone. She tasted like coffee and something sweet, like she'd stolen this moment just for me.

There was no careful this time.

I laid her back on the bed, her laughter dissolving into breathless sighs as my mouth found her throat, her shoulder, the soft skin just beneath her jaw. Her hands tugged me closer, urgent and familiar, like her body remembered before her mind could interfere.

When I joined us, it felt inevitable, like something snapping back into place. She held onto me tightly, forehead pressed to mine, breath shuddering against my lips, and for a few stolen moments it felt like the years between us had never existed.

Later, tangled in the sheets, her head rested on my chest, our legs still entwined. I stared at the ceiling, listening to her breathe, wishing I could freeze time right there.

"Jackson," she said softly. "How are you even here? Shouldn't you be at training camp?"

The question caught me off guard. I glanced down at her, confused. "Training camp?"

She lifted her head, brows knitting together. "Football. What team are you with?"

The weight of what she didn't know settled hard in my chest. I exhaled slowly, pulling her closer. "You didn't... you never looked me up?"

Her gaze slid away. "No."

"Why not?"

"It's complicated."

I swallowed the sting in my throat and let it go. For now. "I played in college," I said finally. "Until I tore my ACL. The surgery went well, but the recovery didn't go the way I hoped. That was it. Goodbye football."

Her lips parted like she wanted to say something, but nothing came out. She rested her cheek against me again, quiet.

After a long silence, I asked, "So why Oakridge? Why are you working there?"

Her body tensed slightly against mine. "It's a job. I like helping people."

"Abby..."

Her phone buzzed.

She sat up immediately, already reaching for her scrubs, smoothing her hair like she'd rehearsed this exit a hundred times.

"Already?" My voice cracked as I pushed up on my elbows.

She nodded, avoiding my eyes. "I have to go."

I watched her tie her hair back, slipping her pristine white shoes on like she'd rehearsed this. She paused at the door, one hand on the knob, and for a second I thought she'd turn back.

But she didn't.

The door clicked shut, leaving me half-dressed and restless, staring at the space she'd just filled.

Whatever she was hiding, it was bigger than me. Bigger than *us*.

And I wasn't leaving until I understood what it was.

When Wednesday came, I told myself not to expect anything.

Still, my heart leapt when the knock came at the same time it had the last two days.

Abby stepped inside, and the moment the door shut behind her, the relief hit me hard and fast. I kissed her like I'd been holding my breath for days, and she kissed me back the same way - urgent, familiar, and impossible to resist.

We didn't talk. We didn't need to.

Later, we lay tangled together, my arm around her waist, her head tucked beneath my chin. The room was quiet except for our breathing, the air heavy with that fragile sense of almost-normal I didn't dare name.

For a few minutes, it felt like this could be a life.

Like this was what life was supposed to be. Me, her, just us.

"God," I murmured, brushing my thumb over her hand. "I can't believe you're really here."

She didn't answer. She only pressed closer, her fingers curling against my chest like she was holding on to something she couldn't keep.

"Do you ever think about it?" I asked softly. "What it would've been like if you hadn't disappeared?"

Her breath hitched.

I shifted, trying to catch her eyes. "You could've come to Falcon Pointe. We would've figured it out. We could've..."

"Don't." Her voice cut sharp, and brittle. She shook her head, hair brushing my jaw. "Don't say things like that."

The words stung, but her trembling gave her away.

I tightened my hold on her. "Abby... come home with me. Let me take care of you. We can make this work."

"I can't," she whispered.

Then she sat up, already reaching for her clothes.

The way she gathered her scrubs - quick, and practiced - twisted something deep in my chest. Like she'd learned how to disappear long before she ever walked into this room.

"You don't have to leave," I said.

"I do." She didn't look at me.

The door clicked shut behind her, and the silence hit harder than anything she'd said.

Three days in a row, and she still couldn't give me anything real. Just her body. Her kisses. The way she said my name like it still belonged to her.

I should've felt grateful.

Instead, all I felt was frustration, sharp and restless and unanswered.

I wanted to believe she loved me, I just didn't know if that belief was saving me... or setting me up to break.

Chapter 16

Abby

What the hell was I doing?

I backed out of the motel parking lot and turned onto the main road, my hands tight on the steering wheel. I didn't have to be back at work for another twenty minutes, but I couldn't stay in that room a second longer. The walls felt like they were closing in on me, on the version of myself I kept pretending didn't exist.

Of course Jackson was right.

We could have been together. I could have run when my parents said they were taking me away from the only home I'd ever known. I could have told him the truth that day on the phone, told him I wouldn't be at his game instead of letting him wait.

But I hadn't.

I never did.

I had always chosen the quiet path. The safer one. The one that asked me to swallow what I wanted and call it maturity.

And now here I was, a married woman, slipping out of a motel room in the middle of the day, my skin still warm from the only man who had ever really seen me. Lying to my husband. Lying to myself. Letting Jackson believe this could be something more when I didn't know how to give him anything without everything breaking apart.

What if Sung-ho found out?

The thought sent a sharp twist through my chest. I knew exactly what that would look like - the cold silence, the calculated cruelty, the punishment that always came later, behind closed doors where no one could hear.

And Cole.

The image of my son flashed through my mind, his careful smile, the way he watched everything like he was always waiting for the air to change. He didn't deserve to be pulled into this. He didn't deserve to lose the only stability he knew, even if it was a fragile, hollow kind.

I parked behind the care facility and shut off the engine, my heart still racing. My hands shook as I dug a granola bar out of my purse, appetite gone. Skipping lunch to see Jackson had been reckless, but I hadn't been able to stop myself.

I needed him.

Not just his touch, but his attention. The way he looked at me like I mattered. Like I wasn't too much or not enough. Like the years hadn't stripped me down to someone smaller and quieter than I used to be.

He didn't care that my body had changed. That I carried myself differently now. He told me I was beautiful like it was a fact, not a favor.

And that terrified me more than anything.

Because how was I supposed to walk away from the one place I still felt real?

By the time I walked through the front door that evening, I'd convinced myself no one could tell what I'd been up to. Not Sung-ho. Not my mother. Not Cole. If I acted normal, if I tucked away the giddy, shameful part of me that was still replaying the sound of Jackson's voice, the feel of his lips and hands, everything would be fine.

Except Cole was already home, sprawled on the living room floor with his schoolbooks, and my mother was perched on the sofa like a hawk. Her eyes flicked up the second I came in.

"You're late," she said.

My throat closed, panic clawing at my ribs. I forced a small cough to cover it, reaching for an excuse. Normally I would have been home long before my mother arrived with Cole. I couldn't tell her I'd been parked across the street from a motel, watching for a familiar truck.

"Mrs. Ortiz was telling me a story about her cat," I lied smoothly, setting my purse on the table with hands that felt damp and shaky. "It would have been rude to leave in the middle of it."

Cole didn't look up, but I caught the way his shoulders hunched tighter. He always knew when something was off.

"You're here early," I said quickly. "What happened to youth group?"

Cole froze, pencil pausing mid-stroke, and my mother rose from the sofa, slow and deliberate.

"Ha-joon does not know this week's Bible verses. I asked him to recite them on the way to the church and he couldn't even tell me which ones he was supposed to be studying."

Her glare burned straight through me. I lowered my head, shame scalding my cheeks. "That's my fault, Mom..." The word slipped out before I could stop it. Once upon a time, I was allowed to call her that. Not anymore. Not since I disgraced the family. "I..."

"Yes. It is your fault," she cut me off, her voice sharp as glass. "But he is also ten years old. He must take responsibility for his studies."

The garage door rumbled open. My stomach clenched. A second later, Sung-ho stepped inside.

His eyes narrowed on me immediately. He turned his focus to my mother, a smile he reserved just for her, painted across his strong face. "Hello, eomeoni. I did not expect to see you this evening."

"Sung-ho. It is so good to see you. I was just telling Ah-bi that Ha-joon has fallen behind in his Bible studies again."

He adjusted his cuffs like he was stepping into a boardroom instead of his own house. His gaze flicked from my mother to me, and back to my mother.

"I'll deal with her," he said coolly.

My mother pressed her lips together, gave the faintest nod, and collected her purse. Her hand lingered on Cole's shoulder before she left, and the look she gave me as the door shut said everything: she had delivered her judgment, and now the punishment was mine to bear.

"Go cook dinner," Sung-ho instructed, his voice as smooth and sharp as the blade of a knife.

"Yes," I whispered, rushing to the kitchen, my mind everywhere except for the task at hand. The only thing that gave me peace was knowing he'd never lay a hand on my son.

My fingers fumbled as I pulled ingredients from the fridge. He'd mentioned wanting bulgogi earlier in the week, but I hadn't marinated the beef. My stomach twisted as I scrambled to throw something together, chopping onions too thick, nearly dropping the soy sauce bottle. I stirred until my wrist ached, tasting, retasting, desperate to make it perfect.

The smell of garlic and sesame filled the kitchen, but it did nothing to ease the tension. We ate in brittle silence, only the scrape of chopsticks against porcelain breaking the air. Cole pushed his food around his plate, eyes darting between us.

As soon as Sung-ho set his chopsticks down, I rose. "Go take a bath," I told Cole softly. "Then study. I'll come in after I clean up."

He nodded, relief flashing in his eyes, and slipped away down the hall. A door clicked shut a moment later.

That's when Sung-ho stood.

Slowly - the way he always did when he knew no one would stop him.

I turned toward the sink, lowering the dishes into the growing suds. My hands trembled, water still running when his shadow fell over me.

"You humiliated me," he said, voice low and dangerous.

"I-I'm sorry," I stammered. "It won't happen again…"

"Look at me when I'm talking to you."

Slowly, I turned to face my husband, and the moment our eyes met, his hand swept out and closed around my throat. He pulled me away from the sink and slammed me against the wall, the air whooshing from my lungs. Panic surged as his grip tightened, cutting off breath, sound, everything. My nails clawed at his skin, but he didn't flinch.

"Sung-ho," my voice scraped out, barely a whisper.

Stars burst behind my eyes. My chest burned with the struggle to breathe.

Just when everything started fading to black, there was a creak in the floorboards and a moment later a door down the hall clicked shut.

He froze. For a beat, his gaze locked on mine, fury blazing there. And then, just as suddenly, he let go.

I crumpled to the floor, knees slamming against the tile, coughing, gasping in ragged lungfuls of air.

"Clean this up," he ordered, his tone flat, already dismissing me as he strode out of the kitchen.

I stayed there until my vision cleared, my throat raw, before dragging myself back to the sink. I washed each dish with mechanical precision, forcing my hands to stay steady even as the rest of me shook.

In the living room, the TV droned on. Sung-ho's low hum blended with the crisp voices of commentators dissecting golf swings. The steady click of his glass against the coffee table said he'd already poured himself a drink.

I wiped my hands on a dish towel, then reached up into the cupboard where he kept the green glass bottle of soju. My fingers hesitated, trembling just a little, before curling around its cool neck.

My dad had let me taste soju once when I was sixteen, the night I won an award for one of my paintings. A special occasion, he said, while my mother scowled in the corner. He'd poured me a splash, just enough to wrinkle my nose and burn my throat. He laughed and said, *"One time only."*

And it had been. Until now.

I unscrewed the cap and poured a shot into the little glass, the smell was sharp and medicinal. My throat ached from where Sung-ho's fingers had pressed, still tender and raw. The liquor burned going down, twice over - first the fire of the alcohol itself, then the sting of bruised tissue. Tears pricked at my eyes, unbidden.

The warmth spread through me, loosening the edge of the tremor in my hands, dulling the pain just enough that I could pretend it wasn't there.

I pressed the empty glass flat against the counter, listening for footsteps, for the sound of him catching me touching something that was off limits. But the golf commentary kept rolling, steady and smug, and I exhaled slowly.

I rinsed the glass quickly under the tap, and slid the bottle back into its place. My hands were still trembling, the burn of the liquor mixing with the burn around my throat, but I didn't dare pause.

The living room glow flickered against the wall as I passed, Sung-ho's voice low and steady as he muttered about someone's swing. I kept my steps light and careful, until I reached the hallway.

Cole's room was dim except for the small lamp by his bed. He looked up when I pushed the door open, his eyes too old for ten. I forced a smile, hoping the soft light would cover what the darkness inside me could not.

"Ready to read, bud?" I whispered, closing the door behind me.

"Mom..." His voice cracked.

I dropped onto the mattress beside him, pulling him close. "Shh. It's okay."

"I-I'm sorry I forgot."

I kissed the top of his head, running my fingers through his damp hair. "It's okay. It's not your fault."

He clung to me, burying his face against my chest like he was six again.

"Why does Dad hate us?" His words were muffled against me.

"He doesn't," I whispered automatically, though the lie cut like glass.

Cole pulled back, eyes red-rimmed but steady. "You don't have to lie to protect me. I know he does. And I hate him. I wish he'd leave. Like some of my friends' dads did. Or... or maybe you and me could run away. Just us." His words tumbled out in a rush now. "We could eat pizza and mac and cheese, play video games, and watch football. I could wear jeans every day and no one would yell at me. We could be free."

My throat closed. I smoothed his hair back, but no words came. What could I say when his dream sounded so much like my own?

So I just held him, my arms tight around his small body, silently wishing for the same impossible escape.

I kissed the crown of his head, breathing him in like I could shield him with the strength of my lungs alone. He shouldn't have to dream of running away. He shouldn't have to wish for a father who loved him or for freedom in pizza and football. He should just be a boy.

But here he was, and here I was, lying through my teeth while inside I wanted the same escape he did.

I tucked him under the covers and sat in the dark until his breaths evened out. Then I slipped into my own bed, my throat aching where Sung-ho's hands had been, my chest burning with shame and longing.

Later, when the house finally went quiet, I lay awake in the dark, my body aching in ways I didn't know how to name.

I thought about Jackson, about the way he looked at me like I still mattered, like I wasn't broken or diminished by the life I was trapped in.

Wanting him felt like standing on the edge of a cliff, where all it would take was a stiff breeze to send me over

But even knowing that, I didn't know how to stop.

Chapter 17

Jackson

Thursday came and I woke before the alarm. Not that I'd really slept. I'd spent half the night pacing the thin carpet, half staring at the ceiling, and listening to the buzz of the neon motel sign just outside my window.

Something wasn't right, I could feel it.

I'd always believed Abby and I were connected in ways I couldn't explain. Time had dulled it, buried it under years of silence, but the moment I held her again, that belief came rushing back, as strong as ever. Maybe it was foolish. Maybe it was just hope masquerading as instinct. But the unease wouldn't let go

I didn't know what was holding her back, I just wished she'd talk to me. Like she used to.

I rubbed the back of my neck, trying to ease the ache. "Must've slept wrong," I mumbled to myself as I stumbled into the bathroom.

I shaved, showered, and dabbed on a bit of the cologne Abby once loved. Then, I paced. I checked the clock, sat, stood, and checked it again. I brewed motel coffee, let it go cold, then poured another cup I barely touched.

When noon came, my pulse spiked.

I stood by the door, heart kicking every time a car pulled into the lot. A red sedan. A blue minivan. None of them were her.

I cracked the blinds, watching, waiting.

By twelve fifteen, doubt started gnawing at me.

By twelve thirty, it was chewing through bone.

What if she'd changed her mind? What if yesterday was a mistake she was already trying to forget?

I dropped onto the bed, elbows braced on my knees, staring at the letter I'd written her, page after page of words I hadn't known how to say out loud. All the reasons we should be together. All the things I wanted her to understand before she rushed off again.

For the first time since I found her, fear dug its claws in.

Not the fear that she didn't love me anymore. No - something worse.

The fear that she was slipping away again, right in front of me, and I was choosing to let it happen.

I scrubbed a hand over my face and looked at the clock again. 12:42.

Should I go?

I pictured her car in the Oakridge parking lot. Pictured her walking out back on her break, scanning the shadows, and finding no one waiting. Would that make her think I'd given up? Or would showing up uninvited spook her more than she already was?

The war in my chest was brutal - wait and risk losing her again or chase her and risk driving her further away.

But the unease wouldn't quiet. It wasn't just doubt anymore. It was a gut-deep certainty that something had happened. Something she wasn't telling me.

I grabbed my keys.

The drive to Oakridge felt endless. Every red light was an insult. Every slow car in front of me tested my restraint. I wanted to floor it, to run the lights, to get there as fast as humanly possible. To do *something*.

Instead, I forced myself to breathe. To slow down. To keep my hands steady on the wheel.

When I finally pulled into the lot, my heart slammed against my ribs.

Then I saw it.

Her car.

Relief hit hard enough to make me dizzy. She was here. She hadn't vanished. She was still going about her life, still moving through the world, even if I wasn't part of it.

For now, that had to be enough.

I didn't get out of the truck. Didn't go looking for her. I sat there for a long moment, letting my pulse settle, and the worst of the panic drain away.

Then I turned around and drove back to the motel.

The unease followed me.

Because even knowing she was still here, still close enough to see if I let myself... I couldn't shake the feeling that this wasn't over.

That waiting might be the right choice.

And that it might also be the one that cost me everything.

Chapter 18

Abby

The turtleneck itched under my scrubs, the collar too high, and too tight. Almost like his hand was still clamped there. But it was the only way to hide the bruises my makeup couldn't cover.

I gripped my travel mug tighter, the tea the only thing that seemed to soothe the ache in my throat. "Come on, bud, the bus will be here any second."

Cole slung his backpack over his shoulders. "Did you sign my permission slip?" he asked around a yawn.

I ruffled his hair, "Yes. I put it in your blue folder."

He nodded his head then turned to look up at me when we reached the curb, the bus just turning onto our street. "Why are you wearing that, Mom?" he gestured to my neck. "It's hot outside.".

I forced a smile, tugging the fabric higher on my throat. "I didn't sleep well. I don't want to catch a cold."

His eyes lingered longer than they should have, as if he could sense there was more to it, but he let it go. When the bus stopped in front of us, he gave me one last look before climbing the steps.

"Love you!"

He shook his head, a smile tugging at the corners of his mouth. "Moom!"

"I know, I know... Have a good day, I'll see you soon."

The bus pulled away in a cloud of smog, and I watched as it disappeared down the road, a longing for my son I hadn't felt since his early days of school - back when separating from my baby boy was something new.

I hated it then, and I hated it now.

At work, I parked in my usual spot and checked myself in the mirror, practicing my "happy" face. I cleared my throat a couple of times and tested my voice, hoping no one would be able to tell something was wrong - or worse that they would suspect I actually was sick and send me home.

Home was the last place I wanted to be.

I smiled as I walked through the front doors, greeting the ladies at the front desk with a smile and a wave, "Good morning."

"Morning, Ah-bi."

I quickly dropped my things off and got to work, prepping the morning meds.

I got a few curious looks as I rolled the cart from room to room, but mostly, everything was normal. That was until I reached Mrs. Ortiz's room.

"What's this all about?" She gestured to her neck, indicating my turtleneck. "Since when are you the one who's cold?" she teased as I passed her a paper cup with her daily medication.

"Since it's September, and I don't want to get sick. Then I'd miss your cranky butt."

"Mmm hmm," she arched an eyebrow.

"I'm serious!" I laughed, the action causing me to cough, the ache in my throat more apparent now. I passed her a cup of water once the coughing subsided.

She shook her head and took her pills. "I don't know what's going on, but I'm not buying it."

"I'm fine, I swear."

The questions didn't stop there though. I fielded curious looks and questions all morning. "Aren't you hot?" One nurse asked.

I laughed like it was nothing, like my skin wasn't burning with the added layer and the heat of their stares.

By noon, my hands were shaking. My body moved on autopilot, sliding charts back into their slots, restocking gloves, nodding at patients. When my lunch break finally came, I walked straight past the cafeteria and out to my car.

The second the door shut, I broke.

Sobs tore through me, ugly and loud. My forehead pressed to the steering wheel, my fingers white-knuckled around the rim. I couldn't walk away from my life, not with Cole depending on me, not with Sung-ho's shadow looming over every decision I made.

Being with Jackson was one of the few things in my life that had always felt like true freedom. Tasting it again, if only briefly, left me insatiable for more.

I covered my mouth with both hands, muffling the sound, but the ache inside me didn't quiet. It only grew louder, until I felt like I was being torn in two.

No matter how much I wanted to run to Jackson, to feel his strong arms wrap around me, hold me, telling me everything would be alright, I couldn't. The risk was too great, not only to me and Cole, but also to him. What would Sung-ho do to him?

I buried my face in my hands, shoulders shaking, the ache in my throat spreading lower, deeper.

When the last of the tears dried, I splashed cold water on my face in the bathroom and forced myself to return to work. I smiled when I had to, charted vitals with steady hands, answered questions like nothing inside me was crumbling.

Pretending.

God, I had gotten so damn good at pretending.

By the time my shift ended, I was running on fumes. The pain in my throat pulsed with every swallow, the ache in my chest worse with every breath. I drove straight to the school, parked at the curb, and waited for the buses to roll in.

Cole bounded down the steps, his backpack bouncing, his grin a small flicker of light in my dark day.

I couldn't take him home. Not yet. I wasn't ready to step back into that house, not with my mother's judgment still hanging in the air and Sung-ho's shadow waiting there.

So, I steered us toward the park.

The air was warm, and the sun was too bright, but he didn't seem to mind. He ran ahead with his backpack bouncing until we found a table and bench, then plopped down beside me and dug out his homework.

I helped him through the math problems, circling the numbers with my pen while he scribbled his answers. Every so often, he'd glance at me, like something heavy was sitting on his chest. Finally, he blurted, "Mom, what if we really did it?"

I looked up, startled. "Did what?"

"Ran away." His voice was quiet, but sure. "What if it was just us? No Dad. No grandma. Just you and me."

My throat tightened. The bruises there still ached; the tenderness sharp every time I swallowed. "Cole…"

"I've been thinking about it," he pressed on, eyes wide, and hopeful. "We could go anywhere," he tapped his pencil against his notebook. "I want to go to Colorado. They've got mountains, and snowboarding, and the Broncos. Did you know they're, like, one of the coolest teams ever?"

A laugh escaped me before I could stop it, thin and trembling. "Yeah, I know."

"You do?" His head snapped toward me, suspicious and curious all at once.

I smiled, thinking back on the hot summers and cool autumn days. The clean air and the corn fields, just blocks from our house. "I grew up in Colorado."

His mouth fell open. "What? No, you didn't. You've always lived here."

"No," I said softly, shaking my head. "Not always."

He blinked at me, the kind of look that said he was rearranging everything he thought he knew. "So… you know stuff about Colorado? About football?"

I swallowed hard, debating how much to tell him. "My best friend played football," I finally admitted. "He wanted to play for the Broncos when he grew up."

Cole's face lit up, brighter than I'd seen in weeks. "Seriously? Did he teach you how to play? Is that why you're so good? You gotta tell me about him!"

Regret hit me like a blow. As much as I wanted to, I couldn't tell him more, not without unraveling everything. And yet, watching the light in his eyes, I felt it - the longing I'd buried for so long. The need for him to know someone like Jackson. To have someone to look up to who wouldn't tear him down.

I forced a smile, brushing his hair back from his forehead. "Maybe another time."

Cole's disappointment was quick, but the spark of hope remained, glowing in his eyes long after we packed up his homework and headed home.

That night, after he was in bed, the house sank into silence. Sung-ho's snores drifted down the hall, steady and indifferent, while I sat in the darkened living room, staring at nothing.

The ache in my throat hadn't eased, and now it spread deeper, pressing into my chest until every breath hurt. I told Sung-ho I wanted to stay up to make a study plan for Ha-joon's Korean school, and he'd smiled, proud of my diligence. But my stomach twisted with guilt, because the truth was, I wasn't thinking of lesson plans at all.

I was thinking of green eyes and a smooth voice. Hands that touched me like I was something precious.

Lips that tasted like forever.

And then I thought of Cole. Of the walls closing in on us.

It wasn't worth it.

The truth cut sharper than Sung-ho's grip ever could. No matter how much I wanted Jackson, no matter how badly I wished for a life that didn't exist, I couldn't risk my son's safety. I couldn't risk him losing the only home he'd ever known - or worse, losing me.

The ache in my throat was no longer the only pain I carried. My chest felt hollow, split wide, my heart poisoned by longing for a man I could never have.

And yet, God help me, I wanted him still.

I closed my eyes, clutching the empty space beside me like it could hold me together. Tomorrow, Jackson would wait, but I wouldn't come. And somehow, I knew that choosing myself, choosing my son, would cost us both.

Chapter 19

Jackson

Tomorrow came, and I waited, longer than I meant to. The hours dragged, heavy and slow, until pacing the motel room felt like punishment. Every car that pulled into the lot made my pulse spike. None of them were her.

By noon, my chest felt like it had been cracked open. She wasn't coming. I felt it in my bones, in the hollow ache where she used to fit.

And God, it broke me.

I couldn't just sit there anymore.

I grabbed my gym bag from the truck and laced up my running shoes, telling myself this was better. Smarter. That I needed to burn off the restless energy before I did something stupid.

The late afternoon air was thick and warm as I took off down the road, my stride long and familiar. Muscle memory carried me forward even as my mind refused to quiet.

I'd forgotten my earbuds.

Every thought I'd been trying to outrun came flooding back; Abby's face, her hesitation, the way she'd pulled away like she was bracing for something I couldn't see. I pushed harder, lungs burning, legs screaming, but it didn't help.

If anything, it made it worse.

By the time I slowed to a stop, hands braced on my knees, my chest heaving, I knew I was lying to myself.

This ache wasn't going to pass.

I turned around and ran back to the motel. I took a hot shower, the scalding water beating down on my skin, grounding me just enough to breathe.

There had to be more to the story. Abby wouldn't just walk away. Not again. Not like before.

Except I still didn't know what happened before...

By the time darkness crept in, I couldn't sit still any longer. I grabbed my keys and drove to her house. If she wouldn't come to me, I'd go to her. Just once. Just to see her, to make sure she was okay.

I parked across the street, heart slamming against my ribs as I tried to work up the courage to knock on her door.

My hand had just closed around the door handle when the garage door hummed to life. A pair of headlights cut across the drive, and a sleek Mercedes slid into the space

I froze.

That wasn't her car. Abby drove something older, practical. This was... wrong.

My gut twisted as I sat there in the dark, questions chewing through me faster than I could chase them. Who the hell was driving that car? Why was it pulling into *her* garage?

Was this why she wouldn't run away with me?

I tossed and turned all night. Sleep wouldn't come, no matter how hard I tried. My mind ran on an endless loop. Maybe it was her parents' car. Maybe she had a roommate.

Maybe I'd gone to the wrong house.

But Abby's beat-up sedan had been right there in the driveway, plain as day. And then that damn Mercedes, rolling right up beside it…

Morning came like an accusation, the sun stabbing through a crack in the blinds, and I gave up. I threw off the blankets and got dressed. I couldn't stay here waiting, couldn't sit like some coward hoping she'd come back to me. I had to move, had to do *something*. Even if it was pointless.

Keys in hand, I jumped in my truck and drove. Half my Saturday gone, tank burning gas, desperately trying to outpace the storm in my chest. But every mile snapped me back to the same place: the Mercedes gliding into her garage, chrome flashing like a taunt. Abby refusing to meet my eyes.

The helplessness slammed into me the same way it had the day the sky ripped open and left me standing in the wreckage.

By noon I was in some highway diner, staring at a burger I didn't want, pushing fries around the plate. The longer I sat there, the more the waitress lingered. She was brunette, cute in a girl-next-door kind of way. She brushed my arm when she refilled my drink, leaning in too close, an offer I knew all too well.

For a flicker of a moment, I almost let myself sink into it, into her. Forget about Abby for a while and drown in someone else's skin, punish myself the way I always used to.

But when I shut my eyes, it wasn't her I saw. It was Abby. Her smile, her laugh, the taste of her mouth on mine. The waitress could've been anyone, and it wouldn't have mattered. My body didn't want strangers anymore. It wanted Abby.

It had always wanted Abby. Everyone else was just a poor place-holder.

As the sun slowly dipped below the horizon, I once again found myself back outside Abby's house, headlights off, parked in the shadows. I couldn't stay away, even if I tried.

Her car was parked out front, but I no longer knew what that meant. Then the garage door opened and the Mercedes rolled out. My mouth went dry, pulse thundering in my ears. For a moment I was wracked with indecision. Do I follow, or wait for Abby to tell me about the mystery car?

I slammed my fist against the steering wheel once, twice, then turned the key.

I pulled out and followed at a distance, my truck rumbling low against the pavement.

The Mercedes led me into town, into the parking lot of a fancy restaurant, complete with an outdoor patio where the tables were all lined with linen tablecloths and flickering candles; through the windows, you could see the glow of a chandelier. I parked at the edge of the lot where I wouldn't be seen.

I kept my eyes glued to that car, not sure what I was hoping to see. And when the passenger door opened, everything around me blurred.

Abby stepped out, one heeled foot, then the other, her smooth legs on display for all to see. As she emerged, I couldn't help but trace the curves of her body, the way her dress clung to her in all the right ways.

She smoothed her skirt with trembling fingers, her hair pulled back neat, her lips painted the soft shade I remembered from high school dances.

My chest caved.

A man stepped out of the driver's side. Every line of him screamed money from the tailored jacket and polished shoes to a watch that probably cost more than my truck. He circled the car without hurry, placing his hand low on her back as though he had every right to touch her.

And maybe he did.

My lungs stuttered. My pulse roared in my ears.

She tilted her chin up and he leaned closer, saying something I couldn't hear. She laughed - soft like she once laughed with me. My stomach flipped, bile rising up in my throat.

The valet opened the glass doors, and she let the man guide her inside, his hand never leaving her.

I gripped the steering wheel so hard it creaked beneath my palms. My vision tunneled, locking on the spot where they disappeared together.

Every instinct in me screamed to storm inside, to rip her away, to demand answers.

Instead, I sat there in the dark, pulse hammering, my chest splitting wide open.

What the fuck was going on?

I sat there just long enough for my vision to clear, and then I roared out of the parking lot, tires squealing against the pavement.

I drove like I was fleeing a crime scene, all the way back to the motel. I had never felt pain quite like this; not when my parents died, not when I lost my dream of playing for the NFL, and not when Abby disappeared eleven years ago.

I was done. Done waiting for her to open up to me, to be honest with me, to *choose* me!

I tossed my bag on the bed and started shoving clothes inside. Fast, rough movements, like if I didn't stop to think, I could actually go through with it.

I could go home and move on.

Keys in hand, I hit the road. One hour, Two. The miles blurred under my tires, the radio nothing but static. I told myself leaving was the smart play; that walking away clean was better than bleeding out slowly.

But the farther away I got, the tighter my chest locked up. That Mercedes kept flashing in my head, chrome glinting like lightning. Abby not meeting my eyes. The helplessness pressing in until my hands were shaking against the wheel.

An exit sign loomed green in the headlights. My knuckles went white as I gripped the steering wheel, fighting myself. Then I wrenched it hard, tires squealing as I cut across the lane.

Back the way I came. Back to Stonehill. Back to Abby.

No matter how far I drove, I could never outrun her.

Chapter 20

Abby

The clink of silverware and low murmur of voices pressed in on me as I sat across from Sung-ho, the linen tablecloth stretched tight between us like a barrier. He'd chosen the nicest restaurant in town, a place with polished glasses and a maître d' who bowed low, like that could undo the knots in my stomach.

Sung-ho looked perfect, of course; tie knotted, his polished cufflinks catching the light. He never came undone, not in public. Especially not here, where appearances mattered. He ordered for both of us without looking up from the menu.

The candlelight flickered against the rim of my glass, his voice a steady murmur that washed over me without meaning. I folded my hands in my lap to keep from fidgeting. My scarf itched against my neck, but I didn't dare take it off. I smiled when expected. Cut neat pieces of chicken I couldn't taste. Smile, pretend, and most importantly, don't let anyone see how badly I wanted to be anywhere else but here.

Inside, my thoughts spun faster than the wine swirling in his glass. The choices I'd made stacked up like accusations. Obeying my parents when they demanded I marry him, even though I barely knew him. Staying after the first time he raised a hand to me. Letting Jackson go without ever saying goodbye.

And worst of all - staying now, giving Cole this life, when I should've taken him and run. Family duty may have chained me, but fear kept me here.

By the time we got home, I was fully acting on autopilot. Shoes off at the door. Lights dimmed. Bed turned down. Sung-ho never wavered from our Saturday night ritual, and tonight was no different.

When he touched me, my body refused to respond. I closed my eyes as his weight settled over me, and when he pushed into me, my body resisted, unyielding. I winced, but if he noticed, he didn't care.

I went through the motions as his thrusts gained speed, but I had nothing left to give, just silent tears rolling down my cheek as I turned away.

"Ah-bi." His hand clamped around my chin, forcing me to look at him. His voice carried a softness I hadn't heard since the last time I took a pregnancy test. His thumb brushed over my tears, and when our eyes met, fury burned beneath the calm.

"Why are you crying? You are my wife." The back of his hand cracked across my face, sharp enough to split my lip. The taste of iron filled my mouth.

Before I could move, he seized my wrists and pinned me to the mattress. "You will give me a son," he said, pressing me down, every second another reminder of the cage I'd built around myself.

When he was done, I turned to the wall, wishing he would roll away. Instead, he held my chin again, brushing my hair from my face with a sick smile.

"I've given you everything. And still, you deny me what's mine. That doesn't happen by accident."

I tried to shake my head, but his grip was unyielding. "I'm not doing anything," I whispered through a choked sob.

He finally pulled away, reaching for his phone on the nightstand. I shifted to get up, but his hand clamped around my arm, shoving me back into the bed.

"You will stay here."

"I-I have to pee. I don't want to get a UTI."

His glare sliced through me. "You will do as I say. You will not deny me my son."

When his breathing evened out beside me, I lay on my back, staring at the ceiling, my bladder aching for relief. The copper tang of blood on my tongue reminded me not to defy him by getting up. My lip throbbed with every heartbeat, but worse was the weight pressing into my chest.

He thought he controlled everything. My body. My choices. My future. But there was one thing he didn't know; one thing I'd hidden deep enough that even he couldn't take it from me. The IUD meant his demand for a son would always go unanswered.

Still, fear gnawed at me. If he found out, if he even suspected...

I closed my eyes and let the debate circle endlessly in my head. Stay and endure or run and risk everything. Either way, the cage held tight.

Relief flooded my veins when I woke and realized I was alone. I picked up my phone and checked the time - it was after 9am - Sung-ho was long gone for another day of golf with his colleagues. Because he didn't have friends; he had business deals dressed up as leisure.

I took a scalding shower, scrubbing until my skin burned, trying to wash away every trace of him. My forehead pressed against the cold tile, my chest aching with the weight of the decision I *had* to make.

When I shut off the water and wiped the steam from the mirror, my reflection stared back, hollow-eyed. The bruises on my neck had started to yellow, but my cheek... my lip. A raw split that mocked me every time I moved my mouth. He had never left such an obvious mark on my face before. That alone steeled my resolve. Cole and I were leaving - if Jackson would have us.

By Sunday afternoon, the house gleamed; floors scrubbed, counters wiped, laundry folded into perfect piles. My suitcase lay open on the bed, waiting for me to finish packing. I just prayed Jackson hadn't already left town.

When the front door opened, my mother ushered Cole inside, her hand resting on his shoulder. Her eyes caught on my lip and lingered for just a moment before sliding away, as if ignoring it could erase it. "Ha-joon's writing has improved," she said lightly, as though we were just two women talking about schoolwork. "Keep doing what you're doing."

Cole's chest puffed with pride. "Really, Mom. She said I'm the best in class this week."

My heart cracked and swelled all at once. Even bleeding, even broken, nothing compared to seeing him smile.

"That's amazing," I told him, forcing brightness into my voice.

"Halmeoni said if I keep it up, she'll get me that rocket I've been wanting."

I glanced at my mother who appeared pleased for once, then back at my son. "Then we better keep practicing," I said, my heart breaking as the words left me. Leaving Sung-ho was one thing. Leaving my parents, taking their grandson away from them...

My mother nodded and smiled down at Cole. "I'll see you Wednesday for youth group."

I swallowed past the lump in my throat. "Thanks, Eomma."

She gave me a soft smile and left without another word.

I turned away from my son, but his gaze lingered on my face. "Why don't you go unpack? Then we'll get some ice cream."

"Mom?"

"Hmm?"

"What happened?"

I smoothed his hair, keeping my voice steady, the lie already falling from my lips. "I slipped in the kitchen when I was mopping and hit the counter. I'm fine."

He didn't look convinced, but he nodded anyway.

The alarm went off at 5:15, but it was pointless. I hadn't slept, too mixed up to fall into the same routine. Something had changed in me, and the only thing I could attribute it to was Jackson. His strength was seeping into me, and I didn't know if that was a good thing or not.

My body ached as I got out of bed and padded softly across the room, careful not to wake Sung-ho. In the bathroom, I stared at my reflection for only a moment, before pulling out my makeup bag.

I rarely wore makeup, my father always said real women didn't need makeup, and Jackson had always loved me the way I was. But living with Sung-ho meant makeup had become a necessity. Unfortunately, after ten years of marriage, I still had not mastered the art of covering bruises.

I gave up after twenty minutes. There was no way I was going to make it to work today - not looking like this.

I went back to my room and dressed quickly then hurried to wake Cole.

The sun had not quite risen yet, so the only light in his room came from his nightlight. Something Sung-ho insisted he was too old for. I sat down on the edge of his bed and brushed my fingers across his forehead. His hair was getting longer, once dark brown, it was now full of lighter streaks and waves I hadn't noticed before.

"Hey, sleepyhead. Time to wake up."

He stirred, throwing an arm over his face. "Five more minutes?"

I laughed, "Having a good dream?"

He nodded, a smile curling his lips. "I was playing football. It was first and ten at the fifty yard line with ten seconds left in the fourth. Kevin hiked me the ball and I launched it down the field, all the way to the end zone."

"And then what happened? Did you win?"

He sat up and rubbed his eyes with the back of his hand. "I don't know - you woke me up before he could catch it."

I ruffled his hair, "I'm sorry. Guess you'll have to make up the ending. What do you think would have happened?"

He sat up on his knees, his solid blue blanket falling off of him. He pulled his arm back, hand positioned as though it held a football. He mimed throwing, jumping to his feet a moment later, and punching the air, "Touchdown!" He whisper-shouted.

"Yes!" I clapped my hands quietly, the smile on his face warming even the darkest recesses of my heart.

He dropped down onto his butt, his smile slipping away. "Do you think dad will ever let me play?"

"I don't know, bud. I'll talk to him again."

"Really? Because Kevin said his mom is going to let him play next year in the community youth league."

I stood up and kissed the top of his head. "I'll look into it."

He threw his arms around me, "Thanks, mom."

"Love you, bud."

"Love you too."

While Cole got dressed and brushed his teeth, I pulled out my phone and called Oakridge, telling them I was sick with a fever, and wouldn't be able to make it in today. I felt bad for lying, but the alternative was even worse.

After the bus pulled away, I went back inside. The house felt too quiet without Cole's chatter filling it. Just me and my thoughts, circling like vultures.

I opened my phone and searched the youth football league he'd mentioned. The pictures made my chest ache - kids in oversized helmets grinning from ear to ear, parents cheering from the sidelines. Cole would love it. He deserved that joy.

Movement in the hall caught my eye and I froze. Sung-ho stepped into the room, his brow furrowing when he saw me. "What are you doing home?"

My throat tightened, but I kept my voice even. "I couldn't go to work like this. Makeup doesn't cover what you did to my face."

His expression hardened. "Don't play the victim. If you behaved like a proper wife, we wouldn't have these problems."

The words stung more than the split in my lip. I almost asked about football, about Cole, but the thought shriveled on my tongue. Not now. Not when the fire in his eyes blazed hot enough to burn us all.

When he finally left for work, the air loosened in my lungs. I slipped into my bedroom, crossed to the far corner of my closet, and pulled out the small lockbox I hadn't touched in years. Inside lay the pieces of a life I'd buried: a dried flower, a childish sketch of sunflowers, a handful of Polaroids with Jackson's arm slung around me, both of us young and breathless with possibility.

My throat burned as I closed the lid. I couldn't say goodbye to him. But I couldn't run to him either. Not yet anyway.

I shoved the box back into the shadows and sat on the edge of the bed, staring at my hands. Trapped between the life I had and the life I wanted.

Chapter 21

Jackson

Jackson

The room reeked of whiskey and stale air when I opened my eyes. My head pounded, and my tongue stuck to the roof of my mouth. I groaned, rolled over, and knocked the empty bottle I didn't remember finishing off the nightstand.

Saturday night after I flipped my truck around and came back to town, I'd stopped at a liquor store, grabbed a few bottles, and told myself it would help. I hadn't left the motel since, not even for food. Just poured glass after glass until the burn dulled and I finally passed out.

It didn't help.

My hand groped for my phone on the nightstand. I unlocked it and flinched, the screen too bright for my eyes. I blinked a few times, trying to focus, when I saw I had a missed call and a voicemail from the last person I expected to hear from - Whitney.

For a second, I couldn't breathe.

I pressed play.

Her voice filled the quiet, small but steady. "Hey, big brother. Why didn't you tell me? All these years, I thought you didn't care. And now I know the truth. I could've been there for you. I should've been. But I guess we both did what we had to do to survive. You deserve this. You deserve to be happy. Call me when you can. I love you."

I sat there, clutching the phone like it might break apart in my hand. It'd killed me that I hadn't tried to get custody of her when I turned eighteen, but I wasn't in a good place back then.

If I was honest, I wasn't in a good place now, either.

Did I *deserve* happiness? I didn't know. But God, I wanted to believe her.

I dragged myself into the shower, twisting the handle until steam filled the room. The scalding water beat down, and I scrubbed until my skin turned red, as if I could wash away the liquor, the guilt, the years of getting everything wrong.

Clean enough to pass, I threw on a shirt and jeans. There was only one person who could give me the answers I needed - Abby.

Keys in hand, I hopped in my truck and drove straight to the nearest coffee shop. I ordered the largest black coffee I could get, then was back on the road, heading straight to Oakridge.

Her car wasn't in the lot when I got there and for a second the old dread, the fear of her disappearing again, rose up. "She didn't run," I told myself, and pushed the thought down.

There could be any number of reasons for her car being gone, I just had to go inside and find out.

The place smelled like antiseptic and coffee. The woman at the front desk looked up, polite but cautious. "Can I help you?"

"I'm looking for Abby Kim."

The woman frowned slightly. "You mean Ah-bi?"

Hearing her real name hit me harder than I expected, a reminder that she wasn't the girl I'd grown up with, not entirely. I nodded. "Yes, thank you. Is she here?"

She shook her head. "I'm afraid not. She called in sick today."

The words dropped straight through me. Not gone. Not avoiding me. Just... not here.

"Is there any chance I could get her number?" I asked, knowing I already had it from the PI, but also not wanting to scare Abby by calling unexpectedly.

She hesitated. "I'm sorry, I can't give out employee information. But I could call her for you."

My pulse kicked. "Yes. Please. Tell her it's Jackson."

I waited while she dialed, staring at the counter like it might crack open and swallow me whole. When she hung up, she smiled softly and reached for a stack of Post-its, scribbling something down.

"She said to give you her number."

I stared at the digits on the paper, my chest tight. For the first time in days, maybe weeks, hope flickered in the hollow space where everything else had been bleeding out.

The drive back to the motel was a blur. My palms slipped against the steering wheel, sweat slicking my grip. I hadn't felt this way since I was a teenager, working up the courage to tell my best friend I had a crush on her. Back then, the risk had been worth it. I prayed it still was.

By the time I made it to the room, my chest was so tight I could barely breathe. I sat on the edge of the bed, my phone in one hand, the post-it trembling in the other. I held my breath as I typed the number in.

For a long second, my thumb hovered over the call button. Then I pressed it, my pulse thundering in my ears.

It rang once. Twice.

"Hello?" Her voice was soft, wary, but it hit me like a punch straight to the ribs.

I swallowed hard. "Abby?"

There was a pause, a sharp inhale. Then, "Jackson."

Just my name. Two syllables, and the years between us collapsed.

I dragged a hand over my face, trying to steady myself. "I didn't think you'd want me to have your number."

"I almost didn't," she admitted. "But... I wanted you to call."

Relief cracked something open inside me, jagged and raw. "Abby, I just... I need to see you. I need to talk to you. Please."

Her silence stretched. I could picture her biting her lip the way she used to, weighing the risk. Finally, she said, "Not tonight. But soon. I'll tell you when."

It wasn't what I had hoped for, but it was still everything.

"Okay," I whispered. "I'll wait."

Chapter 22

Abby

I sank onto the couch, folding my legs beneath me, my phone pressed tight against my chest. My other hand hovered over my mouth as if I could hold the words back, as if I could undo what I'd just said.

I'd given Oakridge permission to hand over my number. To Jackson.

I didn't even know why. The second I heard his name, my stomach dropped, my throat closed, and before I could think better of it, the words had just slipped out.

I couldn't believe he was still in town. I'd vanished on him once already - twice, if you counted all those years ago - and he had every reason to hate me for it. But he hadn't left. He was still here, still looking for me.

And God help me, part of me was glad.

Because no matter how much time had passed, no matter how impossible this situation was, Jackson had always been my safe place. The only place I ever felt like I could breathe.

My eyes drifted around the living room of the place I'd called home for the past ten years, and all I could see was Sung-ho.

White walls, beige carpet, everything spotless and stiff, like the pages of a catalog. Just the way he liked it. The sofa I sat on was too firm, the kind of furniture meant to impress visitors, not cradle the people who lived here.

Then there was the glass-topped coffee table that gleamed in front of me, sharp-edged and empty but for a glossy art book and a vase that had never held flowers.

It wasn't even good art.

The television dominated the wall, enormous and sleek, another status symbol. Above it hung a piece of abstract art - black lines slashing across a canvas in some design that was supposed to mean something.

It didn't. None of it did.

There were no mismatched mugs, no worn blankets, no clutter from a life actually lived. No trace of me. No trace of Cole, unless you counted the rogue crayon that had escaped the box and lay hidden under the entertainment center.

In this house, childhood wasn't an excuse to be messy.

Every corner of this house reminded me how little of it had ever been mine. Even the way I came here hadn't been my choice.

I moved in right after the wedding, a quiet ceremony my parents arranged in a church basement while I was still healing from giving birth. My body ached, my son was barely two weeks old, and instead of resting, I was reciting vows to a man I had only met once. A man who lived in this pristine house in Kansas - far away from everyone and everything I'd ever known.

None of it felt real. None of it felt like mine.

But the truth was, the marriage hadn't begun there. It had been decided years earlier - before the tornado, before Cole, even before I gave my heart to Jackson. While I was still a girl, my parents had already promised me to Sung-ho, the son of one of my father's business associates.

He was five years older. The plan had been to marry after college.

My pregnancy simply moved the date up.

No one asked what I wanted. It didn't matter.

If I'd known sooner, I would have run. I would have told Jackson, begged him to take me anywhere but here. Instead, I hid the truth as long as I could, praying my parents wouldn't find out until it was too late. At least I kept the secret long enough that ending the pregnancy was no longer an option - not that my parents would've risked the shame.

I remembered the exact moment everything unraveled.

The day before Jackson's playoff game, I stood in my bedroom trying to decide what to wear. I wanted to look perfect for him, sitting in the stands, cheering him on. That's when it happened - a strange flutter low in my stomach, so faint I almost missed it.

I pressed my hand there, heart stuttering, then lifted my shirt and turned toward the mirror. My belly was rounder than I'd admitted, even to myself. I smoothed my palm over the curve, awe and terror colliding in my chest.

It should have been a moment I shared with Jackson.

Instead, I was alone.

That was the moment my mother walked in without knocking.

She stopped cold in the doorway, eyes fixed on my stomach. The silence lasted only a heartbeat before she called for my father, her voice sharp with panic. He appeared almost immediately. I yanked the sweater down, but it didn't matter.

He didn't shout. He didn't ask questions. He just shook his head once, slow and heavy with disappointment, and turned away.

By nightfall, boxes lined the hall. Our house was being stripped bare, my life folded into cardboard without my consent. I was pushed into the car, my phone torn from my hand, my protests ignored.

I never got to tell Jackson.

I never even got to say goodbye.

Once, I used to dream of him finding me, saving me. Saving *us*.

But now that he was here, I was frozen with fear. Sung-ho would never let us go without a fight.

My fingers brushed the fading bruises at my throat, then the split in my lip. If he had no problem doing this to me, what would he do to Jackson? To Cole?

The thought hollowed me out.

My phone buzzed in my hand, the sudden ring shattering the silence. I flinched, heart in my throat, staring at the unfamiliar number. With a Colorado area code, it could only be one person.

Jackson.

My thumb hovered, every nerve screaming at me not to answer. But before I could stop myself, I swiped the screen.

"Hello?"

For a moment, there was nothing but static and the rush of my own pulse. Then...

"Abby?"

His voice was rough and hesitant. The sound of it punched straight through the walls I'd been trying to rebuild.

I squeezed my eyes shut, clutching the phone tighter. "Jackson." His name broke out of me before I could stop it.

The silence between us was heavy with everything we hadn't said.

"I didn't think you'd want me to have your number," he said finally, low and careful.

"I almost didn't," I whispered, curling into myself on the couch, nails digging into my knee. "But... I wanted you to call."

"Abby, I just... I need to see you. I need to talk to you. Please."

The desperation in his voice cracked something inside me. I was hurting him. And still, I couldn't stop. Keeping us safe meant keeping my distance.

I crossed the room and pulled the curtain aside just enough to look out at the street. I knew Sung-ho wouldn't be home for hours, but the idea of him finding me on the phone with Jackson sent a chill through me.

"Not tonight," I breathed, letting the curtain fall. "But soon. I'll tell you when."

"Okay," he said. "I'll wait."

I ended the call before I could say goodbye. Every farewell took something from me I couldn't afford to lose.

I wiped away the tear that slipped down my cheek and opened my contacts, saving his number under his sister's name. If Sung-ho ever checked my phone, a woman's name wouldn't raise questions.

Chapter 23

Jackson

For the first time in days, I felt like I could breathe. Hearing her voice, knowing she hadn't run, loosened something in my chest. But the relief didn't last. Every time I closed my eyes, I saw her with another man, laughing, living a life that didn't have me in it.

I gripped the steering wheel tighter, trying to shake the thought. I couldn't sit in that motel room and continue to drown myself in whiskey and what-ifs. Not after hearing her voice. Not after she'd told me she wanted me to call. It may not have seemed like much, but it was everything.

So, I hopped into my truck and drove. No destination, just miles of Kansas roads. I grabbed a burger at a drive-thru, finishing it in just a few bites. I couldn't remember the last time I actually ate something, not just pushing food around on a plate.

On the way back, I slowed as I passed an elementary school. The afternoon sun was low, shadows stretching across the cracked blacktop. You could hear the kids playing from over a block away. From the corner of my eye, I spotted a football soaring across the field. It missed its mark, sailed over the fence, and smacked the hood of my truck.

I hit the brakes, heart thumping, and shoved the gear into park.

Hopping out, I bent and scooped up the ball, its leather worn smooth, laces frayed from use. The kind of ball I'd thrown a thousand times in my own yard.

A moment later, a kid burst through the gate, dark hair flopping into his eyes, breathless from running. He couldn't have been more than ten. He froze when he saw me holding the ball. "This your ball?"

"Yes, sir," the boy said, his voice polite but wary.

"You throw it?" I asked, already knowing the answer.

The boy nodded slowly, "Yes, sir."

I smiled, taking in the grass stains smeared across his slacks and polo. He reminded me so much of myself at that age, and I couldn't help but think his mom was gonna have something to say about dirtying up good clothes.

I held the ball out to him, "You've got a good arm. Next time, try squaring your shoulders and point your foot where you want the ball to go."

He cocked his head, brows scrunched, "That's what my mom always says."

I nodded, "She sounds like a smart lady."

A teacher approached the fence and called out, "Cole?"

The boy, Cole, grinned, quick and shy, "Be right there!"

I gripped the ball in one hand and waved him away. "Go long. I'll show you."

I waited until he was across the street, right next to the gate, then launched the ball at him. He caught it easy, eyes wide.

"Keep working on it. You'll be great!"

His smile lit up his face as he clutched the ball to his chest and darted back toward the playground.

I stood there for a moment, watching him go, a strange ache stirring in my gut. Then I shook it off and climbed back into my truck.

Still, I couldn't stop smiling. Helping that kid felt good. Familiar. Like muscle memory I didn't know I still had.

Driving away, I couldn't stop thinking about him. The way his face lit up when he caught the ball. The way it felt to give him something useful, even in a passing moment.

Football.

Coaching.

Back home, the community center had asked me more than once to help with the youth league. I always turned them down. Football was my first love, and I lost it - something I was reminded of every time the weather changed and that ache in my knee flared up. I couldn't stand the idea of being the washed-up has-been hanging around kids who deserved better than my bitterness.

But today... today had been different.

I loved kids. Always had. And helping that boy with something so small... It felt like more than just tossing a ball. It felt like maybe I still had something worth giving. Maybe it wouldn't destroy me to try. Maybe it would even help me.

By the time I pulled back into the motel lot, the idea had dug its claws in. Before I could second-guess myself, I pulled out my phone and dialed my foster mom, Mrs. Bryant.

"Jackson?" she answered, her voice warm, the same as it had been since I was seventeen and she took me in.

"Hey, Mrs. B." I rubbed the back of my neck, suddenly feeling awkward, especially since I'd missed the last few Sunday night dinners. I never told her I was leaving town, and I made Grady promise not to either. Mrs. B never had much patience for anyone who hurt one of her boys.

And to say that Abby's disappearance hurt me, was an understatement.

I cleared my throat, shaking off the memory. "You still know people over at the community center?"

"Aren't you forgetting something?" She asked, a smile in her voice.

I shook my head, nerves falling away. "Hey, Mrs. B. How are you? I'm sorry I haven't been by, I've been..."

"I know, I know," she said.

My heart stuttered, then she continued. "Grady said you had to leave town unexpectedly to handle something for the bar?"

"Yeah," I lied, grateful Grady had my back and guilty as hell for using him to cover.

"And is everything okay?"

"Yes ma'am. Just finishing some things up, and I'll be home before you know it."

"Good, because Edward and Edie miss you."

I laughed, that lighter feeling working its way back in. Edward and Edie were five-year-old twins she was currently fostering, and a lot of fun to be around. "I miss them too."

"Now. About the community center. Yes, I still have some friends over there. What do you need?"

I swallowed. "I was thinking about maybe helping out with the youth football team. Coaching. If they still need someone."

There was a pause, followed by the obvious smile in her voice. "I'll find out for you, honey. I think that would be good for you."

"Thanks, Mrs. B."

We said our goodbyes, and then I was alone again. Alone in the motel room, with nothing but silence and the echo of my own thoughts.

And once again, the memory of that black Mercedes crept in. Shiny chrome catching the light, sliding into her garage like it had every right to be there.

Abby said she'd call. She said *soon*. But what if soon never came? What if I was wasting my time, waiting for something that was never going to be mine?

I stared down at my phone, thumb hovering. Then I typed the words before I could stop myself.

Me: Who drives the Mercedes?

Chapter 24

Abby

I drummed my fingers on the steering wheel out of rhythm with the beat of the song. Ever since Jackson's call, the house had felt too quiet, too sterile; just me and my thoughts ricocheting off the spotless walls. I couldn't stand it anymore.

I missed him. So much that I found myself digging through the back of my closet until my hands once again held that old lockbox I had gone through that morning. Inside was the mix CD he'd made me all those years ago, his messy handwriting scrawled across the note tucked in its case.

Play track six when you need me close.

Maybe it was a good thing the only CD player we owned was in my car. That's what brought me here, to the pickup line outside Cole's school, "Chasing Cars" by Snow Patrol pouring through the speakers.

For a minute, I let myself sink into the sound. The melody, the lyrics - everything about it was him. The memory of his truck, his laugh, the way the world used to feel so simple.

Safe.

Then my phone buzzed with a single text.

Whitney: Who drives the Mercedes?

For a second I forgot I'd saved Jackson's number under his sister's name. When it hit me, my breath caught. My grip tightened on the steering wheel.

How does he know? Has he been watching me?

A car horn blared behind me, jerking me back. Cole was already halfway into the car, backpack slung over his shoulder, while the line of parents behind me waited impatiently.

"Mom!" he said, giving me a look. "You okay? I thought I was taking the bus."

I forced a smile, still reeling. "I got bored at home. Aren't I allowed to miss my baby boy?"

He groaned, buckling his seatbelt. "Mooom, I'm not a baby."

I laughed, but it sounded hollow. "I know, I know. You're growing up too fast."

As I pulled away, Cole leaned forward between the seats. "What are you listening to?"

It took me a second to realize the CD was still playing. Twenty One Pilots' "Car Radio" filled the car, and my son's ears. I started to turn it off, but his hand on my shoulder stopped me.

"Don't turn it off. I like it," he said, grinning. "It's not like what we usually listen to."

I cleared my throat, unsure what to say.

What could I say?

This is the music your father gave me when we were in High School. The soundtrack to the girl I used to be.

In the end, I went with the safest version of the truth. "This is some of the music I listened to when I was a kid," I said. "I was feeling nostalgic."

He tilted his head. "Nostalgic?"

I smiled. "It's when something reminds you of a time that made you happy. Even if it was a long time ago."

"Like when I see my baby pictures?"

"Exactly."

"So why don't we listen to this music now?"

I turned off the radio, searching for words I didn't have. The problem was, even I didn't fully understand. I just learned to do as I was told. And music - that kind of music - is what got me into this mess in the first place. At least that's what my mother said.

"The music we listen to shapes how we think," I said carefully. "Classical music doesn't have lyrics, so your brain doesn't get distracted. It helps you concentrate and remember things better."

"Well, I like Mozart and R-Ra-Rach..."

"Rachmaninoff."

"Yeah, him."

I smiled and switched the radio back on, "I like them too."

The rest of the drive home blurred by in a haze of sunlight and noise. After the music conversation, Cole chattered about school, telling me a story about throwing a football over the fence and some guy giving him advice, while my thoughts spun somewhere else entirely.

By the time we pulled into the driveway, the text still glared up at me from my phone screen, like an accusation I couldn't ignore.

At home, Cole spread his homework across the kitchen table while I started dinner, my phone burning a hole in my pocket. I needed to respond, but every possible answer felt dangerous. What could I say? What *should* I say?

The front door opened and Sung-ho's voice cut through the hum of the kitchen. "Mmm, what's that smell?"

"Japchae," I said, my voice bright, *too* bright. "It's almost ready."

He hesitated, studying me longer than usual. Then, apparently satisfied, he nodded and sat down, scrolling through his phone while I plated dinner.

All evening, I smiled too much. Laughed too easily. Overcompensated so hard my cheeks hurt. Anything to keep him from seeing the tremor underneath. Anything to keep him from asking about my day.

He couldn't find out about Jackson.

By the time we got to bed, my nerves were stretched thin. And when he rolled over, touching me, I didn't protest.

I couldn't.

If this was what it took to keep him calm, to keep us safe, then that's what I'd do. Even though it killed me a little more with each thrust of his hips.

Afterward, I stared at the ceiling in the dark, wide awake beside a man who would never love me, replaying that text over and over in my mind.

Who drives the Mercedes?

I picked up my phone and rolled onto my side, covering the screen with the blanket so it wouldn't wake Sung-ho. I opened the text and quickly typed out a response.

Chapter 25

Jackson

The new message chime sliced through the dark motel room.

I grabbed my phone, pulse kicking, half-expecting her name on the screen.

Steven: Hey, Jax. I uploaded the inventory counts. Let me know if you need anything else

"Fuck." I scrubbed a hand over my face and dropped the phone on the bed. Of course it wasn't Abby. She was probably busy with *Mr. Mercedes.*

What the fuck was I still doing here? She was obviously doing fine without me. She had a nice house, a good job, some fancy-ass rich guy taking her out on dates.

What did I have to offer?

A house I shared with my foster brother. An old bar I also shared with my foster brother - though we had been fixing it up...

My chest ached - an old, restless ache I hadn't felt in years, and I rubbed it with the heel of my hand.

I should just go home.

I picked up my phone and looked at Steven's text.

Steven.

God, that man...

Back in high school, I used to think Steven was a closeted nerd - quiet, observant, driving his mom's station wagon while everyone else was chasing noise. I told myself his girlfriend was just a cover, a beard, a way for him to move through the world without questions.

I never expected him to walk in on us at that party. I remember thinking he'd bolt. That he'd look away, pretend he hadn't seen anything. Instead, our eyes locked, and something in me snapped before I could think better of it.

"Stay," I said.

I don't know why.

He closed the door behind him.

I'd never shared a girl with another guy before. I let go of her hips, leaned back, and watched as Steven crossed the room, calm and unreadable. The way he looked at me made my chest tighten. Not intimidated. Not impressed. Just... curious. Like he was seeing something I didn't know how to name yet.

When he turned his attention to her, I couldn't look away.

It wasn't jealousy.

It was something worse.

Watching him with her cracked something open in me - the way he moved, the way his focus never fully left me. I told myself it was the thrill of being watched. Of control.

But when he finally looked back at me, I knew that wasn't it.

It was recognition.

And God help me, I wanted him to see me that way.

He dismissed her gently at first, then firmly when she started to protest.

I hardly heard the door slam.

The room changed after that, becoming both quieter and heavier. Like we'd crossed a line without speaking it out loud.

I thought for sure he'd leave.

But he didn't.

He came closer instead, eyes never leaving mine. When he said my name, *Jax,* it landed differently. No one else ever used it. No one else was *allowed* to.

But from his lips...

I should have stepped back. Instead, I reached for him first - fingers curling behind his neck as I pulled him in, choosing this before I could talk myself out of it.

The kiss wasn't rushed. It wasn't hungry. It was careful. Like he was checking in even as his mouth found mine. Like he already knew I was standing on the edge of something and he didn't want to push me.

When I shifted closer, he followed my lead, not the other way around.

The rest of the night blurred together in a mix of heat and confusion and the terrifying relief of being wanted without explanation. There was no label that fit, no version of myself I recognized.

I stayed longer than I meant to.

Steven didn't rush me. Didn't fill the quiet with jokes or questions. He just lay beside me, his shoulder warm against mine, breathing slow and steady like he was anchoring something that wanted to drift.

My pulse eventually followed his.

For the first time in weeks, maybe months, the noise in my head dulled. The pressure I carried in my chest eased, just a little. I hadn't realized how tightly wound I'd been until his thumb traced slow, absent circles against my wrist - not possessive, not demanding. Just there.

I let my eyes close.

Steven pressed his forehead to my shoulder, close enough that I could feel his breath. "You okay?" he asked quietly.

I nodded, though the truth was more complicated than that.

And that was the problem.

That's when the panic crept in - subtle at first, and then sharp. The sense that if I stayed any longer, this would become something I didn't know how to walk away from.

Steven must've felt it.

He didn't stop me when I sat up. Didn't ask me to explain. He just watched me pull my jeans on, his expression open and unreadable.

"Jax," he said quietly.

"I've never done anything like this," I admitted, staring at the floor.

He took my hand, his smooth skin so much different from my own. "Me neither," he smiled, soft, and disarming.

I laughed once, sharp and humorless. "This can't happen again."

He nodded and released my hand. No argument. No hurt. Just understanding. "I won't tell anyone."

When I reached the door, he came up behind me - not touching, just there.

"But, if you ever change your mind," he said, voice low. "I'll be here."

I turned back. I don't know why. I kissed him again - slow, grateful, and so damn dangerous. For a second, I almost stayed.

Then my phone buzzed, Grady's ringtone slicing through the haze and pulling me back to the world I was supposed to belong to...

The memory faded as fast as it came, leaving me flat on my back in a dark motel room - alone in a way I hadn't been back then, breath unsteady and heart pounding like it used to after a game. The ceiling fan hummed above me, blades cutting through the silence.

I picked up my phone again, staring at my message thread with Steven for only a second before typing out a response.

> **Me:** Thanks, man. How's everything going over there?

His reply came almost instantly.

> **Steven:** Good, good. Your sister's a little firecracker. She's keeping Grady on his toes.

A laugh slipped out before I could stop it. Some things never changed.

> **Steven:** How are you holding up?

I debated telling him the same thing I've been telling Grady: *It's good. I just need more time.*

But I didn't want to lie to him.

Grady was family - my brother, my best friend - but there were things I just couldn't share with him, like my relationship with Steven. Like this...

Steven though... Steven had been there when I needed someone the most. He knew everything. My darkest secrets. My fears. After that night, it wasn't just about sex. What he gave me was support, the kind I didn't even know I needed, and that only he seemed capable of giving.

As much as I loved Grady, he would never understand that.

> **Me:** I think there's someone else.

> **Steven:** Has she seen your ass? I swear, it's the ass that launched a thousand ships.

> **Steven:** She'd be an idiot not to come running back to you.

I barked out a laugh. Leave it to Steven to make my ass into the next Helen of Troy...

> **Steven:** On top of having the greatest ass known to man, you're kind, sweet, sensitive, smart, generous, sexy as hell.

Warmth bloomed in my chest; the first I'd felt in days. Sometimes I wished I could let go. Let go of Abby. See what this thing with Steven might become if I weren't already ruined for anyone else.

But I couldn't.

> **Me:** Thanks for the kind words.

> **Me:** And yes, she's seen my ass. Up until a few days ago, I was fucking her pretty regularly

> **Steven:** So what makes you think there's someone else?

I typed out a reply. Deleted it. Typed another. Deleted that too.

The silence of the motel room felt heavier than before, pressing in from all sides. I checked the time, it was a little after nine. Monday night. The Hideaway would be dead by now.

Before I could talk myself out of it, I hit *video call.*

Steven answered immediately, his handsome face filling my screen, making me miss home that much more.

"I'm taking my ten!" he called out, stepping through the door and into the brisk night air. He kept walking until he was in his car, away from prying ears. "Hey, baby. What are you wearing?"

I angled the phone, showing him the open fly of my jeans.

"Fuck, you're hot. You sure you don't just want to come home?"

I smiled, despite the storm twisting inside me. "Hey, Steven."

He leaned back in his seat, grin softening. "So, spill. What makes you think there's someone else?"

And I did. Everything - from finding Abby, to sleeping with her again, to seeing her out with some rich schmuck driving a Mercedes.

"They could just be friends," he offered.

I sighed. "Friends don't cozy up in fancy restaurants like that."

"I'm sorry, man."

"All this time, I've been pining for her, turning away the best thing that's ever happened to me since she left, and after I finally find her, she lets me believe what we had is still there? That there's hope?" I swallowed hard, the words scraping my throat. "I don't want to be her side piece. The loser she hooks up with on her lunch breaks. Her dirty little secret."

"I know. I get it," Steven said quietly.

"Fuck, Steven. I'm sorry. I shouldn't be complaining about this to you."

"Jax, it's okay. I get it." His tone was steady, almost gentle. "As far as you and I go - I've always known where I stood. Did I hope for more? Yeah. But I can't blame you for how I feel."

I rubbed a hand over my face, guilt clawing at my chest. "You deserve better than this. Better than me unloading all my crap on you every time I screw things up."

Steven shook his head, the faintest smile tugging at his lips. "You're not screwing things up, Jax. You're feeling something. That's what you do. It's one of the reasons I..."

He stopped himself, looking away for a second before meeting my eyes again. "It's one of the reasons I care about you."

Silence stretched between us, filled with everything we'd never said. His breath fogged the window of his car; mine caught somewhere between regret and relief.

"I love you, Steven," I said quietly. "You know I do."

His eyes softened. "I know." He smiled - small, real, and full of understanding. "I love you too, Jax. Always."

Jax.

He was the only person I ever let call me that. The name softened something in me, even as guilt threaded through my chest. I breathed a little easier, hearing him say it, but I still worried I was playing with his heart.

Then my phone buzzed. A new notification flashed across the top of the screen. My pulse spiked.

I sat up in bed, the world narrowing to that one glowing line of text.

"Whoa, hey... what just happened?" Steven asked, concern breaking through the haze.

I swallowed hard, then looked into Steven's warm hazel eyes.

"She texted me back."

Chapter 26

Abby

The glow of my phone faded to black, leaving me alone with the echo of what I'd just done.

I shouldn't have sent that text. *God, what was I thinking?*

I lay on my side, staring at the framed wedding photo on the dresser - the one where my smile was forced almost as much as the marriage. The room was dark except for the faint spill of light from the hallway. Beside me, Sung-ho breathed slow and steady, his back turned - solid, and unmoving, like a door I'd stopped trying to open.

I pressed the phone to my chest, as if I could take the words back through my skin.

I'll explain everything, but not like this.

What if he thought I meant never? What if he thought I was string-ing him along? What if he didn't care at all?

The house creaked with every passing gust of wind, the refrigerator humming in the kitchen, the heater clicking on and off. Each sound reminded me the world kept moving - even if I couldn't.

I shut my eyes, willing sleep to come, but my mind refused to quiet. Every time I drifted close, Jackson's voice, low and rough, pulled me back like a song I'd never stopped knowing the words to.

What if he texts back?

What if he doesn't?

Both possibilities scared me.

When the clock on the nightstand blinked past two, I finally gave up and rolled onto my back. My phone screen was dark. No new notifications. Just silence.

Maybe he hadn't seen it yet. Or maybe he was long gone - leaving me behind, the way I once left him.

I told myself that was what I wanted.

But the ache in my chest said otherwise.

By morning, I had barely slept a wink. My head pounded, eyes gritty from hours of staring at the ceiling.

The house was quiet. Too quiet.

Sunlight slipped through the blinds in thin, perfect lines, painting stripes across the bedspread. Sung-ho was gone, his side of the bed cold and untouched; as though he'd never been there at all.

He never left before me.

I tried not to think about what that meant and reached for my phone, unable to stop myself.

No new messages.

A part of me sagged in relief. The other part felt hollow.

I went through the motions like it was any other day, waking up Cole, packing his lunch, triple checking his homework. I kissed the top of his head before sending him off on the school bus.

I should've gone to work. Should've showered, put on the uniform of normalcy and pretended everything was fine. But the thought of facing anyone, of trying to smile and make small talk while my skin still felt raw from the inside out, made my stomach turn.

I dialed the number for Oakridge instead. My voice came out scratchy when I told them I still had a fever. They didn't ask questions. They never did.

After I hung up, I sat on the edge of the bed, my hands trembling in my lap. I had the whole day ahead of me - nothing but time, silence, and the weight of my conscience.

So, I cleaned.

I filled the sink with hot water and bleach until the smell burned my nose and scrubbed every surface in sight.

Every motion was an attempt to quiet the noise in my head - the part replaying Jackson's voice, the memory of his hands, the way he made me feel like I was still worth something.

By noon, my body ached, but the house gleamed.

I made tea I didn't drink, wishing it was coffee. I turned on the TV for background noise, some daytime soap I couldn't follow.

Eventually, I ended up on the couch, wrapped in a blanket, staring at my phone.

Still nothing.

Maybe that was for the best. Maybe this was the universe telling me to stop before I ruined everything.

But deep down, I already knew - if he texted, I'd answer.

And if he didn't... I'd find a reason to text him first.

By Wednesday morning, the bruises around my neck and cheek had started to fade.

They weren't gone, not completely. The purple had softened to yellow, and with enough foundation and powder, I could almost pretend they'd never been there.

The mirror was unforgiving. No matter how much makeup I brushed on, I could still see the cracks beneath it; the dark circles, the tightness in my smile, the person I didn't recognize anymore.

When I got to Oakridge, the mix of disinfectant and coffee hit me all at once, a smell I'd always associated with routine, with safety. Now it just made me feel small.

"Hey, Ah-bi," one of the nurses called from the break room. "Feeling better?"

I nodded, offering a quick, practiced smile. "Much better. Just a little bug."

No one questioned me. After all, I was Ah-bi Kim, hardworking and dependable. Never late, always ready to take on an extra shift...

I fell into the rhythm of the day - checking charts, changing linens, soothing patients - my movements mechanical, almost graceful from practice. I even managed to joke around with Mrs. Ortiz.

She watched me for a long moment as I adjusted her blanket, her sharp eyes softer than usual.

"You're very good at pretending, you know," she said.

My hands stilled. "Pretending?"

She nodded once. "Like everything's fine when it's not." Her gaze flicked briefly toward my face, then away again, polite enough not to stare. "I did that for years."

I swallowed. "We all do."

She hummed, unconvinced. "Not like you." Then, gently, "Yesterday, you didn't look like someone carrying this much alone."

My chest tightened. "Yesterday, I wasn't here."

She smiled, faint and knowing. "Exactly."

I straightened, forcing a breath, murmuring something about getting her lunch tray. She let me go without another word.

But the thought stayed with me.

You didn't look like this yesterday.

By lunchtime, my mask felt too heavy to keep wearing.

I carried my lunch out to my car, claiming I needed fresh air, and sat in the driver's seat. The radio hummed low, a familiar piano line slipping through the speakers before I realized what it was - "Fix You" by Coldplay, one of Jackson's songs.

I shut it off, but the ache remained.

My hands shook as I unwrapped my sandwich, but I couldn't bring myself to eat.

My phone sat on the console, the same black screen that had mocked me for two days.

There were still no new messages.

I tried to convince myself that it was good, that his silence meant he'd moved on, that I could breathe again, go back to pretending this version of my life was enough.

That I could keep Cole safe.

But I couldn't stop thinking about him. About the boy who couldn't climb trees, yet was the strongest person I'd ever known. The boy who didn't understand the difference between chalk and charcoal, but always took the time to admire the beauty in the art.

The man who had searched for me for years when it would have been easier to move on with his life and find someone new.

Whatever had made me lighter that day hadn't been freedom. It had been him.

Before I could talk myself out of it, I unlocked my phone and opened our message thread. My heart thudded so hard I could hear it in my ears.

Are you still in town?

My thumb hovered over the send button.

I stared at the message until the screen dimmed, my reflection ghosting across the glass, tired eyes and too much hope.

My breath caught, sharp and shallow, like I'd already said too much.

Then I locked the phone without sending it.

I didn't know what answer I wanted.

Only that I was terrified of needing one.

Chapter 27

Jackson

The sun was high enough to bake the hood of my truck, but I barely noticed. Autumn was in full swing, and in Kansas, that meant cold nights and warm days. Sweat slicked my neck as I leaned over the open engine, phone cradled between my shoulder and ear.

"Yeah, that's right," I muttered, tightening the oil cap with one hand. "Same order as last week, but throw in an extra case of whiskey. And yeah, yeah, I know what that means for the invoice."

The rep on the other end chuckled, his voice muffled by static. I half listened, half drifted. I hadn't slept much - just enough to dream of Abby, and that message that wouldn't stop replaying in my head.

I'll explain everything, but not like this.

She wanted to see me again. That had to mean something.

But then Steven's voice cut in, quiet and steady like always: *Leave the ball in her court, Jax. If she wants you, she'll come to you.*

And I'd tell myself that's what I was doing - giving her space. Letting her come to me. But I couldn't keep the doubt from creeping in. I'd gotten that message Monday night. It was Thursday now, and not a peep. I was waiting for a woman who, deep down, I knew was making me a fool.

"Uh, Jackson?" the rep said. "You still there, man?"

"Yeah, sorry," I said quickly, wiping my hands on a rag tucked into my back pocket. "Just a little distracted."

I reached back under the hood, wrench in hand. A bead of oil dripped onto my forearm, hot enough to sting. I hissed and wiped it away, squinting against the glare off the chrome. The whole truck needed a tune-up, but it gave me something to do, something to focus on that wasn't my spiraling thoughts.

"Alright," the rep said. "I'll send over the confirmation this afternoon."

"Sounds good," I said, tugging on a stubborn bolt. "Appreciate it."

That's when it happened.

A light touch on my shoulder, soft, and hesitant.

I jerked in surprise, my head slamming into the raised hood with a solid clang. "Shit!"

The phone slipped from my grip, hitting the concrete with a hollow crack. A tiny voice still mumbled through the speaker.

I straightened, rubbing the back of my head, already halfway to snapping at whoever thought sneaking up on me was a good idea.

Then I saw her.

Abby.

The wrench slipped from my hand, landing near my boot with a dull thud.

She stood just a few feet away, sunlight catching in her hair, her fingers twisted together like she wasn't sure she belonged there. Beneath the scent of oil and asphalt, there was a faint trace of something softer - her perfume, the one I hadn't realized I still remembered.

Her lips parted like she wanted to say something, then closed again.

"Hey," she finally said, her voice soft.

Everything in me went still. The hum of cars on the main road, the faint voice on the phone, even the wind. It all disappeared.

"Hey," I breathed, the word catching in my throat.

For a long second, we just stood there. Me gripping the edge of the hood, her clutching her purse strap like it might hold her upright. The air between us buzzed, thick with everything we hadn't said.

"Can we talk?" she asked at the exact same time I said, "How are you?"

We both froze, then laughed, quiet and nervous, the sound more exhale than humor.

"You first," I said, rubbing the back of my neck with a grease-stained hand.

She hesitated, glancing toward the road, then back at me. "Can we talk? Somewhere private?"

I nodded, wiping my palms on a rag. "Yeah. Of course."

I lowered the hood, the metal clanging shut louder than it should've been, then turned toward the row of rooms behind us. She fell into step beside me, her pristine white shoes scuffing against the cracked concrete.

Halfway to the door, a faint voice called from somewhere near the ground.

"Jackson? You still there?"

The sales rep.

"Shit." I turned back and scooped the phone off the pavement. The screen was cracked, the guy still talking. "Hey, sorry about that," I said quickly. "Yeah, we're good. Thanks man."

I ended the call before he could ask questions and slipped the phone into my pocket. Abby stood a few feet away, watching me like she wasn't sure if she should stay or run.

I opened the door and gestured for her to go in first.

"Thanks," she whispered, stepping past me.

As the door shut behind us, the world outside went quiet again, just the sound of my heartbeat and the faint creak of floorboards as she crossed the room.

Inside, the air felt too still. The hum of the mini fridge, the faint tick of the wall clock, all of it grated against the silence that had fallen between us. I motioned toward the table by the window and pulled out a chair for her.

"Have a seat," I said, trying to sound casual.

She sat, her hands folded in her lap, eyes fixed on the table like she was afraid to look at me.

"Can I get you something to drink?" I asked, already reaching for a glass from the counter.

She shook her head. "No, thanks."

I filled the glass anyway, just to have something to do. My palms were slick, my throat dry, and when I sat across from her, I couldn't make myself speak.

For a while, neither of us said a word. The silence stretched so long, I started to think she'd changed her mind about talking at all.

She swallowed. I watched her throat work, the way her eyes darted away and then back again. Then she took a breath, shaky and uneven. "You asked about the Mercedes," she said.

My pulse kicked. "Yeah."

Her eyes lifted, meeting mine for the first time. "His name is Sung-ho." She hesitated, like she wanted to stop right there. "He's my husband."

Everything in me went still.

I blinked, like maybe I'd misheard her. But she didn't take it back. Didn't laugh. Didn't say it was a bad joke.

She just sat there, her shoulders drawn tight, waiting for me to react.

My mind was suddenly full of noise; static and half-formed thoughts. Husband. She said *husband.*

I forced out a breath, slow and careful, because if I spoke too fast, I might break. "Your... husband."

"Yes."

The word echoed in my head, loud and hollow.

"You're married," I said.

She nodded once, the movement barely visible. "My parents arranged it when I was young, before you and I..."

I closed my eyes, the ache in my chest flaring back to life.

"After you were gone, my parents took the opportunity to move us to Kansas where he lived. I didn't have a choice, Jackson."

I sat back, the chair creaking beneath me. Every part of me wanted to look away, to stop seeing her sitting there, looking at me like she was sorry but not sorry enough. "You're telling me," I said slowly, "that you've been married this whole time."

My heart was pounding so hard it hurt.

"You let me find you," I said. "You let me touch you. You let me believe this was... real."

"It was real," she said. "It was to me."

The glass in my hand was slick with condensation, my fingers gripping it too tight. "What about all of our plans? Were you ever going to tell me?"

"I didn't know. I swear I didn't know." A single tear rolled down her cheek.

I wanted to feel bad for making her cry, but I just couldn't. "And after you found out? Why didn't you tell me then?"

"I wanted to," she said softly. "I just didn't know how."

Something sharp tore through my chest. I laughed, not because it was funny, but because my body didn't know what else to do. "You've had eleven years, Abby. I think that's enough time to figure it out."

Her face crumpled. "It's not that simple."

"Yeah," I said, swallowing hard. "Guess it never is with us."

For a long moment, all I could do was stare at her, the girl I'd obsessed over, the one I built my hope around, sitting across from me, wearing someone else's ring.

The air felt thinner now, the room smaller, the walls closing in.

For a long moment, I couldn't move.

Couldn't think.

I stared at her, waiting for something to make sense. But nothing did.

My chest hurt, sharp and deep, the kind of ache that didn't stop when you breathed.

All I could see were flashes - her in my bed, her breath on my neck, the sound she made when I touched her like she was mine. The way she looked at me. The way she *came back* to me.

God. How could she?

"You're married," I said again, because I needed to hear it out loud, to make it real. "You're telling me that after everything that happened, after what we *did,* you went home to your husband?"

Her chin trembled. "Jackson, please..."

"Don't," I cut her off. My voice came out rough, like gravel. "Just answer me. Are you in love with him?"

She hesitated, and that hesitation was enough.

I looked away, a humorless laugh escaping before I could stop it. "Guess that's my answer."

"It's not that simple."

"Yeah, you keep saying that." I rubbed my hand over my face, my palm catching on the stubble along my jaw. The sound of my own breathing filled the room, uneven and ragged. "You could've told me. You *should've* told me before any of this started."

"I know," she whispered.

"Was I just a mistake you needed to get out of your system?"

Her eyes went wide, hurt flashing across her face, but I couldn't stop. The pain had tipped into something sharper.

"Jackson..."

"Because that night," I said, my throat tightening, my anger collapsing under the weight of it all, "those days we had together... They weren't just sex, Abby. Not to me. They were *everything*."

"They mattered to me too," she whispered.

"Then why?" I asked. "Why let me fall back into this knowing you'd already built a life without me?"

"I was scared," she said. "I still am."

"Of him?" I asked.

"Yes."

"And of me?" I held her gaze. "Because that's what it feels like."

She shook her head, tears spilling now. "I was afraid of losing everything."

I nodded slowly. "And I was the thing you could afford to lose." The words tasted bitter the moment they left my mouth, but they rang true anyway.

The room went quiet again. The only sound was the low hum of the heater and my pulse pounding in my ears.

I dragged a hand through my hair and turned away, pacing a few steps, then stopping when my knees threatened to give out. "You told me to wait," I said quietly. "All this time, I thought maybe there was still a reason to. But now I just... I don't know what the hell to believe."

She didn't answer, and maybe that was worse than any lie she could've told.

I stared at the wall for a long time, my jaw locked tight, trying to get my breathing under control. I could feel her eyes on me - waiting, maybe hoping I'd say something that would make it all okay. But there wasn't a single damn thing left to say.

Finally, I turned back to her, my voice quieter now, but still rough around the edges. "Are you happy?"

Her brow creased, confusion flickering across her face. "What?"

"With him," I clarified. "Are you happy?"

The question hung there, heavy and impossible.

She opened her mouth, but I couldn't bear to hear what she had to say, not if she said yes.

"Never mind," I said, shaking my head. "I can't do this."

Her lips parted, but no sound came out.

"I waited eleven years for you," I said. "I would've waited longer if I thought it meant something."

"It did mean something," she said.

I looked at her then, really looked. Not the girl I loved. Not the woman I'd found again. Just someone standing in the wreckage with me.

"Yeah," I said. "That's the problem."

I grabbed my keys from the table. The room suddenly felt too small, too full of everything we'd lost.

"Jackson," she said softly, rising halfway out of her seat.

I stopped with my hand on the doorknob, but I didn't look back. If I did, I'd never walk out.

"Take care of yourself, Abby," I said, the words barely more than a whisper. Then I opened the door and stepped out into the daylight.

The sun hit me hard, too bright and too hot. I stood there for a moment, blinking against it, trying to breathe.

Behind me, I thought I heard her crying. Or maybe that was just my imagination.

Either way, I didn't go back.

Chapter 28

Abby

The door shut behind him and I flinched, the echo snapping through the silence like a gunshot. It would have hurt less if he slammed it.

For a long moment, I didn't move. *I couldn't.*

The air was still heavy with him; his scent, his heat, the quiet weight of all the words we didn't say. His glass of water still sat on the table between us, half full, a smudge along the rim from where his lips had touched it.

I stared at it, at the way the light caught the ring of condensation pooling beneath it, and my chest squeezed so tight I could barely breathe.

He was gone. And this time it was my fault.

My throat burned, and before I could stop it, tears blurred my vision. I hadn't cried for Jackson in years. Not when I married Sung-ho. Not when I found out what kind of man he really was. Not even when I realized my life was never going to be my own again.

But now, sitting in this motel room, surrounded by the ghost of him, I couldn't stop.

I pressed a trembling hand to my mouth to muffle the sound, but the sob broke loose anyway. It felt like grief and guilt and relief all tangled together, because even after everything, even after I'd destroyed him all over again, part of me was grateful he'd come back.

He wasn't supposed to find me.

He wasn't supposed to still care.

And yet, the second I saw him, I remembered what it felt like to belong somewhere.

I'd let go of that future years ago. The girl who dreamed about running away with him and building a life together - she'd died the day my parents packed our lives into boxes and drove me out of Colorado. I thought I'd buried her for good.

But Jackson had dragged her back to the surface, gasping for air.

Why did he have to come back?

Why couldn't he have stayed gone?

The questions looped through my head, sharp and useless. I couldn't change anything. I couldn't undo what I'd done - to him or to myself.

But one truth cut through all the noise, sharp and terrifying: the thought of losing him again felt unbearable.

Not this time.

When the tears finally slowed, I wiped my face with the sleeve of my sweater and forced myself to stand. The mirror above the dresser caught my reflection - eyes red, mascara smudged, skin blotchy. I barely recognized the woman staring back.

I turned away, heading for the bathroom. His scent hit me as soon as I opened the door, faint but unmistakable. Soap. Aftershave. *Jackson.*

My knees nearly buckled.

I gripped the counter and leaned against it, closing my eyes as I breathed it in. For a second, I was seventeen again, sitting beside him in his old truck, the windows down, his hand brushing mine on the gearshift. The world had been so simple then. So full of maybes.

A bitter laugh escaped me.

"Get it together, Abby," I whispered.

I splashed cold water on my face, scrubbing away the salt of my tears, then stared at my reflection, the smeared makeup no longer concealing the faint, but visible bruises underneath.

With a shaky breath, I reached into my purse and pulled out the makeup I had packed, just in case. Layer by layer, color by color, I replaced my mask. By the time I had finished, I looked almost normal again. The same old, unbothered, perfectly composed Ah-bi.

Like nothing inside of me had been cracked open.

No one would ever know.

I left the motel without looking back.

Outside, the sun was sharp against the pavement, too bright after being in the dim room. I blinked through the glare, climbed into my car, and started the engine. The clock on the dash read 12:47. If I left now, I'd make it back to Oakridge just before my lunch break ended.

As I returned to my life, I couldn't help looking for Jackson in every truck I passed. I don't know what I expected would happen when I told him I was married, but I certainly hadn't expected this.

By the time I turned into the employee parking lot, the numbness had started to set in, an old, familiar armor settling over me. I put the car in park and caught my reflection in the rearview mirror.

The makeup had held, but my expression hadn't. My lips were trembling, my eyes too wet, too soft. They weren't *her* eyes. Not Ah-bi's.

I took a slow breath and practiced my smile. Once. Twice. Again. Until it reached my eyes just enough. Until the woman in the mirror looked composed. Capable.

Perfect.

I fixed a loose strand of hair, dabbed the corners of my eyes with a tissue, then straightened my shoulders.

By the time I stepped out of the car, my mask was firmly back in place.

The automatic doors of Oakridge opened with a rush of cool air and the sharp scent of disinfectant. I pasted on my smile and walked inside, every step a performance.

No one would ever guess I'd spent my lunch break falling apart.

No one would ever know that my hands were still shaking.

Or that, behind the mask, I was already trying to figure out how to fix the unfixable.

Chapter 29

Jackson

The road blurred ahead of me, a long stretch of nothing that went on forever.

The kind of road meant for thinking... or forgetting.

I didn't know which one I wanted more.

The sun perched high in the sky, mocking me with its warm comforting rays. I'd been driving for an hour and still hadn't turned on the radio. The only sound was the hum of the tires and the rattle of the old truck every time I hit a pothole.

I didn't know where I was going. Didn't care.

Anywhere but that motel. Anywhere but the room that still smelled like her skin.

Anywhere that wouldn't remind me of her, which was impossible when wild sunflowers had popped up everywhere I looked.

My phone sat on the passenger seat, silent. I'd thought about calling Grady, hell, even Steven, more than once. But what was I supposed to say? *Hey, guess what, she's married. To some rich asshole who probably doesn't even know how lucky he is.*

For all I knew, he was actually really nice...

No. This one I had to figure out on my own.

By the time I rolled into the next town over, I was still no closer to an answer. A neon sign buzzed outside a liquor store, the *Open* light flickering like a beacon of hope. My truck stuttered, like it was trying to warn me off. I almost listened.

Almost.

The bell above the door chimed when I stepped inside. The place smelled like dust and stale beer, like every small-town liquor store I'd ever set foot in. I didn't look around. I didn't need to. I went straight for the whiskey.

The good kind.

The kind I hadn't touched in months.

The clerk barely looked up when I dropped the bottle on the counter. He rang it up, handed me a brown paper bag, and told me to have a good night.

"Yeah," I muttered. "You too."

Back in the truck, I sat there for a long minute, the bottle heavy in my hand. I shouldn't. I knew I shouldn't. But knowing and doing were two very different things.

The cap twisted off with a soft crack.

The first swallow burned like hell.

The second went down easier.

By the third, I didn't feel much of anything.

I nursed it, let the burn fade just enough before I turned the key.

I drove. Miles blurred into more miles. The bottle rolled against the seat with every turn, clinking against my phone.

I told myself I'd stop after one more sip. Then one more.

Then the bottle was half-empty, and I was right back where I'd started - stuck in my head, stuck in the past, chasing a ghost I could never have.

When I finally turned back toward Stonehill, the streets were quiet. Parents still at work while their kids kept busy in school.

I slowed as I neared the elementary school, then pulled into a parking lot across the street. I hadn't meant to, I needed to go pack and head home, but something held me there.

The sound of laughter carried across the field, high, wild, and free.

And then I saw him.

That kid from the other day, the one with the strong arm and determined face. He dropped back, ball in hand, shoulders squared just like I'd shown him. His foot planted, his arm arced... and the ball cut through the air in a perfect spiral, landing right in his friend's hands.

I smiled before I could stop myself.

For the first time all day, something warm broke through the fog.

"Nice throw, kid," I murmured, even though he couldn't hear me.

I sat there a while, watching them play until the whistle blew and they started to pack up. For a second, I almost got out of the truck. Almost walked across the street just to tell him he did good. But I didn't.

I couldn't.

The sun dipped lower, catching on the bottle in the passenger seat. I picked it up, took another pull, and drove off.

By the time I made it back to the motel, it was dark. My hands were steady enough to turn the key, but my head wasn't. I dropped the bottle on the nightstand, sank onto the bed, and stared at the ceiling.

The room spun a little. The air was too still.

I told myself I'd pack up in the morning, head home to Falcon Pointe, pretend this trip never happened.

But the longer I lay there, the louder the silence got.

It pressed on my chest, filled my throat, until I couldn't take it anymore.

I reached for my phone. My thumb hovered over her name.

Don't do it, I told myself. Don't be that guy.

But I was already typing.

> **Me:** Are you happy?

I stared at the message for a long time before hitting send.

The three dots never appeared.

So, I took another drink.

And waited.

Chapter 30

Abby

The smell of garlic and soy filled the kitchen, the hum of the vent fan soft against the sound of Cole's voice.

He sat at the table, arms flailing as he told me about recess, his face lit up in that way that made my heart ache.

"My throw was perfect! It must have been fifty yards, and Kevin caught it! I told you, Mom. I'm gonna be a quarterback one day."

I smiled as I stirred the japchae, even though I already knew this story. He'd been telling it since the moment I picked him up from school. "A quarterback, huh? That sounds like a lot of responsibility."

"It is," he said proudly. "But remember that man I told you about? He said if I keep practicing, I'll get better."

His excitement, normally contagious, filled me with dread. I kept my back to him, stirring the noodles like it mattered. "That's good advice," I said softly.

There was no world where Sung-ho would let him play. I didn't have to ask, and honestly, I was afraid to try.

Cole beamed, tapping his pencil against his notebook as he talked. For a few moments, everything felt almost normal...

Until the low rumble of the garage door broke through the noise.

Cole froze mid-sentence. The joy drained from his face. He closed his notebook, stuffed it into his backpack without looking at me, and stood.

"Go wash up," I said gently, even though he was already halfway down the hall.

A moment later, the door opened and Sung-ho stepped in, removing his shoes neatly by the mat.

"You're home early," I said, forcing brightness into my voice.

He smiled, a thin, measured thing. "Traffic was light." He glanced at the table. "You made dinner."

"I did."

He nodded, satisfied, and walked into the dining room while I began plating the food.

My phone buzzed on the counter, lighting up the dark granite.

One glance and my breath caught.

Whitney: Are you happy?

My fingers trembled. Whitney...

No, not Whitney... Jackson - his name hidden where it didn't belong.

The number still sat in my contacts like a lifeline I wasn't supposed to touch.

I swallowed hard, stuffing the phone into my pocket just as Sung-ho called from the other room.

"Ah-bi?"

"Coming!" I said quickly, grabbing the plates.

By the time I stepped back into the dining room, Cole had reappeared, his face blank.

We sat together, the three of us, eating in a silence broken only by the scrape of chopsticks and the faint ticking of the clock.

Sung-ho cleared his throat and turned to Cole. "Your mother and I were talking about adding someone new to the family. Wouldn't you like a little brother?"

Cole's head shot up, surprise and hope mingling in his eyes. "Really?"

"Maybe," I said quickly, before Sung-ho could answer.

"Of course," he said smoothly, looking at me. "If your mother tries a little harder."

The words struck me, though I kept a smile fixed in place, pretending not to feel the blow.

After dinner, I helped Cole with his homework, then followed him to his room. He'd already climbed into bed, the football plushie he'd had since he was a baby tucked under his arm.

"Mom?" he said quietly as I sat beside him. "If you have a baby, do you think he'll like me?"

I brushed his hair back from his forehead. "Of course he would."

"I'll be the best big brother. I'll teach him everything I know."

Despite my frustration with Sung-ho for bringing this up with Cole, I couldn't help but smile. "I know you would."

"Do you think..." He hesitated then tried again. "Do you think maybe if there's another kid, Dad will be happier? Do you think if I helped out, he'd love me more?"

My heart cracked. I pulled him close and kissed the top of his head. "You're enough, Cole. You'll always be enough."

He fell asleep still clutching the football. I sat there a while, listening to the steady rhythm of his breathing.

When I finally stood, I went straight to the bathroom and locked the door behind me.

I leaned against the sink, staring at my reflection, at all the things makeup couldn't cover. Tired eyes, heavy shoulders, the faint tremor that never seemed to leave.

I turned on the water and wet a washcloth. With careful, measured strokes, I cleared the makeup from my skin, revealing the faint bruises on my cheek and neck.

My mind reeled, unable to get Cole's words out of my head. *Do you think he'd love me more?* I didn't know how to tell him that if we had a baby, there was a good chance Sung-ho would love him less - if he even loved him at all.

A new baby would be *his* baby, and he wouldn't need Cole anymore.

I pulled out my phone and unlocked the screen. Jackson's message was still there, waiting for my reply.

Are you happy?

I stared at it until my eyes blurred. Then, with a shaking thumb, I typed:

> **Me:** Sometimes. Ask me if I love him

I didn't wait for a reply. I stuffed the phone back into my pocket, turned off the light, and stepped back into the hall.

The bedroom light spilled into the hallway, a narrow slice of gold. Sung-ho sat on the edge of the bed, his tie gone, his expression calm. Almost gentle.

He looked up as I entered. "You've been quiet tonight."

"It was a long day."

He stood, closing the distance between us. His hand brushed my arm, light, and deliberate before pulling me into his arms.

I wrapped my arms around his waist, because it was expected, and waited to see what would happen next.

He pressed a soft kiss to the top of my head. "I made an appointment," he said. "With a fertility specialist."

The word *specialist* lodged in my chest like shrapnel. I pulled away just enough to see his face. "You what?"

He smiled faintly, his fingers tracing the edge of my sleeve. "It's time, Ah-bi. We've waited long enough."

The words hollowed me out, my world crumbling all around me.

He wanted me to see a specialist. They would know about my IUD. And if I didn't tell them, they'd find out as soon as they examined me.

What would he do when he learned the reason I couldn't get pregnant wasn't bad luck, but me?

I pushed my worries down and smiled softly, protecting myself while there was still time.

"Of course," I whispered.

And let him believe it.

Chapter 31

Jackson

The ringing wouldn't stop.

It drilled through my skull, sharp and relentless, until I realized it wasn't in my head, it was my phone.

I groaned, throwing an arm over my eyes to block out the sunlight pouring through the motel curtains.

It didn't help.

Nothing helped.

My head throbbed in time with my heartbeat, my mouth dry as dust. I groped for the phone somewhere on the nightstand and answered without looking.

"Yeah?"

"You sound like death." Steven's voice came through, too bright, and way too loud. "Rough night?"

I rolled onto my back with a groan, pressing the phone tighter to my ear. "Define rough."

"Considering the four voicemails you left me last night, I'd say 'rough' covers it."

I winced. "Shit. I did that?"

"Oh yeah," he said, amusement thick in his voice. "You were very philosophical, by the way. Something about how whiskey tastes like regret and how you think you want kids."

That pulled me up short. "What?"

"You asked if I wanted kids," Steven said. "Then told me you do. That you'd probably be a good dad, once you got your shit together."

I dragged a hand over my face. "Fuck. I don't even remember that."

"Don't worry, you didn't cry or confess your undying love for me this time."

"Thanks," I muttered. "That's comforting."

"Seriously, Jax." His tone softened. "You okay?"

I stared up at the ceiling, squinting against the light. The empty whiskey bottle sat on the dresser, half-tipped, like it had tried to make a run for it. "Yeah," I said finally. "Just... paying for bad decisions."

"Story of your life," he said, half teasing. "Call me later, alright?"

"Yeah. Later."

I hung up before he could say more and let the phone rest on my chest. The room was spinning just enough to make me queasy. I closed my eyes, trying to remember everything from last night.

The liquor store.

The road stretching out like it would never end.

The bottle, heavy in my hand.

Abby's face in my mind.

Her voice.

Her confession...

I groaned again and sat up, the room tilting before settling back into place. I unlocked my phone to check the time and frowned. I rubbed my eyes and looked down at the screen. At the text from Abby...

Abby: Sometimes. Ask me if I love him

I looked up at the text I sent her first, and for a second, I couldn't breathe.

The words blurred, refocused, then blurred again. My pulse hammered in my temples, the hangover fading beneath something sharper, something that hurt worse.

She didn't answer the question.

She couldn't even say she loved him.

My hand tightened around the phone until my knuckles ached.

"Damn it, Abby," I whispered.

The sound of my own voice was too loud in the silence.

I scrubbed a hand over the rough stubble on my face. I didn't have to remember my drunken phone calls to know what I wanted, no, *needed* to know. Once I accepted that Abby was married, there was only one logical choice left for me.

Go home, back to Falcon Pointe, and move on.

Apparently, my drunken mind thought I should move on with Steven - and have kids...

But once again, here was Abby, throwing a wrench in my plans, in my life.

Against my better judgement, I opened the text thread and responded.

Me: Do you love him?

I didn't wait for a response, just got up and headed for the shower.

I turned the water on as hot as I could stand it, then stepped under the stream and let it burn.

The sting felt good. Clean, punishing, and honest.

I braced my palms against the tile, bowing my head as the water ran down my face and neck, turning the skin along my shoulders red.

Maybe I deserved this.

For drinking. For staying. For chasing a woman who didn't belong to me anymore.

"Why couldn't you just let me go?" I muttered, voice drowned out by the rush of water.

I wanted to hate her. God, I wanted to. But I couldn't. Even now, after everything, I still loved her. I still wanted her.

And that made me hate myself even more.

By the time the water started to cool, the mirror was fogged and my head was pounding again. I turned the faucet off and grabbed a towel, dragging it over my face and chest.

My reflection looked worse than I felt - eyes bloodshot, skin pale, the weight of years of mistakes staring back at me.

I dressed on autopilot, jeans and a plain black T-shirt, running my hand through my hair to shake out the water. The motel room felt smaller than before, the air heavy with regret.

When I reached for my phone on the bed, the screen lit up with two new messages.

> **Abby:** No, I don't love him

Another followed almost instantly.

> **Abby:** Ask me what I want

My chest tightened.

I sank onto the edge of the bed, towel still draped over my shoulders, hair dripping onto the carpet. My thumb hovered over the screen.

There were a thousand things I wanted to say. Accusations. Pleas. Questions.

But none of them mattered.

I scrubbed a hand through my hair, water flinging against the wall, and typed the only thing that made sense.

> **Me:** What do you want?

Then I set the phone down beside me and waited, the silence in the room pressing in on all sides.

I checked the time again.

1:07 p.m.

It was too late to drive home today; not that I was going to stay. I just needed to figure out how the hell to walk away without feeling like I was leaving a piece of myself behind.

My phone buzzed against the comforter.

> **Abby:** You

The breath caught in my chest. For a second, I thought I'd imagined it.

Then I typed a response before I could think better of it.

> **Me:** Then run away with me

Her reply came almost instantly.

> **Abby:** I can't

My stomach twisted.

> **Me:** Why?

Abby: It's complicated

Me: Because of your husband?

Abby: Yes. And also my family

I shoved to my feet, pacing the small space between the bed and the door, the floorboards creaking under my feet. My pulse thudded like I'd been running for miles.

Me: Come over. Let's talk

Abby: I can't

I clenched my jaw, the bitterness spilling out before I could stop it.

Me: Because of your husband?

Abby: It's complicated

I ran a hand through my hair and let out a shaky breath. She was driving me insane; the way she pulled me in just to push me away again. Then another message came through.

Abby: I never expected to see you again. I thought you were lost to me forever, so I moved on like my family demanded. It doesn't change the fact that I still love you. That I want a life with you

Abby: I just don't know how to make it work. Not yet anyway

Abby: Will you wait for me?

The air went still.

I stared at the screen, thumb hovering. The words blurred in front of me. *Will you wait for me?*

I wanted to laugh. Or scream. Or throw the damn phone across the room.

I started typing, "*I moved on too.*"

Then stopped.

I couldn't do that to her. Not when she was being honest. Not when I knew exactly how it felt to be trapped and wanting something you couldn't have.

I deleted the message and tried again.

Me: How long?

The typing bubble appeared, disappeared, then came back.

Abby: In a hurry to be rid of me?

Despite myself, I smiled, that soft, familiar ache settling right under my ribs. Even through text, she still had that bite.

That spark.

That piece of my heart I'd never gotten back.

For a while, I just sat there, staring at the last message.

In a hurry to be rid of me?

But the warmth that came with it faded fast.

My thoughts drifted back to Steven.

Those voicemails. The stupid, drunken things I said.

Kids.

Fuck, *had I really asked him about kids?*

My chest tightened. He'd laughed it off earlier, but I knew Steven. He didn't joke unless he was trying to hide something.

What was I doing to him?

What was I doing to any of them?

An hour ago, I was ready to drive home, ready to leave all this behind. Now I was sitting here again, tangled up in the same damn web, waiting for a woman who couldn't even promise me tomorrow.

And then there was Grady. My best friend, my brother. He didn't deserve this either, me leaving him with everything at the bar, plus my sister, while I chased ghosts and guilt across state lines.

Hell, *I* didn't deserve it.

I picked up my phone again, thumb hovering over Abby's name. My pulse kicked hard in my chest as I typed.

Me: Don't play with my heart. I can't take it. Either tell me you want me and let's find a way to be together. Or let me go

I stared at the message until the words blurred, then set the phone down. I didn't wait for her reply this time.

Instead, I grabbed my keys and called Grady.

Straight to voicemail.

"Hey, man. It's me," I said, rubbing the back of my neck. "Just checking in. Haven't heard from you or Whit. Call me when you get this."

I hung up and immediately called again. Same thing.

By the third try, I was pacing, heart thudding harder than it should've.

Then I tried Whitney.

She answered on the second ring. "Jackson? Is it really you?"

Relief hit me so hard I had to sit down on the edge of the bed. "Who else?"

She asked where I'd been, why I hadn't answered any of her calls or texts, and for a moment I almost told her everything. About Abby.

About the way finding her had cracked me open all over again. But the truth stayed lodged in my throat, too sharp to touch.

"I've got so much to tell you," I said quietly.

"I'm all ears," she teased.

I laughed, something in my chest easing for the first time all day. "I figured. But now's not the best time. Soon."

"Promise?"

"I promise." I hesitated, then asked about Grady.

"He's right here. Want to talk to him?"

"Please."

My stomach knotted. The longer I stayed away, the harder it would be to come back. "Wait," I said quickly.

"Yeah?"

"I love you, Whitney. Thank you for being there for him. It's the only reason I can stomach being away so long."

Her voice softened. "Love you too, big brother."

"Okay," I said, a weak laugh slipping out. "Now hand him the phone."

"Grady?"

A second later, Grady's voice came through, deep and familiar. "Yeah. I'm here."

Relief washed over me and I raked a hand through my hair. "God, man. It's good to hear your voice." And it was.

I closed my eyes.

By the time the call ended, my chest felt hollowed out, like something vital had been carved away and left behind. Grady had trusted me with the truth. About his now ex-girlfriend, Emily. About Whitney. About feelings he didn't want but couldn't deny.

And somehow, impossibly, I'd given him my blessing - to date my sister.

When the silence returned, it settled heavier than before.

I sat there for a long time, unmoving, staring past the wall, past the cracks in the ceiling, letting the weight of it all sink in. How easily I'd told Grady to be patient. To be careful. To do the right thing.

Funny how advice comes easy when it isn't your own heart on the line.

Eventually, the room felt too empty to ignore.

I reached for my phone.

Still nothing from Abby.

Somehow, the quiet felt heavier than before.

Chapter 32

Abby

His words wouldn't leave my head.

Don't play with my heart. I can't take it. Either tell me you want me and let's find a way to be together. Or let me go.

I didn't need to see his face to know what that message had cost him. I could hear it in my mind; how low and raw his voice would sound, breaking the way it always did when he'd reached his limit. It had been years since I'd seen Jackson cry, but the memory of it still haunted me: the set of his shoulders, the way his jaw tightened as he tried to stay strong.

And now I'd made him walk away all over again.

The rest of the day passed in a blur. I kept myself moving - checking vitals, signing charts, smiling when patients thanked me... But my mind was somewhere else entirely.

With him.

By the time my shift ended, I was exhausted in a way that was so much more than *tired*.

When I picked Cole up from school, he climbed into the car and immediately began telling me about his day. I nodded and smiled at the right moments, but his words barely sank in. The traffic lights bled together, Vivaldi playing softly beneath his voice - measured and precise.

Everything I wasn't.

At home, I tried to focus on dinner. *Tried* to remember how to be the version of myself that fit the mold of this life I'd made. But my thoughts wouldn't stop or even slow down. My hands shook as I stirred the pot, and I didn't notice the smell until it was too late - sharp and bitter, filling the kitchen with the stench of something burned.

"Mom?" Cole wrinkled his nose. "I think it's smoking."

"Yeah," I muttered, pulling the pan off the burner. "Guess it is."

Part of me wanted to laugh. Part of me wanted to cry. Mostly, I just didn't care. If it were up to me, I'd order a pizza, crawl into bed, and forget the world existed.

I couldn't even remember the last time I'd eaten pizza.

Instead, I scraped what was salvageable onto plates and set them on the table, bracing myself for whatever version of Sung-ho would walk through the door tonight.

When he finally came in, he didn't say a word. He hung his jacket on the hook, straightened it with precise care, and sat down. His eyes flicked to the food, then to me.

My stomach clenched, waiting for the furrow of his brow, the tightening of his lips - for the anger of a spoiled dinner to lash out at me. But there was nothing. Just a quiet, assessing look that chilled me more than yelling ever could.

Like he already knew my secret.

Dinner passed in silence, the sound of chopsticks against ceramic too loud in the still air. When Cole asked if he could be excused, I nodded, relieved.

Afterward, as he focused on his homework for Korean school, carefully tracing the Hangul characters one by one, I leaned over his workbook, forcing my mind to focus on the words instead of the ache in my chest. It helped for a while. I couldn't help smiling at the way his tongue poked out in concentration as he whispered the sounds under his breath - ga, na, da, ra - his pencil wobbling at the corners of each box.

By the time I tucked him into bed, the house was quiet again. The television hummed faintly from the living room, and my chest tightened with the sound of the occasional clink of ice against glass.

Sung-ho was drinking, and for once, I wasn't entirely sure what that meant.

I climbed into bed alone, clutching my phone to my chest like it was the only thing keeping me tethered. My heart raced as I opened our message thread. His last text sat there, waiting, the words feeling heavy and final.

Don't play with my heart.

I traced the words with my thumb, wishing I knew what to say. Wishing I knew how to make things work.

Would he understand that I couldn't leave?

What would he do if he knew what Sung-ho did to me? That he voiced his displeasure with scathing words and closed fists?

Would he hate me if he knew the truth - that he has a son, who doesn't even know he exists? A son who calls another man *Dad?*

My throat tightened.

Could I keep that secret forever?

I lay there in the dark, the ceiling blurring above me. My phone was still warm against my chest, my fingers tracing the edges of it like it was something fragile.

If I was going to keep him, I had to say something. I had to *give* him something.

Not everything, not yet, but enough.

My thumbs hovered over the keyboard. The screen glowed pale against the shadows, lighting my hands, my breath, the tremor in both.

He'll think I'm weak.

He'll hate me for staying.

He'll try to save me, and I can't let him do that.

I started typing anyway.

It's not what you think.

I paused, then deleted the words. Though it was true, it was too vague, bordering on what I hoped he already understood.

I tried again.

Me: My marriage isn't what it looks like. He's not… kind. Not always

The words made my throat ache. I read them twice, my thumb shaking over the send button. From the living room came the faint clink of ice against glass, the low murmur of the TV.

I waited until I was sure he wasn't moving before hitting send.

The message bubble blinked back at me. I typed more before I lost my nerve.

I can't just leave. It's complicated. I wish it wasn't.

I sucked in a deep breath, then deleted it and typed a new message.

If I walked away, he'd find me. He always does.

My breath hitched at the truth in my words. Words I hadn't shared with anyone. I squeezed my eyes shut; it was too much. I erased the last sentence, leaving only the first part.

> **Me:** If I walked away, he'd find me

It still felt like standing on a cliff, but I hit send anyway.

I stared at the screen, at the tiny block of text that said both too much and still not enough. What I really wanted to write was *I still love you.*

What I really meant was *don't stop loving me yet.*

Instead, I typed:

> **Me:** Please don't give up on me. I just need time

My thumb hovered for a heartbeat before I pressed send.

The message whooshed away, tiny and irreversible, like a spark vanishing into the dark.

I locked the phone and slid it beneath my pillow. My heart wouldn't slow. I could still feel him out there somewhere, waiting, hurting.

From the living room came the sound of the TV shutting off, followed by heavy footsteps.

I turned off the lamp, rolled to my side, and closed my eyes just before the bedroom door creaked open.

The mattress dipped behind me, the familiar weight settling close enough for me to feel his breath on my neck.

"Still awake?" Sung-ho's voice was quiet, smooth, the faint, sweet burn of soju clinging to his breath.

I kept my breathing steady. "No."

He exhaled a faint laugh, his hand resting on my hip, heavy and possessive.

I lay perfectly still until his breathing slowed, until I could almost believe I was safe.

Only then did I let the smallest whisper slip through my lips, so soft even I barely heard it.

"Don't give up on me."

Chapter 33

Jackson

The world outside was too bright for the way my head throbbed.

I hadn't slept more than a couple of hours. The motel heater groaned, trying to drown out the sunlight slicing through the curtains. I threw an arm over my face, but the hum only made the pounding worse.

My hand brushed against something cold and solid on the nightstand, another empty bottle. The third in as many days.

I told myself I wasn't that guy anymore, the one who drank to cope. Steven had pulled me out of that hole once. Hell, *twice* - yet here I was again, halfway down it before I even noticed.

I reached for my phone, the glass slick under my fingers, and brought it close. My pulse jumped, her name alone was enough to jolt me upright.

> **Abby:** My marriage isn't what it looks like. He's not… kind. Not always

> **Abby:** If I walked away, he'd find me

> **Abby:** Please don't give up on me. I just need time

I blinked at the messages, trying to make sense of them through the fog in my head. The words hit like a punch and a plea all at once. She didn't have to spell it out.

Her husband wasn't just possessive.

He was dangerous.

Was she safe? How long had this been going on?

And where the *hell* were her parents? The ones who'd supposedly "arranged" this whole fucking thing?

I scrubbed a hand down my face, jaw tight. I needed answers.

I needed to see her.

I swung my legs over the edge of the bed and sat there for a long minute, elbows on my knees, head in my hands. The sour taste of whiskey coated my tongue, thick enough to turn my stomach. My reflection in the mirror across the room looked rough. Bloodshot eyes, days-old stubble, and beneath it all, a cloak of guilt.

If I was right… if her husband really was hurting her… then I couldn't show up like this.

I turned on the shower as hot as it would go. The pipes groaned before steam filled the room. I stepped under the water and let it burn, scrubbed until the sting drowned out the pounding behind my eyes. It didn't sober me up completely, but it gave me something that almost felt like control.

By the time I got dressed, jeans, clean shirt, and boots, my mind was set. I didn't think, I just moved. The keys jingled as I snatched them off the nightstand, catching the light like a challenge.

The drive across town blurred together in a wash of heat and hangover. The air outside was warmer than it had any right to be for early October, the kind that made your shirt stick to your back and your thoughts twist in on themselves. The road stretched long and flat, nothing but dry grass and the hum of tires beneath me.

Every mile between me and that motel felt like one more I couldn't take back. I told myself I just needed to see her. Just needed to know she was okay. That she was telling the truth.

But deep down, I knew better. I wasn't looking for proof...

I was looking for her.

The neighborhood came into view before I realized I'd even entered it. Perfect lawns, trimmed hedges, and houses that looked more like display models than homes. Even the trees stood unnaturally neat, their leaves still clinging stubbornly to branches while the rest of the world was turning gold and letting go.

Her street looked exactly the same as the last time I had been here.

I slowed, pulling to the curb across from the white home with black shutters. Abby's car sat in the driveway, looking out of place.

There it was. The life that wasn't mine.

I cut the engine but didn't move, just sat there with both hands on the steering wheel, pulse hammering behind my ribs. The heater ticked as it cooled. My reflection stared back at me from the rearview mirror and I winced.

I didn't belong in a place like this.

Once upon a time, Abby didn't either. It wasn't the life we had talked about. It wasn't the one we *dreamed* about.

Minutes passed, maybe longer as I sat unmoving.

Then the front door opened.

Abby stepped out, dark hair catching the sunlight, movements clipped and tense, like she was running on nerves alone. She didn't look at first, just walked, her bare feet striking the pavement in sharp, steady beats.

Then her eyes found me.

Her pace faltered. For half a second, she froze.

Then she marched straight toward the truck.

"Jackson, what the *hell* are you doing here?"

I reached for the door handle, but Abby was faster, shoving it shut before I could even open it an inch.

"Abby..."

She glanced around, checking the street, then ran around the truck and climbed into the passenger seat. Too stunned to speak, I just watched as she slid across, and then her lips were on mine.

For a heartbeat, it felt like we were kids again. Parked outside her parents' house. Lost in our own world.

Except we weren't kids.

And this wasn't her parents' house.

I gripped her shoulders and broke the kiss, cursing myself for every second she wasn't in my arms, but I needed answers.

"Jackson?"

I dragged in a breath and closed my eyes. "I-I need to know..."

Her hand brushed my cheek, and I leaned into it.

"What?"

I swallowed and caught her hand, pulling back so I could see her face. "Does he... does he hurt you?"

She recoiled, practically jumping to the other side of the seat.

And that's when I saw it - the yellowed shadows of fingerprints around her neck.

Rage flooded me, sharp and blinding. It took everything I had not to march into that house and tear him apart.

"Did he do that?"

Creases formed between her brows before her hand flew to her neck, realization dawning too late. The loose T-shirt she wore showed more than the scarves and turtlenecks she'd been hiding behind.

"I, um..." She looked away, fingers curling around the door handle.

I stopped her, gentle but firm, my hand closing around her upper arm. "Tell me the truth. Does. He. Hurt. You?"

She swallowed and nodded, looking anywhere but at me.

Something in my chest cinched tight. Heat crawled up my neck, a copper taste burning my throat. Every instinct screamed at me, *get him, threaten him, burn his world down*, but I watched Abby shrink with each violent thought.

She wasn't asking me to fight for her.

She was asking for time.

Time so she could fight for us.

"I need you to understand something," I said quietly. My hands were shaking now, and I didn't bother hiding it.

"I waited once. I told myself staying calm was the right thing to do. That not pushing, not making noise, was safer."

I swallowed. "And while I was waiting, everything I loved was taken from me."

The words hung between us, heavy and raw.

Abby's breath caught. She looked down at her hands, then back up at me, exhaustion etched into every line of her face.

"I'm not asking you to disappear," she said softly. "I'm asking you not to make this worse."

Something in her voice - steady, scared, and resolute - hit harder than any argument could have.

I closed my eyes. Drew in a slow breath. One. Two. Three. Forced the animal in me back under a thin layer of control.

"Okay," I said finally, my voice rough. "We'll do it your way."

Her shoulders sagged, just a little.

"But promise me one thing."

Her eyes lifted, wary but listening. "What?"

"You call me when it's safe. You tell me when you can get out." I paused, choosing my next words carefully. "If anything changes... If he..."

I stopped, fury licking at the edges of my voice, then forced it back.

"If anything changes," I said more evenly, "I will come. I won't wait."

She hesitated, then nodded, small but fierce. "I will. I'll make a plan. I just... not yet. I can't just walk out."

Her voice cracked and she steadied it. "I promise."

Every part of me wanted to argue. To grab her and run until this life couldn't touch her anymore. But I saw the fear in her eyes, the terror of being seen, of a neighbor's whisper.

So, I swallowed it. Folded the wanting into something sharper.

"Fine," I said. "Call me. Text me. Tell me when I can take you home."

She turned toward the door, then paused.

Our eyes met, just for a second, and whatever she saw there made her look away first.

She climbed out of the truck and headed for the house, her shoulders already set like armor. Her hand hesitated on the door for just a moment before she went inside.

I didn't move.

I sat there with the engine running, hands locked on the steering wheel, watching the front of the house like it might give something away.

When the door finally closed, the shaking started.

Not fear - control.

I leaned forward, resting my forehead against the wheel, breathing through the burn in my chest until my pulse slowed and my fingers stopped curling into fists.

Waiting had cost me once.

I wasn't going to let it cost her.

Only after the porch light flicked on did I put the truck in gear and pull away.

Chapter 34

Abby

I reached for my chair, but Sung-ho stopped me with a light touch on my shoulder. He pulled the chair out and waited while I sat, then helped scoot me in. "Th-thank you," I stammered, the words unfamiliar on my tongue. It was the first time in years he had made such an effort.

He simply nodded as he took his seat across from me, immediately lifting the menu. I followed his lead, going through the motions, playing my part in this charade like I did every Saturday night.

I flipped through the glossy pages, the words and images all blurring together. My mind wasn't here, at dinner with my husband. It was miles away, at an old motel on the other side of the city. Jackson's face flashed in my memory, the fear in his eyes when he saw the bruising on my neck, the realization that my husband was a monster.

He wanted to drag me away, right then and there. And I would have gone with him, if it was only me.

But Cole...

The waiter arrived for our drink order. Sung-ho didn't bother looking up. "Whiskey, neat," he said. "She'll have water."

I nodded when the waiter looked to me for confirmation, and as soon as his back was turned, my thoughts returned to my son.

Cole didn't know the truth. He had no idea Sung-ho wasn't his father. How would he take the news? Would he be upset?

Or relieved?

And what about Jackson? He didn't know he had a son. Would he be angry?

Angry because he had a child he didn't know about?

Or angry because he didn't want kids and I didn't give him a choice?

When the waiter returned for our entrées, Sung-ho ordered steak, like usual. But then he turned to me, "What would you like?"

For a second, I just stared at him. He'd never asked before, Sung-ho always ordered for me, usually a salad or... I quickly glanced over the menu. It might as well have been in another language for all the good that did me. I forced my eyes to focus, and ordered the first thing that made sense. "Uh... I'll have the chicken, please," I managed.

"Very good," Sung-ho said, an unexpected smile twisting his features from sharp and cold, to almost... handsome and kind.

The waiter disappeared, and for a moment the clatter of silverware and low murmur of conversation filled the silence between us. Candles flickered in the glass centerpieces, throwing restless shadows across the tablecloth.

Sung-ho watched the flame, not me. When he finally spoke, his voice was smooth. Too smooth.

"Monday afternoon," he started, swirling the whiskey in his glass, "we have an appointment with Dr. Han, the fertility specialist."

My stomach tightened. "But... I have to work."

His gaze lifted then, sharp and deliberate. "You will quit."

I gripped the edge of the table, pulse thudding in my ears. "But..."

He smiled faintly, a practiced imitation of warmth. "You won't need it much longer anyway. Once you're pregnant, I want you home where you belong."

The words hit like cold water. "You can't mean that. We've always agreed that I could have my job..."

He shook his head, taking a sip of his drink. "You didn't work when Ha-joon was little. You'll do the same with our son."

Son?

The word landed like a blow, like he could control the sex of the baby.

He was delusional if he thought I would give him a child... But then it hit me like a punch in the stomach - the reason I hadn't already. A specialist would know, they'd tell him I've been sabotaging him all these years.

I sucked in a deep breath. "Monday is a little soon, couldn't you give me a little more notice?" I needed more time. Time to find a clinic that would take me without insurance. Time to get rid of my IUD.

"I've already called your supervisor. You're taking a leave of absence."

My throat went dry. "You did what?"

His smile didn't falter. "It's best for you. For us. Stress isn't good for conception."

I wanted to argue, to tell him I loved my work, that I needed it, but my tongue felt heavy, caught between fear and fury. "You should have asked me," I managed.

He set his glass down, the sound crisp against the table. "I don't have to ask, Ah-bi. I make the decisions that are best for this family. You'll thank me later."

I dropped my gaze to the candlelight trembling between us. My hands wouldn't stop shaking, so I folded them in my lap, pressing them together until my knuckles ached.

"Monday afternoon," he repeated, his tone softening in that way that always made my skin crawl. "We'll see the doctor, and we'll finally start moving forward. A fresh start."

A fresh start.

The words rang hollow, like something he'd practiced in the mirror.

The waiter reappeared with our food, breaking the moment. Sung-ho thanked him politely, immediately cutting into his steak with neat precision. I stared at my plate, the chicken I barely remembered ordering, my appetite gone.

I forced a smile, small and brittle. "Of course," I said, because it was safer than silence.

But inside, something sharp and certain took root.

He thought he owned every piece of me - my body, my choices, my future.

I couldn't wait any longer, it was time to take back my life. I knew my parents wouldn't help me - they knew about the abuse, and stood by quietly, reminding me that Sung-ho was a good man, and that no other man would have a tainted woman like me.

As much as it would hurt to leave them behind, I knew what I had to do, for me and Cole. I just prayed Jackson would have us.

Both of us.

I lay back in the tub, my head resting against the cold porcelain, a wet cloth draped over my eyes.

Sung-ho had been especially rough last night.

The doctor said the deeper it is, the better, he'd groaned in my ear as he slammed into me over and over. It didn't matter that I cried out that he was hurting me. It didn't matter that I knew his words were lies.

Every part of me ached. The deep, lingering kind that didn't fade with hot water or time.

I shifted carefully, wincing as my body protested, and stared at the faint bruises blooming along my hips and thighs, marks I'd already started cataloging in my mind.

I pressed the cloth harder against my eyes and focused on breathing, counting each inhale until the shaking stopped.

All that mattered was he was desperate to put a baby in me.

And I couldn't let that happen.

But I also couldn't let him find out about the IUD. Not now. Not ever.

I pulled the cloth away from my eyes and stared at the bathroom door, my chest tightening as I checked the lock again. Once. Then Twice. Cole would be home soon, and I needed this done before he was.

My gaze drifted to the edge of the tub.

The hemostats sat there, old and stiff from lack of use, salvaged from my medical bag and scrubbed clean until they gleamed under the harsh bathroom light. Tools meant for helping. For healing.

I told myself this was the only way. That I'd handled worse. That I knew my own body well enough to survive this too.

But when I reached for them, my hands betrayed me, trembling so badly I had to curl my fingers into fists to steady them.

"I should have been stronger," I whispered. "I should have said no. I should have run before it ever got this far."

Tears blurred the edges of my vision, regret pressing so hard against my ribs it stole my breath. I wasn't strong enough to fight him. Not out loud. I wasn't brave enough to leave.

So this...

This was all I had left.

The next moments came in flashes; panic, pain, a gasp that caught halfway between breath and cry. Then silence followed by a heaviness that felt like shame settling over my skin.

When it was done, I sank lower in the water, trembling. The small pink piece of plastic sat discarded on the side of the tub, while the red that colored the water between my legs slowly thinned to pink.

Regret hit harder than the pain. Not because of what I'd done, but because this was what I had allowed my life to become. Living a lie, every action nothing more than a reaction to the fear that consumed me.

I pressed the cloth back over my eyes and whispered to no one, "I can't live like this anymore."

***

"Mmmm..." Cole groaned, his voice muffled by the blanket. "Five more minutes."

"Sorry, bud. It's already six-thirty," I said softly, pulling the curtain back just enough to let in a sliver of gray light. "Come on, sleepyhead."

He rolled over, rubbing the sleep out of his eyes. "Mom?"

"Hmm?"

"You keep holding your stomach. Are you sick?"

"Just a little stomach ache," I lied as I sat on the edge of the bed and brushed his hair back. "Nothing pancakes can't fix."

He grinned. "Extra chocolate chips?"

"Always."

When he finally dragged himself out of bed, I lingered by the doorway, pressing a hand to my abdomen once his back was turned. The ache was sharp this morning, a little deeper than before. I swallowed it down, the same way I swallowed everything else. I had to keep it together, for both of us.

After breakfast I helped him with his jacket and then we headed out the door, his backpack slung over one shoulder. He talked my ear off, chattering about a science project and the class hamster while we waited for the bus. I nodded in the right places, and when the bus pulled up, I kissed the top of his head, and watched him climb on.

The taillights disappeared around the corner and for a second, the silence felt merciful. Then the weight of what was coming came crashing back.

By ten, Sung-ho's Mercedes was idling in the drive.

I had showered, praying there was no trace left of what I'd done. Leaning back into my medical training, though nowhere near as involved as a doctor, I logically knew I was fine.

Even still, that fear lurked in the back of my head.

I took a calming breath and left the house, rushing down the sidewalk to the car.

Sung-ho's hand rested on the gearshift, his tie perfectly knotted, his smile tight. "You're late," he said mildly. "Let's not embarrass ourselves."

I swallowed, folding my hands in my lap. "Yes, sir."

He drove one-handed, the other drumming against the wheel. The city outside was abuzz with activity. Every pothole jarred through my body, sending dull waves of pain through my abdomen.

"When we see the doctor," he began, "you'll let me handle the conversation. No nervous fidgeting. Be respectful."

I nodded, eyes on the passing buildings.

"After today," he continued, "we'll start properly. You'll rest, eat better, and stop wasting energy at work. I spoke to your supervisor this morning, told her you'd be taking an indefinite leave."

My stomach turned. "You did what?"

He kept his eyes on the road. "It's for your health. For the baby we'll have."

A chill rolled through me, the leash of control tugging a little tighter.

He glanced over, expecting gratitude. I folded my hands in my lap so he wouldn't see them shake.

The fertility clinic was small, neat, and blindingly white. The air smelled like disinfectant and citrus.

A receptionist smiled from behind the desk. "Good morning, Mr. and Mrs. Kim. You can fill these out while you wait."

Sung-ho thanked her in that smooth, public voice that fooled everyone while I took the clipboard she held out.

One look and my stomach clenched, the questions swimming before my eyes.

Current medications. Previous contraception.

My pen hovered above the line. I hesitated only a second before writing the lie: *None.*

Sung-ho's thumb brushed once against my knuckles - slow, and approving. Then he placed his hand over mine, light enough for the receptionist to mistake it for affection.

To me, it felt like a threat.

We didn't have to wait long before we were welcomed back to Dr. Han's office. I had to fight to keep from wrinkling my nose at the smell of stale coffee.

I sat in a brown leather chair in front of his desk, unable to miss the framed photo of his family sitting beside the computer, their smiling faces too warm for this cold room.

"Good to see you again, Mr. Kim," Dr. Han shook Sung-ho's hand first, then mine. He gave me a soft smile, "I understand you've been trying to conceive?"

"Yes," Sung-ho said quickly. "As I said before, we're ready to begin as soon as possible."

White noise filled my head as I realized my husband knew Dr. Han. And not just from his work as a fertility doctor. They had discussed me before, without me even knowing about it. My hands clenched in my lap, my stomach ached with every heartbeat.

Their voices faded away, replaced with static. It wasn't until Sung-ho squeezed my shoulder that I realized Dr. Han was asking me something.

"I'm sorry, what?"

"I asked, when was your last menstrual period?"

My throat went dry. "About... two weeks ago." The lie came out steady, practiced. I honestly couldn't remember the last time I had had my period.

"Good. Any history of contraception?" he asked, now seated in front of his computer, typing in my responses.

What was the point of the paperwork I filled out if he was just going to ask me the questions?

I felt Sung-ho's hard gaze on me like a hand around my throat. "No," I said.

Dr. Han nodded, making a note. "We'll start with some baseline bloodwork and a pelvic ultrasound today. That will tell us if everything looks healthy before we proceed with hormone testing. Simple and painless."

Simple, I thought. *If only he knew.*

Sung-ho leaned forward. "And after that? How long until she conceives?"

The doctor offered a polite smile. "That depends on the results. We'll review them together and decide next steps. For now, patience is important."

Patience. I almost laughed.

Dr. Han turned back to me. "We'll take a quick look at your uterus and ovaries today. You may feel some pressure. Is that alright?"

I nodded because I had to. What I really wanted was to run.

When he stepped out to prepare, I stared at the tray of sterile equipment. My pulse thundered in my ears. Every clamp, every glint of metal made my stomach twist tighter.

Sung-ho's voice cut through the buzz in my head. "Smile," he said softly. "You don't want him thinking there's a problem."

I looked up at him, and for a moment I thought I might scream. Instead I forced the corners of my mouth up, a cheap imitation of calm I didn't feel.

The door opened again, and Dr. Han gestured toward the curtained exam area.

"Whenever you're ready, Mrs. Kim."

I slid off the chair, legs trembling, the pain a dull echo of yesterday's action. *Don't let him see. Don't let anyone see.*

Behind the curtain, the paper crinkled beneath me. The light overhead hummed, too bright, too clean.

When the exam began, I held my breath and prayed he wouldn't be able to tell.

And if he did, if he looked up with confusion in his eyes, I already knew what I'd say.

That it was nothing.

That I was fine.

Chapter 35

Jackson

I sat on the edge of the motel bed, the same damn spot I'd been glued to all night, breathing the same stale air, feeling the same damn knot in my chest. I needed Abby like I needed air to breathe, and the only thing that made not having her, not knowing if she was okay, was sitting on the dresser, mocking me.

The bottle of Jack caught the morning light like it was waving me over. I didn't even remember buying it, and that alone was a big enough red flag for me to reconsider my actions.

But the craving was still there, humming under my skin, as familiar as breathing.

And as much as I wanted to call Steven, to lean into his strength, I couldn't do that to him. Not this time.

Not when I knew in my heart that what he and I had, while perfect in so many ways, wasn't the future I had dreamed of.

He deserved better than me. Someone who would put him first and not constantly drag him down with their bullshit.

I picked up my phone, hoping for a new message from Abby, but wasn't surprised when there was nothing.

I didn't understand what was so hard, why she couldn't just run away with me. Why she couldn't go to her parents, to the police. Tell everyone what was going on.

Her parents had to know something was wrong.

They couldn't possibly be okay with what her husband was doing to her.

My thumb hovered over our text thread as the anger drained out, replaced with that same raw fear I'd been fighting since Friday.

I typed without thinking.

> **Me:** Good morning, beautiful

I stared at the screen, waiting for those three little dots to appear.

Waiting for any sign she'd seen it, that she was okay.

But the message just sat there staring back at me.

Nothing.

I shoved the phone into my pocket before I could stare at our text thread any longer. Staying in that room was driving me insane. I was so used to being on the go, always moving, and here, I sat frozen in more ways than one.

I grabbed my keys, ignored the bottle on the dresser, and walked out before the craving dug its claws in me again.

The morning air slapped me awake - cold, dry, almost metallic. The air here smelled different than home. Less pine, more dust. More... nothing.

I climbed into the truck and fired up the engine. It coughed, then settled into its familiar low rumble. The old Chevy had seen better days, but I could never part with it. It was all I had left of my dad. The truck he had taught me to drive in. The truck he had taught me to work on.

I rolled my neck from side to side, trying to alleviate some of the pressure, then backed out of the lot. "Breakfast," I muttered to myself. "I just need some breakfast."

I said it once more on the drive to the diner, like maybe saying it out loud would make it true. And maybe real food, not convenience store grab-and-go snacks, was the answer.

The place was quiet, half-empty except for the old-timers in the corner drinking coffee that looked older than they were. I sat at the counter, ordered eggs and toast, and watched them pile powdered sugar on pancakes like it was the key to immortality.

My phone sat face-up on the counter. There was still nothing from her.

I poked at my food, desperate to feel something other than dejected, and failing miserably. I sighed, my appetite gone.

The waitress gave me a sympathetic smile I didn't deserve and topped off my coffee.

When I paid and stepped back into the sunlight, I already knew where I was going, and I wasn't proud of it.

But I couldn't stop myself either.

I'll just drive by, I told myself.

I just needed to make sure she wasn't lying in a ditch or something even worse.

The closer I got, the tighter my grip became on the steering wheel.

Her neighborhood rose up like a damn postcard with its perfect lawns and perfect hedges. But I knew there was more to it - an ugly side hiding just beneath the surface. At least at one house.

I slowed before I meant to, my foot easing off the gas.

Her house sat quiet, like it was still asleep. Windows closed, the blinds drawn in the front window, the kind of stillness that made my shoulders tense.

Abby's car was parked in the driveway.

Relief hit first. Then something colder.

I checked the time. It was after ten, and yet there didn't appear to be any movement coming from her house.

The quiet didn't feel peaceful. It felt watched. Like the whole place was pretending nothing was wrong.

As much as it pained me, I kept my head straight, eyes forward, and drove past. I didn't even let myself glance in the rearview mirror until I'd made it halfway down the block.

My chest burned with the ache of not knowing.

I exhaled through my nose, shook my head, and turned the truck around. Not back toward her house, but toward the motel.

It felt wrong, like diving deeper when all I needed was air.

Back in the parking lot, I sat in the truck, hands still gripping the wheel. The engine ticked as it cooled.

"I'm trying," I said to no one. Maybe to myself. Maybe to her.

Back in the room, I dropped onto the chair and pulled my laptop toward me. I opened The Hideaway's inventory spreadsheets, Steven's neatly typed notes staring back at me. Rows and rows of liquor counts, food orders, backstock levels. He color-coded everything - green for good, yellow for low, red for *order this or we're screwed.*

My vision blurred for a second before refocusing.

"Alright," I muttered. "Easy stuff."

I clicked into the whiskey column. The brand I'd been eyeing all morning sat at the top of the list, a half-empty case flagged in yellow. That alone made something sour tighten in my stomach.

We never go through that much in a week.

Not even on busy weekends.

I scrolled. Vodka low. Tequila low. Even the beer kegs were marked as "check levels."

"What the hell..." I rubbed my thumb against my palm, trying to make sense of it. Steven wasn't sloppy. If anything, the guy was annoyingly meticulous.

Which meant either business had exploded while I was gone...

or I was looking at these numbers wrong.

Probably the second one.

I tried to ignore it. I tried to focus. I tried to be better than the man staring back in the motel mirror.

But the numbers kept slipping.

"Fuck," I grumbled, dragging my hand down my face.

I closed the sheet and opened QuickBooks instead. Payroll, invoices, supplier emails, auto-reorders - none of it stuck. My brain lagged two steps behind my fingers.

I triple-checked last week's beer order. Then I accidentally submitted a new one for a keg we didn't need.

Great. Real great.

I sat back hard, exhaling through my teeth.

I wasn't doing The Hideaway any favors this morning. Hell, I wasn't doing *anyone* any favors.

I glanced over at my phone, sitting beside the keyboard, its screen still dark.

I said I would give her time. Time to figure out whatever it was she needed to. But it was hard. Harder than I could have imagined.

"Get it together," I whispered to myself. "She needs you to be solid."

I forced my fingers to move again.

Typed in inventory counts.

Cross-checked pricing.

Sent in another order.

Did all the things I knew how to do blindly, on muscle memory.

And then, in the forefront of my mind, was the question I just couldn't shake.

Why won't she text me back?

A noise escaped me, half a groan, half a laugh at how ridiculous I sounded inside my own head.

I slammed the laptop shut and scrubbed a hand down my face.

"God, Abby," I whispered. "Just give me something."

And then, as if hearing my plea, my phone lit up, buzzing against the table top.

My pulse launched straight into my throat.

Abby: Hey good lookin' ⊠

It was like the sun cracked open inside my chest. I didn't even bother trying to play it cool, my thumb was already moving across the screen.

Me: Well hey there ⊠

Me: You always start conversations like that or am I special?

The typing bubbles popped up instantly and my heart damn near tripped over itself.

Abby: Don't get cocky

Abby: I just figured you needed a smile

She wasn't wrong.

I sank back into the chair, tension sliding off me like someone had finally loosened the vise around my chest.

Me: It worked

Me: Haven't stopped smiling since your name popped up

I held my breath, waiting for her response, grateful she didn't make me wait long.

Abby: Remember when I wrote that on your locker?

Abby: "Hey good lookin'" in pink Sharpie?

Abby: Coach made you clean it off before practice. 🫠

I snorted. Out loud.

Me: You mean the morning I thought I was being stalked by a ten-year-old with a crush?

Me: I almost reported you to the principal

Abby: Please

Abby: You LOVED the attention

Me: I loved YOU

The words were out before I could stop them; unapologetically honest. I stared at the screen, my pulse hammering in my ears.

Her typing bubbles appeared... disappeared... then appeared again.

Abby: I know

Abby: And I never stopped loving you either

I stopped breathing for a full second, then typed out, "Then why aren't you here?" Then quickly deleted it, replacing it with:

Me: What are you doing today?

Abby: Oh, you know...

Abby: It's Sunday

Abby: I'm home, pretending I'm still good at art even though I haven't painted anything in months

That last line punched me someplace soft.

Me: Hey

Me: You ARE still good at art

Me: You could out-draw half our high school blindfolded and hopped up on Pixy Stix

Abby: That's... oddly specific. ☒

Abby: But thank you

Me: What about your sketches?

Me: Still carrying around that beat-up notebook?

Abby: Not really

Abby: Art isn't...

Abby: Useful

It hurt to see her talking about something she loved so much, something that fueled her very being, in such a negative light.

It wasn't like her and only reinforced the distance between us.

Me: Art doesn't have to be useful, Abby. At least not in the traditional sense

Me: Do me a favor and open it today

Me: Even if it's just to doodle

Me: Can you do that for me?

For a long moment, I was greeted with nothing but my own words staring back at me. Maybe I had pushed too hard, but then again, it was never like me to hold back with her.

Then finally those three dots appeared, followed by a message.

Abby: Okay

Abby: For you

I blew out a heavy breath and let myself grin like an idiot.

Me: Remember when you drew the mural behind the bleachers?

Me: The one with the stars and the mountain line?

Me: You never signed it

Abby: Didn't have to

Abby: You knew it was mine

Yeah.

I always did.

Then, before I could respond, another text came through.

> **Abby:** I should get going, I've got a busy day tomorrow

My heart sank at her words, but a glance out the window told me it was getting late.

> **Me:** You know you can text me any time, right?

> **Me:** I don't care if you think it's dumb or random or 3am

> **Me:** I'm here

There was a much shorter pause this time.

> **Abby:** I know

> **Abby:** I'll text you tomorrow morning. Busy day. But… I'll try

> **Abby:** Thank you for checking on me

> **Me:** Always

> **Me:** Goodnight, beautiful

> **Abby:** Goodnight, Jackson

The motel room was still dark when my phone buzzed against the nightstand. For a half-second I thought I'd dreamed it.

Then it went off again, the sound soft and insistent, pulling me out of the only real sleep I'd had in days. I reached for it blindly, then blinked blearily at the screen, my heart thudding stupid-fast.

Abby: Morning

Abby: Got a really busy day today, but I'll text you when I can

Abby: Hope you slept well 🖤

I sat up so fast, the room tilted.

It didn't matter, I'd never been wide awake so quickly in my life.

I read her messages again, slower this time, making sure they were real and not some dream my brain cooked up because missing her had become a physical thing.

A grin spread across my face. She was thinking about me enough to send this before the sun was even up.

For the first time since she climbed out of my truck and ran back into that house, I felt like things were going to be okay.

I typed back:

Me: Morning, beautiful

Me: Take your time today. I'll be here

Me: Always

I tossed my phone onto the blanket beside me and scrubbed both hands over my face, grinning like an idiot. That tiny sliver of hope cracked my whole world open.

I lay back on the pillow, staring up at the stained motel ceiling, and for the first time in eleven years, let myself picture it.

All of it.

Abby in Falcon Pointe.

Abby in my truck, feet on the dash, singing off-key.

Abby curled up on my couch, sketchbook in her lap.

Abby at The Hideaway on a busy Friday night, rolling her eyes at Grady while he pretended not to be amused.

A house.

Not the one I shared with Grady - God, the thought of him listening to us fight over dishes or hearing her walk around in the mornings made me almost laugh.

No, we'd need our own place. Something small. Something... ours.

And maybe...

Hell, maybe someday I'd get to see her walk toward me in white, bare feet if she insisted. Her hair, loose and wild, eyes brighter than the sun bouncing off the mountains.

Mrs. Abby Taylor.

The name fluttered across my mind so easily I almost whispered it out loud.

I pressed my palms against my eyes, smiling like it was stitched into my bones.

I wasn't stupid, I knew she still had to get away. I knew things were going to get ugly before they got better.

But for the first time...

I let myself dream about a life where I didn't have to lose her again. Where she didn't have to run. Where she was mine. Where we could be *us* again.

My phone buzzed and I grabbed it without breathing.

Abby: Have a good day, okay?

Abby: And don't drink that garbage you like. Get coffee instead ☒

Chapter 36

Abby

The gentle humming of the tires against pavement was a welcome reprieve from the list of instructions we had just been given.

Schedule a hormone panel. Schedule another ultrasound. Track my cycle using an app. Take prenatal vitamins...

The list went on and on.

I glanced over at Sung-ho. He was gripping the steering wheel at ten-and-two, his posture perfect, his jaw tense. He didn't look at me, not once, just stared ahead like the road was a test he couldn't afford to fail.

I wonder if he's thinking about the doctor's other *suggestion... That maybe* he *was the problem.*

"Dr. Han said intercourse should be regular," he began, his calm voice cutting through the quiet like a knife. "Every two to three days is optimal. We'll adjust our routine accordingly."

I closed my eyes and sank back into the seat, ready for the onslaught of information I'd already had recited to me.

"He also emphasized rest," he continued. "Your energy needs to go toward conception. It's a good thing you're already taking a leave from work."

Of course it was... But good for who? Certainly not me.

"And the vitamins - don't forget those. Dr. Han was very clear. Folic acid daily. I expect you'll go to the store and pick some up. You'll start that tonight."

We came to a stop at a red light, and he turned to look at me for the first time since we left the doctor's office. "And you'll use that app he recommended to track your cycle. Obviously, what you've been doing hasn't been working. I want everything documented."

I pressed my fingers lightly to my stomach, relieved and aching at the same time. The exam was clean. There were no tears, no bleeding, nothing to raise suspicion.

My secret was safe.

But relief lasted only a moment before something heavier settled in its place.

How was I supposed to avoid getting pregnant now? How long could I fake ovulation pain or headaches or exhaustion before he noticed? How many excuses could I make before he started asking questions I couldn't answer?

"Dr. Han said nothing is wrong," Sung-ho added, as if reading from a script. "So, the rest is just discipline and timing."

Discipline.

Timing.

He made it sound like a military operation.

I wonder if this discipline will include fewer bruises, or if it's just me who needs to change?

I kept my eyes on the window, watching the blur of buildings pass by. But inside, my mind drifted miles away.

Back to Jackson. Back to earlier in his truck. Back to the way his voice softened when he said my name.

Back to the life I used to imagine I'd have - mountains, sunlight, paint-stained fingers, a boy who loved me before I even knew what that meant.

How was I supposed to get there from here?

How was I supposed to get Cole out, *get myself out*, without tipping everything over?

How was I supposed to leave my parents behind when I'd been raised to believe that everything they did was for me?

———

Sung-ho pulled up along the curb in front of the house, pausing just long enough for me to get out, before speeding off - eager to get back to whatever the hell it was he did all day.

The moment the front door clicked shut behind me, the entire house felt too big and too quiet.

I stood there in the entryway for one long, breathless second - holding my purse, holding my stomach, holding myself together by sheer force of will.

Then the silence cracked.

My knees went weak, and I pressed a hand against the wall, sucking in sharp breaths that didn't feel like enough. A wave of panic swelled up my spine, hot and suffocating.

This was my life.

This house.

This marriage.

This plan I never agreed to.

And I had no idea how the hell I was supposed to escape it.

I forced myself to move. One step, then another, into the kitchen. My hands shook as I opened the junk drawer beneath the microwave and pulled out the little pad of paper I used for grocery lists and school reminders. The pen felt slippery between my fingers.

I stood at the counter, staring at the blank page until my vision steadied enough to write.

> To figure out:
> 1. How to keep from getting pregnant without birth control
> 2. How to pull Cole from school without them alerting anyone
> 3. How to get a divorce
> 4. How to tell Jackson the truth

I stared at the fourth line until my eyes burned.

I almost didn't add the last one - but the doctor had said it, so I wrote it out too:

> 5. Folic acid

I let out a shaking breath and leaned my forehead on my hand.

The list didn't fix anything.

But it made the chaos inside my head line up into something I could understand, even if only for a moment.

When the panic loosened its grip just enough, I pulled out my phone. I stared at the name I'd given him, my thumb hovering over the edit contact button. Then I changed it - from Whitney to Jackson - and hit save before I could talk myself out of it.

I let out a slow breath, a feeling of calm settling a little deeper as I typed out a message.

Me: I miss you

The response came almost immediately.

Jackson: Miss you more. Can I see you yet?

A pull in my chest tightened, gentle and sharp at the same time.

Me: Soon

Just that.

A promise I didn't know how to keep yet, but I would.

I folded the list in half and slid it into my purse, right behind my wallet.

Then I grabbed my keys and headed out the front door and climbed into my old car.

The steering wheel felt cold in my hands.

I backed out of the driveway, careful, cautious, the way I always was. A little spark burned in my belly thinking about the day when I could finally let go.

At the end of the street, I turned toward the grocery store, my sense of self-preservation still intact for the moment.

As the neighborhood faded behind me, I whispered under my breath, "I'll find a way out. I swear I will."

And for the first time in years...

I almost believed myself.

That scared me as much as it gave me hope.

Chapter 37

Jackson

I woke to sunlight stabbing through the cheap curtains and the vague smell of burnt coffee drifting from somewhere. For once, I wasn't waking up with a knot in my stomach or my heart pounding out of my chest.

I woke up smiling.

Smiling like an idiot.

Her messages from last night were still open on my phone, the little white heart, the "Goodnight, Jackson."

God, I couldn't remember the last time I'd felt this kind of quiet inside my head.

I stretched, scrubbed a hand through my hair, and swung my legs off the bed… and froze at the sound of a soft knock on the door.

Two taps, then nothing.

My heartbeat leapt like someone plugged me into a damn outlet.

Nobody ever knocked on my door here. Nobody except…

I was already crossing the room before my thoughts caught up with me.

It can't be her. It won't be her. She said she'd text.

But some part of me, the part that had never stopped loving her, already knew.

I pulled the door open and there she was.

Abby.

Her usual navy scrubs traded in for a pair of jeans and a light sweater. Her neat bun was replaced with hair half pulled up, the rest falling over her shoulder.

Her breath puffed in the cool morning air, and her eyes - God, those eyes - lifted to meet mine, and every bone in my body went weak.

"Hi," she whispered.

I didn't move, I *couldn't*.

My hand stayed on the doorknob because I was terrified if I let go, she'd disappear.

"Abby," I finally managed, voice rougher than I meant. "What-what are you doing here?"

She lifted one shoulder in the smallest shrug.

"I just... needed to see you."

That was it.

That was all it took.

I reached for her - slowly, carefully, like she might break - and she stepped right into me, right into the circle of my arms, pressing her forehead to my chest like she'd been holding herself together for days and finally didn't have to anymore.

The breath left my lungs in a rush.

I wrapped her up without thinking, without question, without hesitation.

For a minute, just one, we were in our own world again.

"Come in," I said against her hair.

She nodded, just once, and I guided her inside, closing the door behind us like I was shutting out the whole damn universe.

"You want to sit?" I asked softly, nodding toward the bed.

Her eyes flicked up to mine - wide, searching - and she nodded.

I walked over and sat on the edge, leaving plenty of room, not quite sure how to act. Knowing what her husband had done, what she'd endured, made every memory of touching her replay differently in my head.

She hesitated only a second before crossing the room and sinking down beside me. Not touching, but close enough that the heat radiating off her arm made my chest tighten.

She let out a breath. One long, shaky exhale that sounded like the first air she'd had in days.

"You okay?" I murmured.

Abby nodded, but her eyes stayed on the carpet. "I just... needed to be somewhere that wasn't that house."

"Yeah," I whispered. "You're safe here."

She closed her eyes like that meant something. Like she believed me. A moment passed, quiet and gentle, then she leaned into me. Just a little. Barely there. But I felt it like a damn shockwave, her head brushing my shoulder.

I didn't move at first, afraid anything more might be too much. But then she shifted, turning toward me, resting her cheek just above my collarbone like it was the most natural thing in the world.

My arm slid around her back before I could think better of it.

She melted instantly, her body softening, breath slowing, finally letting herself relax.

"Jackson," she whispered, voice muffled by my shirt. "I've missed you."

God.

I didn't even try to hide the sound that escaped me, half a breath, half a prayer.

"I've missed you, too."

She moved again, slowly, like she was testing whether I'd pull away. She tucked her knees up onto the bed, angling her body toward mine. I shifted with her, guiding us back against the thin pillows until we were lying on our sides, facing each other.

Her fingers slipped into the fabric of my shirt, holding on lightly. "Is this okay?" she asked.

I swallowed hard. "Abby... this is more than okay."

She smiled and it was small, tired, and real.

God, I'd forgotten what that looked like on her.

We both scooted closer until our foreheads touched. Our legs tangled lazily, and comfortably. No rush. No fear. No weight.

Just two people who'd spent too much time apart finally remembering how to breathe again.

I brushed my thumb across her cheek, the softest touch I'd ever given anyone. "You don't have to talk," I murmured. "We can just... be."

Her hand found my chest, right over my heartbeat.

"I want to be here," she whispered.

"Then you're here," I said. "As long as you want."

We lay there for a long stretch, wrapped in each other, listening to the motel heater tick along the wall. The morning had gone soft and slow, like the whole world had decided to hush around us.

Abby's fingers brushed absently over the fabric of my shirt, tracing shapes I couldn't see. Her breathing had evened out, but she hadn't fallen asleep, not really. I could feel the tension in her muscles, the secret worries weighing down her shoulders even as she rested against me.

After a minute, her voice came quiet and hesitant.

"H-he made me take a leave from work."

My chest tightened. "Your husband?"

She flinched. It was small, but I felt it.

"Yeah," she whispered. "He said I needed to 'focus.' On... every-thing."

She didn't elaborate and I didn't pry, afraid to know what that meant.

I brushed a strand of hair from her cheek. "I'm sorry, sweetheart."

She let out a humorless little sigh. "I mean... maybe it's not the worst thing. I have time I didn't have before. Time to think. Time to figure things out."

That landed harder than I expected.

I couldn't help feeling hopeful and terrified all at once.

"Figure out what exactly?" I asked softly.

She hesitated... then lifted her head just enough to meet my eyes.

"Do you know how to get a divorce?"

The words hung between us, fragile and terrifying.

The way she said it - a half-laugh, half-cry - hit me like a punch and a kiss at the same time.

I couldn't help the grin that cracked across my face.

"No, baby," I said, shaking my head. "Because I've only ever wanted to marry you. And once I do, there'll be no getting rid of me."

She let out a startled laugh, a real one, bright and sudden as she buried her face into my chest. The sound warmed every cold corner inside me.

"Oh my god," she groaned. "You can't just say stuff like that."

"Why not? It's true."

She swatted at me, half shy, half delighted. "You're such a...

"Charmer?" I teased.

Her eyes sparked. "More like a Golden Boy."

I felt myself blush like a damn teenager.

"Abby..."

"What?" she said innocently. "It's not my fault you were the pride of Cedar Valley High. Mr. Perfect. Straight A's. Football star. Teachers' favorite."

I groaned into her hair. "I was *not* the teachers' favorite."

"You photocopied your butt and taped it to every locker in the senior hallway," she reminded me, laughing into my shirt. "And you didn't even get in trouble. If that doesn't scream favorite, I don't know what does..."

I covered my face with one hand. "I was sixteen. And pissed off."

"And weirdly proud of your..."

"Don't say it," I warned.

"...sweet cheeks."

I rolled onto my back, mortified. "God, Abbs..."

She grinned wickedly. "Oh, come on. You earned that nickname."

I tickled her side before I could think it through.

She squealed, twisting her body in an attempt to get away.

"Jackson! Stop... stop! I hate being tickled!"

"Say you're sorry."

"Never!"

I caught her wrists gently, holding them above her head just long enough to make her breath hitch - not from fear, but from laughing too hard. Her cheeks were flushed, eyes bright, chest rising and falling in soft, uneven breaths.

God, she was beautiful.

Alive.

Free, if only for this moment.

I released her immediately, letting her settle back onto the pillow, both of us still breathless. She rested her hand over her heart, trying to catch up.

"Mean," she murmured, smiling.

"You started it," I said, brushing my thumb along her knuckles.

Silence fell again, but this time it was warm and comfortable. The kind that felt like an old blanket pulled over both of us.

Abby shifted closer, tucking her leg against mine. Her head settled back on my chest.

After a long moment, she pulled her phone from her pocket and sighed. "I should... set an alarm. Just in case."

My stomach sank. "Yeah," I said quietly. "Before he notices you're gone?"

"Something like that," she whispered.

I pressed a soft kiss to the top of her head.

She closed her eyes, and we lay there together, wrapped in thin motel blankets and old memories, building a future neither of us were ready to say out loud

Chapter 38

Abby

I lingered in the motel doorway a moment longer, not quite ready to leave.

Jackson wrapped his arms around me and nuzzled into my neck. "I love you, Abby."

I brushed my lips against his, "I'll text you later."

I fought tears the whole way home and by the time I pulled into the driveway, the warmth from Jackson's arms had already begun to fade. I held onto it anyway, the smell of him still in my sweater, the way his heartbeat had steadied mine.

I needed a plan. A real one.

By the time I got home, the house felt smaller than it ever had.

Not because anything had changed, but because I had.

I moved through the familiar rooms quietly, my body still buzzing with the echo of Jackson's hands, his voice, the way he'd looked at me like I was something worth holding onto. It made everything else feel sharper. Louder. Harder to ignore.

Until I found a way out, I was trapped here, playing the dutiful wife to a man I despised.

The house was silent, the kind of quiet that always made my stomach twist. I went to my bedroom and opened my nightstand drawer. I pulled out the old spiral notebook I used when I couldn't sleep, to write down the things that weighed heavily on my mind. The pages were soft at the edges, some smudged with old ink or fingerprints.

Today, it would serve a different purpose.

I flipped to a blank page and just... stared.

My mind was too full and too empty at the same time.

Where do you even begin when your whole life needs to change?

My hand moved before my thoughts could catch up:

    Needs:

    1. Important papers - birth certificates, etc.

    2. Cole's school records? Vaccine records?

    3. Money - cash

    4. Clothes/shoes/coats

    5. Where do we go? What about Cole?

I stared at the last one until my throat tightened. *What was Jackson going to say?*

I was a grown woman, plotting how to run away like a sullen teenager. I should be able to tell my parents that I'm not happy. I should be able to tell my husband that I want a divorce. I should be able to go after the life I've always wanted.

Right?

I wanted to laugh and cry at the same time, and just when it started feeling like too much, the front door opened and closed softly.

Cole.

I closed the notebook and shoved it back into my drawer.

"Mom?" he called.

"In here," I said, wiping my face with the heel of my hand.

Cole stood in my doorway, backpack still slung over his shoulders, his hair sticking up in all directions. I couldn't help but smile as warmth spread through me.

"Good day?" I asked.

He shrugged.

My smile began to slip. "What happened?" I patted the bed beside me.

He dropped his backpack at the door, trudged across the room and hopped on the bed. "Why can't I go out for Halloween?"

And just like that, my heart sank. "What brought this up?"

"All the guys were talking about it today - they're all dressing up as zombie football players."

"And you want to dress up with them?"

His shoulders slumped, "Well yeah, but they didn't even ask me. They acted like I wasn't even there."

I wrapped my arms around him and pressed a kiss to the top of his head. "I'm sorry, that must have been hard."

He shook out of my hold, "It sucked!" he snapped. "It's not fair, mom! Why can't I ever do anything I want to? Why can't I just be a kid? Why do I always have to..."

I waited for him to finish his sentence, but it never came. Tears rolled down his flushed cheeks. His hands tugged the ends of his hair, just like his father always used to when he was frustrated and didn't know what to do.

"Why do you always have to what?" I asked, my voice calm, encouraging him to say whatever he needed without fear.

He closed his eyes and shook his head. "Why do I always have to be perfect?"

I stood and pulled him into my arms, his tears soaking the front of my sweater. "Oh, baby. I'm so sorry." My heart broke for him.

"I just want to be normal," he cried.

I knew then, more than I had before, that leaving was the right thing to do. I'd be taking him from his friends, but letting my boy be himself, enjoy his childhood, was worth more than anything I could give him here.

I smoothed my fingers over his hair, taming the unruly length. "I know," I sighed. "I know, and I want that for you too."

He turned his head, looking up at me. "Why doesn't dad? Why does he hate me?"

I didn't know what to say. I didn't know that Sung-ho hated him, but I knew he definitely didn't love him the way a father should. I didn't want to lie to my son, but what else was I supposed to say? "Things are going to change, I can promise you that."

The rest of the evening fell into its familiar rhythm. Cole took a shower and dried his tears before laying out his math homework across the dining room table while I cooked chicken and rice. After dinner, he spread out his Bible notes for Wednesday youth group, and I helped him look up verses. We washed dishes together, all the while, talking about nothing.

We acted normal.

But underneath it all, dread pulsed like a bruise.

I was wiping the counter, the lemon cleaner sharp in the air, when a hand clamped around my upper arm.

I flinched hard and Sung-ho's grip tightened.

"Tonight," he said, voice low and calm in the way that made my stomach drop, "we begin working on the baby."

My mouth went dry, I still hadn't looked at that app. The numbers blurred as I tried to calculate my cycle in my head, panic blooming too fast to control. "I'm still sore from the exam yesterday," I whispered. "The doctor..."

He didn't care what the doctor said. He didn't care what I said. His fingers dug harder into my arm. "Be ready," he said simply, and released me like I was something dirty he didn't want to touch for too long.

The rest of the night passed in a blur; helping Cole brush his teeth, checking his backpack for tomorrow's homework.

Turning off hallway lights.

I went through the motions of mother and wife while my mind spun with fear and calculations. Timing. Risk. Consequences. Escape.

By the time Sung-ho entered the bedroom, I was already checked out. As he pressed into me, my mind began to slip somewhere safer.

A golden field.

Long grasses brushing my knees.

Jackson beside me, his dirty blonde hair too long, a crooked grin, ten years old and all trouble and sunshine.

We were picking wildflowers for his mom.

He told me in a scandalized whisper that he'd heard strange noises coming from his parents' room the night before. How he snuck out of bed and peeked through the crack in their door.

How confused he'd been.

How we giggled about it for hours, trying to make sense of a grown-up world we didn't understand.

It was warm there.

Safe.

Easy.

A grunt ripped me back to the present.

Reality slammed into me like cold water. The room, the smell of him, the weight of fear pressing into every corner of my mind. I lay perfectly still, trying to breathe around the knot in my throat, the memory of sunlight and wildflowers slipping away like a dream I couldn't hold onto.

When he was finished, he barked his usual order, "Legs up."

Despite the humiliation I felt, I obeyed, because to disobey was worse.

Later, when his breathing evened out beside me, I slipped out of bed and padded to the bathroom. I shut the door softly, turned on the sink to cover the silence, and braced my hands on the edge of the counter.

I refused to look at myself in the mirror.

I washed with shaking hands, desperately trying to erase every part of him I could. The shame, the panic, the helplessness clawed at my chest, but I swallowed it all down because I had to survive tonight to survive tomorrow.

Then I went back to bed.

I lay on the very edge of my side, closed my eyes, and pretended the field was still there.

Chapter 39

Jackson

Wednesday

The motel room felt colder without her.

I woke to the memory of Abby's body on the sheets beside me, her scent lingering on the pillow - vanilla lotion and something warm that always pulled me back to seventeen.

I reached for my phone before I even took a breath.

Me: Morning, beautiful

The three dots didn't appear right away. In fact, they didn't appear for a while.

I stared anyway, until finally, the screen lit up.

Abby: Good morning, Golden Boy

Abby: Busy day ahead, but I'll text when I can

Abby: Promise

I smiled like an idiot, the kind of smile I hadn't had in years.

I set the phone on my chest and let myself breathe. She was okay. She was still choosing us. And sometime soon - days, maybe weeks, I'd be taking her home.

She texted that evening.

Abby: Miss you

Me: Miss you more. Come see me?

Abby: Soon. I promise

Something about the last part tightened in my chest, like she was reassuring herself, not me.

Thursday

Fuck QuickBooks.

Everything was a mess, and as much as I didn't want to admit it, I really needed to be back home, at The Hideaway, where I could see the problems instead of guessing at them from a motel room.

I knew Whitney had gotten the stage up and going for open mic night - Steven had asked if he could pass my plans for the space along to her, and of course, I said yes. But that was supposed to be *my* thing, and while I was proud of her for not only getting it done, but getting Grady up there performing, I'd be lying if I said I wasn't a little jealous.

I started to call Steven, then stopped. The man was already shouldering enough; he didn't need me adding to his burden.

Instead, I texted Abby, because right now, she was the only reason I was still here.

> **Me:** You alive over there?

I stared at the walls until my phone buzzed.

> **Abby:** Look

> **Abby:** *[a photo of her hand holding a coffee mug with a smiley drawn on the foam]*

> **Me:** You trying to make me fall harder?

> **Abby:** You already fell. Don't pretend you didn't

I laughed, like really laughed, and the sound startled me.

Saturday

Abby was supposed to come by, but she canceled at the last minute.

> **Abby:** I'm sorry. I can't get away today

> **Abby:** I swear I'll make it up to you

My stomach twisted.

Something felt off, but she promised everything was okay.

Later that night, I got a voicemail from Grady.

"Hey man. Call me when you get this. I need to talk... about the bar, but also... Whitney."

My chest squeezed.

I should've called him back, should've checked in. I could hear it in his voice, something was wrong.

But all I could think about was Abby canceling. Abby hurting. Abby trapped in that house.

I told myself tomorrow.

Tomorrow I'd call him.

I never did.

Sunday

Abby: Busy morning. Tell me something stupid from high school

Me: Like the time you dared me to eat that ghost pepper and I threw up on Principal Schaefer's shoes?

Abby: 😂😂😂 I forgot about that!!

Abby: He banned you from the cafeteria for a week

Me: Worth it

Abby: Sweet cheeks

I nearly dropped my phone laughing.

Me: Don't call me that

Abby: Yes sir ▢

I grinned until my cheeks hurt.

Tuesday

The motel felt too small, too quiet.

Even the bed seemed colder without her tucked up against me.

I looked up houses in Falcon Pointe. Starter places, townhomes... and then I found a tiny blue one with a wraparound porch she'd love.

I imagined her cooking breakfast in our kitchen.

I imagined buying a ring.

I imagined her last name next to mine on the mailbox.

It was dumb - I knew it was dumb.

But hope was making me reckless.

I didn't hear from her again until late that night.

Abby: Love you

Abby: So much

The message was short, tired, like she'd written it curled into herself.

I played it off in my mind, insisting she was just worn out.

Thursday

I stopped by the hardware store for something pointless - super glue, I think - just to get out of the room. I caught myself picking up a small pack of picture hooks, imagining her art hung on our future walls.

I put it back, I couldn't help but wonder if I was getting ahead of myself, if things were ever going to happen for us.

> **Me:** When can I see you?

I waited five minutes.
Ten.
Fifteen.

> **Abby:** Soon

> **Abby:** I promise

Friday

My phone buzzed at 6am, waking me from a restless sleep.

> **Abby:** Tomorrow night

> **Abby:** Just us

> **Abby:** I'll come to you

> **Abby:** I swear

I sat back on the bed and let the relief wash through me so hard I nearly laughed out loud.

Tomorrow.

Finally.

I didn't know what had changed. Only that the thought of seeing her again loosened something in my chest and tightened something else right beneath it.

Still, I let myself believe it.

Maybe, just maybe, we were finally getting our future.

Chapter 40

Abby

Sung-ho stood in the bedroom doorway with that familiar expectant look I knew all too well. The one that meant *he wanted something done before he had to ask.* His suitcase lay open on the bed, clothes already arranged in stiff, precise stacks.

"Make sure the blue dress shirt is steamed," he said without looking at me. "And fold the black slacks properly this time. The dry cleaner creased them wrong."

"I'll take care of it," I murmured.

Internally, I was rolling my eyes. I didn't bother to ask why he couldn't do it himself, or why a man going away for a weekend golf event needed three pressed shirts.

I didn't ask anything. I could only imagine his response if I did...

I lifted the shirt from the bed, carried it to the bathroom, and turned on the steamer. The familiar hiss filled the small space, fogging the mirror, softening the air. My hands moved automatically - tug, smooth, release - my mind somewhere else entirely.

Tomorrow.

Jackson.

His motel room.

A whole night where I could breathe easy and just... exist.

"Ah-bi," Sung-ho called sharply. "My cufflinks."

"They're on your dresser," I called out to him, realizing my mistake a second too late.

He made a dissatisfied sound, the kind that wasn't quite a sigh and wasn't quite a rebuke, yet somehow managed to be both, but at least he let it go.

By the time I finished steaming his shirts, his suitcase was nearly packed. He stood in front of the mirror adjusting his watch, checking the time again - 9:12 a.m. His car would arrive any minute.

He glanced at me. "You'll keep the house clean while I'm gone. And focus on resting so we don't lose any progress."

Progress.

I'd checked my tracker Tuesday night. I wasn't due to ovulate for another couple of weeks.

Instead of saying what I wanted to say, I replied with a simple, "Yes, sir."

A black sedan pulled into the driveway, and he snapped his suitcase shut.

"Carry this out," he said, as if the task required someone other than the fully grown man standing beside it.

I lifted the suitcase, heavier than it should have been, and followed him to the door. He took it from me only when the driver stepped forward. He didn't kiss me goodbye, he rarely did, and I was grateful.

"I'll message you when I arrive. Don't be late responding."

The door shut behind him and the car disappeared down the street.

And with it, the air in the house finally loosened, freedom thin and temporary, but real enough that I could breathe.

I exhaled so hard my knees nearly buckled. The silence left in his absence wasn't the thick, watchful kind I'd grown used to.

It was *relief*.

I pressed a hand to my stomach, steadying myself.

He was gone.

Tonight would be just me and Cole.

And tomorrow... Tomorrow, I'd see Jackson.

By the time Cole got home from school, I'd already opened windows, lit a candle, and whispered a tiny prayer of thanks to God.

"Pizza?" I asked, leaning against the kitchen counter like it wasn't a dangerous suggestion.

Cole froze mid–backpack drop, his mouth twisting like he'd already tasted it. "Squid?"

I shook my head and tried not to smile too big. "Delivered."

His eyes widened like I'd just offered him a golden ticket. "Are we allowed to do that?"

"We are tonight," I said. "Just you and me."

He grinned so hard it scrunched his freckles together.

"Can we get pepperoni and sausage?" he asked, bouncing on the balls of his feet.

"Yeah, baby. We can do that."

I placed the order and when the doorbell rang a little while later, he ran to get the pizza, pausing only at the last second to look back at me.

I nodded. "Go ahead."

He opened the door with the kind of confidence I wished I'd had at ten.

We ate on the living room floor, straight from the box, grease soaking into paper towels, laughter filling places in the house that had forgotten how to hold it. Cole talked with his hands, his whole body alive in a way I hadn't seen in a long time.

After dinner, he settled onto the couch beside me. "Remember when I told you I had a friend who played football?"

"Yeah."

I pulled up an old CU Boulder football game on my phone - one where Jackson threw an 86-yard completion to win the drive. I'd watched it countless times since finding out where he played.

I hit play and tilted the screen so we could both see.

"Is that him?" Cole asked, leaning in.

"Yeah." My voice softened. "That's Jackson."

"Wow," he whispered. "He's really good."

I nodded, warmth blooming in my chest. "Better than he ever gave himself credit for."

I restarted the clip, and we watched the entire thing together - our shoulders touching, the faint smell of pizza mingling with his shampoo. He didn't say anything else, but he didn't have to. His eyes said enough: curiosity, admiration, and something unspoken.

It pressed against my heart, sharp and aching.

Halfway through a second video, I took a breath. "Hey... if we ever moved... how would you feel about that?"

He blinked up at me. "Moved? Like to another house?"

"Maybe. Another town."

He considered it, not alarmed exactly, just thoughtful. "I'd miss my friends. And Grandma and Grandpa. Would they come too?"

My throat tightened. "Maybe not right away."

"And what about... the other grandparents?" His voice dipped with uncertainty.

Halmeoni and Harabeoji.

Sung-ho's parents. The ones Cole only saw on holidays, and even then, rarely enough that they always seemed relieved when the visits ended.

"We'd figure it out," I said softly, brushing a hand over his hair. "Nothing would ever happen without you and me deciding together. Okay?"

He studied me, eyes searching for whatever I wasn't saying. "What about dad?"

My breath stalled. "We'd..." I paused, choosing the safest version of the truth. "Work through that too."

Before he could ask more, he tilted his head. "You're acting weird."

I laughed lightly and pulled him into a hug. "I'm just tired, baby."

He didn't press further.

We fell asleep easily that night, him tucked under my arm, the TV playing highlights in the background, the room warm and safe and ours.

For the first time in a long time, I felt almost... happy.

***

Cole woke up buzzing with energy, excited for Korean school and his overnight at my parents' house for the first time in a long time. I packed his bag, double-checked he had last week's homework, and smoothed his shirt collar until he swatted my hand away.

"Mom," he groaned, "I'm not five."

"You'll always be five to me," I teased, kissing the top of his head.

When my mom pulled into the driveway, he ran out to meet her, backpack bouncing.

"Call me if you need anything," I told my mom.

She nodded, but was already distracted, asking Cole about school, about his friends, about a dozen other things.

Cole waved from the back seat as they drove off, his little face bright behind the glass.

I stood there until the car disappeared down the street.

I waited one minute.

Long enough to prove to myself that I could.

Then I pulled out my phone.

> **Me:** You still up for some company?

> **Jackson:** Yours? Always

> **Me:** See you soon, Golden Boy

I grabbed my bag, locked the door behind me, and headed for the car.

Tonight, for the first time in years, I wasn't just surviving.

I started the engine and pulled away from the curb.

Chapter 41

Jackson

I didn't sleep, I couldn't. I was too wired, too anxious, too damn ready to see her after a week of nothing but texts, daydreams, and my own fucking hand.

After weeks of sending away the cleaning services, I'd finally gone to the office and asked to have the room cleaned. When I came back, the bed had fresh sheets, the bathroom had fresh towels, and for the first time in God knows how long, the place didn't smell like sweat and whiskey.

It still wasn't a five-star establishment, not even close to what Abby deserved, but it was what we had. And as long as I had her, I didn't need anything else.

I paced back and forth over the threadbare carpet, every sound outside making me check the window. Every car door made my pulse jump.

When her text finally came, my hands actually shook

Abby: You still up for some company?

Me: Yours? Always

Abby: See you soon, Golden Boy

I sat on the edge of the bed. Stood up again.

Checked myself in the mirror.

Ran a hand through my hair.

Sat back down.

The knock on the door nearly stopped my heart.

I crossed the room in three steps and opened it.

There she was, looking beautiful in her soft sweater, her cheeks flushed from the cold. Something bright and terrified and hopeful tangled together in her eyes.

"Hi," she whispered.

I didn't even realize I was smiling until her shoulders relaxed.

"Get in here," I said quietly.

She stepped inside, and the second I closed the door, she was in my arms, like her body remembered mine without asking permission. I wrapped her up, lifting her just slightly off the floor, and she made a sound I felt in my chest more than I heard.

"I missed you," she murmured into my collarbone.

"I missed you more," I said, because it was true and because she needed to hear it.

We sank into the bed like it was our own private sanctuary. She curled into me like she'd been waiting years to do it, her leg draped over mine, her head tucked under my chin. My fingers slid into her hair automatically, slowly stroking the dark, silky strands, like if I touched her wrong she might disappear.

"This feels like no time has passed," she whispered. "Like we're still... us."

"That's because we are," I murmured into her hair. "This is where we're meant to be. Together."

She didn't answer, not with words anyway.

She pressed closer, fitting perfectly into the space I'd kept empty for her.

We talked for hours about everything and nothing. High school memories, college, the stupid things we did as kids. She asked if I still slept with my arm over my head. I asked if she still hated the endings of sad movies.

She snorted. "I never hated the endings. I hated crying in front of you."

"Why?" I teased.

"Because you always laughed."

"I laughed because you cried at *commercials*, baby."

She hit me with a pillow. I pretended it hurt. She pretended she didn't love me for it.

The room stayed warm, soft, and easy.

Hours passed without either of us noticing.

I ordered delivery - Chinese, spreading the takeout boxes across the foot of the bed.

Abby ignored the fork I handed her and reached for the chopsticks.

"Show off," I muttered, rolling my eyes.

She laughed.

"There's something I've been wondering," she said, nibbling on an eggroll.

"What's that?"

"How come you're not married?"

I nearly choked on a grain of rice.

"Sorry! I wasn't trying to kill you," she laughed, patting my back.

I cleared my throat and took a long drink of Coke. "It's fine. You just caught me off guard."

"So it's okay that I asked?"

I wrapped an arm around her and kissed her shoulder. "You can ask me anything."

I thought about my life before her. The blank spaces and temporary hookups.

Marriage had never crossed my mind.

"I guess I just never pictured myself with anyone but you," I said quietly.

"You have to have had girlfriends, though. Didn't any of them want to get married?"

I scratched the back of my neck. "I didn't really date. Don't get me wrong - I wasn't a saint. But I never had a girlfriend. There was only ever you."

The words sat between us, fragile.

"And..."

I knew the moment I said what came next, something would shift. Not break, but change. And I didn't know if I was ready to see her look at me differently.

She waited, patient.

I released a breath I hadn't realized I was holding. "And Steven."

"Steven?"

Her voice wasn't judgmental, just curious.

"I met Steven in high school. He was kind of this nerdy guy, but... there was something about him. We ended up hooking up. A lot." My face went hot.

"What happened with him?"

I hesitated. Long enough that my chest started to ache. "You're not creeped out?" I asked, honestly stunned.

Her hand came up, cupping my cheek. Steady and warm. "Why would I be creeped out?"

I swallowed. "Because it wasn't what you thought. What I was supposed to be." I blew out a heavy breath. "Because... I was with a man."

The truth I'd never spoken out loud, eased something in me, like a weight I didn't know I was carrying.

She studied my face for a moment, then shrugged lightly. "Was he good to you?"

I nodded. "Yeah. He's one of my best friends."

Her brows lifted. "Are you still... together?"

I shook my head. "No. It was never really like that. Steven always knew where he stood with me."

"And where's that?" she murmured.

I tucked a strand of hair behind her ear. "I've only ever wanted you."

In the late afternoon, her sweater slipped off her shoulder and she shivered. I pulled the blanket up around her and pressed a kiss to the curve of her neck.

She inhaled sharply.

"That okay?" I asked.

Her nod was barely there, just the smallest tilt of her chin, but something about it wrecked me. Like she was trusting me with the parts of herself she didn't show anyone. The parts she'd been forced to bury just to survive.

I brushed my thumb along the curve where her neck met her shoulder, and she shivered beneath my hand. God, I'd missed this - missed how responsive she always was, missed the way her breath quickened before she even realized it had.

"Come here," I whispered.

She shifted, slow at first, then with purpose, swinging one leg over my hips until she was straddling me. Her sweater slipped even lower, baring one collarbone completely, and I swear to God, my heart actually stuttered.

"You're so beautiful," I murmured before she could look away. "You always were."

Color rose in her cheeks, soft and warm, and she ducked her head like she didn't believe me. Like no one had told her that in years.

I slid my hands up her thighs, over denim worn soft from time and movement, until my palms found her waist. She exhaled sharply, fingers curling into my shoulders.

"Jackson," she breathed, and the sound of my name from her lips, the way it trembled, the way it pleaded, sent heat straight through me.

I pulled her closer, my hands settling on the small of her back, and she melted into me. Her mouth brushed mine once, a soft, testing kiss that tasted like hesitation and hope twisted together.

The second kiss wasn't hesitant.

She cupped my jaw with both hands and kissed me like she was drowning and I was the only thing keeping her above water. I met her halfway, deepening it, letting years of wanting her - years of what-ifs and maybes and never-should-have-beens - pour into every movement.

She sighed against my mouth, the sound soft but hungry, and I felt her fingers slide into my hair, tugging just enough to make my breath catch.

"God, I missed you," she whispered between kisses.

I touched my forehead to hers, breathing her in. "You have no idea."

Her hips shifted, just a small movement, barely anything, but it pulled a groan from my chest before I could stop it. She froze for half a second, startled, then did it again, slower this time, more sure.

"Abby…" My voice cracked, her name a plea.

She kissed the corner of my mouth, then my jaw, then the hollow beneath my ear. Her breath was warm, her lips soft, and my grip tightened on her waist without meaning to.

"You're shaking," she whispered.

"So are you," I said.

And she was - tiny tremors running through her, like her body couldn't decide if it was terrified or desperate or both. I ran my hands up her back beneath the edge of her sweater, skin warm and soft against my palms, and she made a sound I'd never forgotten - a breathy little whimper that had lived in my bones for more than a decade.

She lifted her gaze to mine, eyes dark and glassy.

"Tell me this is okay," she said softly. "Tell me you want this."

I cupped her face, my thumb brushing the corner of her mouth.

"I've wanted you every day for as long as I can remember, Abby. I never stopped."

Her exhale shuddered out of her, and then she kissed me again - slow, then deeper, then hungry. Her hands were everywhere, sliding under my shirt, dragging across my stomach, up my chest, like she couldn't get enough.

I sat up, keeping her in my lap, and tugged her sweater over her head in one smooth motion. She gasped when the cool air hit her skin, then wrapped her arms around my neck and pulled me close, her forehead pressed to mine.

She wasn't shy. She wasn't timid.

She wanted me, all of me, the same way I wanted her.

"Jackson…" she whispered again, the sound rough with need.

I lay her back gently, kissing a trail down her neck, her collarbone, the faint rise of her chest. Her fingers threaded into my hair, guiding me, encouraging me, her breathing uneven and frantic.

"Please," she whispered, arching into me.

That one word - soft, breathless, trusting - nearly undid me.

I kissed her, slow and deep, my hands sliding along the curve of her waist as her body curled toward mine. The heat between us built, electric, undeniable, years of longing finally spilling over.

Clothes shifted. Touches deepened. Her breath mingled with mine, her soft gasps filling the tiny motel room until it felt like the whole world had narrowed to just this - her, me, and everything we were finally allowed to feel.

Her fingers hooked in my belt loops, tugging me down to her, and I went willingly, my forehead pressed to hers, our breaths mingling in the smallest space between us.

"Abby," I managed, voice thick and shaking. "Tell me if you need me to stop."

She lifted her hips, meeting mine with a slow, pleading push, eyes locked on mine.

"I don't want you to stop," she whispered. "Not tonight."

And as her hands slid down my back and her lips met mine again...

The rest of the world fell away.

We fell asleep wrapped together, her body curved into mine like it belonged there. Her breath was warm against my throat, our legs tangled under the sheets. I hadn't slept that peacefully in years.

Orange light spilled through the gap in the curtains as Abby shifted against me. Her hair brushed my chin, warm and soft, and I pressed a kiss to the top of her head. I still couldn't believe we were here, really here, after all the years I'd imagined it.

She stirred, tilting her face up toward mine, a sleepy smile tugging at her mouth.

"What time is it?" she murmured, voice scratchy and warm from sleep.

I reached for my phone on the nightstand. The screen lit up, and the first thing I saw wasn't the time. I had a text from Whitney.

My stomach tightened.

"It's 7:32," I said absently as my thumb slid over the notification and opened the message.

Whitney: Hey. Can we talk sometime soon? It's about Grady

Abby lifted her head fully now, propping her chin on my chest.

"Is everything okay?"

I tried not to let my expression give too much away, but Abby read me like she always had. Her hand slid over my ribs, gentle and grounding.

"It's Whit," I said softly. "She wants to talk. Says it's about Grady."

Her brows pulled together. "That's your foster brother, right? That doesn't sound good."

"No," I admitted, staring at the message a little too long. "It doesn't."

But I didn't want to leave the warmth of her body or the quiet bubble we were still wrapped in. I didn't want reality slamming back in yet.

Abby traced a line across my chest with her fingertip.

"You should call her," she said gently. "Your sister wouldn't reach out if it wasn't important."

She was right. Of course she was.

I sighed, brushing a thumb along her jaw. "I will. Just... give me a minute?"

Her smile was small and knowing. "Take all the minutes you need."

She tucked herself against me again, and for a moment I let myself breathe her in - vanilla lotion, warmth, the faint comfort of home I'd been missing for eleven years.

But the worry in Whitney's text gnawed at me, and I knew I needed to talk to her.

I hesitated for a moment before hitting the call button, my heart beating faster with each ring.

"Hello?" Whitney answered, her voice rough with sleep.

"Hey. Sorry for calling so early."

"It's okay. I didn't think you'd call so soon."

I cleared my throat. "Your text... Is he okay?"

"I don't know," she said quietly.

I exhaled, sitting up carefully so I wouldn't jostle Abby. "What happened?"

"He got drunk last night. Really drunk. Steven had to bring him home. I don't even know why he left. We were fine, and then... he just disappeared."

"Fuck," I muttered.

"Steven said you could help me understand."

I closed my eyes, scrubbing a hand over my face. *Oh, Grady...*

"I don't know where to start," I finally said. "But if you're serious about him, Whit... you need to know that he's not just moody or guarded. He's scarred. Deep."

"I've figured that much out."

"I don't know what you endured during your time in the foster system," I said softly. "But for him, it goes back, even before that."

"What do you mean?"

I didn't know how much I should tell her, but if she was there with him, if I was trusting her to take care of him in my absence, she needed to know.

"Grady was adopted when he was a baby. His adoptive parents were…" I paused, searching for words that didn't feel heavy enough. "Very religious."

"He mentioned that."

"Right. Well. There was this choir teacher, Miss Becky. Has he ever said anything about her?"

"No, I don't think so."

Beside me, Abby shifted, her brows knitting with worry. The memory of all the pieces Grady had entrusted to me hit harder than I wished it would.

"He never told anyone for a long time," I said quietly. "But she molested him. When he was a kid. He didn't understand what was happening. He thought he was the one doing something wrong. And when he was thirteen, his mom walked in on him… just being a normal teenage boy. But she saw it as proof. That he was broken. That he was…" my voice faltered. "Tainted.

"She blamed him," I continued. "Told him he was a sinner. That he needed to pray for forgiveness. She called a social worker. Said she didn't want a defective son."

I felt Abby's hand slide to mine, squeezing gently, grounding me.

"He never said anything, but I always knew something was wrong. He'd go silent for days, flinch when people touched him. I just didn't know what it was."

Guilt gnawed at me. It always did.

"Nobody protected him, Whitney. Not when it counted. So now he protects himself, by shutting down. By running. And yeah, sometimes by drinking until he can't feel anything."

I took a long breath. My voice softened. "But he's not defective. He's not broken. He just doesn't know how to believe that yet. Please be patient with him. He's worth it."

There was a long silence on the other end.

"When are you coming home?" She finally whispered.

I looked down at Abby curled in my lap - safe, warm, needing me in ways she didn't have the strength to say out loud.

"I... I'm not sure yet. Soon."

Whitney inhaled shakily. "I have to go."

"Call me later, okay?"

"I will."

The call ended, leaving the room too quiet, the screen blank and heavy in my hand. Guilt churned in my stomach - toward Grady, toward Whitney, toward the man I wished I could be for everyone at once.

Abby shifted again, slow and soft, then lifted her head just enough to kiss my stomach.

"I'd ask if everything was okay," she murmured, "but that's a dumb question."

I brought her hand to my lips and kissed it.

"I need a minute," I whispered, sliding out from under her and crossing the small space to the bathroom.

I closed the bathroom door behind me, letting it click softly in the frame. The room was dim, lit only by the weak daylight sneaking through the cracked blinds. For a second I just stood there, hands braced on the edge of the sink, head hanging low.

Whitney's voice echoed in the back of my mind.

He got drunk. Steven had to bring him home.

I don't know what happened.

Can you help me understand?

I swallowed hard.

I hated that I wasn't there. Hated that I'd missed the signs. Hated that Grady was hurting and I wasn't beside him the way he'd always been beside me.

I turned on the faucet, not because I needed water but because the noise filled the silence pressing into my skull. I splashed some onto my face, watching the droplets roll off my chin and break apart in the sink.

Then I lifted my head.

The reflection staring back at me looked... tired. Older than I remembered. My eyes were rimmed with worry. My jaw set tight and my shoulders were heavy with all things I couldn't carry at once.

"Are you even a good man?" I whispered to my reflection.

It sounded pathetic out loud.

What kind of brother wasn't there when his best friend spiraled?

What kind of son didn't know how to fix the pieces of a broken childhood?

What kind of man ran off to chase the girl he loved instead of staying home to help the people who depended on him?

I pressed my palms into the counter until it groaned.

I had always promised myself I'd never fail Grady the way everyone else had. But I left. Again. Not because I wanted the wrong thing, but because I wanted the right thing at the wrong time. And a part of me wondered if that made me unworthy of the woman still warm in my bed.

My chest tightened.

Was I doing the right thing?

Had I built my whole life on the idea that I had to save everyone except myself?

The sound of movement caught my attention - just a tiny shift, the creak of the motel bed springs, the soft inhale of someone fully waking.

Abby.

The sound wasn't loud, but it broke through all the noise in my head, snapping something back into place.

Grady had Whitney.

He wasn't alone.

He had people around him who loved him, who could support him while I was gone. Maybe for the first time in his life, he wasn't drowning in the dark by himself.

But Abby...

Abby didn't have anyone else.

She had a husband who watched her like a prison guard.

Parents who didn't see her slipping into the shadows.

And me.

She had me.

Maybe for the first time in eleven years, *she* wasn't alone either.

I exhaled slowly, gripping the edge of the sink until my knuckles turned white.

I couldn't be everywhere at once.

I couldn't save everyone.

But I could choose who needed me *right now*.

And right now?

It was the woman in my bed.

The woman who whispered "I love you" like it hurt.

The woman fighting every day just to survive.

I shut off the water and wiped my face with a rough motel towel. Then I took one last look at the mirror, at the man in it questioning whether he was enough, and whispered, "you're doing your best. It has to be enough."

When I stepped back into the room, Abby was half-sitting, hair tousled, blinking sleepily as she reached for me under the blanket.

And just like that, all the doubts quieted.

She needed me.

I climbed back into bed and pulled her close, pressing my face into her hair, letting the promise settle in my chest where it belonged.

Chapter 42

Abby

I kissed Jackson goodbye at the motel door, the taste of him still warm on my lips. His hand lingered at my waist like he wasn't ready to let go, and God, neither was I.

"Text me when you get home," he murmured, brushing his thumb along my jaw.

"I will," I whispered. "And I'll... I'll talk to you later."

Later.

It suddenly felt like such a fragile word.

I forced myself to turn, to walk back across the parking lot with my heart still tangled up in the sheets behind me. A tiny, stupid smile kept tugging at the corner of my mouth, one I had to physically fight down as I drove home. If anyone saw me like this, glowing like a teenager sneaking in after curfew, they'd know something was different.

Something was *dangerously* different.

Something I couldn't afford.

I pulled into the driveway just as my parents' car rounded the corner. Perfect timing. Cole jumped out the second the car stopped, waving at my parents before sprinting toward me.

"Hey, mom! Look! Grandma got me that model rocket kit I told you about!" he yelled, nearly tripping over his own feet. "Can we build it today? Please?"

His excitement was contagious. I laughed, catching him as he crashed into me. "Yeah, baby. Of course we can."

My mom smiled from the passenger seat but didn't linger; she and my dad waved, then pulled away before I could wonder if she noticed anything different about me.

Cole tugged my hand. "Come on! I wanna start it now!"

Inside, we spread newspapers across the kitchen table and opened the box. Cole talked nonstop about school, about the museum my parents took him to last night, about how badly he wanted to go to his friend Kevin's Halloween party even though he wasn't allowed.

I let Cole take the lead, handing him parts, glue, and steadying the pieces when his hands shook with excitement.

But my mind kept drifting.

Back to Jackson's arms around me, to the motel bed still warm with us. Back to the plan taking shape in my notebook, nothing more than half scribbles, half prayers.

Back to Falcon Pointe, the place I was hoping we would call home.

I pulled out my phone when Cole disappeared for a bathroom break.

> **Me:** What's Falcon Pointe like this time of year?

> **Me:** Is it colder than Stonehill?

> **Me:** Are the leaves still changing?

I ran my finger over the now-dry design Cole had painted along the rocket's side, remembering a time when I used to do the same thing, back when dreaming was second nature.

> **Jackson:** It's a lot like where we grew up. A little smaller, fewer farms, but the weather is pretty typical for Colorado

> **Jackson:** The trees are usually pretty bare this time of year, and we should have already had some snow

> **Jackson:** It's my favorite place in the world, the only thing missing is you

I couldn't keep the stupid grin from spreading across my face as I tucked my phone away, just as Cole got back to the table.

By late afternoon, the rocket was half-assembled, and Cole had paint smudged across his cheekbone.

"This is the best day ever," he said proudly, and the words cracked something in my chest.

Best day ever.

Was it because his father wasn't home? Because for a few hours, he could just be a kid?

Cole's laughter rang through the kitchen, bright and unguarded.

I have to get him out, the thought came sharp and clear, slicing through every doubt still lingering inside of me.

I have to be the one to save him.

Sung-ho arrived home just after six.

The door opened with that familiar click, and the house lost a degree of warmth almost instantly. Cole stiffened. I straightened.

"Ah-bi," he called, like a test.

"In the kitchen," I answered, wiping glue from my fingers.

He appeared in the doorway, his expression flat, eyes scanning the counter like he was performing some sort of inspection. Cole avoided his gaze completely, busying himself with rinsing paintbrushes.

Sung-ho didn't ask about our weekend. Didn't acknowledge the project covering the table. Didn't ask Cole a single question.

But he also didn't say anything cruel.

And for reasons I didn't fully understand, not even that could ruin the buoyancy inside me.

It lasted until bedtime.

He closed the door, folded his arms, and said, "Tonight, we try again."

The bubble burst.

I tried to get out of it. I tried everything I could think of. I said I was tired, said my back hurt from leaning over the rocket for hours, but he didn't care. He never cared.

The contrast slammed into me, hard and cruel. Jackson's gentle hands, his whispered *You okay?* versus the way Sung-ho pushed, took, and pressed me down into a world I didn't belong in.

For the first time, I let myself think it fully, not about escape, but about choice.

And being with Jackson made me remember what that felt like.

The thought scared me almost as much as it thrilled me.

Cole... he had come from love. Real love. A love I never let myself admit existed until now. Having a child with Jackson - having *another* - felt like reclaiming something that had been stolen from me.

But I couldn't.

Not yet.

Not like this.

Not with this secret between us.

Still, the idea lingered long after Sung-ho rolled away and started snoring.

I fell asleep hopeful, imagining another life, another family, another future.

My alarm went off at 5:15, but for the first time in a long time, I didn't wake before it. I silenced it quickly, stealing a peek at Sung-ho, still fast asleep beside me.

Today was going to be a good day - I could feel it.

I padded quietly down the hall and into the bathroom. When I looked at myself in the mirror, I no longer saw Sung-ho's obedient wife. I saw a spark of the old me, the strong me, the *defiant* me.

The me that had been buried deep inside for the past ten years.

I splashed water on my face, brushed my teeth, and returned to my room to dress. I grabbed my phone from my nightstand, my heart racing at the thought of what message might be waiting for me.

I didn't even bother checking my notifications, instead going straight to our message thread.

> **Me:** Goodnight. I love you more than all the stars in the sky

> **Jackson:** I love you more than life itself. Goodnight

And then there was a new one.

My breath caught as I read it - then reread it.

> **Jackson:** I have to go home - something happened with Whitney

> **Jackson:** I love you more than anything in this life and the next. I'll be back for you

The room felt suddenly colder, the shadows sharper.

He was leaving.

And I...

I couldn't go with him.

Not yet. Not without risking everything.

Chapter 43

Jackson

I woke up smiling.

Actually smiling.

The kind that catches you off guard because you don't remember the last time it happened.

The room was quiet, the sun slipping around the edges of the curtains in soft golden streaks, and for a moment, one perfect moment, I let myself stay in that haze of warmth, replaying the day before. Abby's laugh. Abby's mouth. Abby's body curled into mine like she belonged there and nowhere else.

Today was the day we were going to start planning. Really planning. No more stolen hours. No more fear. No more hiding.

I reached for my phone on the nightstand, ready to send her a good morning message or maybe even call, and that's when I saw it.

A missed call.

From Whitney.

My stomach dipped, I never even heard it ring.

Then I saw the voicemail icon.

"Shit," I muttered, hitting play.

Her voice came through shaky, quiet, and too soft to be anything good.

"Hey, Jackson. I wanted to wait till you got back, but I can't do this anymore. I love you."

The bottom dropped out of my stomach.

For a second, I couldn't move. Couldn't breathe.

It was like my body hadn't caught up to the words yet.

"Whit?" I breathed uselessly at the phone, like saying her name would call her back through time. I sat up straight, sheets pooling around my waist, heart racing.

I hit call.

Straight to voicemail.

"No, no, no - Whit, come on." I tried again. And again. Same result.

I dialed Grady next, and just like all my recent calls to him, it went straight to voicemail.

"Fuck!" Panic surged hard and sharp.

I called Steven. He picked up on the third ring, his voice rough with sleep.

"Jax?" he rasped. "It's early, babe, is everything okay?"

"Have you seen Whitney?" I asked, desperation dripping from every word. "Is she with you?"

There was rustling, then a pause.

"She... she was here," Steven said slowly. "She came over last night. Stayed on the couch. She was upset about Grady."

My pulse hammered. "But she's not there now?"

More rustling. I pictured him walking through his tiny apartment, checking the rooms.

"No," he said, suddenly awake. "She's not here. I'm sorry, I didn't even hear her leave."

Fear punched me so hard I nearly doubled over.

"Fuck, fuck, fuck." I was already out of the bed, grabbing jeans, shoving things blindly into my bag. "I'm coming home. Keep trying her."

"Jax, wait," Steven's voice cut in. "Don't freak out yet. She was upset, sure, but..."

"She left me a voicemail telling me she loves me and can't do it anymore," I snapped, more harshly than he deserved. "I'm not waiting."

Silence.

"Okay," Steven said quietly. "I'll keep calling. I've got a branding consult this morning, but I'll keep trying her between clients."

I zipped the bag and slung it over my shoulder. "Thanks. And Steven?"

"Yeah?"

"Thank you."

"Always. Be safe. I love you."

I hung up, grabbed my keys, and bolted for the door. I didn't bother checking out. I didn't look back. I just ran.

The engine roared to life. I peeled out of the parking lot, heart pounding so hard I could hear it. Every red light felt like an attack. Every mile felt like failure.

At the next stoplight, with my hands shaking on the wheel, I opened my text thread with Abby.

I owed her something.

Anything.

The truth I could give her without pulling her into the chaos.

The light turned green.

I drove like hell.

All the way back to Falcon Pointe, I kept calling - Whitney, Grady, Whitney again - but no one answered. Steven checked in a couple of times, saying he still hadn't heard anything.

By the time I pulled into The Hideaway's parking lot, my fear had curdled into something hotter. Sharper.

I slammed the truck door so hard the whole frame shook and stormed toward the bar.

I knew Grady was inside, and I was damn well going to get answers.

The bell over the front door clattered against the glass as I shoved it open, barely aware of how hard I'd hit it. My heart was still racing from the drive - five hours of white-knuckling the wheel, calling Whitney over and over, getting nothing but silence.

I didn't feel the cold October air on my skin.

I didn't feel the stares from the regulars.

I could only feel one thing. *Panic.*

"Is she here?" I barked.

Grady froze mid-sip, a mug of coffee hanging in the air like someone had pressed pause on him. His eyes widened when he finally saw me.

"Jackson?"

It was the first time I'd seen him in over a month. Hell, the first time I'd been home in more than that. And if things were normal, if today were any other fucking day, I might've stopped to talk, might've clapped him on the shoulder, might've asked why he hadn't answered any of my calls.

But nothing was normal.

I stalked across the bar, adrenaline pounding through every vein. "Where is she?"

He blinked, still trying to catch up. "What?"

"Whitney," I snapped. "Where is she?"

He set the mug down and stepped out from behind the bar, dread already creeping into his expression.

"She... she stayed at Steven's last night. Said she needed a girl's night."

My jaw clenched so hard it hurt. I pulled my phone from my pocket, tapped the voicemail, and set it on the bar between us. Whitney's voice filled the space.

"Hey, Jackson. I wanted to wait till you got back, but I can't do this anymore. I love you."

The words hollowed me out all over again.

Grady's face went gray. His knees actually gave a little, like he had to force himself to stay upright.

"What the hell happened, Grady?" I asked, voice low but razor-thin. Not angry - yet - but stripped down to bare fear.

He sank onto a stool, head in his hands. I'd never seen him look so goddamn lost.

"I-I don't understand," he whispered. "She said she needed space. That it was just a girls night."

But he didn't believe himself.

Neither did I.

"She wouldn't just leave," he said suddenly, desperation cracking through his voice. "Not without saying goodbye. Not without telling me why."

I rubbed the back of my neck, trying to ground myself, but the fear clawing inside me wasn't letting up. "She's not answering my calls. I drove straight here the second I got her message."

Grady opened his mouth, closed it, then swallowed hard. "There was a message on my phone... from Emily."

I felt the temperature inside me drop.

"A picture," he added, voice barely audible. "Naked. On my lap."

Every muscle in my body tensed. "Grady..."

"It's from a couple nights ago," he rushed out. "She just showed up at the bar. I was already drunk. I didn't even see the message until this morning. It had already been read."

I stopped breathing.

"She saw it," I said, not a question.

"I think so."

"What the fuck were you doing with Emily?" My voice came out sharper than I meant, but underneath it was something else - hurt. Fear. Not for me. For him.

"Nothing. I swear." His eyes were glassy with humiliation. "She forced her way into the office, tried to pull her usual shit, but I told her no. I didn't touch her, Jackson. Sh-she took a photo. I didn't really think about it after I kicked her out."

I shoved the stool back so hard it screeched across the floor. "Goddamn it, Grady. You let her get close enough to do this?"

He flinched, shame rolling off him in waves.

Then he looked up and said quietly, "Why haven't you been returning my calls?"

"What?" I snapped.

He pulled out his phone, thumb trembling as he scrolled, then held it out. A string of unanswered calls. Messages. Weeks' worth.

"Grady... I've replied to every single one," I said, frowning. "I swear to God."

I took the phone from him to double-check and froze.

I turned the screen so he could see.

"I'm blocked."

His whole face drained. "How the hell..."

"When was the last time Emily had your phone?" I asked.

"Never..." he began, and then stopped. Completely stopped.

His eyes went wide.

"That night at her apartment," he whispered. "I left my phone on the nightstand."

I exhaled a curse, dragging a hand down my face. "That fucking bitch."

He nodded numbly, throat working like it hurt to swallow.

The silence that followed was brutal.

We weren't just dealing with heartbreak.

This was a full-blown sabotage.

Manipulation.

A damn ambush.

And Whitney, who already carried too much, saw that photo and believed the worst.

"Do you think she's okay?" Grady asked, his voice breaking around the words.

I stared at the ground, feeling the weight of a hundred failures on my shoulders. "I don't know, man. I wish I did. But if she's going back to Utah, back to that asshole Eric... I don't know if we'll ever see her again."

His breath hitched, raw and painful.

"I thought I'd already lost everything once in my life," he whispered.

"I know," I said, softer now. "Me too."

We stood there, surrounded by the smell of coffee and old wood polish, two men gutted by the same storm.

Two men who loved her.

Two men who weren't enough to save her from her past.

I stayed with Grady until his breathing evened out, until the shaking in his hands stopped. He wasn't okay, not even close, but at least he wasn't falling apart alone anymore.

Eventually, he drifted into that blank, numb stare he used to wear in the worst years of our childhood. I hated seeing it again. Hated knowing there was nothing I could do or say to fix it.

But staying here all night wouldn't fix it either.

I squeezed his shoulder once, firmly. "I'm not going anywhere. We'll figure this out."

He nodded without looking up.

I stepped outside into the cold, evening air. It bit at my skin, clearing my head just enough to remind me that my life wasn't only here. Someone else needed me too.

I unlocked my truck and slid into the driver's seat, letting the engine rumble to life. For a long moment, I just sat there, gripping the steering wheel, staring through the windshield like answers might magically appear.

They didn't.

So I reached for my phone.

I didn't know how to tell Abby any of this. Didn't know how to explain the storm I'd just walked into. But I knew one thing...

I needed her voice.

Her reassurance.

Her hope.

My thumbs moved before I could overthink it.

> **Me:** Made it back to Falcon Pointe

> **Me:** Things are… rough. But I'm okay

> **Me:** Just… miss you

I stared at the screen, the way I had a hundred times in the motel, waiting for those three little dots.

Nothing.

Then…

> **Abby:** I'm glad you made it home

> **Abby:** I miss you too

My chest loosened, just enough to breathe.

I leaned back against the headrest, closing my eyes for the first time since I'd walked into The Hideaway.

Hearing from her didn't fix anything.

But it gave me something solid to hold onto when everything else felt like it was falling apart.

I needed to be strong for Grady.

I needed to be steady for Whitney, wherever she was.

But Abby… she was the thing pulling me forward when everything else felt like sinking.

I put the truck in gear and drove home. To my house. My responsibilities. My mess.

Because until I could go back for her, I had to get my shit together here.

And I meant what I told her.

I wasn't going anywhere.

Chapter 44

Abby

My phone buzzed just as I stepped out of the shower, steam rising around me, but my mind was still tangled in the warmth of him from Saturday. I smiled before I even picked it up.

Jackson.

I opened the message, already imagining him safe back in Falcon Pointe, maybe stretched across his bed after the long drive, that soft, tired voice he only used with me...

And froze.

> **Jackson:** Made it back to Falcon Pointe

> **Jackson:** Things are... rough. But I'm okay

> **Jackson:** Just... miss you

The steam suddenly felt colder.

My heartbeat stumbled, then steadied, then ached in a way I hadn't been expecting.

I sat on the edge of the toilet, towel loosening around me as the weight of his words settled into my chest. Rough could mean anything. Everything. And I wasn't there to help him. I wasn't there to *be* with him the way he'd been with me - even if only for a single night.

I typed a reply, erased it.

Typed another, erased that too.

I knew how important his sister was to him, yet every reply I typed felt wrong - too needy, too small, too much.

Finally, I sent something simple, something I hoped would carry everything I didn't know how to say.

> **Me:** I'm glad you made it home

> **Me:** I miss you too

I didn't add the rest.

That I missed waking up in his arms.

That I missed believing, even for a second, that I belonged somewhere good.

The three dots appeared.

Flickered.

Disappeared.

I set my phone on the sink and pulled my knees up, wrapping my arms around them. The house was quiet - too quiet. The kind of quiet where my thoughts grew loud enough to scrape at the inside of my skull.

Rough.

He'd said things were rough.

Was Whitney okay?

Was *Grady* okay?

I hated the distance. Hated that he was hurting and I couldn't reach him. Hated that the only thing I could give him right now were small words typed on a screen because anything bigger, anything real, would unravel the illusion that my life was still functioning.

I wiped a hand over my face, the steam on my skin cooling into something almost like sadness.

I wanted to be there.

I wanted him to come get me.

I wanted to pack a bag and take Cole and never look back.

But wanting wasn't enough.

Not yet.

A soft knock on the bathroom door pulled me back.

"Mom?" Cole called sleepily. "Are you done? I need to brush my teeth."

I took a breath, smoothing the expression on my face before opening the door. "Yeah, baby. All done."

He shuffled past me, half-asleep, his hair sticking up, and I forced myself to focus on him - on the life I was still responsible for protecting.

Teeth brushed, I kissed his head, tucked him in, and turned out the light.

Then I went to bed myself.

But sleep didn't come easy.

I kept turning, shifting, reaching for a body that wasn't there. For arms that had held me like I was made of something precious. For a voice that whispered I was safe.

Instead, the only voice in the room was Sung-ho's soft snore beside me, a sound that had always felt suffocating, but tonight they felt like a warning. A reminder. A cage.

I turned my face toward my pillow, exhaled shakily, and let myself whisper into the darkness, "Come back to me."

Even though I knew he already had.

Even though I knew I was the one who still needed saving.

Somewhere between the ache and the longing, exhaustion won.

My days began to blur together, each morning unfolding like the one before it.

Up before the alarm.

Shower. Lotion. Hair combed into a neat, tidy bun.

Dress in slacks and a neutral sweater.

Prepare breakfast with quiet, practiced hands.

My body felt heavy, like I'd borrowed someone else's bones.

Nothing in the house had changed outwardly, but something inside me had shifted, and I could feel Sung-ho sensing it. His glances lingered a little too long. His silences sharpened. The air around him felt charged and watchful.

"Your mood has been unstable," he commented one morning, his voice cool and assessing. "Perhaps you should nap today."

Instinctively, my hand drifted toward my stomach.

"I'm fine," I murmured.

He studied me for a moment, something calculating in his eyes... then turned away.

Later, folding laundry with the dryer masking the thud of my heartbeat, I slipped two twenty-dollar bills beneath the lining of my purse. It wasn't much, but it was something.

I started driving Cole to and from school - any sliver of autonomy mattered. In the rearview mirror, he drummed his fingers against his backpack, humming tunelessly, his world still bright in places where mine had gone dim.

"Mom?" he asked as we approached the drop-off lane. "Can you... stay till the bell rings?"

His cheeks flushed as soon as he said it, like needing me was embarrassing.

"Of course," I said.

Relief softened his whole face, and something cracked inside me. After he climbed out, I parked around the corner, gripping the steering wheel as a wave of fear washed through me so strong it numbed my fingers.

I can't let him grow up like this. And I can't let Sung-ho take him from me.

At home, I pulled down an old tote bag that I never used from my closet shelf and quietly packed the bottom - Cole's spare shoes, pajamas, a t-shirt he'd outgrown but loved, the picture he drew of us last year that made me cry in the parking lot.

I buried the bag beneath a pile of grocery sacks in the trunk of my car. Then I slid my passport into a hidden pocket in my purse, my hands trembling the entire time.

That night, Sung-ho picked up my phone from the counter, entered the code he insisted on having, and scrolled.

Just scrolled.

He didn't say a word.

My pulse roared in my ears as I tracked the slow movement of his thumb, counting contacts, prayers caught in my throat. One name. Just one wrong name, and everything would burn.

I didn't breathe until he set the phone down and I heard the water turn on in the bathroom down the hall.

For the first time all week, I was grateful I hadn't heard from Jackson. Grateful I'd once again changed his name in my contacts.

Saturday arrived with fresh snow blanketing the neighborhood. In the past, I would have assumed that was the reason for Sung-ho's clipped, sour mood. Now I wasn't so sure.

He stood in the kitchen doorway as I made his tea, watching the exact angle of my pour, the way I aligned his cup on the counter.

"You've been… distracted," he said. "That is not acceptable."

A chill slid down my spine.

"I'm sorry," I whispered. "I'll do better."

He nodded once, satisfied.

That afternoon, after Cole finished shoveling the driveway, I went grocery shopping if only to breathe freely for ten minutes. Sung-ho called twice to ask why it was taking so long, then told me which brand of pregnancy test to buy.

"Take it as soon as you get home," he instructed.

My stomach churned.

At home, I paced the short length between sink and tub, as I waited for the result.

My hand flew to my mouth when it came up negative. The relief hit so sharply tears sprung to my eyes and my knees wobbled.

That night, Sung-ho touched me again, his breath sour with rice wine, his movements mechanical and unyielding. When he finished, he rolled away and fell asleep instantly.

I stared up at the ceiling, grief hollowing me out from the inside. Grief for a life I hadn't yet escaped.

Afterward I stared at myself in the bathroom mirror. I barely recognized my own reflection.

My eyes weren't mine. My face wasn't mine. My life wasn't even mine.

I braced my hands on the counter and whispered to the woman looking back at me, "Hold on. Just a little longer."

Sunday came with soft light and the scent of snow melting in thin patches across the street. It had been a week since I'd seen Jackson, a week since I'd felt safe in someone's arms, a week since anything felt like hope.

My parents' house was warm, filled with sesame oil and toasted rice and the sound of my mother humming as she laid out plates. Cole hurried ahead, thrilled that Korean school had been canceled yesterday, prompting my mother to promise him kimchi pancakes for breakfast.

For a moment, just a moment, I let myself feel safe.

My mother poured tea and set the pot between us. She studied my face the way only mothers can.

"You're quiet today," she said softly in Korean. "More than usual."

My throat tightened. "I'm fine."

She reached across the table and touched my hand, a small gesture that nearly undid me.

"Ah-bi," she murmured, "you look tired. Is everything okay?"

Suddenly, unexpectedly, it rose inside me - the truth, sharp and desperate, clawing its way toward my mouth.

He hurts me. I'm scared. I need help. I need to save my son.

But then I pictured my father. His pride. His unwavering respect for Sung-ho. The shame this confession would bring. The consequences. The danger.

The wave receded.

"I've just been... stressed," I whispered.

She squeezed my fingers, regret flickering in her eyes. "If you ever need anything," she said quietly, "you can come home."

I nodded, even though we both knew it wasn't that simple. Or safe. Or possible.

Not yet.

Across the table, Cole lifted his chopsticks, cheeks pink from the steam rising off the food. He laughed at something my father said, eyes bright, wholly unaware of how fragile our lives had become.

I watched him and knew, with painful certainty:

We were not staying. Not in this house. Not in this marriage. Not in this life.

It wasn't a question of *if*.

Only *when*.

Chapter 45

Jackson

Days at The Hideaway were busier than ever. Word about Open Mic Night had gotten around, and the place filled up fast - tourists, locals, regulars, all waiting to see if Grady might show up and sing again.

Most days, he didn't.

He stayed in the back room, staring at the wall, shoulders tight, eyes hollow.

And when he did come out, he poured drinks like a ghost wearing his skin.

I checked on him constantly.

"Eat something," "Take a break," "You want to talk?"

The answers were always the same.

No.

And he never asked about Whitney.

I knew better than to push. What Whitney was doing was cruel, sure - but heartbreak makes people do stupid, desperate things. God knows I'd done enough of both.

I just wish she'd stop freezing us out.

Steven was my lifeline, sliding behind the bar beside me, picking up slack without being asked. He didn't pry, didn't ask questions he knew I wasn't ready to answer.

Just gave me that soft, knowing look, making me love him that much more.

"You okay?" he asked one night, tapping my arm.

"No," I admitted. "But I'm trying."

He squeezed my shoulder once. "Then you're already doing better than most."

***

We were drowning in customers, which meant we needed help - fast.

Steven posted an ad and stuck a sign in the window. Twenty minutes later, the bell over the door jingled and Xander walked in.

He was tall and broad with dark hair that hung just long enough to look dangerous. His eyes were as sharp as a switchblade, his jaw set like he didn't know how to relax.

"Ever bartended?" I asked.

He shrugged. "Picked up shifts at a dive back home. Learned fast."

"Where's home?"

Another shrug. "Don't really have one right now."

He said it so simply, it felt like a warning.

Steven leaned closer to me. "We need the help," he murmured.

He wasn't wrong.

I nodded at Xander. "Fine. You start tomorrow."

Xander gave a quick, single nod, no smile, no relief, just acknowledgment. He walked out as quietly as he came in.

Steven watched him go. "He's... something."

"Yeah," I said. "Something."

I didn't know what yet, but I knew a storm when I saw one.

At night, I crashed onto my bed and checked my phone.

Still nothing from Whitney.

I tried calling her twice, each time it went straight to voicemail.

My stomach twisted every time.

Then I switched to the message thread beneath hers, guilt flooding my system that I hadn't been able to talk to Abby nearly as much as I wanted.

> **Me:** How are you holding up?

She called instead of texting. I could hear the quiet snick of a door closing, followed by her soft, tired voice.

"Long day. But hearing you helps."

We didn't talk long - couldn't, not with her husband always nearby, but it was enough. Enough to ease something sharp inside me. Enough to remind me why I needed to keep going.

Another night, she called just to hear me breathe for a minute.

"I miss you," she whispered.

"I miss you more."

We said goodnight like a vow.

Two days later, during the dinner rush, I checked my phone again.

Nothing from Whitney. Nothing from Grady who refused to talk about her. And nothing that told me I wasn't about to lose everything at once.

Abby's name sat near the top of the screen, the only part of my life that still felt steady, though the ground we were standing on felt shaky at best.

God, I wanted to go back to her.

Wanted to get in my truck and drive to Kansas and take her away from all of it.

But the bar needed me.

Grady needed me.

Whitney... wherever she was... needed me too.

For now, it was all I could do to keep everything from falling apart.

I shoved my phone back into my pocket and grabbed another set of pint glasses.

"Hey, boss," Xander said as he walked past with a tray balanced effortlessly on one hand. "Where do you want me after this - bar or tables?"

"Bar," I said.

He nodded once, already pivoting back toward the floor, all silent strength and controlled movement, a guy who took up space without trying to.

"Hey, wait," I called after him.

He paused, one eyebrow lifting.

I studied him for a beat. Something about him - the way he carried himself, the roughness softened by something unspoken - made a thought spark in my mind.

"You ever sing?" I asked.

Xander blinked, surprised. Then his mouth pulled into the smallest, driest half-smile.

"Yeah," he said. "I can."

I jerked my chin toward the small stage. "Open mic's been pulling crowds. Grady's not... up for it lately. If you want the slot, it's yours."

He hesitated, like a man weighing whether stepping into the light was worth being seen.

"Sure," he said finally. "I can take a set."

Steven leaned against the cooler beside me, arm pressed against mine, eyebrows raised. "Well damn," he murmured. "This should be interesting."

I watched Xander walk toward the stage, rolling his shoulders back once, quietly, like he was settling into an old skin he hadn't worn in a while.

Steven nudged me. "Think he'll be any good?"

"I don't know," I said. "But we could use a win."

What we really needed was a miracle.

Because inside, I was slowly unraveling - one unanswered message, one missing girl, one distant love at a time.

And I didn't know how much longer I could keep this place together.

Xander stepped up onto the little Hideaway stage like he'd done it a thousand times but also like he didn't want anyone to notice he had.

He didn't head for the mic right away.

Instead, he crossed the stage and picked up the old acoustic that lived there - Grady's backup, its strings slightly out of tune from too many different hands.

He tested one chord, winced, and adjusted a peg.

Then he glanced up at the room like he was just checking something.

"Hope this is okay," he said, already settling the strap over his shoulder.

He cleared his throat and began to sing.

His voice wasn't loud. It wasn't flashy.

It was *rough* around the edges, low and smooth in the center, like whiskey poured over gravel. A voice that carried stories he wasn't ready to tell and bruises no one could see.

The entire bar shifted.

People turned.

Forks paused.

Conversations stilled mid-sentence.

Steven's mouth actually fell open.

Mine wasn't far behind.

Xander didn't look at the crowd.

Didn't smile.

Didn't even seem aware of the way every person in the room leaned toward him, caught by the quiet gravity of someone who didn't ask for attention, but *commanded* it anyway.

He finished the song in under three minutes.

Silence held the bar for a breath, and then applause broke out like a storm.

Xander stepped back from the mic, barely nodding once in acknowledgment, and walked offstage exactly the way he walked on - calm, steady, all shadows and unspoken things.

He passed me behind the bar, expression unreadable.

"Good?" he asked simply.

"Better than good," I said. "You just tripled our crowd."

He shrugged like it meant nothing.

But something flickered in his eyes, something haunted and hopeful in the same breath, before he turned back to the floor.

Steven elbowed me. "Well," he said under his breath, "I think I'm in love."

"Get in line," I muttered.

Because suddenly, without warning, the bar had a new heartbeat.

But even that wasn't enough to jump start mine - still waiting on a woman an entire state away and a sister who refused to call me back.

Chapter 46

Abby

Footsteps in the hall were the first sign that something was wrong.

"I have to go," I whispered into the phone, praying Jackson understood the urgency.

"Goodnight, Abbs. Love you."

I hung up, turning the phone off and setting it on the nightstand just as Sung-ho closed the bedroom door.

He didn't say a word at first - he didn't need to. His intentions filled the room like smoke.

He stood near the foot of the bed, unbuttoning his shirt. "Come," he said finally, and it wasn't a request.

I tried the only excuse I hadn't used yet. "My stomach's a little upset. Maybe tomorrow..."

I started to leave when his fingers clamped around my wrist, firm and punishing.

"You're ovulating," he said, proving that he had been monitoring it just as closely as I had. "It will be tonight."

He guided me backward, his grip tightening whenever I hesitated. With deft fingers, he shoved up my nightgown and yanked my panties down my legs.

And then there were no more words, just the sound of his pants hitting the floor followed by the rough weight of him, the smell of his cologne burning my nose, the sting of tears I didn't let fall. I lay still, staring at the ceiling, letting my mind fracture away - the only freedom left to me.

When he finished, he rolled off me without a glance and turned out the light.

I stayed awake for a long time afterward, staring at the ceiling fan as if it might spin fast enough to pull me out of my own body.

I don't know when I finally slept, only that when I woke, the decision was already there, solid and cold inside me.

I will not have his child.

I will not be tied to him forever.

I will not let this be my life.

The next morning, I dropped Cole off at his friend Kevin's house, since there was no school, and headed for the highway before I could talk myself out of it.

The drive to Overland Pharmacy took about an hour, but I couldn't remember a single turn. Every mile blurred together under the weight of what I was about to do. I kept imagining someone I knew walking in behind me. My mother. A church elder. One of the Korean school moms. The pharmacist looking at me and knowing.

The only thing that kept me moving forward was the memory of last night.

Sung-ho's hands pinning me down.

His breath in my ear like a declaration of ownership.

His voice reminding me that my body was a duty, not a choice.

My fingers shook when I reached for the box.

Plan B.

Behind a thick, clear plastic security box.

Of course it was.

I wrapped my hand around the cold, unforgiving plastic. My throat tightened. Anyone passing by could see exactly what I was holding. Anyone could judge. Anyone could assume.

But I couldn't care about that now.

I lifted it off the hook.

It felt heavier than it should.

Carrying it to the front register felt like walking a tightrope, every step more dangerous than the last.

The cashier, a girl who couldn't have been older than nineteen with bright blue eyeliner and chipped black nail polish, glanced at the box in my hand and blinked.

"Oh-uh, yeah. I'll just call someone to unlock that for you."

She grabbed the phone beside the register and pressed a button.

"I need a key at checkout three. A key at checkout three."

Her voice echoed across the store.

My stomach dropped.

A man from the back appeared, moving at the slow, bored pace of someone who had no idea he was holding a stranger's entire life between his fingertips. He didn't even look at me as he unlocked the case, just popped it open and handed me the small cardboard box inside.

"There you go."

Cold. Indifferent. Completely unaware of the war taking place inside my chest.

"Thank you," I whispered.

He walked away before the words even finished leaving my mouth.

The cashier rang it up without comment. The beep of the scanner sounded too loud.

"That'll be $49.99."

My fingers fumbled the bills once before I got them flat enough to hand over.

She didn't say a word, just gave back my change and the small paper bag with practiced neutrality. Maybe she'd seen this a hundred times. Maybe she didn't care.

Or maybe she understood more than she said.

I didn't breathe until I was back in the car.

The bag sat in my lap like a confession, my fingers curling around the top of it until the paper crinkled.

I closed my eyes.

Last night's memory flashed again - the weight of a body I didn't want, didn't choose. The sickening echo of his voice telling me it was my duty. The grief of knowing I had once made a child out of love... and that this man would destroy any chance of that happening again.

My hands trembled as I opened the box and swallowed the pill with the last sip of lukewarm water from the bottle in my cupholder.

I set my hands on the wheel, breath shaking, heart pounding in the small, enclosed space.

He will not take anything else from me.

For the first time in a long time...

I felt the spark of something like control. A sense of command, a rush of power, and a taste of freedom.

I felt it all.

It was terrifying, but it was mine.

I drove home in silence, the pill dissolving somewhere deep in my stomach, its promise and its consequences settling into the same place.

Chapter 47

Jackson

The roar of Xander's debut still pulsed through The Hideaway days later. Word spread fast, and by midweek the bar was packed before we even unlocked the doors.

Xander filled the stage twice more - cool, steady, unreadable - but everyone knew who they were really waiting for.

Grady.

Every time someone stepped onto the small staircase to the stage, conversations dipped, people leaned forward, phones lifted.

Then they'd see it wasn't him, and disappointment rolled through the room like a wave.

It was killing him.

He tried to hide it, but I saw the flinch every time the chant broke out:

"Grady! Grady! Grady!"

He'd freeze, just half a second, barely noticeable, then disappear into the back room like the sound physically shoved him there.

Steven tried talking to him. I tried. Every attempt bounced off him like we weren't even speaking the same language anymore.

By mid-week, the crowd was the biggest yet - shoulder to shoulder, buzzing with anticipation. And tonight, they weren't letting it go.

The chant hit so hard I felt it in my teeth.

"Grady! Grady! Grady!"

Beside me, Grady stiffened, a coffee mug halfway to his lips. He didn't blink. Didn't breathe.

"Come on, man," I murmured, squeezing his shoulder. "You have to play."

He still didn't move.

The last few weeks had gutted him. He'd been silent, hollow, barely functional. And Whitney's disappearance... it was written in every line of his face.

"She's not answering my calls either," I admitted quietly. "I'm giving her time, but I figured she'd at least text by now."

"Maybe she has you blocked," he muttered. "She's punishing me. She saw Emily's photo and thought the worst."

I exhaled slowly, rubbing the back of my neck. "Yeah, well, I can't blame her. The timing was shitty, man."

But what hurt him most wasn't that she left.

It was that she didn't ask for the truth.

"I can't go up there," he whispered.

I jerked my head toward Xander, who was nursing split knuckles while moving inventory like nothing hurt. "Xander can't cover this time. Smashed his damn hand trying to fix his car. Or so he says."

Grady snorted. "You believe him?"

"Not even a little. Knuckles are split. Looks like whoever he hit got a few licks in too."

"He ever say why he came to Falcon Pointe?"

I shrugged. "Said he needed a change. Place to lie low."

"Lie low from what?"

"That's the part he didn't say."

"He's running from something," Grady muttered, latching onto anything that wasn't the stage.

"Probably. But he's a hard worker. Keeps to himself. Doesn't start shit, just seems to find it."

"Sounds familiar."

I didn't argue. We'd both been that kind of stray once.

A beat passed.

"So... you're saying I'm the only one left to cover?"

I gave him a pointed look. "Unless you want me up there singing country covers from the early 2000's, yeah. You're it."

He groaned. "I can't go up there, man. Not tonight."

"You can. You just don't want to."

He glared at me, but I wasn't backing down. "They're not here for me, Grady. They're here for you."

His shoulders sagged like something inside finally gave way.

"She wouldn't want me to keep hiding," he whispered.

I clapped his shoulder. "Exactly."

"Fine," he muttered, relenting. "But I'm not smiling."

I grinned for the first time since coming home. "Wouldn't expect you to."

Slowly, reluctantly, he pushed off the bar and made his way toward the stage.

Phones lifted instantly. People screamed. Chanted. Reached for him.

He looked like a man walking into battle.

I stood just behind the bar, arms crossed, heart pounding as he sat on the stool and adjusted his guitar on his lap.

He didn't say a word.

He just played.

And the room went silent.

Every. Single. Person.

By the time he finished, the applause was so loud it shook the bottles on the shelves.

He didn't bow. Didn't smile.

He just stood, looked at the door like he half-expected Whitney to walk through it...

And when she didn't, he walked offstage.

Past the cheers.

Past the cameras.

Straight into the back room, where his heartbreak didn't have to be seen.

I followed him, because someone had to.

***

The week before Thanksgiving passed in a blur of noise, spilled drinks, and too many people wanting what I didn't have to give.

Xander stepped up when he could, and the whole damn place leaned in to listen.

Working with him was... interesting.

He didn't smile much. Didn't talk unless he needed to. Didn't ask for praise or attention.

But he showed up early.

Stayed late.

Never complained.

And when he sang - low, gritty, quiet but impossible to ignore - the room held its breath like they were afraid to break whatever spell he cast.

One night, I caught him polishing glasses behind the bar, his hair falling into his eyes, jaw tight with some private anger he'd never share.

"Bar tonight or tables?" he asked without looking up.

"Tables," I said. "We're short again."

He nodded once, all silent efficiency, a solid presence in the middle of chaos.

"Hey, kid," Steven called as Xander passed him. "Your fan club's here again."

Xander didn't flinch. Didn't react at all. Just kept moving.

Steven watched him go, shaking his head. "I swear he's either a serial killer or a future rock star."

"Why not both?" I muttered.

Steven laughed, then leaned against the cooler beside me, his shoulder brushing mine. "You doing okay?"

"No," I said honestly.

He bumped my arm, warm and steady. "I'm here for you - whatever you need."

I nodded, unable to speak. The words jammed in my throat, blocked by exhaustion and worry and everything I was holding together with two damn hands and a fraying will.

Dinner at the Bryants' house was the first calm thing I'd had in weeks.

Mrs. B sat across from me, elbows on the table, watching me with those soft, all-seeing eyes. Edward and Edie were tucked at the little kids' table behind us, working on a puzzle and arguing over edge pieces. The smell of pot roast and fresh rolls clung to the air - warm, steady, and familiar.

It felt like coming up for air.

Like stepping back into the kind of life I used to picture late at night - a life where love wasn't so damn complicated, where people didn't disappear without a word, where "family" wasn't a wound that still hadn't healed.

Mrs. B took a slow sip of her iced tea before setting it down with purpose.

"Alright," she said, leaning back in her chair. "You've been home for about a month now. I gave you time to come clean on your own, but since you haven't..." she tipped her chin at me, "care to tell me where you disappeared to?"

I rubbed a hand over the stubble on my jaw, stalling because... hell, what was I supposed to say?

"I was..." I exhaled. "Chasing a ghost."

Her brows rose. "This ghost have a name?"

All I could do was nod. "Abby. After all these years, I finally found her. I had to go. I had to see..."

"And?" Her voice softened just barely. "Was she okay?"

That did it.

I leaned forward, bracing both arms on the table. "No, ma'am."

Mrs. B didn't react right away. She studied my face the way she always had, like she was reading past the words and straight into my chest.

"So," she said quietly, "it wasn't about closure."

"No," I admitted. My voice cracked before I could stop it. "It was about someone I love being hurt."

Her whole face fell.

She reached across the table and took my hand in both of hers, her thumb brushing my knuckles the way it used to when I was seventeen and scared of my own shadow.

"Abby," she whispered, as if quietly forgiving the girl from my youth for the pain I suffered at her loss.

I nodded. "Yes, ma'am."

Something in my chest loosened and broke at the same time and I found myself telling her everything I could. Not the dangerous pieces, not the parts that weren't mine to share, but enough. Enough for her to understand the weight of it, the helplessness, the fear, the hope I'd been white-knuckling since the moment Abby opened that motel door.

And damn, it felt good.

Like finally setting down a load I'd carried so long I forgot it hurt.

Mrs. B didn't interrupt. Didn't judge. Just listened the way only she could, as if nothing I said could ever change how she saw me.

When I finally ran out of words, she squeezed my hand.

"Oh, baby," she murmured. "You've been carrying this alone."

My throat burned. I could only nod.

"And you love her," she said - not a question.

"I never stopped," I rasped.

She smiled then - not happy, not sad, but proud.

"Then you hold on," she said. "You hold on until she's ready. And when she is... you make damn sure she knows she has a home waiting here."

Home.

That word hit me right in the center of my chest.

Before I could respond, my phone buzzed on the table.

Whitney's face lit up the screen.

My stomach dropped.

I picked it up, thumbed the screen open, and said her name like a prayer I wasn't sure I believed in. "Whitney?"

Mrs. B went still. Even the twins quieted behind us.

I couldn't hear her words, but the tension hit me like a punch to the ribs - her voice fast, cracked, panicked.

"Whoa, whoa. Slow down," I said, leaning forward. "What happened? I came home as soon as I got your message..."

"I-I'm moving. To Vegas."

"Vegas?" I repeated, sharper than I meant to. "Why Vegas?"

"It-it's not my choice. Eric has a job... He..."

My heart sank clear through the floor.

She went quiet, letting the words hang as though she couldn't bring herself to say the rest.

Long enough that I could hear her breathing on the other end.

"Jackson," she said softly, "before I go... I need to know some-thing."

My stomach tightened.

"Is Grady okay? I know he hurts himself."

Cold shot through me. The fact she knew that meant something had happened while I was gone. Something Grady didn't tell me. Something he didn't tell *anyone.*

"No," I whispered. "Not really. I think... I think you should talk to him."

"I can't. I can't be what he needs. I'm moving on. With Eric. He *loves* me. Tell me you understand."

I turned slightly away, shielding Grady from the unraveling on the other end.

"Is that really what you want?" My voice cracked. "You can come back, Whit. You'll always have a home here."

"It's what has to be. I love you, Jackson."

Then, so soft it hollowed out my chest, "I love you, too."

And then the line went dead.

I wasn't ready to face him.

Not with this.

Not when he was already drowning.

But before I could say anything, he rasped, "She's not coming back, is she?"

I didn't answer.

He was already gone, the front door slamming behind him.

Mrs. B looked at me, concern written all over her face. Even the twins watched me with wide eyes.

"She's moving to Vegas," I finally said, voice barely holding. "I... I have to go check on him."

Mrs. B pulled me into a hug and told me to call her later.

I ran out the door, across the frost-crusted lawn, lungs burning as my feet pounded the pavement toward the only place he'd go.

When I reached his tree, I couldn't help but grin when I saw my rope ladder already down and waiting for me.

I climbed up and settled across from him. He didn't look at me. Didn't move. Didn't breathe.

I waited.

"She's not happy," I said finally, voice low. "I could hear it in her voice. She's trying to convince herself going back was the right thing. But it's not. You know it. I know it. Hell, deep down, *she* knows it too."

Wind rattled the branches above us, brittle and dry.

"But even if she never comes back," I added, nudging his knee, "I need you here, man. I need you breathing, okay? I already lost Abby. I can't lose you too."

Silence stretched too long and too heavy.

Then finally, barely audible, he managed a simple, "One day at a time."

I nodded. "Yeah. One day at a time."

***

The next time the crowd at The Hideaway chanted Grady's name, he didn't run.

He didn't hide.

But he did something even I didn't see coming.

He stepped onto the stage like it was a place he'd been avoiding his whole life and finally got tired of running from.

"Good evening, everyone," he said, voice rough but steady as he settled on the stool, guitar held like something sacred. "I know I never do this, but tonight I wanted to try something a little different."

My brows lifted.

Different?

From *Grady*?

He glanced across the bar and locked eyes with me.

There was something in his look - fear, hope, surrender. I couldn't tell which. I just knew it mattered.

Then he strummed his first chord.

"This is a song I wrote," he said softly, "for a girl who came into my life like a wildfire."

And just like that, the entire bar fell still.

The first notes of *Addicted* peeled him open from the inside out - raw, painful, and honest.

His voice cracked in the places where the truth lived too close to the surface, and the lyrics poured out of him like a confession whispered in the dark.

People cried.

People held their breath.

People fell in love with him right in front of me.

He wasn't singing a song.

He was bleeding onstage.

And everyone knew it.

When he finished, the silence that followed hit hard - heavy and reverent - before erupting into applause so loud the bottles on the back shelf rattled.

From that night forward, The Hideaway exploded.

Every single evening, the place overflowed - tourists, locals, influencers with phones held high - everyone hoping to catch the boy with the voice who'd melted TikTok for fifteen seconds at a time.

Because someone in that crowd, some random stranger with shaky hands and too much hope, had recorded the performance...

Posted it...

And it blew the hell up.

Who the fuck would've guessed?

Not me.

***

Two days later, Steven yanked me into the office like the place was on fire.

"You need to see this," he said, shoving his phone at me with zero explanation.

On the screen, a paused clip showed Grady sitting on a bright Good Morning Denver set, lights washing out the shadows under his eyes. He looked smaller somehow. Softer. Like someone trying not to show how badly he was shaking.

Steven hit play.

The anchor was smiling at him, all polished warmth. "So, Grady - quite the week you've had."

Grady ducked his head, giving a shy half-smile I hadn't seen on him in... hell, years. "Yeah, it's been... overwhelming."

A montage of his viral clip played beside him, the one from The Hideaway, his voice cutting straight through me even in a cheap studio recording.

Then the camera cut back to him on set.

"Would you mind giving us a little something live?" the anchor asked.

Grady swallowed once, then nodded.

And when he opened his mouth to sing, even through Steven's tiny phone speaker, it hit me right in the chest.

Pride.

Fear.

A punch of guilt I couldn't shake.

My best friend was breaking open on live television, and I wasn't sitting beside him. I didn't even know he was going.

"Fuck," I whispered.

Steven folded his arms, leaning against the desk. "Man's a damn comet."

Yeah.

A comet - bright, beautiful, and burning himself alive for everyone to see.

When the clip ended, I exhaled slowly, feeling the weight settle in my ribs.

"I hope she saw this," I murmured.

Steven didn't have to ask who *she* was.

Because if Whitney saw him, really saw him, maybe she'd remember the truth she'd tried to run from.

Chapter 48

Abby

Thanksgiving had always been a loud holiday in my family - pots clattering, my mother scolding my father for sneaking bites too early, Cole hovering like a hungry shadow.

But today, everything felt... wrong.

Sung-ho had barely spoken to me all morning, his silence cold enough to frost the edges of the counters. I moved carefully around him, trying to avoid the tension radiating off his skin, but I didn't understand the source.

My parents arrived first. Then his parents. Cole bounced between the adults, chattering about school, his model rocket, the snow - blissfully unaware of the undercurrent running through the room.

We sat. We prayed.

We began to eat.

And then...

"Ah-bi," Sung-ho said calmly, passing the kimchi dish to his father. "Did you enjoy your trip to Overland Pharmacy?"

The words froze the air.

My chopsticks slipped in my hand, hitting the plate with a clatter.

He looked at me with polite curiosity, the kind that meant danger.

Everyone else looked too.

My mother paused mid-bite.

His father raised an eyebrow.

Cole's head swiveled between us, sensing it, feeling it, even before the adults did.

My mother finally spoke, her voice soft. "Ah-bi, darling… is everything okay?"

My pulse hammered hard and high in my throat.

"I-I went to get cold medicine," I said softly.

Sung-ho reached into his pocket and pulled out a crumpled receipt. He smoothed it once between his fingers, then set it beside my plate.

I looked down.

Plan B.

$49.99.

My breath left me in a silent rush.

For a heartbeat, no one else noticed.

Then my mother leaned closer, her eyes narrowing as she read the bold print. Her inhale caught sharp in her throat.

Sung-ho's mother stiffened beside her husband, gaze dropping to the table as if the porcelain itself had offended her.

My father's shoulders went rigid - not in defense of me, but in fear of what this moment meant.

The silence thickened, spreading seat by seat.

Cole tugged lightly at my sleeve. "Mom?"

I couldn't look at him.

I couldn't look at anyone.

Sung-ho's voice stayed calm - conversational even.

"Tell them, Ah-bi," he said mildly. "Why would a married woman need this?"

My stomach twisted so violently I thought I might be sick.

"This is not the place," I whispered.

"This is exactly the place," he said softly. "Family deserves the truth."

Except he had no interest in the truth.

He wanted humiliation.

Control.

A public confession of guilt he already believed.

My hands shook under the table. "I didn't want to get pregnant yet," I whispered.

His jaw tightened a fraction, only a fraction, but I felt the danger spike in the air.

"So," he said, "you tried to prevent what God intended."

My mother put a hand over her mouth. "Ah-bi…"

His father looked away.

My father's lips pressed into a thin, scared line.

And Cole…

Cole reached under the table and grabbed my hand.

I squeezed back - once, lightly, a secret apology in the form of touch.

The rest of the meal unraveled.

My parents insisted they should go.

His parents excused themselves quietly.

Cole kept glancing at me like I might disappear.

When the door finally shut behind them, the house fell into a silence that roared.

I took one step toward the kitchen. Sung-ho followed.

Another step. He was right behind me.

Another…

His hand snapped around my arm, yanking me backward so hard pain shot up my shoulder.

"You humiliated me," he hissed. The calm voice was gone. This was the real one. The one I heard in the dark. "You humiliated *yourself.*"

"I'm sorry," I whispered, trembling. "Please..."

His hand flew.

The slap cracked across the kitchen tile like a gunshot.

My vision went white, then red, then sharp and ringing.

I stumbled, caught myself on the counter, and tasted blood.

"S-stop," I breathed.

But he didn't.

He hit me again - a closed fist this time. My cheekbone erupted in fire. The room tilted sideways. Pain bloomed bright in the corner of my eye.

And then...

"STOP!"

Cole.

My boy.

My ten-year-old baby boy.

He ran toward us, fury burning across his face, tears streaking down his cheeks.

He pushed at Sung-ho's arm.

Tiny hands. Trembling hands.

"Don't hurt her!" he screamed. "DON'T TOUCH MY MOM!"

Everything in me shattered.

Sung-ho turned on him.

It happened too fast.

His hand lashed out.

Caught Cole across the face.

Sent him stumbling into the pantry door with a thud that split something open inside me.

Cole cried out - a sound so raw it ripped through the walls of my chest.

My knees gave out, and I was on the floor before I realized I'd fallen.

And in that moment - bruised, bleeding, dizzy - something inside me snapped into terrifying clarity.

We are leaving.

I don't care what he does to me.

I don't care if I die getting out.

But Cole will *not* grow up like this.

My son will not learn fear from the man who claims to father him.

I crawled across the floor, dragging myself toward Cole as he curled into my lap, sobbing into my shirt.

I pressed a shaking hand to the back of his head.

"It's okay," I whispered into his hair, even though nothing was okay. "I've got you. I've got you. I've got you."

My cheek throbbed.

My ribs ached.

My vision blurred.

And then, quiet footsteps.

Sung-ho stood above us.

Not remorseful.

Not uncertain.

Calm.

As if he had simply completed a task.

"This is what happens when there is disobedience," he said flatly, adjusting the cuff of his sweater. "Both of you should reflect on that."

Then he turned, smoothed his hair, and walked out of the kitchen.

The bedroom door closed with a soft, deliberate click.

No apology.

No hesitation.

No humanity.

I held my son tighter and made him a promise.

We're not staying.

We're done.

We're gone.

No matter what it takes.

I held Cole against me until the tremors in his small body eased, until his breathing settled into uneven, shuddering breaths instead of sobs. My own tears had dried on my face, stinging the split skin along my cheekbone.

When I finally pulled back enough to look at him, his left cheek was already swelling. A red mark spread across the soft skin near his temple.

I brushed his hair back gently. "Baby," I whispered, "does your head hurt?"

He nodded once, fast - more afraid of doing the wrong thing than of the pain itself.

That broke me in a way nothing else had.

"We're going to clean you up," I murmured, "and then you're going to sit with me, okay? I'm not leaving you alone."

I helped him stand, my ribs screaming with every movement, but I didn't let him see the way I winced. I carried him to the bathroom, lifting him onto the counter like I'd done when he was little. The light was bright and merciless. His reflection made me nauseous.

He sniffled. "Mom... is it my fault?"

My throat closed.

"No," I said fiercely. "Look at me, Cole. This is not your fault. Do you hear me? Not ever."

He nodded again, but I saw doubt flicker in his eyes. A doubt that man had planted.

I cleaned the tender spot on his forehead with a damp cloth. He held so still, so brave, like he was trying to make it easier for me. When I was done, I kissed the unhurt side of his face.

"Come on," I whispered. "Stay with me."

Back in the kitchen, the table was still set - half-eaten plates, spilled kimchi, abandoned chopsticks. The untouched rice looked like a funeral offering.

I sat Cole at the far end where I could see him and pressed my phone into his hands.

"Here," I said quietly. "Play your soccer game."

His eyes widened. He never got to play games unexpectedly. "Are you sure?"

"Yes," I said. "Just stay where I can see you."

He nodded and curled into the chair, clutching the phone like a lifeline.

I turned to the dinner mess, forcing my shaking hands to move. Stacking plates. Rinsing dishes. Throwing away the ruined food. Every task became a distraction from the pain. The fear. The rage. The truth.

He could have killed my son.

He *wanted* to break us.

And once, I would have let myself shatter. I would have apologized, begged, convinced myself it wasn't that bad. That I could endure it. That staying was safer.

Not anymore.

By the time the kitchen was clean, my body felt hollowed-out but steady. For the first time, every step forward felt like a decision, not a reaction.

"Mom?" Cole asked softly.

I turned. His feet dangled from the chair, hands still clutching the phone. His cheeks were blotchy. He looked younger than ten. Older than ten.

Broken in ways no child should be.

"Can we... can we go to bed?" he asked.

My chest cracked open.

"Yes," I whispered. "Let's go."

I took the phone back gently and carried him to his room. He climbed into bed, but as soon as I started to pull away, he grabbed my wrist.

"Stay," he whispered. "Please."

I slid under the covers beside him, pulling him against me. His small body fit into the curve of mine like it always had, but tonight, something was different.

Tonight, he wasn't just my son.

He was the reason I would not die in this house.

I lay awake long after he drifted into exhausted sleep. I watched the shadows shift on the ceiling, listened to the hum of the heater, to the distant sound of Sung-ho moving down the hallway - calm again, controlled again, restored to the version of himself everyone else believed in.

But I knew better.

And I wasn't afraid of him anymore.

I turned my face into Cole's hair, inhaling the familiar boyish scent of shampoo and paint and innocence he was still fighting to keep.

"We're leaving," I whispered into the dark, the words a vow carved into bone. "I promise, baby. I promise. I will get you out."

And even though morning felt impossibly far away...

For the first time since the world broke apart around me,

I believed myself.

Chapter 49

Jackson

On Thanksgiving, while Grady stayed behind at the Bryants' to play with the twins, I made an early escape to The Hideaway, mumbling something about needing to finish inventory.

It was a lie.

What I needed was space.

And my phone.

And a sign Abby was okay.

I hadn't heard from her in a few days. Her silence had started as a flutter - small, ignorable, something I told myself not to read into.

But by this morning, it felt like a fist slowly closing around my ribs.

I stood in the storeroom, surrounded by cases of beer and stacks of plastic cups, staring at my phone like I could force it to ring with nothing but sheer will.

Nothing.

A hollow ache pulsed at the base of my throat.

She wasn't able to talk much - I knew that. She was being careful. She *had* to be careful.

But this wasn't just distance.

This felt wrong.

I thumbed her name and lifted the phone to my ear.

It went straight to voicemail.

My breath stuttered.

I waited for the beep, heart pounding.

"Hey," I said quietly. "I just wanted to hear your voice. I hope you're okay. Call me when you can, baby. I just want to know you're okay."

I stood there a second longer, listening to the silence on the other end, then hung up before the worry could swallow me whole.

I shoved the phone into my pocket.

And forced myself to wait, because if she was still fighting for air, the least I could do was not add to the weight on her chest.

Chapter 50

Abby

Sung-ho left for work before the sun had fully risen, straightening his tie in the hallway mirror like last night had never happened. Cole and I stood in the kitchen doorway, silent and stiff, two shadows waiting for the storm to pass.

"Clean the house today," he said, slipping into his shoes. "And make sure Ha-joon reviews his Korean lessons."

"Yes," I answered automatically.

He didn't look at my bruised cheek.

He didn't look at Cole's swollen eye.

He just opened the door and left.

The moment the latch clicked, Cole flinched. I did too.

Then I placed a hand on his back, steady and gentle.

"Go get your coat, baby," I whispered. "We're going for a drive."

He blinked up at me, confusion flickering behind the hurt. "To Grandma's?"

"No," I said softly. "Just... somewhere safe."

He didn't understand. But he nodded.

I moved quickly, grabbing an extra duffel and stuffing it full of clothes for Cole and myself, then shoved it beneath his feet in the car. We had everything we'd need, at least for now.

I kept checking the driveway, the street, even the neighbor's windows. Every shadow looked like it could swallow us.

"Seatbelt," I whispered.

Cole clicked it into place. His lower lip trembled, but he didn't cry. He was used to being brave, and he needed to be now more than ever.

I backed out of the driveway without turning on the radio, without breathing, without risking a last glance at the house we were leaving behind. Whatever memories it held were no longer enough to make us stay. None of it mattered anymore.

I stayed off the interstate, choosing narrow county roads that wound through farmland and long stretches of nothing - roads with no cameras, no traffic, no witnesses. And still, I couldn't stop checking the rearview mirror. Every car behind us felt like a threat. Every mile felt like a countdown.

We made stops, not because we needed them, but because unpredictability was a kind of safety.

A gas station outside an abandoned grain elevator.

A church parking lot.

A diner where no one looked up from their pancakes.

My cell started ringing sometime around lunch, Sung-ho's name lighting up the screen like a warning flare. I silenced it, turning the screen so I wouldn't have to look at it.

The notification sound chirped, signaling a new voicemail.

My stomach twisted. I stepped harder on the gas.

Cole watched me, quiet but attentive, questions pooling behind his eyes.

"You okay, Mom?" he asked softly after our third stop.

"Yeah," I said, forcing a smile. "I'm okay," though I wasn't sure I'd ever be okay again.

His hand crept across the center console, fingers brushing mine in a gesture that was more comfort than a child should ever have to offer.

"Are we running away?"

My throat tightened. "We're... getting distance."

"From Dad?" he whispered.

I swallowed hard. "Yes."

He didn't look at me again for a long time, just stared out the window at miles of winter fields drifting by.

Then, quietly - bravely, he said, "I'll go wherever you go. I don't care where."

A sob clawed up my throat.

I squeezed his hand tighter.

Because I knew he meant it.

And because I knew I had no choice but to keep going.

The motel we stopped at was small and sagging, tucked behind a closed-down lumberyard in the middle of nowhere - the kind of place no one would think to look.

The VACANCY sign flickered, a red pulse against the fading daylight. Normally it would have made me uneasy, but seeing the lot empty except for one pickup truck felt like a mercy.

I checked in, paying cash, keeping my head down.

Then I parked around the back, far from the road, and led Cole into the room.

It smelled like old carpet and bleach.

"Go ahead and get comfy," I said gently. "I just need to make a phone call."

He nodded and climbed onto the corner of one of the beds, pulling his model rocket from the bag and hugging it to his chest like it could keep him safe.

I stepped outside, shutting the door behind me with a soft click.

My phone screen lit up.

37 missed calls.

My stomach dropped.

I opened my voicemail.

Message after message spilled through the speaker - Sung-ho's voice shifting from confused, to apologetic, to irritated, to furious.

Then the final message played, and everything inside me froze.

"Ah-bi. I don't know who you think you are or where you've gone, but listen carefully. You better enjoy it, because when I find you, it will be the last time you see Ha-joon."

A bolt of ice shot through me.

I stopped the message mid-sentence, hands shaking violently.

I bent at the waist, squatting down, forcing my breathing to steady.

I could not go back.

I *would not* condemn Cole to this life - to fear, to silence, to a childhood shaped by fists and control.

I only had one person I could call.

My fingers trembled as I hit Jackson's name.

He answered on the second ring.

"Abby?" His voice cracked. "Baby, what, where are you?"

"I left," I whispered. "I left Sung-ho. I'm at a motel a couple hours out."

"Oh my god... are you safe?"

"I'm okay for now. But I don't know how long."

"Text me your location," he said instantly. "I'm coming. Right now."

My eyes slipped shut, his voice the only steady thing in the world.

"Please hurry," I whispered.

"I'm already on my way."

We hung up, and a second later, my phone buzzed again.

I didn't even think - I answered, believing it was Jackson calling back.

"Where."

Just that one word. Low. Icy.

Sung-ho.

I froze.

"Where are you?" he demanded.

My pulse thundered in my ears. "We're not coming back."

A beat of silence.

Then...

"That's your choice, Ah-bi. But hear me clearly..." His voice slid into a quiet, venomous whisper. "I will do everything in my power to make your life a living hell. You want out? Good luck. Marriage is forever," he said calmly. "You know how this ends."

A sob clawed up my throat. "Why?"

He didn't answer the question.

"And just so we're clear - you will give me my son. And until you do, I'll take yours. Say goodbye to Ha-joon until you learn how to behave like a proper wife."

My knees buckled.

"You won't touch him," I choked. "I won't let you."

"You think you can run?" he hissed. "You think anyone will believe you? I will ruin you. I will kill him before I let you poison him against me."

The line cut out.

I stared at the phone like it was on fire.

I staggered back inside.

Cole stood the moment he saw my face, little fists balled tightly.

"Mom?"

I collapsed to my knees in front of him.

"Baby... there's something you need to know." My voice wavered. "Your dad... he isn't your real father."

He blinked. "What?"

I took his hands. "Sung-ho... He isn't your father."

His brow furrowed, confusion twisting into fear. "What do you mean? If he's not, then who is?"

I cupped his face, tears spilling freely now. "Someone who loves you. Someone who will protect you. Someone I should have told a long time ago."

I swallowed hard. "Do you remember my friend? The one who played football?"

He nodded slowly. "Yeah. We watched his game videos."

A broken smile tugged at my lips. "Jackson was my high school boyfriend..."

He looked down at his rocket, gripping it so tightly his fingers turned white. "I don't understand."

I pulled him gently into my lap, smoothing his hair with trembling hands.

"It's a long story, baby," I whispered. "But here's what matters - Jackson, your father, is coming."

He swallowed, voice tiny. "Why are you telling me now?"

Because we may never have another moment.

Because if Sung-ho found us here...

Because I might die protecting him...

But all I said was, "Because things have changed. And I... and I have to go."

His whole face crumpled. "What do you mean?"

"I love you so much, Cole. More than anything in this world." Tears blurred my vision. "And that's why I have to go back."

"But..."

"I called Jackson. He's on his way."

His voice cracked. "I'm coming with you." He grabbed his bag.

I stood, lifted the bag from his hands, and set it on the bed. "No, baby. You can't. You have to stay here."

"But what about you?!"

I forced a smile I didn't feel. "I'm going to straighten things out with Sung-ho, and then I'll come find you."

Something in him broke. Tears poured down his cheeks. "No, mom. No! I want to stay with you!"

I gathered him into my arms, holding him so tightly I could feel his heartbeat against mine.

"I want that more than anything," I whispered. "But it's not safe for you there. If anything happened to you, I..." I couldn't even finish.

He sobbed harder, face buried in my shoulder. "But what about you? Who's going to protect you?"

My heart shattered.

But there was no other choice.

I pulled back and placed my phone in his shaking hands.

"I need you to take this. Only answer for Jackson."

He shook his head desperately. "No... No, Mom... Please..."

I cupped his cheeks and kissed his forehead, memorizing the feel of him, the warmth, the weight, the miracle that was my son.

"I love you," I whispered fiercely. "More than anything. More than my own life."

Then I stood, walked to the door, and opened it.

Cold air rushed in as Cole broke again behind me.

"Mom!"

"Lock the door," I whispered. "Don't open it for anyone but Jackson."

And then I stepped out.

The door closed behind me, and his sobs were muffled instantly.

I walked through the dark toward my car, each step heavier than the last.

I slid behind the wheel, started the engine, and stared at the empty road ahead.

I was leaving everything I loved behind.

But it was the only way to save him.

The only way to guarantee my son had a future.

A future *without fear.*

The road stretched out endless and empty, the night swallowing everything behind me.

My hands were numb on the steering wheel, my heartbeat echoing loud enough to shake my ribs.

Cole's voice still rang in my ears.

Who's going to protect you?

If only he knew.

He already had.

He was the reason I found my strength.

He was the reason I chose to run.

He was the reason I finally believed I deserved more than the life I had been sentenced to.

A tear slipped down my bruised cheek.

"Be brave for me," I whispered into the dark, not sure if I meant it for him… or for myself.

Then my phone, now Cole's phone, flashed in my mind.

Jackson was on his way, racing toward a motel for a boy he didn't yet know was his.

A boy who would change everything.

I pressed harder on the gas.

"I'm coming back for you," I whispered.

"Both of you."

The road didn't answer.

But for the first time since the world fell apart, I felt something flicker inside my chest.

Hope.

Chapter 51

Jackson

T he Hideaway was buzzing - loud, messy, and alive.

And of course, we were short handed.

Xander was behind the bar, sleeves rolled up, tattoos peeking out as he moved like he'd been born in the chaos. As for me - I was doing my damndest to just keep up.

Grady had something to take care of.

Steven was weirdly MIA - which never happened.

But somehow, we were holding things together, and for the first time since I left Abby behind, I felt something almost like hope.

I'd just finished wiping down a table and was carrying a tray of dirty cups across the bar when the front door swung open.

The noise dipped.

Not much, just enough for me to look up.

And there she was.

"Holy shit," I blurted, my jaw actually dropping. "Are you....?"

Whitney stood in the doorway like the storm she was - eyes bright, cheeks flushed, hair tousled from wind or tears or both. But she was *here*. Back in Falcon Pointe. Not a dream. Not a voice on a phone.

And strolling in behind her was Steven, looking smug like he'd personally escorted a stray angel home.

She slapped my arm before I could say anything else. "Don't make me cry or I'll ruin my makeup."

I barked out a laugh and pulled her into a hug. "You don't need it. You're perfect."

Her breath hitched, and when she looked up, her eyes were glassy.

It hit me then - she'd been through hell. And she came home.

A shadow fell beside us.

Xander.

He took one look at her, nodded once like he'd just solved some long-standing equation, then disappeared toward the back room without a word.

"That's Xander," I muttered. "Don't mind him."

Whitney stood on her tiptoes, scanning the bar, probably looking for the one person who wasn't here.

"I'll be right back," she said, ducking into the bathroom.

Grady was doing okay. Whitney was here, and for the first time in weeks, things felt like they might actually be shifting.

And then my phone rang.

Her face lit up my screen.

Abby.

My heart slammed into my ribs so hard it hurt.

I stepped away from the bar, chest tightening. "I-I'm sorry. I need a minute."

I ducked into the office, jammed my thumb against the screen, and lifted the phone to my ear.

"Abby?" I breathed. "Baby, what? Where are you?"

Her voice was a whisper made of fear.

"I left," she said. "I left Sung-ho. I'm at a motel a couple hours out."

"Oh my God." My voice cracked. "A-are you safe?"

"I'm okay for now. But I don't know how long."

My heart fell straight into my stomach.

"Text me your location," I said, already grabbing my keys. "I'm coming. Right now."

"Please hurry," she whispered.

"I'm already on my way."

I hung up and practically ran back through the bar. Steven was halfway across the floor, taking one look at me and going still.

"Cover me," I said. "I have to go."

He nodded once, eyes sharp. "Everything okay?"

"No," I said, voice shaking. "I'll explain later."

I pushed out into the freezing November air, heart pounding so hard I could barely breathe.

A single text pinged.

A motel address.

I jumped into my truck and tore out of the lot like the road belonged to me.

It only took a couple of hours, but it was still the longest damn drive of my life.

I called Abby twice.

No answer.

I told myself she was afraid. Hiding. Saving her battery.

But fear still crawled up my spine anyway.

By the time I turned down the long, cracked road leading to the motel, my hands were shaking on the wheel.

Her car wasn't there.

My stomach dropped, hard and violent. "No, no, no..."

I circled the lot once.

Twice.

Pulled around back.

Checked every shadow, every dark corner.

Nothing.

Cold air tunneled straight into my chest.

I yanked out my phone and hit call again.

One ring. Two...

"Hello?"

A small voice answered. A kid.

My breath snagged. "Uh... hey, buddy, I think I have the wrong number..." I pulled the phone away and checked the screen. Abby's name glowed back at me.

"Don't hang up!" he cried, loud and scared. "Please don't hang up!"

The fear in his voice hit me like a punch.

I pressed the phone harder to my ear. "Hey, hey, okay. I'm here. What's your name?"

"C-Cole," he stuttered, followed by a shaky sniff. "You're... Jackson, right?"

My pulse stuttered.

"Yeah," I said slowly. "I'm Jackson."

"She said you'd call." His voice broke. "My mom said... only answer if it was you."

His *mom*.

My lungs seized with questions I didn't have time to ponder. "Where's your mom now?"

"She had to go. Dad called and... she didn't know I was listening..." His voice cracked completely. "He said he'd kill me if we didn't come back."

My legs nearly gave out. I had to brace myself against the truck.

"I'm scared," he whispered.

Something inside me broke open. Clean and sharp.

"Hey," I said softly, keeping my voice calm for him. "Where are you?"

"I'm... I'm still in our room."

I jogged toward the row of rooms, gravel crunching under my boots, heart hammering so loud I could barely hear my own footsteps.

"Hey, Cole?" I said quietly. "I'm almost there."

A breath.

A quiet, trembling breath.

Then...

"Are... are you really my dad?"

The world stopped.

My heart didn't beat. It *dropped*. "I-what did you say?"

"She told me," he whispered. "Tonight. Right before she left. She said... she said you're important. That you'd come."

There was a pause then, "She said you're my dad."

My vision blurred.

My throat burned.

I pressed my fist to my mouth, trying to breathe.

I didn't know what to say...

Dad?

But if Abby said it... It had to be true, didn't it?

But why didn't she tell me?

I reached Room 14.

I lifted my hand and knocked three times.

Soft. Careful. Absolutely terrified.

The door opened a moment later, and there he was.

The kid from the elementary school.

The kid I'd helped with his throwing stance.

The kid who had looked up at me with bright eyes and trust, and I'd had no idea...

He stared at me, jaw trembling. And then recognition flickered across his face.

"You," he whispered.

My heart cracked wide open.

One look, and I knew.

I just knew.

Dad.

The word didn't fit. Didn't make sense.

And yet, nothing had ever felt more true.

He was mine.

"Yeah," I said, voice breaking. "Me."

He launched himself forward before I could even react.

Small arms flung around my neck.

Face pressed into my chest.

Sobbing like the whole world had gone dark and I was the only light he had left.

I held him so tight my arms shook.

"Hey," I whispered, kissing the top of his head because I couldn't not. "I've got you. I swear, I've got you."

He cried harder.

And I held him like he was the last piece of Abby I'd ever get to touch.

My son.

My boy.

When he finally loosened his grip, I knelt in front of him.

"We're gonna go somewhere safe," I said softly. "Okay? I'm gonna take care of you."

He nodded, wiping his cheeks with the back of his hand.

I grabbed his bag from the bed, took his small hand in mine, and walked him to my truck. I buckled him in myself because my hands needed something to do besides fall apart.

I checked my phone one more time.

No messages.

No texts.

No Abby.

My chest squeezed painfully, but I forced myself to breathe.

I couldn't go after her yet, not until Cole was safe.

Not until my son... my *son*... was out of danger.

I started the engine.

"Where are we going?" he asked, voice small and scared.

"Home," I said, voice steady and certain. "Falcon Pointe, Colorado."

And I drove.

For him.

For her.

For the family we should've had all along.

Chapter 52

Abby

The drive home blurred into nothing.

Headlights. Darkness. The steady hum of the engine.

My body felt like it was made of sand and nerves, held together by nothing but the thought of Cole's face pressed against my shirt when I said goodbye.

I shouldn't have left him, I knew that.

But staying... staying would've killed us both. And there was no way I was bringing him back to this...

By the time I turned onto our street, my hands were so numb I could barely grip the wheel. Snow drifted across the pavement in thin white sheets. A neighbor's wind chimes tapped like brittle bones.

And my house...

It rose out of the darkness like a warning - black windows, porch light off, shadows thick as oil pooling beneath the eaves.

It looked like a crime scene before anything had even happened.

My stomach twisted.

I pulled into the driveway and sat there, forehead pressed to the steering wheel, whispering a prayer I wasn't sure belonged to God or desperation.

Then I stepped out.

The air cut through my jacket, sharp enough to sting. Every crunch of gravel under my boots felt like it echoed all the way to the door.

My key slipped once in my shaking hand before it finally slid into the lock.

The lights were off inside. The house smelled like stale tea and something bitter underneath; sweat, anger, control.

Then a voice rose from the darkness.

"Ah-bi."

I froze.

Sung-ho sat in the armchair by the window, the faint glow of the streetlamp outlining his silhouette. His hands were folded neatly in his lap, his tie still on. Always the picture of composure.

Except for his eyes.

His eyes burned.

"You came back," he said softly. "I admit... I wasn't certain you would."

My throat closed. "I..."

But the words dissolved.

He lifted one finger.

"Lights."

The lamps flicked on.

And suddenly the room wasn't dark or mysterious.

It was exposed.

Merciless.

Every inch of him visible, his rage disguised as calm, the certainty that I belonged to him.

"Where is Ha-joon?" he asked.

The question dropped like a stone.

I swallowed. "He's safe."

His jaw ticked. "That was not my question."

I stood in the doorway, bag still over my shoulder, as if I'd need to run again at any second. "He's safe," I repeated, voice firmer this time.

He studied me. Slowly. Like examining a broken object to determine whether it could still be repaired.

"Sit," he said.

"I'd rather stand."

A beat of silence.

Then...

"You took my son," he said quietly.

"He's not your son," I whispered before I could stop myself.

The stillness that followed was worse than yelling, filling me with dread.

He rose from the chair.

Not quickly, not dramatically.

Just... stood. Like a man deciding the weather.

"You forget yourself," he murmured. He stepped closer and I stepped back until the door pressed into my spine. "You forget your duty. Your vows. Your place."

My breath shook.

"Marriage isn't supposed to be a place you survive," I whispered.

His eyes hardened into stone.

"And yet here you are. Alive enough to defy me."

He reached out, one finger pressed beneath my chin, forcing my face up.

The touch made my skin crawl.

"Where is the boy."

It wasn't a question, it was a demand.

"He's safe," I repeated, voice cracking. "And you're never touching him again."

Something in him snapped, not loudly, but cleanly, like a wire pulled too tight.

He moved past me then, pacing once through the living room as if considering his options.

Then he stopped at the far wall, hand braced against it, shoulders rising and falling with measured breaths.

When he spoke again, his voice was almost gentle.

"You will tell me where he is, Ah-bi. You will bring him home. And you will apologize for this shame you have brought upon our house."

I felt my spine straighten.

"No."

He turned. "No?" he echoed, like he was tasting the word.

My pulse pounded in my ears.

"I'm not your possession," I whispered. "And Cole will never suffer under you again."

The lamp beside him shattered.

He'd hit it.

I didn't even see his hand move.

The room plunged half into shadow again, glass glittering across the carpet like tiny stars fallen into hell.

He took one step toward me, then another.

I braced myself. Not to fight him, I wasn't strong enough.

But to survive him long enough for Jackson to get here.

Because Jackson had said he was coming.

I'd heard it in his voice. *I'm on my way.*

The memory steadied me, knowing he would already have Cole with him, that our son was safe. That he would come for me next.

At least I hoped he would.

Sung-ho stopped inches from my face.

"One question," he said, voice tightening enough to reveal the rage beneath. "Did you take him because you wanted to leave me? Or did you leave me because of the boy?"

"I left," I whispered, "because you hurt him."

His eyes darkened.

The temperature in the room seemed to drop ten degrees.

"Children need discipline."

"He is TEN!" I snapped, finally, *finally,* letting something inside me ignite. "And you HIT him. You terrorized him. You..."

My back hit the hallway wall.

I hadn't even seen him move.

He hovered inches from my face, breath steady, like he'd practiced every step.

"You think," he said softly, "that you can take what is mine and walk away?"

A tremor climbed my spine.

He touched my cheek.

Right where the bruise was.

I flinched.

He smiled.

Not with his mouth, but with his eyes.

"You think you can run?" he whispered.

His breath ghosted against my cheek, poisonous and suffocating.

"Ah-bi," he said, my name like a curse on his lips, "you don't understand yet. There is no life without me."

Something in me lifted its head, the girl I'd been before him - hopeful, defiant, alive - pushed her way to the surface.

"That's where you're wrong," I whispered. "There *is*."

His expression changed.

And for the first time...

I genuinely feared he might kill me.

Chapter 53

Jackson

The highway blurred past in streaks of white and yellow, but I barely saw any of it.

My brain was stuck on one loop:

Abby left.

Abby ran.

Abby went back alone.

My son is in the seat beside me. My *son*.

Every few minutes, I checked the rearview.

Cole slept curled on his side, one arm wrapped around his rocket, cheek smashed into the pillow I'd wedged against the door.

He looked small.

He looked braver than he should've had to be.

He looked like *her*.

Fuck.

I had a son.

My chest squeezed so tight I had to roll down the window and breathe cold air just to stay upright inside my own skin.

I thumbed my phone and hit call.

Steven answered on the second ring, voice thick with exhaustion. "Jax? What's wrong?"

"I need you," I said, the words cracking out of me before I could soften them. "Can you meet me at my house? In twenty?"

"Yeah, of course. Are you okay?"

"No," I said honestly. "But I'm coming home, and I'm not alone."

A pause.

Then Steven's voice gentled, quiet and sure, "I'll be there."

I hung up and kept driving.

By the time Falcon Pointe's familiar streetlights rose out of the dark, Cole was awake, blinking through sleep with confusion and fear tangled together.

"Is this your house?" he whispered.

"Yeah," I said. "It's home." *For both of us,* I wanted to add, but I didn't want to scare him with promises I wasn't allowed to keep yet.

When I pulled into the driveway, Steven's car was already there. He was pacing the porch, coat half-zipped, hair wind-tossed, like he'd run the whole way.

His eyes went wide when he saw the little boy in my passenger seat.

"Holy shit," he breathed. "Jax, that's..."

"My son," I said, voice quiet but certain.

Saying it out loud nearly knocked me flat.

Steven didn't freeze or freak out or bombard me with questions.

He just nodded once and whispered, "Okay. I've got you. Whatever you need."

I swallowed hard and opened Cole's door.

"Hey, bud," I said softly. "This is Steven. He's a good friend of mine."

Cole clutched his rocket but didn't shy away. "Hi."

Steven lowered himself to eye level, softening in a way I rarely saw. "Hey, Cole. You like mac and cheese? I can make some. I make *terrible* mac and cheese, but I try really hard."

Cole blinked, then nodded faintly.

I could've kissed Steven for that.

Inside, the house was quiet.

Grady's door was closed. Whitney's laugh drifted faintly through the walls. She sounded... *happy.*

I didn't want to disturb that.

Not tonight.

Not with the mess I was carrying.

I led Cole into my room, grabbed an old t-shirt he could sleep in, and helped him change into it. He didn't say much, just watched me with wide, worried eyes.

When I pulled the blankets back for him, he hesitated.

"Will... will she come back?" he asked, voice wobbling.

My throat tightened. "I'm going to find her," I said, kneeling beside him. "With my life, Cole. I'm going to bring her home."

He crawled under the blankets, the rocket tucked beside him.

I clicked on the lamp, dim and warm, a nightlight substitute, and brushed the hair off his forehead.

"Sleep," I whispered. "I'll be right outside."

He nodded, eyes heavy but afraid.

I stayed until his breaths evened out.

Steven waited in the hallway, arms crossed, shoulders tense. When I stepped out, he exhaled like he'd been holding his breath.

"You want to tell me what the hell is going on?" he asked softly.

I leaned my head back against the wall and closed my eyes. "Abby ran. She took Cole and ran. Something happened last night, something bad, and she went back to that asshole alone."

Steven's jaw tensed. "And the boy... Cole? He's yours?"

I huffed a humorless laugh, "Yeah. Look at him, there's not a doubt in my mind that he's mine."

"So, what's your plan?"

I laughed, nothing more than a broken sound. "I don't have one. I'm gonna drive to Kansas and pray I don't get arrested or shot."

Steven snorted, the tension cracking for a moment. "Well, it's a good thing neither of us owns a gun, because right now? You look like you'd use one."

"Yeah," I muttered. "Probably."

Then I sobered, meeting his eyes. "I need you to stay with him."

Steven didn't hesitate. "Of course. I'll take care of him."

Something in my chest unclenched.

Because if I lost Abby tonight...

At least my son would be safe.

I grabbed my keys from the table, shoved my jacket on, and took one last look at the closed bedroom door.

"Bring her home," Steven said quietly. "Whatever it takes."

"I will," I said, and meant it with everything I had left.

Then I stepped back into the freezing night, climbed into my truck, and floored it toward the only woman I had ever loved.

The road stretched dark and endless, but it didn't matter.

I was coming for her.

And God help anyone who stood in my way.

Chapter 54

Abby

Sung-ho sat in his armchair, jacket off, sleeves rolled up, hands steepled beneath his chin like he'd been waiting hours. Days. A lifetime.

He rose with measured precision, smoothing the front of his shirt, reclaiming that perfect, practiced posture he wore like armor.

"Where is Ha-joon?"

I didn't answer.

A muscle in his jaw ticked once. Then he turned away from me, walked into the kitchen, and began making tea.

Every movement careful and practiced.

The kettle filled.

The burner clicked on.

The ceramic cup placed neatly on its saucer.

He stirred the tea even though nothing needed stirring.

This was his ritual, order in place of control.

"You know," he began, voice as calm as the steam rising from the cup, "I have been patient with you tonight."

He brought the tea to the table but didn't drink it.

"But patience has limits. And you…" His gaze slid to me. "You have crossed every one."

I stayed silent.

His smile vanished.

"You will tell me where my son is."

I kept my mouth closed, because silence was all I had left.

Sung-ho set the tea down without a sound and walked toward me, slow and calculated

"When I married you," he said, "everyone told me I was a fool."

My stomach twisted.

"I remember what your mother said. That you were ruined. Tarnished. That no respectable man would take you after what you'd done." His eyes hardened. "But I did."

He stepped closer.

"I saved you, Ah-bi. I saved your reputation. Your dignity. Your future. I took in another man's child as my own, and this…" his hand swept through the air, sharp as a blade. "This is how you repay me?"

Ungrateful.

Selfish.

A wife who forgot her place.

Every word came at me like a lash.

"You ran." He shook his head slowly, expression twisting into something ugly. "With my son. And you think I will let that go?"

My knees trembled, but I remained still.

I didn't break.

And that… God, that was what finally snapped something inside him.

He turned abruptly, grabbed my purse off the counter, and dumped it on the floor. The contents scattered - keys, lipstick, receipts. His face mottled with rage as he realized my phone wasn't there.

Then he unplugged the router. He locked the back door and dragged a kitchen chair in front of the front door and sat.

Blocking the only other exit.

"Sit down," he ordered.

I sank onto the edge of the couch because my legs wouldn't hold me much longer anyway.

The night stretched.

Minutes.

Hours.

The silence thick enough to choke on.

Every time my eyes drifted shut, he flicked his finger against the wall.

A sharp, punishing click.

I forced myself awake.

1 a.m.

2 a.m.

3 a.m.

He didn't move.

He didn't raise his voice.

He didn't lose control.

That made it worse.

"You don't understand what you've done," he murmured around 4 a.m., leaning forward, elbows on his knees. "You've ruined my name. Our family's name." His voice cracked - not with grief, but with ego. "Do you know the shame you have brought to me?"

I said nothing.

He laughed softly, a sound without any warmth.

"You are still that stupid girl," he went on. "The one who opened her legs for a boy who didn't even stay."

Jackson stayed. Until the world tore us apart.

I didn't say that either.

Dawn crept through the blinds, pale and cold.

Sung-ho's mask began to slip.

His hair was mussed, his tie loosened. Eyes red-rimmed with obsession, not exhaustion.

"Tell me where he is."

Soft.

Sharp.

Lethal as a whisper.

I shook my head once.

His breath shuddered out of him, and then something inside him fractured loud enough I could feel it.

He began searching the house.

Every room.

Every closet.

Every cabinet.

As if Cole might magically be hiding in a drawer he'd already checked twice.

He muttered in Korean, half curses, half frantic prayers. *Ungrateful woman... you think you can shame me... you think you can win...*

He was unraveling. All sharp edges and crumbling control.

And I just sat there.

Silent.

Still.

Terrified... but steady.

Because my silence was the only weapon I had left.

Around mid-morning, he stopped pacing.

Stopped muttering.

Just stood in the middle of the living room, chest heaving, looking at me with pure hatred wrapped around something far more dangerous:

Fear.

Fear of losing control.

Fear of losing the narrative.

Fear of losing what he believed he owned.

And then...

A sound.

Barely there. So faint you almost couldn't hear it.

A car door closing.

My heart slammed against my ribs.

Sung-ho's head snapped toward the window.

Slowly, silently, I drew in a breath that felt like the first oxygen I'd had in hours.

Because I knew that sound.

I knew that engine.

I knew the way those footsteps sounded as they approached a door - with purpose, with force, with love.

Jackson.

For the first time all night...

Hope hurt worse than fear.

Chapter 55

Jackson

By the time I turned onto Abby's street, I was vibrating with adrenaline.

I hadn't slept, hadn't eaten. Hadn't done anything but drive and breathe and pray she would still be alive when I got here.

The houses looked too normal. Quiet. Saturday-morning quiet.

Her car sat parked in the driveway.

Good.

It meant I had found her, though what condition she was in, I had no idea.

My truck barely came to a stop before I was out of it, boots hitting the pavement harder than I meant. Every step felt like it carried a year's worth of fear.

I climbed the porch steps, raised my fist, and knocked three times, the way I used to knock on her window at seventeen.

Inside, something shifted. A shadow. A rustle.

I braced myself, and there he was.

Sung-ho.

His expression was tight, calm on the surface, but wrong underneath. A kind of wrong that told me Abby had not had a peaceful night.

We stared at each other for one long, loaded second.

Then his upper lip curled. He clearly knew who I was...

"You need to leave," he said, voice clipped, quiet, poisonous. "Now."

I didn't move.

I didn't blink.

"Where is she?" I asked.

His eyes narrowed. "This is my home. And she is my wife..."

"Where," I repeated, "is Abby?"

Something flickered behind him. Small, and fragile.

Abby.

She stood a few feet back, bruised, exhausted, eyes wide like she couldn't believe I was real.

Our eyes met, and everything inside me locked into place.

I stepped forward.

He stepped in front of her.

"No further," he snapped.

Wrong answer.

I leaned in, voice low enough that it barely carried over the threshold. "Move."

He actually laughed, small, humorless, and deranged. "She isn't going anywhere with you."

And then...

Soft, breaking, barely above a whisper.

Abby said, "I'm going."

I didn't look at him anymore.

I looked at her.

Her chin trembled, but her spine was straight. Brave in a way I'd never seen on any battlefield, any football field, anywhere.

She wasn't choosing me.

She was choosing *freedom.*

And that made me feel something raw and holy in my chest.

She stepped forward again and Sung-ho snapped.

He lunged toward her.

I moved on pure instinct. Without thinking, I caught him by the front of his shirt and drove him back into the wall, just far enough to stop him.

"You touch her again," I said, voice shaking with the effort of not killing him, "and I swear to God..."

He shoved against me, but he didn't stand a chance.

I didn't hit him.

Didn't break his nose. Didn't throw him across the room like every cell in my body was begging me to.

Because Abby didn't need that.

She needed out.

I lowered my face toward him, voice like steel.

"You're done," I said. "Stay where you are."

Then I reached behind me, never taking my eyes off him, and found her hand.

Her fingers slid into mine like they had been waiting a decade to find their place.

"Come on," I told her quietly. "Let's go get our son."

Her breath hitched, and we backed up together.

Sung-ho didn't follow, he just stood there shaking - not with fear, but with the kind of rage cowards get when they realize control is slipping through their fingers.

The door shut behind us with a quiet click.

Not a slam.

Just an ending.

We made it to the truck before Abby's knees buckled.

I caught her, pulled her against me, and felt her breath shudder into my chest.

"Cole," she whispered. "Jackson, I have to get to Cole…"

"He's safe," I told her instantly. "He's with Steven. He's okay."

Her fingers dug into my sleeve like she was anchoring herself to something solid, then she sagged, her forehead pressing into my collarbone.

I helped her into the truck. Her hands were shaking so badly she couldn't buckle the seatbelt. I gently took it from her hands and did it for her.

I shut the door softly and walked around to the driver's side.

As soon as the engine started, she grabbed my sleeve.

"We have to go to the police," she whispered. "But he… He'll twist everything, I know he will. But I have to, I have to at least try. For Cole. For…" Her voice cracked. "For everything."

"I know," I murmured. "Let's find someplace safe and we'll call from there."

She nodded, wiping her face with the back of her hand.

We drove half a mile.

A mile.

Two.

I turned into a deserted church parking lot - wide open, empty, and neutral.

No neighbors watching.

No interference.

No narrative Sung-ho could control.

I put the truck in park and turned to her.

"You ready?" I asked softly.

She closed her eyes, took one shaky breath, and then nodded.

I dialed 911 and pressed the phone into her hand like it weighed more than either of us.

Her fingers curled around it, trembling but determined.

The dispatcher answered, and Abby, finally, bravely, devastatingly, began to speak the truth out loud.

I sat beside her, hand on the back of her neck, grounding her, steadying her, loving her in the only way I could while she rebuilt her life from the ashes.

And when the call ended and the report was filed and the next steps were set in motion, I whispered, "We're going home. All three of us."

Her breath broke, but she nodded.

And for the first time since she left me at seventeen...

She didn't pull away.

Chapter 56

Abby

I didn't realize I'd fallen asleep until the truck slowed beneath me.

The rumble of the engine softened. Gravel crunched. A porch light glowed through my eyelids.

I was safe. The kind of safe I never let myself dream about.

I blinked awake just as Jackson threw the truck into park. My neck ached, my face stiff from dried tears, but the moment I saw him, all of that slipped into the background.

"Hey," he whispered, his hand brushing my knee. "We're home."

Home.

The word barely made sense... at least, not until I looked past him and saw the house. Warm lights filled the windows, a soft glow spilling across the snow-dusted yard. A place that didn't hurt to look at.

Before I could process anything else, the front door flew open.

"Mom!"

Cole bolted out of the house so fast, the man behind him had to lunge to grab the railing. Too late. My son was already tearing across the snowy yard, feet slipping, breath puffing in panicked bursts.

"Cole, hang on, buddy..." Jackson tried to reach the handle first.

But Cole was faster.

His fingers curled under the door frame, he hauled himself up with a sound that was half-sob, half-laugh, and then his arms were around me.

No hesitation. No fear. Just pure, broken relief.

"Mom," he cried again, burying his face in my neck, shaking. "Mom, you came back. You came back."

My whole body folded around him.

"I told you," I whispered, kissing his hair, my vision swimming. "I told you I'd find you."

Truth be told, I wasn't sure I ever would. But I wasn't letting go now. Ever.

He clung tighter, small fingers knotted in my jacket like letting go might undo everything we'd survived.

Behind him, the other man slowed to a stop, breathless, eyes wide and wet. Jackson stood beside him, chest heaving, exhaustion, fear, and love written all over his face.

But no one said a word, not yet.

This moment belonged to us.

Cole pulled back just far enough to touch my cheek with shaking fingers.

"Did he hurt you?" he whispered.

It broke me in a way nothing else ever had.

"No," I said softly, cupping his face. "I'm okay. You saved me. You were so brave."

He nodded, but fresh tears spilled anyway. "I didn't want you to go back."

"I know," I whispered. "But I had to. And now we're here."

He sniffed, wiped his face with the back of his hand, then blinked up at Jackson.

"She really came back."

My heart didn't break this time, it healed.

Slowly, sweetly, right there in the cab of a muddy old truck in Falcon Pointe.

Jackson swallowed hard, his voice cracking when he stepped closer.

"Yeah, buddy," he whispered. "She did."

Cole reached for him, and in one seamless motion, Jackson lifted him into his arms. Cole wrapped around him like he'd been doing it his whole life.

Watching them together was... indescribable. Like watching the world tilt onto the right axis for the very first time.

Jackson looked at me over Cole's shoulder.

Something fierce and gentle and absolutely forever lived in his eyes.

"You ready to go inside?" he asked.

I exhaled, shakily.

For the first time in a decade, the answer didn't terrify me.

I nodded. "Yeah. I'm ready."

He extended a hand, and this time, *finally*, I took it.

The moment we stepped through the door, warmth wrapped around me so suddenly my eyes stung.

Not just temperature. Warmth.

The kind that comes from being in a place where people *love* each other.

Where no one flinches at footsteps and the air doesn't vibrate with fear.

Cole slipped his hand into mine, his little fingers tight, trembling with exhaustion. Jackson stayed close, one hand hovering at my back like he wasn't ready to stop protecting us yet.

A figure appeared in the living room doorway, wild blonde hair, warm eyes, familiar in a way that made something deep inside me break open.

Whitney.

She was grown up now, but still had the same soft features, the same wide, earnest eyes I remembered from when she was eleven, always peeking around corners when Jackson and I were together.

Her breath hitched. "Abby?"

My throat tightened. "Hey, Whit."

In two steps she had her arms around me, not cautious, not tip-toeing around the bruises on my face. Just holding me like she'd been waiting eleven years.

"You came home," she whispered against my shoulder.

For a moment, for the first time all night, I let myself lean.

When she pulled back, another man stood behind her - tall, sharp-jawed, eyes both gentle and haunted.

Grady.

We'd never met, but I felt like I already knew him. From the way Jackson talked about him like a brother. From the sad, raw song that somehow found its way across the internet.

"Hi," he said softly. "I'm... Grady."

I managed a small nod. "I know."

He looked at Cole, something aching and protective flickering across his face. "You're safe here," he said quietly. "Both of you."

Then the man from the porch stepped into view again, dark hair, slightly mussed, wearing a CU Buffs Football hoodie, like he probably slept in it half the week. His expression was open, worried, a little frazzled.

Cole's face lit up. "That's him," he whispered. "That's Steven. He stayed with me."

Steven blinked like he hadn't expected the introduction. "Uh... hey." He raised a hand awkwardly. "I don't usually... babysit. But he kicked my ass at Madden, so... We bonded."

A tiny smile tugged at Cole's mouth.

I stepped forward, offering my hand. "Thank you. For taking care of him."

But Steven shook his head. "He didn't need taking care of. Just... someone around." His voice gentled. "You don't need to thank me."

I nodded, even though we weren't talking about the same person.

My eyes prickled again.

Jackson cleared his throat, drawing my attention back to him, soft-eyed, worried, and trying so hard to keep it together.

"We, uh..." he rubbed the back of his neck. "We only have two bedrooms." He looked around the room, at the group we had gathered, and exhaled. "You and Cole can take my room. I'll take the couch."

I shook my head before he even finished. "No. Jackson, you haven't slept in..."

"Abby." He stepped closer. "You need your rest. And I'm not putting Cole anywhere he's not comfortable, where you can't easily check on him."

Cole pressed closer to me. "Can he sleep with us?"

Jackson's face softened, like he hadn't expected to be so openly accepted. *Loved.* "If your mom says it's okay."

I nodded. Because right now? Cole needed the safest place he could find, as did I. And that was wherever Jackson was.

We got Cole settled, shoes off, covered up, his hand wrapped tight around mine. His eyes kept slipping shut, but he fought sleep until Jackson sat on the edge of the mattress and brushed a hand through his hair.

"I'm right here, bud," Jackson murmured. "You can sleep."

Cole's fingers loosened and his breathing deepened.

He was safe, and for the first time in eleven years, so was I.

Steven hovered in the doorway, hands in his pockets, looking like he wanted to say something but didn't want to intrude.

"Steven," I said softly. "You don't have to stay up."

He shrugged. "I'm not leaving until he," he pointed at Jackson, "looks like he's not going to collapse."

Jackson rolled his eyes. But affection softened every line of his face.

He walked back to me, reaching for my hands, holding them carefully, like he was afraid I might break.

"Abby," he whispered, voice cracking, "you're home."

And in that moment. standing barefoot in a warm house that wasn't mine, surrounded by people who had every reason not to accept me but did anyway, I realized something. I believed him.

The house slowly grew quiet.

Whitney and Grady moved to his room.

Steven dimmed the lights and murmured something about starting coffee for the morning.

Cole finally drifted into a deep, heavy sleep.

Jackson caught my eye across the room and nodded gently toward the hallway. "You need to rest," he said softly. "Come on."

I followed him through the narrow hallway into the small bathroom. He shut the door behind us, careful not to let it click too loud. The space was warm, faintly smelling of cedar soap and old tile.

Without a word, he turned on the bathtub faucet.

Warm water poured in, steam rising, filling the air between us. He tested it with his fingers, adjusted the heat, then reached up into the cabinet for a towel.

Everything he did was slow. Gentle. Like he was afraid any sudden movement might make me shatter.

The house had gone quiet again. No raised voices, no slammed doors. Just running water and breathing.

My throat tightened. "You don't have to..."

"Abby."

His voice was soft but firm.

"Let me take care of you."

No one had said that to me in eleven long years.

Not with love.

Not with tenderness.

Not without strings.

My eyes burned.

When the tub was full, he turned off the water and straightened, finally facing me fully. His jaw clenched when he really looked at me, the bruises, the swelling, the split skin near my cheekbone.

He lifted his hands to my face, cupping my cheeks without pressure.

"Tell me if anything hurts," he whispered.

"Everything hurts," I said truthfully.

His eyes softened. "Let me help anyway."

He reached for the hem of my shirt.

"Is this okay?" he asked quietly.

I nodded, lifting my arms, letting him peel away the fabric. My ribs ached, and he froze when he saw the mark there, the dark, ugly, proof of what had transpired.

He sucked in a breath like it physically hurt him.

"Abby…" His voice cracked.

He pressed his forehead to my shoulder, breath trembling.

"I'm okay," I whispered, though neither of us truly believed it.

He helped me into the bath, lowering me slowly into the warm water. Heat wrapped around me, loosening knots I'd carried for years.

He knelt beside the tub.

Not leaving.

Not stepping away.

Just… being there.

The water lapped softly against the porcelain as I leaned my head back, exhaustion washing over me in waves.

Silence stretched until I couldn't take it any more. "Jackson," I murmured, "I need to tell you something."

He lifted his gaze, eyes dark and steady. "Whatever it is… I'm here."

I swallowed, gripping the edge of the tub.

"Cole is yours."

He didn't flinch.

Didn't lose his breath.

Didn't look shocked.

He looked… wrecked.

Wrecked with relief.

Wrecked with grief.

Wrecked with love.

"I figured," he whispered.

A tear slid down my cheek. "I'm sorry I didn't tell you. My parents, my mother, she found out I was pregnant. She dragged me away before I could... before I even knew what I wanted."

His hand curled over mine, warm and sure.

"They said you wouldn't want it," I whispered. "That you had a whole future lined up and telling you would destroy it. And I believed them. I didn't even know if you wanted kids. You were supposed to go play football, go to college, go chase your dreams and I..."

"Abby."

His voice cut through the spiral.

I looked up.

His eyes were shining.

"You were my dream," he said quietly. "You. Not football. Not college. Not anything else they told you."

I swallowed a sob.

"And Cole?" I whispered.

He smiled, emotional and unsteady and soft in a way I'd never seen.

"I would've given anything," he said, voice breaking, "to know he existed. To hold him. To raise him. To be his dad from the start."

I covered my face with my hands, crying silently into the steam.

Jackson gently lowered them, cupping my cheeks again.

"I'm here now," he said. "And I'm not going anywhere."

I leaned forward, resting my forehead against his.

"What if he hates me, for keeping this from him all this time?" I whispered.

"Oh, baby, he could never hate you for that," Jackson murmured. "Abby... he ran into my arms. He clung to me. He looks at me like... like he's been waiting his whole life to meet me."

My breath hitched.

"And I..." his voice shook, "I love him already."

The words hit me like a warm flood, filling the cracks inside me.

He pressed a soft kiss to my forehead.

"Let me take care of you," he whispered again.

And for the first time since I was seventeen...

I let him.

By morning, my body felt borrowed. Too light, too heavy, and too not-my-own.

Jackson had insisted I sleep, but sleep came in pieces; flashes of headlights, the scrape of a chair on hardwood, Sung-ho's voice hissing, *I will ruin you, I will kill him.*

But then Cole's arms wrapped around my waist again in a dream, and I found myself clinging to that instead.

When I stepped out of the bedroom, the house smelled like coffee and something warm, like hope trying to exist where it hadn't been allowed in years.

Jackson stood by the front door, keys in hand. His eyes softened the second he saw me.

"You ready?" he asked quietly.

No, not even close.

"Yes," I said.

He squeezed my hand once, and we walked outside together. Cole was still asleep, and Steven sat alert on the couch, like a guard dog who'd never blink.

The drive to the Falcon Pointe police station took all of five minutes.

My thundering heartbeat lasted all five.

Inside, the fluorescent lights felt too bright, too honest, and all too revealing.

The woman at the front desk looked up, took one glance at my face, and her expression changed instantly - softening, but sharpening too. A look like she'd seen thousands of women like me, and had never once stopped caring.

"How can we help you?" she asked, voice low.

Jackson answered for me.

He didn't speak loudly.

He didn't have to.

"We need to report domestic assault and threats against a child."

Her eyes flicked to my bruised cheek.

My swollen jaw.

My knuckles, scraped from gripping a steering wheel until my skin split.

"Come with me," she said.

She led us down a quiet hallway to a small room with a round table, two chairs, and a box of tissues already sitting in the middle.

Someone had placed it there intentionally. Someone who knew.

A sergeant entered a moment later - older, calm, the kind of steady presence that feels like a held door.

"I'm Sergeant Alvarez," he said gently. "You're safe here. We're going to take this one step at a time."

Safe.

I tried to breathe that word in, but it caught on something sharp in my ribs.

Jackson stood with me immediately.

Inside his small office, he motioned us to sit. He didn't waste any time.

"I understand you've been through significant trauma," he said gently. "We're going to go slowly."

I nodded, fingers twisting together in my lap.

"There's something I should tell you," I managed, my voice cracking. "I... already talked to the police in Kansas. Last night. Before I left. I told them what happened, and they said they'd send someone."

Sergeant Alvarez nodded, flipping open a slim file already waiting beside him.

"I'm aware," he said. "Kansas contacted us early this morning. A welfare check was attempted at your residence."

My breath caught.

"They reported that lights were on and someone was inside," he continued, "but because you weren't present to give a statement, and your husband refused entry, their options were limited."

I stared down at my shaking hands.

"So... it didn't change anything," I whispered.

"It did," he corrected firmly. "It created documentation. A timeline. A record of risk. And now that you're physically here, safe and able to give a full statement, we can take steps Kansas could not."

Jackson's jaw tightened, his hand finding mine.

Sergeant Alvarez pulled a form forward.

"First, we'll file an emergency protective order here in Colorado. Then we'll coordinate with Kansas law enforcement for cross-state enforcement. Domestic violence cases cross jurisdiction lines all the time. You are not trapped by geography."

I exhaled a shaky breath, half disbelief, half relief.

"And Cole?" I whispered.

His expression softened. "As soon as the order is processed, custody defaults to the protective parent. Kansas will be notified that Cole is with you and safe."

Jackson's fingers squeezed mine, grounding me.

"Now," the sergeant said, lifting his pen, "start wherever you need to. We're not in a rush."

I told him everything.

Not the way I would tell a friend. Not in fragments or whispers.

But clearly. Chronologically. Without minimizing or apologizing.

The threats. The monitoring. The humiliation. The hitting. The night he struck Cole. The escape. The motel. The call. The way his voice turned into something that still lived under my skin.

Sergeant Alvarez didn't interrupt. He didn't blink away in discomfort or disbelief. He just wrote, nodding at the right places, grounding the story in ink and law.

When I finished, Jackson slid his hand up my back and rested it there, steady and warm.

"And Abby," the sergeant said quietly, "you did everything right. Leaving was the most dangerous moment of your life. Survivors rarely make it this far. You protected your son. You protected yourself. And now, we will protect you."

My throat closed, hot and tight.

"I was so afraid," I whispered. "He said he'd kill Cole."

His voice didn't change. "And now we have that threat documented. That matters."

He stood and printed the first protective order.

Jackson took it before I could, like he needed the paper in his hands to believe it was real.

"We'll escort you out," he said. "You're safe to go home."

Home.

Falcon Pointe.

Jackson.

Cole sleeping in a bed that smelled like fresh laundry and hope.

As we stepped back into the waiting room, I felt Jackson's arm wrap around me, pulling me gently into his side.

"You're not alone anymore," he murmured into my hair.

Jackson's arm stayed firm around me as we walked out, and for the first time, my feet didn't hesitate at the doorway.

The house was quiet in a way that felt earned.

Not the brittle, held-breath silence I'd learned to survive inside, but something softer. A pause. A space where nothing bad was waiting to happen.

Cole was asleep in Jackson's room, the door cracked just enough for me to hear his breathing. I'd checked on him three times already. Jackson pretended not to notice.

I sat at the kitchen table with a mug of tea I'd forgotten to drink, my hands wrapped around it more for grounding than warmth. The light over the sink hummed faintly. Outside, snow dusted the edges of the porch, the world muffled and still.

For the first time in years, I wasn't afraid of the night.

The paperwork sat in a neat stack beside my elbow.

Protective order. Temporary custody. The report I'd given until my voice went hoarse, until the words lost their sharp edges and became facts instead of confessions.

Sergeant Alvarez had been calm. Steady. He'd looked me in the eye when he said it mattered, what I'd done, what I'd survived.

"It establishes a pattern," he told me. "And it gives us leverage."

Leverage. A word I'd never had before.

Sung-ho hadn't been allowed near me. Or Cole. Not within a hundred yards. When the officer said it, something inside me loosened - not relief exactly, but validation. Proof that I hadn't imagined the danger. That it had been real enough to name.

Real enough to stop.

I thought I would feel victorious.

Instead, I felt... finished.

The version of my life that revolved around him was over. No drama. No final confrontation. Just a door closing quietly behind me.

Jackson moved behind me, his presence familiar now in a way that didn't steal my breath. He set a folded blanket over my shoulders without asking, his hand lingering just long enough to check in.

"You okay?" he asked.

I nodded. "I think I finally am."

He didn't push. Just kissed the side of my head and leaned back against the counter, arms crossed, watching me the way he did when he was making sure I was really steady.

The phone buzzed on the table.

My mother's name lit the screen.

I stared at it longer than I needed to before answering.

"Ah-bi," my mother said, her voice tight and controlled. "Your father told me what's happening."

Of course he did.

"I need to know what you're planning," she continued. "You can't just disappear. People are talking."

I closed my eyes.

"I'm not disappearing," I said quietly. "I left."

There was a pause. I could picture her pressing her lips together, the way she always did when something didn't fit the life she'd imagined for me.

"And Ha-joon?" she asked. "You took him?"

"Yes."

"That isn't..."

"Up for discussion," I finished.

The silence stretched between us.

Finally, she exhaled. "Your father says Sung-ho is embarrassed. He's furious."

I felt nothing. Not fear. Not guilt. Just distance.

"That's not my responsibility anymore," I said.

She didn't argue, and that was the most telling part.

"We'll need to talk about arrangements," she said eventually. "Visitation. Holidays."

I considered that, but truth be told, Sung-ho had no claim to Cole. And as for my parents, well...

"We can talk later," I said. "When things are settled. When boundaries are clear."

Another pause.

"Ah-bi," she said, softer now. "You've made things very difficult."

I opened my eyes and looked at Jackson. At the life waiting patiently for me to choose it.

"I know," I said. "But I'm done making them easier for everyone else."

When I hung up, my hands were steady.

I didn't cry.

I stood and moved quietly down the hall, easing Cole's door open just enough to check on him. He slept deep and trusting, safe in a place that wasn't permanent, but wasn't dangerous either.

When I turned back, Jackson was there, filling the narrow hallway with his solid, familiar presence.

I leaned into him, resting my forehead against his chest. His arms came around me without urgency, without expectation.

And tomorrow, when the sun rose, when the world started asking things of me again, I would keep going.

One choice at a time.

Jackson

10 Months Later

The September sun hung low over the Falcon Pointe Youth Football Field, warm enough to smell the grass but cool enough to remind everyone that fall was coming.

Eleven-year-olds in oversized helmets sprinted across the grass, tripping over their own feet, shouting plays that made zero sense but sounded like pure joy. I stood on the sideline, whistle in my mouth, clipboard in hand, pretending these kids weren't working me harder than any college coach ever had.

Cole stood at the front of the huddle.

My son.

Helmet slightly crooked, chin lifted, eyes bright with that same fire I'd carried when I was his age. He bounced on his toes, tapping the ball twice like we practiced.

"Trips right!" he yelled. "On my count! Ready - break!"

They scattered like happy chaos.

Up in the bleachers, Abby watched with her hands tucked inside her jacket sleeves, a smile softening her whole face. She looked like home, she always had. Beside her sat Whitney and Grady, arguing over something on the scoreboard, and Steven leaning forward with his elbows on his knees, yelling out encouragement like the boys could hear him from thirty yards away.

A few seats down, Mrs. B sat with Edward and Edie bouncing beside her, the twins' feet swinging in unison as they waved homemade signs that read *GO COLE!* Mrs. B clapped with quiet pride, eyes shining, like she'd waited a lifetime to sit in these stands.

And then there was Xander.

Sitting a row above them, hood up, legs spread, elbows resting on his thighs. He looked like he belonged nowhere and everywhere all at once, quiet, steady, and unreadable. One of the kids tripped near the sideline, and Cole jogged over to hand the boy his flag belt.

As Cole ran back into the lineup, he passed the bleachers.

Xander's hand lifted automatically, a small ruffle to Cole's helmet.

And for the briefest second, something flickered across Xander's face.

Not a smile.

Something rawer. Sharper. Like the echo of a loss he'd never put words to.

The moment passed as quickly as it came and he went still again, shadowed, watching the field like he was memorizing it.

Yeah. Trouble might've followed Xander to Falcon Pointe... but so had hope. Maybe one day he'd figure out which one he wanted more.

"Coach!" Cole called out. "Can we run it?"

His voice was bright. Brave. Too much like mine.

"You tell me," I called back. "What's the play?"

He grinned and nodded to his teammates, lining them up. God, he was growing so damn fast I could barely keep up.

The ball snapped, and Cole ran.

Feet pounding the turf, arms pumping, grin wide enough to break me in half. The whole field roared as he crossed the end zone, a swirl of cheers, laughter, proud parents, and teammates trying (and failing) to tackle him in celebration.

He turned immediately, searching the sideline until his gaze locked with mine.

His face lit up like the sun.

That's my boy.

I jogged onto the field, lifting him into my arms as he barreled into me, shouting, "Dad! Did you see that?!"

"Yeah, buddy," I choked out. "I saw everything."

When I carried him back toward the bleachers, Abby stood and stepped down to meet us. She touched Cole's head, then my cheek, her eyes soft in a way they hadn't been for years, not since we were kids dreaming about futures we never thought we'd get back.

"Good run," she murmured.

"Good life," I whispered back.

Her fingers curled into my jacket, pulling me closer as she kissed me, slow and certain, a promise sealed under a sky we'd both once prayed under for different reasons.

I kissed her back, long enough to taste everything we survived, everything we fought for, everything we refused to lose again.

Behind us, the boys shouted for another play.

Ahead of us... the rest of our damn lives.

We drove home after the game, down the winding road on the outskirts of town, to the house I bought the minute I knew they were mine for good - a white farmhouse with a wraparound porch, a red barn, and an acre of wild grass that glowed gold in the evenings.

Sunflowers grew everywhere.

Everywhere.

Like they'd bloomed just because Abby finally had space to breathe.

She climbed out of the truck while Cole ran ahead to open the door.

"I wanna go see my mural!" he yelled, helmet bouncing in his hand.

Abby laughed, soft, free, and followed him inside.

I stood on the porch for a second, just taking it all in.

The farmhouse.

The sunflowers.

The barn with paint drying on its windows.

The life I never thought I'd have.

I walked inside to find Cole dragging her down the hall.

He flung open his bedroom door, revealing the mural that had taken Abby three straight days of painting, stopping only when her eyes blurred...

Something he'd been trying to sneak a peek of ever since she started, but hadn't been able to.

A night sky, deep and royal blue.

Planets and constellations ringed with subtle gold.

A rocket ship, hand-painted with the same orange stripe as the model he'd carried everywhere.

And shooting stars, three of them, one larger, two smaller.

He walked over to it, his fingers brushing over the dried paint.

I love it," he whispered.

Abby turned to me then, eyes shining, warm, full, and alive.

"Yeah," I said softly, taking her hand. "Me too."

But we weren't done.

"Come on," I said, brushing a kiss to her temple. "I wanna show you something."

We walked out to the barn, sunlight warming the weathered wood. Sunflowers bowed in the breeze as if they knew her name.

Inside, the space smelled like turpentine and lavender.

Brand new canvases stacked against walls.

Fresh brushes in mason jars.

A drop cloth splattered with the colors of every feeling she'd ever swallowed.

Her art.

Her heart.

Her freedom.

Her new studio.

She stepped inside and covered her mouth with her hand, breath shaking.

"Jackson... it's perfect."

"No," I said, stepping behind her, sliding my arms around her waist. "You're perfect."

She melted against me, letting out a soft, sound that went straight through my ribs.

"Thank you," she whispered. "For this. For everything."

"I'd give you more," I murmured against her neck. "Anything."

Her breath hitched. "Show me."

So, I did.

I turned her gently, lifting her onto the wide wooden worktable. Her paint-stained fingers curled into my shirt, pulling me closer. Her knees parted for me like she'd been waiting years to breathe in this room.

"Jackson..." she whispered, and fuck, that voice...

I cupped her cheek and kissed her slow, deep, and thorough.

Not rushed.

Not desperate.

Not running.

Claiming.

Returning.

Home.

Her legs wrapped around my hips. I lifted her higher, her back arching beneath my hands, her breath warm at my ear.

"You saved us," she whispered.

"No," I murmured, kissing down her throat as she shivered. "You saved yourself. I just came when you called."

She laughed, soft and shaky, fingers sliding into my hair.

I kissed her again, tasting sunflowers and paint and the life we were finally building with our own hands.

And in the quiet between our breaths, I knew one thing with absolute certainty. I was never letting go of her again.

Later, when the sun dipped behind the barn and the house glowed warm across the field, Abby leaned her head on my shoulder, paint smudged across her forearm, lips kiss-swollen, eyes soft and certain.

Cole slept inside.

The world was finally right.

She slid her hand into mine and I squeezed back. For the first time in my life, the future didn't scare me.

It felt like a promise.

I used to think I was obsessed with Abby Park.

Turns out I was just in love. The kind that lasts, the kind you fight for, the kind that brings you home.

Glossary of Korean Terms

Umma – Mom; an affectionate, informal term for mother.

Eomeoni – Mother; a more formal and respectful term, often used in traditional households.

Appa – Dad

Halmeoni – Grandmother

Harabeoji – Grandfather

Annyeonghaseyo – Hello; a polite greeting.

Annyeonghaseyo, Eomma – "Hello, Mom."

Annyeonghaseyo, Appa – "Hello, Dad."

Galbijjim – Braised beef short ribs, often served during family gatherings or special occasions.

Bulgogi – Marinated beef, grilled or stir-fried.

Gimbap – Rice and fillings rolled in seaweed; similar in appearance to sushi but typically made without raw fish.

Japchae – Stir-fried glass noodles with vegetables and sometimes meat; commonly served at celebrations.

Acknowledgements

To my family – thank you for loving and supporting me while I spent my days and far too many evenings lost in my head, talking to fictional people like they were real, and imagining lives that slowly turned into something beautiful. Your patience, encouragement, and quiet belief in me mean more than you know.

To my readers – thank you for showing up. For reading, for feeling, and for reminding me why I keep writing even on the days when imposter syndrome is loud and the words feel hard-earned. Your support gives me the courage to keep going.

And finally, to the love of my life – God rest his soul.
You were woven into this story in ways you'll never know. Part of you lives in Jackson. Part of you lives in Sung-ho. You were my best friend, my greatest inspiration, and at times, my hardest lesson. Our story didn't end the way Abby's does, but you shaped me, and through me, you shaped these pages. This book carries pieces of what was, what hurt, and what I survived. Thank you for the love we shared, the years we had, and the mark you left on my heart.

Falcon Pointe

Addicted

Small Town, Brother's Best Friend, Forced Proximity

Obsessed

Small Town, Friends to Lovers, Second Chance Romance

About the Author

What happens when your inner child "forgets" to choose a career? Suddenly, the princess, doctor, lawyer, and mechanic all come looking for their piece. Without a cloning machine, what's a girl to do?

Write.

As a writer, I live vicariously through the characters I create and the stories they tell. Every day is an adventure to be had, and if I can't do it myself, I'm going to put my daydreams to work.